The Widow's War

Books by Alan Williams

LONG RUN SOUTH

BARBOUZE

SNAKE WATER

THE PURITY LEAGUE

THE TALE OF THE LAZY DOG

THE BERIA PAPERS

GENTLEMAN TRAITOR

A BULLET FOR THE SHAH (SHAH-MAK)

THE WIDOW'S WAR

The Widow's War

ALAN WILLIAMS

RAWSON, WADE PUBLISHERS, INC.
NEW YORK

This work was originally published in Great Britain by Granada Publishing in Hart-Davis, MacGibbon Ltd., London

Library of Congress Cataloging in Publication Data

Williams, Alan, 1935-
The widow's war.

I. Title.
PZ4.W714Wi 1980   [PR6073.I4258]   823'.914   79-67643
ISBN 0-89256-128-9

Copyright © 1978 by Alan Williams
All rights reserved
Manufactured in the United States of America
by Halliday Lithograph Corporation.
First American Edition

For Antonia and Owen

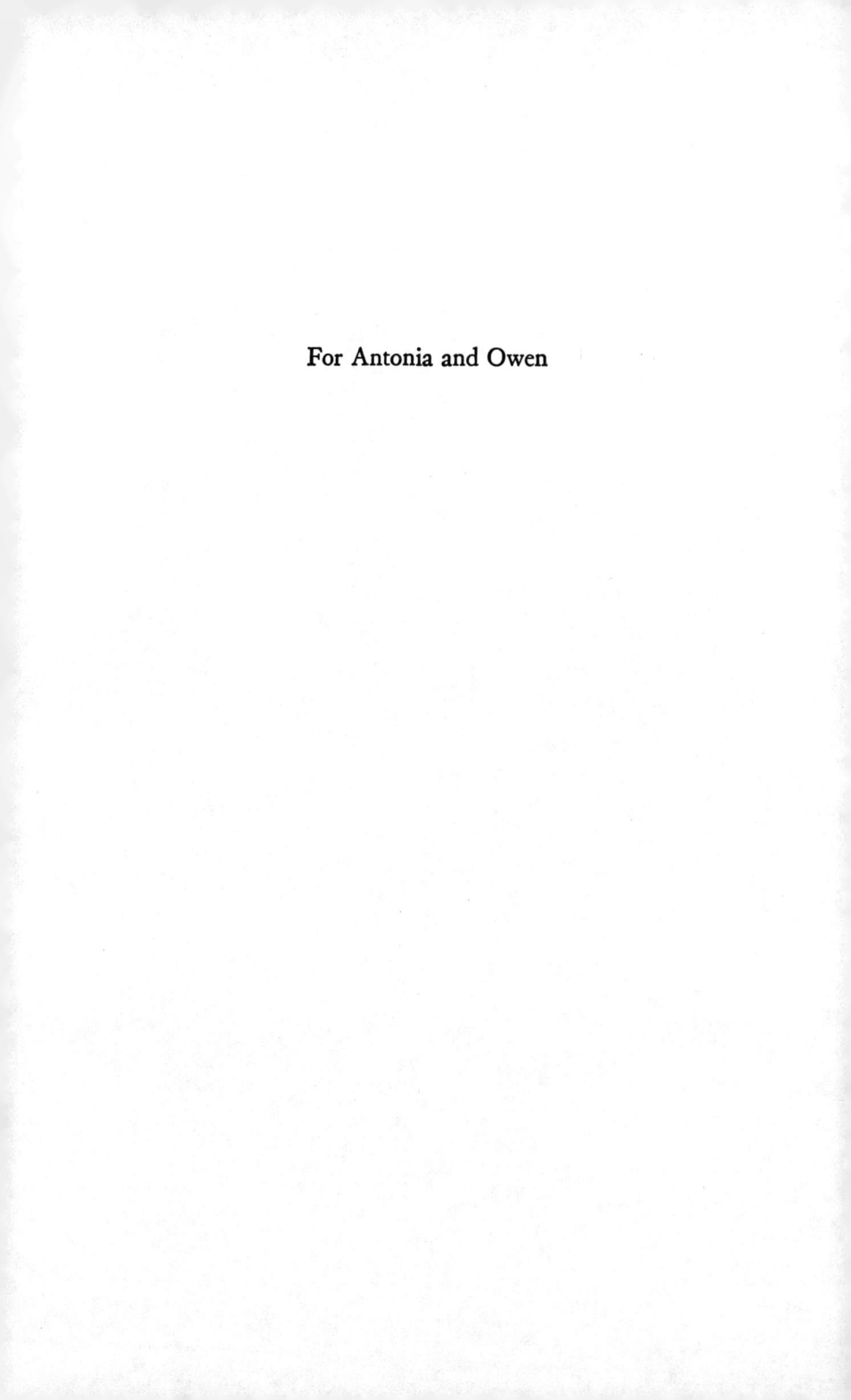

'Thinkers prepare the revolution; bandits carry it out.'

MARIANO AZUELA

Contents

Chapter One	A Quiet Place in the Country	1
Chapter Two	The Night Callers	31
Chapter Three	The Set-Up	58
Chapter Four	The Point of No Return	92
Chapter Five	The Island	118
Chapter Six	First Blood	167
Chapter Seven	A Touch of Triumph	199
Chapter Eight	The Widow Returns	220
Chapter Nine	'Twixt Cup and Lip	238
Chapter Ten	Exit	271

The Widow's War

CHAPTER ONE

A Quiet Place in the Country

At precisely 5.57 p.m. by his grandfather's gold watch, Hugh Dermot Ryan flicked the wall-switch that controlled the thermostat on his bath. It took just three minutes for the bath to fill. He undressed at leisure, folding his clothes over the Sheraton couch, before the radio switched on with the time-signal for the Six o'clock News.

He sank into the water and listened to the headlines. Something called Devolution had caused a mild disturbance and evoked a few clichés from a shadow minister: there was also trouble in Cyprus, the City, and an item about an island in the Caribbean that had recently dispatched a huge armed force to Central Africa, and where there were reports of riots, following the arrival of several troop-ships carrying the bodies of dead soldiers who had been fighting for the liberation of Black Africa.

Ryan listened to this with some interest. Things had changed since he had been stationed out there, in the Island's capital, Montecristo, as a double-agent in German uniform working for the British in World War II.

But Ryan was more concerned by a later item: a vague — and, to Ryan's mind, ambiguous — reference to security measures round the Rushdale Experimental Research Centre near Oxford. This annoyed him because his own establishment relied largely on seclusion: and he was acutely conscious that while experiments in biological warfare might be necessary to the national good, he preferred them to be carried out more than fifteen miles from his own parish.

Ryan listened through the financial report, heard that the weather was continuing dull and cold, then stirred his big toe against the thermostat control below the automatic tap. He had already read all he wanted from the telex in his study. The Index was down again over four points, but this hardly worried him, since he spread his money shrewdly – and usually quite legally – while keeping his 'grubstake' in a reputable banking firm in Geneva.

He climbed out of the bath and wrapped himself in a towelling gown. He was a compact, strongly-built man, well into middle-age, but his muscles were still hard, his belly flat, his chest, arms, and legs flecked with greyish-blond hair.

As he entered his dressing-room, a valet in a white coat appeared and handed him his glass of Jack Daniels, without ice or water. Hugh Dermot Ryan drank slowly, steadily, allowing his body to dry of its own accord under the towelling wrap.

He had been born, sixty years ago, Hugh Dieter Ryan, in Ennis, Co. Clare, son of an Irish civil servant and a second-generation Austrian mother. Later, under a bizarre train of circumstances – some voluntary, others fortuitous – he had become Hans Dieter Reien, later Colonel Reien of the Waffen-SS, with special responsibilities to the Abwehr and Sicherheitsdienst in Central America. As far as anyone knew, he was the only man to have emerged from World War II with both the Iron Cross, First Class, and the DSO.

Ryan finished his drink and began to dress. His clothes were subdued and faultless. His fingers, which were strong and broad-tipped, were extraordinary in a single respect: they bore no fingerprints. These had been surgically, painfully erased at a German military hospital outside Arras, in the Spring of 1942, before he had been parachuted into Britain as an enemy agent.

His appearance was unremarkable. Apart from the grey at his temples, he looked younger than his age: his skin was smooth, his teeth in perfect condition, his eyes wide-spaced, almost colourless, a pair of pale stones. He was the kind of man who, in England, sometimes had trouble cashing a cheque, while on the Continent and in America he rarely found it necessary to reserve at even the most exclusive hotels and restaurants.

In 1947, following a traumatic incident at the Central Criminal Court of the Old Bailey, he had been offered a small fortune by a Sunday newspaper. He had declined – not out of any modesty, but because his memoirs would have constituted a breach of the Official Secrets Act.

From his childhood in Ireland, Ryan had graduated to the shifty, feckless, then largely-redundant activities of the IRA.

But he had no time for politics. With his natural skills in the use of firearms and explosives, he had embarked upon a career in safe-breaking. He specialized in what he called 'tin-opening jobs', and, within twenty months, was one of the most wanted men in London.

By 1939 he had amassed a small fortune, mostly in heirlooms and melted-down family silver, and had discreetly taken up residence in France, just north of Boulogne. Here he was on nodding terms with P. G. Wodehouse, had a large farm, and a lucrative criminal activity in French land deals. In the early summer the latter was exposed and Ryan was arrested. He was just starting his term of five years' imprisonment when the Germans arrived. Since he spoke their language fluently, he was offered recruitment into the Waffen-SS.

He accepted. His options were not numerous. But he was a man who had learned to exploit the most improbable opportunities. His knowledge of German and his impressive personality, together with his skills as a criminal and a hit-and-run man, seemed to qualify him perfectly for service in the victorious armies of the Reich; and although he was not a snob in the social sense, he had always been an elitist. In the Waffen-SS he found his own level.

His first assignment was Paris. The war was going well for Germany, and also for young Major Dieter Reien. His duties were neither heavy nor dangerous. Food, champagne and girls were cheap and plentiful. He enjoyed preening himself in his dreaded black uniform in the smartest restaurants and cafés.

In the middle of June 1942, he was chosen to be dispatched on a hush-hush mission to England. He was to be dropped into Kent and stake out a top-secret factory which was manufacturing a new fighter-aircraft. His task was to pin-point the factory's position and send out a radio-bleep to direct in a Luftwaffe airstrike.

Instead, he boarded a train for London and went straight to Scotland Yard. Here he was arrested and promptly charged on seventeen counts of breaking and entering. It was three days before he managed to get a message out to the War Office. Eventually someone informed the Cabinet of his presence.

From then on, to the fury of the Metropolitan Police, Ryan's case became the special perquisite of Number Ten. Ryan was set free, and within seventy-two hours the aircraft factory outside

Maidstone had been dismantled and reconstructed three miles away; while in its place stood a perfect copy of the original buildings, together with a mock-up prototype of the aircraft. At dusk Ryan made his way through the wire, and at a pre-arranged signal he switched on his high-frequency radio.

The damage was so accurate and extensive that German aerial photographs, taken next day, convinced the authorities in Berlin that the factory had been totally destroyed. The operation was equally successful for Ryan. He was granted a Free Pardon from all his crimes – suspended on the proviso that he committed no more – and was then invited, by the PM himself, to return to France.

Ryan agreed, but only on condition that the sum of 50,000 gold sovereigns be paid into a numbered Swiss bank account in his name. Although the Old Man assumed an air of outrage, he was privately tickled by Ryan's effrontery: he agreed. Ryan was made to sign the Official Secrets Act, awarded the DSO, flown secretly to Lisbon, whence he made his way by boat to Malmö in Sweden. From there he reached the Third Reich, where he was awarded the Iron Cross, First Class, and later promoted lieutenant-colonel.

After that Hugh Dermot Ryan spent a comfortable war. He was sent as SS aide to the Abwehr in charge of the Caribbean theatre. Here he rose to the rank of full colonel, stayed at the plushest hotels, frequented the most exclusive clubs, while regularly supplying British and American Intelligence with detailed movements of U-Boats in the North Atlantic. At the same time he became as fluent in Spanish as he was in German and English.

But sooner or later Ryan knew that his luck would run out: the Allies were winning, and he finally gave himself up to the British consulate in Caracas. He was repatriated to England where he finished the war as a major in the Brigade of Guards. On being demobbed he drew out some of his capital from Switzerland and bought a nice Tudor bungalow, complete with heated swimming-pool, on the South Coast.

The only thing he had failed to anticipate, as a civilian, was boredom. After a year in his redoubt near St Margaret's Bay he decided to try his hand at a few of his old skills. He selected the home of an elderly couple who were away for the weekend in Cannes. But just as he was leaving the house with a bag of valuables, he was apprehended by the local policeman who had spotted a light in the front-hall.

Ryan's carelessness cost him two months on remand, before he was once again in the dock at the Old Bailey. His chief counsel advised him to plead guilty, and to ask for his other seventeen pre-war cases to be 'taken into consideration'. The trial lasted one day, and the jury returned a unanimous verdict of 'Guilty'. The judge reserved his judgement until the morning.

The next day, at 10.20 a.m., a small fat man was seen to be remonstrating with the officers at the door of the court. He eventually reached the judge and handed him an envelope. The judge opened it, turned purple, then rapped for silence. His address to the court was an odd one. His voice was sour: 'The accused will go to prison for ten years.'

There was total silence. Ryan stood steady and quiet between the two policemen, watching the judge. His lordship's next words came in a hurried whisper: 'Sentence to be suspended. The court will rise.'

Knowledge of the letter, and the identity of its two authors, only reached Ryan a few days after his release. The letter had been signed by the former Prime Minister, Winston Churchill, and by the king.

Ryan, the pre-war Mayfair safebreaker, now found himself in a drab post-war Britain to be both famous and fashionable.

He had capital and influential friends – or rather, contacts. For Ryan was one of those rare creatures who had never had any true friends. It was not that he was a withdrawn or cold man: just that beneath that deceptively relaxed, beguiling exterior was a restless spirit that craved uncertainty and excitement. The placid company of his fellows meant nothing to him, unless he could use them. In all his relationships – both male and female – he behaved with the emotionless self-gratification of a man enjoying a prostitute.

His first excursions into legitimate commerce were not altogether happy. He started by setting up a luxurious floating restaurant on the Thames, but soon found that in a world dominated by Sir Stafford Cripps and ration-books, the venture was doomed. He bought a quarter-share in a nightclub, which went broke within five weeks. (It was not Ryan's fault that at the same time a fire destroyed the premises, thus enabling him to recoup most of his losses from the insurance company.) He had even, at one time, considered starting a prep school, with the emphasis on Outdoor Activities.

His final decision was an inspired one. The rule of life in Britain during those hard days was enshrined in the single word: austerity. Ryan calculated that if people wanted to be austere, they should pay for the privilege: he bought a country house in the Cotswolds and established an exclusive health farm. At first he catered for overweight men and fat plain ladies with varicose veins. For a couple of glasses of lemon or carrot juice a day, a sauna and the attentions of a short, elastic man who rubbed and slapped and pummelled them with his rubbery hands, Ryan was ensured of a steady clientele, all of whom were prepared to pay, in order to be starved, at least five times the country's average weekly wage.

In later years Ryan shrewdly extended his scope. While still keeping within the law – as well as occasionally using it – he offered his establishment as a discreet place of recreation to the high and mighty: politicians, film stars, visiting Heads of State, the famous and the infamous, all could be certain of finding sanctuary, and a little diversion, at Ryan's place, known as The Hermitage.

By 1977 Hugh Dermot Ryan was deriving from his various sources of income around £100,000 a year, and was paying derisory tax. Yet he was not a contented man. In his sixty-first year he was still a bachelor and a lecher; he enjoyed good living, fast cars, a wide variety of women. But what he most wanted seemed no longer available. He yearned for the stimulating scent of danger – something that he was unlikely to sniff in the heart of the Cotswolds.

He finished his whisky and pressed a bell on the desk. His secretary and chief assistant, an unsmiling State Registered Nurse, appeared in the doorway.

'Is he here, Miss McKinley?'

'He arrived about ten minutes ago, sir.'

'Tell him to wait. I'll have another whisky.'

The man who was finally shown into Ryan's leather-padded study had a reptilian stillness about him. He was dressed in dove-grey – a sharp narrow man with flat eyes and shiny black hair like a bathing-cap. His manner was arrogant, and he made the initial mistake of complaining that he had been kept waiting.

Ryan sipped his drink, deliberately not offering one to his visitor. 'What do you want, Mr Sargas?'

'Mr Ryan – I am not here on my own behalf. And you will accept, of course, that what I have to say to you is in the most absolute confidence.'

Ryan's eyes lifted slowly from his whisky. 'Mr Sargas, you represent the interests of my new client, Madame Achar. As for confidence, you know my reputation. And as to fees, you have no doubt seen my brochure? £250 a week – excluding such extras as hairdressing, facials, ultra-violet treatment, and so forth.'

The man's eyes slid downward; he smiled and examined his fingernails. 'Mr Ryan, my client has instructed me to offer you 2,000 American dollars a week – for six weeks, payable in advance.' He put his hand into his jacket and drew out a plain buff packet the size of a small paperback. He let it drop down on the desk in front of Ryan, who looked at it without interest. 'Do you not wish to count them, Mr Ryan?'

'Mr Sargas, you are prepared to trust me – why should I not trust you? But since you are paying this amount, there must be special considerations. These I must know. It is a condition I always make. There are no exceptions.'

The man stiffened. 'Mr Ryan, you are not perhaps suggesting that my client has done anything – illegal?'

'I am not suggesting anything, Sargas. I just want the truth. Otherwise, you can start knocking on someone else's door.'

'My client has an alcohol problem.'

Ryan gave his visitor a bland stare. 'You must know that I am not medically equipped to treat alcoholics here, Mr Sargas.'

'Yes, I know that. That is why I am offering you 2,000 dollars a week. All my client requires is rest and privacy.'

Ryan sipped his whisky; then said, in a silky voice: 'Mr Sargas, please don't fool around with me. I know exactly whom you represent and who your people are. Accept my conditions, and we will both remain satisfied men.'

There was a brief pause. 'You know who I am?' Sargas said.

'You are banker and financial adviser to the widow of a notorious political gangster. I didn't spend half the war knocking around the Caribbean for nothing, you know. Your dead boss might not yet have reached the top in those days, but we all knew his name.'

Sargas gave a cold smirk: 'You called my client's late husband "notorious". Do you think him more notorious than the man who now runs my country?'

'I'm not here to argue about Latin American politics, Mr Sargas. The subject is academic. We are discussing a purely business proposition.'

Ryan's visitor sat contemplating the long-haired white rug; then straightened up. 'I agree. My client will be admitted under your conditions.'

'$3,000 a week for six weeks – in advance.' Ryan finished his drink and grinned: 'Take it or leave it, sonny boy. Neither I nor your client are beggars, so we're both free to choose.'

Sargas stood up with some dignity. 'My client can go elsewhere, Mr Ryan.'

'Very well, let her go.' Ryan waved his hand.

His visitor looked at him passively. Just as he was standing up to leave, Ryan laughed:

'Sit down. If you haven't got a sense of humour, at least have a sense of proportion. You and I know that it doesn't matter a bugger – to you or your client – whether the fee is $2,000 a week, or, 5,000. Either way, the woman can afford it. And I won't insult you by calling you a pimp – because I'm a pimp myself. I just want the money in advance, in cash, and in return I'll guarantee that your client is not disturbed. Above all, that nothing appears in the newspapers, or anywhere else.'

His visitor had paused by the door. 'Mr Ryan, the lady is in a highly nervous state. She requires much care. Above all, she does not want to be bothered with questions. Any questions you have, you will put to me.'

Ryan rose and laid a hand gently on Sargas's elbow, and guided him through the door. 'It's a pity, Mr Sargas, that you can't get me some of those excellent cigars they make in your country. The green ones, I mean – not the ones they export.'

Sargas gave him a quick look, as though about to say something, then left with a nod. Miss McKinley showed him to the front door.

At his health farm Ryan did not usually appear until during the eleven a.m. coffee-break. He would move among the tables and armchairs, patting a rinsed head here, a raddled brow there, or tweaking the parched cheek of some ageing matron whose bank account was in excellent condition, but whose body required skilful repairs.

He made it a rule never to dwell too long on any one client, and always to spread his charm in equal measure. Young people were rare at The Hermitage. Those that did appear were almost invariably girls. Ryan would size up each of them with the dispassionate expertise of a good housewife at the butcher's: and if one pleased him, he would seduce her. Sometimes he entertained them in the sauna; more often on the rug in his study; and, in special cases, in his cork-lined bedroom.

The Hermitage offered Ryan a comfortable life, but a dull one. The arrival of Mr Sargas, and the negotiations over his unusual client, at least promised Ryan a slight diversion. As soon as the man had gone, he called his secretary. 'Miss McKinley, bring me the particulars on Madame Achar. I don't expect there'll be many, but I'd like to know what doctor she may have in England. And make your inquiries with the utmost discretion. If the woman does have a doctor over here, I'd prefer you to pretend that you're making a routine check on behalf of some official organization. On no account do I want The Hermitage mentioned.'

As soon as she had gone, Ryan began to make a number of phone calls – all person-to-person – some to London, some to the Continent; and by the time Miss McKinley returned, he was reasonably satisfied with his inquiries. He was also intrigued.

'Well?'

'Madame Achar has also been consulting a Dr Childs – Dr Ivor Childs, of Wimpole Street. As you know, he specializes in psychiatric problems.'

Ryan nodded. 'Did you speak to him?'

'Yes, sir. He was not helpful. In fact, he was most unhelpful.

He asked if I was acting for a Dr Lopez. When I told him I was not, he became, sir, frankly abusive. He accused me of being impertinent. Then he hung up.'

Ryan stared at the desk-top. 'Miss McKinley, what have you written up for Madame Achar?'

'The usual night sedation, and ten milligrams of Valium three times a day.'

Ryan sat inspecting his thick knuckles. 'She arrived this morning? And she still hasn't left her room?'

'She hasn't even been down for a facial, sir.'

'But she's not on a strict regime?'

'No, sir.'

'Which means she is eating?' Ryan asked, with a dull smile.

'Her appetite is not good, sir.'

'Miss McKinley, I think it's time I had a little professional chat with our Madame Achar. But again I want you to be especially discreet. Our client appears to be unusually jealous of her privacy. So make it quite clear that it's to be a professional call, entirely at her own convenience.'

The Scotswoman departed with a faint rasp of starch.

Hugh Dermot Ryan had drunk half a bottle of whisky – with no visible effect – when the house phone sounded on his desk. He spoke into it, glanced at the thick buff package still lying on his desk, then sat back to wait.

It was a full ten minutes before the knock come on the door. He called out and Miss McKinley opened it. Ryan stood up, smiling graciously.

The woman who entered was of medium height, fine-boned and slim, with copper-dark hair. With his practised eye Ryan put her age in the early forties. Although her figure appeared to be exceptionally well cared for, with the ankles of a young girl, she was betrayed by her mouth. This had a hard downward line, set in an exquisite oval face, and her skin was slightly taut about the cheeks and impeccably varnished. She wore a plain black dress and large dark glasses.

'Madame Achar, how kind of you to come!' His big smooth hand crept forward and clasped hers, which was tiny and very cold. He went on, smiling: 'I apologize for not having called on you in your room, but I felt that this meeting would be better held officially, in my office. I confess,' he added, as he led her to a black leather armchair, 'that I'm a trifle embarrassed to know how to properly entertain you.' As he sat down, his expression became grave. 'I am afraid that it would not be entirely ethical of me – in my professional capacity, you understand – to offer you anything to drink. Except coffee.'

She had carefully crossed her legs so that Ryan saw just enough, but no more. 'I am not interested in your professional capacity, Mr Ryan. You are not a doctor. You are an administrator, a bureaucrat.' Her accent was distinct, with that sharp cosmopolitan inflection that can be heard in every bar from St Moritz and Cannes to Acapulco and Copacabana. As Ryan sat watching her, a series of imaginative speculations crossed his mind – of what he would like to do to her. He was not used to being insulted, even by rich spoilt women, however famous. Yet he was neither surprised by her nor angered. He already knew, from his various researches, enough of her past not to expect a woman of refinement.

He sat back, steepled his fingers together, and gave the woman a non-committal stare.

'Madame Achar, I must point out one thing to you. As proprietor of this establishment, I am directly responsible for the health and well-being of every one of my clients. There are, of course, no rules by which I can force you to follow medical advice. However, in your case, Madame—'

Her voice snapped at him, small and hard across the room: 'All you doctors are charlatans, pill-merchants! I have no illusions about your establishment, Mr Ryan, but I have certainly not come here to be drugged. I have come here to be alone – and I am paying handsomely for the privilege.'

He smiled. 'Very well, Madame. Under the circumstances I will make a special exception. I have a well-chilled Krug sixty-four.'

'I am bored with champagne. Have you any Château d'Yquem?'

Ryan moved across to a cabinet. He chose the wine reluctantly. He was not a mean man, but he had a decent respect for objects of value; and above all, he hated dispensing hospitality to people he did not like.

He opened the ancient bottle and poured the slightly misty

yellow wine into two chilled glasses; carried them both over and handed one to the woman with a mock bow. 'You understand, Madame, that I take no responsibility for this?'

'Who reported to you on me, Mr Ryan?'

'I have my sources.'

The edges of her mouth tightened: then she seemed to accept the inevitable. She was too far from her home ground now, and even if her influence could be made to extend this far, she already knew – from her own researches – that the man behind the desk was not one who would break easily, and would be almost impossible to intimidate, even as a result of the most subtle and exhaustive pressures. Her only hope was that he could be bought.

She suddenly smiled, showing two rows of perfect teeth behind blood-red lips. 'Mr Ryan, you are one of the most impudently self-confident men I have met for a long time. I am a foreigner. When things have improved back home, I shall enjoy inviting you to my country. You will at least have the opportunity to learn some manners.'

Ryan said nothing; her smile grew bleak. 'I understand that you were extremely insulting to my friend and close adviser, Monsieur Sargas? I do not tolerate bad behaviour, Mr Ryan.'

Ryan drank his wine. 'I was under the impression, Madame, that your friend Sargas is a man who is not unaccustomed to bad behaviour.'

She was sitting very straight. 'Monsieur Sargas also informed me that you raised the agreed price for my stay here to $3,000 a week. That is exorbitant. $3,000 a week for a diet of lemon juice? A scandal! It should be exposed.'

'You would be quickly exposed with it, Madame.'

She stood up in front of him and smoothed her dress. 'What is there to expose about me?'

Ryan sighed; got up and refilled her glass. When he sat down again his eyes did not move from her face; and although her dark glasses were impenetrable, he knew that she was watching him just as closely.

He spoke now in his fluent Spanish: 'You ask what I have to expose about you, Señora? May I assure you, with all respect, that in my profession I make it my business to be well-informed. I know who you are – where you come from – your whole history. Most of it is public property. Every newspaper office in the country has a thick file on you, and on your late husband. What I do not know is why you are here. But that is not my business. That is, after all, why you will be paying me $3,000 a week.'

She replied, also in Spanish: 'And what have you heard about me – unofficially?'

'That your identity is to be strictly concealed while you remain in my care. Also, that you are suffering from intermittent bouts of dipsomania.'

She flushed visibly under her careful maquillage. 'Who told you that?' Her voice was tight with fury.

'Does the diagnosis offend you? It is not uncommon in my experience.'

'Who told you?'

Ryan noticed that the hand holding her glass was not quite steady. 'A gentleman called Dr Lopez,' he lied.

Madame Achar's mouth dropped open and her drawn, disciplined features assumed a slack, almost ugly appearance. 'You cannot have talked to Dr Lopez. It is impossible! You talked to a Dr Childs in London. Didn't you? That pompous little fool,' she added; then went on, before Ryan could reply: 'Perhaps you sweetened his tongue with some of my dollar bills?'

Ryan made a gesture towards the unopened package on the desk. 'I made a few phone calls, Señora. They were sufficient to confirm your identity. Also, that your present condition is the result of extreme nervous exhaustion. Perhaps even fear?'

'Fear?' The word was spoken in a hushed tone. 'What have I to fear?'

Ryan rose again to refill her glass, but she stopped him.

'You are not, by any chance,' she said, 'playing a comedy with me, Señor Ryan?'

'By no possible chance, Señora. I take my work seriously.'

'I have no doubt of that. I would not have been fool enough to come to you in the first place.'

Ryan ignored the ambiguous compliment. He finished the last of the Château d'Yquem, then paused, thinking hard. What intrigued him was not so much the involvement of Dr Ivor Childs, but the relevance of the mysterious Dr Lopez. Ryan had floated the second name as a kite, and had been agreeably surprised by the response. He would like to know more about

Dr Lopez, but felt he had pressed the woman far enough for the moment.

He decided to conclude the interview. 'Señora, I think it is not yet time to exchange confidences. For my part, you may remain assured that your privacy is in good hands. Neither Dr Childs nor Dr Lopez are of any interest to me.' He leaned across the desk, his eyes fixed on the black lenses which obscured half her face. 'I can promise you that from now on your interests are mine.'

'My interests?'

'Señora, you may think me an impudent and arrogant man. But do not think me a stupid one. You are alone in this country. Your ultimate interests may differ from mine, but at least we both now have one common objective. You wish to remain incognita while in my care. I wish to be paid for my services for as long as possible. As I have promised Señor Sargas, I guarantee you total privacy – from the other clients, from my colleagues, and above all, from any hint of exposure to the public and the press.'

'And the police?'

He looked at her. 'Señora, I do not answer questions from the police. I assure you, in all honesty, that if I did I would not have you sitting here in this room with me, talking to you as I am.'

She put her empty glass down on the desk in front of him. 'Señor, I answer you by saying that if I had thought it necessary to confide in certain people about *you*, you would certainly not be sitting here in this room, either.'

'And you, Señora, would not be staying at The Hermitage.'

She took a step back. 'Señor Ryan, it has been interesting meeting you. You are a hypocrite, but a charming hypocrite. We shall have the pleasure of meeting again.'

Before Ryan could reach her she had opened the door and was halfway through. She turned, giving him a sharp white smile: 'I am your client, Señor Ryan. Remember that.'

'I shall remember it when Señor Sargas has paid me the balance of $6,000.' He bowed to take her hand, but she flinched away from him.

'Hijo de puta!' she hissed; and he felt her fingers tremble and stiffen under his grip. 'But at least,' she added, 'you are a man of character.'

Ryan drew back. He said in English, 'Madame Achar, I am always at your service. Please contact me any time you wish.' And as he watched her walk away, he thought again of how he would like to spend an hour with her in his secluded bedroom.

Half an hour later Madame Achar took her purse, which was heavy with ten-new-pence pieces, and made a long call to London from the pay-phone in the front hall.

Although every bedroom at The Hermitage had its own telephone, which went through the switchboard, Madame Achar did not want to risk having her call monitored – very probably by Ryan himself. The pay-phone was in a sound-proofed box and she could be reasonably sure that it was not tapped. She took one further precaution, however: she spoke French this time, in a series of brisk euphemisms. Not once did she use the name of the man at the other end; nor did she name a third party who was referred to by both of them several times.

Although there was no hint of menace in the call, a suspicious eavesdropper might have noticed that the woman was not at ease.

An hour and a half later a short man, with moist features and a well-tailored paunch, left the Gothic entrance of the Eden Lodge Nursing Home near Swiss Cottage, got into his Rover 2000, and headed towards the Finchley Road. He had no reason to take more than usual notice of the traffic.

The other car kept a skilful distance, closing in only when a set of lights was about to turn red. The man in the Rover had switched on the radio and was listening to a Brahms concert. He enjoyed music, especially at the end of the day. His hands still smelt of ether; and he reflected that it was strange, even after a scrubbing with carbolic, that the pervasive odour of the Treatment Corridor still lingered, like the smell of premature death.

That afternoon Dr Ivor Childs had administered electro-convulsive therapy to a total of fourteen patients, at £30 a head; and this evening, as he drove back to his house in South Audley Street, he had nothing much on his mind. Business at the three private hospitals he attended, as well as his own private practice in Wimpole Street, was thriving; and his relationship with both his bank manager and his patients was excellent.

The only thing which might have disturbed the doctor's peace of mind was the phone call he had received shortly before leaving the nursing home. It had been a request from one of his most recent clients, a Mr Sargas, who wished to see him at 9.00 p.m. sharp. The man had said only that he had urgent business to discuss.

To the doctor it was more of a bore than a worry, because he himself had other business to attend to – a potentially profitable dinner-party on the other side of London. The thought of being delayed distracted him; and he failed to notice the reflected cube-shaped head-lights swimming in his mirror.

He parked in his reserved doctor's space in South Audley Street; locked the car, carefully checking each door before taking out his house-keys. He was a fastidious man, and in this neighbourhood he had taken the usual rigorous precautions against burglary. The stout panelled door was fitted with three patent locks, and the window-catches were all attached to an alarm system wired up to the local police station.

He let himself in, collected the evening newspaper from the hall table, where his houseboy had left them before going off duty at six o'clock.

It was now 8.43 p.m. The carriage-clock on the mantelpiece in the drawing room was three minutes fast. Dr Childs adjusted it, mixed himself a drink, then prepared to wait for Mr Sargas.

The two men in the car, parked fifty yards up the street, also waited.

At exactly 8.58 p.m. one of them reached into the back and picked up a leather bag. Both then got out and walked leisurely down the street. They reached the panelled door under the Georgian fanlight as the drawing-room clock inside was striking nine.

Dr Childs was just finishing his gin when he heard the chimes of the front door. He was accustomed to punctuality, a virtue he admired. He did not bother to fix the chain before opening the door, and was almost knocked over as the heavy timber swung against him and the brass latch struck him a painful blow in the chest.

He felt himself lifted off his feet, rushed backwards, his arms strapped to his sides by a pair of massive hands. The door closed. In the stillness he heard himself trying to shout. A strip of thick clammy tape was stretched across his mouth, and he felt his lungs contract in panic as he began to breathe through a congested nose.

Neither of the men spoke. Their expressions were vacant and businesslike. Through a mist of pain and shock, the doctor saw that they both had the broad, flat features of the Latin American Indian.

They went to work in a silent, methodical manner which, in a wild moment of terror, reminded Dr Childs of his own profession. They had pinned him on his back, spreadeagled on the Aubusson carpet. One of them removed his shoes, while the other opened the leather bag and took out a hammer and three stout six-inch nails.

The first nail was driven through Dr Ivor Childs's left wrist, just above his Patek Phillipe watch, biting through the carpet and at least two inches into the floorboards. Dr Childs made a choking noise and mucus streamed from his nostrils; but he had lost consciousness before the second nail had crunched through his right wrist. They hammered the third nail through both his stockinged feet, slightly buckling one leg above the other. The blood was quickly absorbed by the carpet.

The man with the hammer replaced it in his bag, and the two of them let themselves out, just as the doctor's carriage-clock showed 9.06 p.m.

Next morning Ryan learned from Miss McKinley that Madame Achar had ventured into public for the first time. During the eleven o'clock coffee-break she was sitting downstairs in one of the chintz armchairs. Most of the clients were reading newspapers and magazines, but she had open on her lap a morocco-bound copy of the *I Ching*; and while the others were dressed in towelling gowns and slippers, she wore the same black dress and high-heeled shoes.

As Ryan came into the room he noticed a heavy front-page headline in a newspaper: MAYFAIR DOCTOR CRUCIFIED. The story itself was full of horrified speculations. Ryan gathered that the police had no clues.

But unlike the police, who were used to more conventional forms of urban violence, Ryan recognized the ritual South American punishment for traitors and informers, which had originated with the Aztecs and spread to the Caribbean. Although, even to his sanguine temperament, Mayfair seemed a trifle outré for such practices.

As he neared the beautiful, taut-cheeked woman who sat studying the ambiguous philosophies of ancient China, he felt a ripple of revulsion.

'May I join you, Madame?' He spoke in English, just out of earshot of the other guests, and without waiting for her reply drew up a chair. She was without her dark glasses, and for the first time he saw her eyes: large and sloping, flecked like quartz.

'You are not taking coffee?' he added.

'I hate decaffeinated coffee without sugar.'

'But you're satisfied with your regime?'

'I have no complaints, Mr Ryan.'

'Are you also satisfied with the old Chinese oracle?' He smiled at the fat leather book in her lap.

She glanced down at it. 'You are familiar with the *I Ching*?'

He sat back and crossed his arms. 'I am always prepared to give credit to ancient beliefs. Providing they are the beliefs of civilized and humane societies. I abhor all acts of senseless barbarism.'

She looked up at him. 'Barbarism is like sin, Mr Ryan. What offends one person may be acceptable or necessary to another.'

They sat watching each other like cats.

Ryan spoke at last. 'I was referring to the barbarism of medieval Spain – to the so-called civilizing mission of the Church of Christ, for instance. You are a Roman Catholic, Madame?'

'I was brought up a Catholic.'

'But you will not be offended if I speak of the influence of your Church over many simple, primitive peoples?'

'What peoples did you have in mind?'

'I was thinking of the Aztecs, Madame. When the Conquistadores first arrived in Central America, they brought with them the Bible. The Aztecs were greatly influenced by it – especially by the details of the Crucifixion.' He paused. Not a muscle of Madame Achar's face stirred.

'I should point out, Mr Ryan, that crucifixion was common

among the tribes of Central America long before the arrival of the Spaniards.'

'That may be so. It is also irrelevant. The fact is, among simple people these habits die hard.'

Madame Achar snapped shut the book in her lap and stood up. Ryan followed: and this time he noticed that she did not look him in the eye. 'I am not sure, Mr Ryan, that I understand what you are trying to say. You have not, perhaps, been drinking?'

Ryan inclined his head, with cold courtesy. 'Madame, at the risk of sounding conceited, I will tell you that I can drink a whole bottle of whisky and not turn a hair.'

'Then let me tell you this, Señor Ryan –' she had broken quietly into Spanish – 'I never trust a man who does not drink, and I never trust one who drinks without getting drunk.'

'It is a broad philosophy, Señora – surely not one you got from the *I Ching*?'

She whispered an elaborate insult which sounded, above the rustle of newspapers and clink of coffee cups, more comic than offensive. Yet if Ryan had not been surrounded by his limp ageing clientele he might well have struck her. And the thought of avenging himself on this proud, neat, immaculate body caused his pulse to quicken.

He spoke calmly. 'You have heard, no doubt, that a certain fashionable London doctor was murdered last night?'

'What doctor?'

Ryan ignored the question. 'It appears that he actually died as a result of congestion of the lungs. He was gagged and must have swallowed his vomit. Not a pleasant death, even for a man with a loose tongue.'

'I do not know anything about this doctor.' Madame Achar's voice was still and cold. 'I do not read your English newspapers or watch your television. They do not interest me.'

'For a woman in your position, you are surprisingly isolated. Unfortunately, however, I do not believe you.' He had drawn closer to her, aware that several of the clients were beginning to take an interest in them.

'You have ruthless friends – or servants – who will obey whatever orders you give them – even if it is only by telephone. And when you say you do not know about this murdered doctor, you are lying.'

'Are you accusing me of murder, Mr Ryan?' Her voice had become menacingly quiet.

'I am not accusing you of anything. I am simply informing you that you have until this evening to explain exactly what you are doing here, and why. If you refuse, I shall ask you to leave.'

'You cannot. You have been paid.'

'I shall pay you back. Good day, Madame. Till this evening.'

He watched her walk out of the room, then followed at a discreet distance.

He did his routine rounds, then returned to his study where he selected a book entitled *A Brief Dictionary of Modern History*, and turned to the chapter on the Caribbean.

Although he had come to know the area well during the war, and still spoke Spanish, with a Latin American accent, as fluently as a native, he had neglected to follow the fiery convolutions of the local politics. He selected the entry he wanted and began to refresh his memory with recent events in a certain Island in the Caribbean.

He read:

In 1955 an army officer, Juan Ramon, seized power at the head of what was to be known as the *Ramonista Movement*. It was inspired by Fascist principles, with a strong Populist appeal. During its first years the Movement was increasingly dominated by Ramon's wife, known as *La Consuelita*, whose premature death was an occasion of national mourning.

Her place was taken by a second wife, a Venezuelan actress who herself became a popular heroine, known as *La Vuelva*.

At the same time the regime became increasingly oppressive and corrupt; and during the next few months the Movement rapidly lost control of the country. Inflation and unemployment soared; widespread strikes and riots followed; while a Left-Wing guerrilla force, led by a former schoolmaster, Fulgencio Gallo, made steady progress in its ten-year struggle, waged from the mountains in the south.

In the summer of 1968 Gallo's troops captured the second-largest city on the Island, Santiago y Maria, and two days later the capital, Montecristo, fell. What followed was called *'La Revolucion Barbuda'* – so named on account of Dr Gallo's famous black beard.

Ramon and *La Vuelva* escaped on the last plane to Miami, and are believed to have taken with them a vast fortune. They lived mostly in Madrid until Ramon's death in 1975. However, his widow continues to enjoy extensive support among the Island's exiles, and even, some say, among people on the Island itself.

Meanwhile, Gallo quickly revealed himself to be a Communist, fully committed to Moscow. Owing to a trade embargo by most of the Western countries, the Island's economy is reported to be in trouble. There is also a serious shortage of manpower, since last year the Soviet Union persuaded Gallo to send a large portion of his conscript Army to assist the liberation movements in Africa.

The entry ended here. It had contained only the bare facts of the Ramon phenomenon, and did not fully explain the political magic which the man – and particularly his two wives – had possessed for their people; nor did it explore the continuing legacy of influence still enjoyed by his exiled widow, La Vuelva. And Ryan reflected, only half-seriously, that this lovely ambitious woman might well be in need of a second 'President-Regent' in whose shadow she could perhaps regain power.

That evening Ryan broke his self-imposed rule and called on Madame Achar in her room.

It was the time known as 'the cocktail-hour': that pause following the afternoon treatments, while the customers relaxed in their rooms, sipping single glasses of lemon juice in anticipation of their night sedation.

Ryan's only concern was that he might catch Madame Achar while at her *toilette*; but she opened the door to him immediately. She was wearing an ankle-length Chinese silk gown patterned with flaming dragons, and in her hand, instead of the statutory fruit-juice, was a thin black cigar. He noted also that the toenails of her tiny feet were painted the colour of blood. She had removed her make-up, which left her face looking scraped and purified; while her rich-tinted hair was hidden under a red scarf. Again she wore no jewellery: and for a perverse moment Ryan wondered what priceless baubles might be locked away in this room.

'Señora, you must excuse me. My visit is not entirely social.'

She stood back and let him pass, then closed the door, locked it, and blew a mouthful of smoke in his face. Without expression he walked over to a chair opposite the double-bed. It was one of the finest rooms in his establishment: only the atmosphere of scent and cigar-smoke jarred; and to Ryan's sensitive nostrils it invested the room with the vulgar elegance of that nightclub in Caracas where General Ramon had picked her up more than fifteen years ago.

Madame Achar had spread herself, without embarrassment, on the bed. She crossed her feet and rested her head against an extra pair of pillows. She looked at him with indifference. 'You will be happy to learn that I cannot offer you a drink. I am obeying the rules.'

'I am delighted, Madame. You would be surprised at how many of my clients quickly lose control and drive to the nearest public house. They invariably return drunk. Indeed, it has often occurred to me that severe abstinence is only a short-cut to excess.'

Madame Achar tapped a finger of ash into an onyx bowl beside her. 'It is you who are full of philosophies this evening, Mr Ryan. Why are you not more direct? Is it because a direct man has nothing to hide?'

'What should I have to hide from you, Madame?'

'Either say what you have come to say, or leave my room.'

Ryan did not look at his client as he sat down. 'Madame, you ask me to be direct. Very well. It is now nearly a quarter-to-seven. I will give you precisely thirty minutes in which to answer my questions. And I must warn you that a great deal of what I ask will only be to confirm what I already know. I would therefore advise you to be as frank as possible. If you refuse, or lie, or in any way fail to satisfy me, I shall ask you to leave my establishment.' He paused, watching her over his cigarette. 'And I have an idea that such an order would be most inconvenient to you at the moment.'

Her only movement was to squash what remained of her cigar. When she spoke, her voice was quite steady: 'Firstly, Mr Ryan, I insist that *you* answer *my* questions. What else do you know about this doctor who has died?'

'Probably less than you. He was an expensive psychiatrist who was treating you for what we might call "a slight drink problem". He was a contact of your business associate, Señor Sargas. Sargas's wish was to hide you in a safe place – somewhere that would combine the advantages of a remote hotel with those of a private hospital. But Sargas is not a subtle man. When I demanded of him the ridiculous sum of $3,000 a week for your stay here, he agreed. An innocent client – even the greatest celebrity who wished to dry out in complete privacy – would not pay half as much.

'And unfortunately for you, Madame, Dr Childs was also not a discreet man. After I made my inquiries, and found out that he had been treating you, I deliberately mentioned the fact to you. I also mentioned something else.'

She lit another cigar and watched him through the smoke.

'I gave you another name, Madame. Dr Lopez. When I did so, you seemed quite upset – just as Dr Childs had done when he blurted out the same name to my informant. You told me that I could not possibly have spoken to Dr Lopez. You were right. Until then I had never heard of any Dr Lopez – I had only heard of him *en passant* from Childs.'

Ryan sat back, at ease. 'And only a few hours later this same Dr Childs is tortured to death at his private house. It is a bad story. It is crude and brutal and totally lacking in finesse.' He shook his head. 'Who are you and your friends trying to impress, Madame? This is a civilized country. Yet the tactics you and your accomplices have used are common to the lowest elements in our criminal society.'

The woman on the bed did not appear at first to be listening; then a tiny smile twitched at the corners of her mouth. 'You speak of criminal elements, Mr Ryan. It has not occurred to you that such elements might have killed this doctor? You yourself suggested that the man was not entirely ethical. Perhaps he was a trafficker in drugs? That way a man can make many enemies.'

Ryan saw in the woman's argument a certain specious logic. 'Now, Madame, you will please answer my questions. And I repeat that I know who you are – where you come from – your whole history.' His face took on a hard, dead look. 'Who is Dr Lopez?'

To his surprise she answered this time without hesitation. 'He is a political adventurer. He is not a doctor of medicine, but of philosophy and economics. He studied at Harvard, in London, and in Berlin.'

'East or West Berlin? I only ask because there's a large institution in the East called the Humboldt University. Some very troublesome people have passed through its doors.'

She laughed suddenly. 'You are suggesting that Dr Lopez might have Communist tendencies? Mr Ryan, you may be a very clever and successful businessman, but your political judgements are simplistic. You know nothing. Or rather, you know a little. A dangerous little.'

Ryan lit another cigarette and smoked for a moment in silence. 'Madame, if I had reason to fear you, I would not have been fool enough to visit you this evening. And I have no wish to meddle in your squalid ritual murders. I have rather more ambitious interests.'

'So?' Her face remained immobile, but the word held a chill sneer.

'It is perhaps unfortunate for you and your Movement, Madame, that the present leader of your country, Fulgencio Gallo, seems to hold many of the same views and the same aims as you. The only difference between him and your late husband is that Gallo has been successful and your late husband was not. But then Gallo is a Communist, while General Ramon was a Fascist.'

'Gallo!' she whispered. 'Don't talk to me of that Whore of the Kremlin! You know what *gallo* means in Spanish? It means a cockerel, a rooster. A bearded rooster!'

She had let the ash drop this time onto the pillow beside her, eyes grown dull. She spoke with slow anger: 'Señor Sargas has paid you well in cash, six weeks in advance, in exchange for my absolute peace and privacy. Not only have you deprived me of both, but you have the impertinence to demand even more!' She shifted her bare feet from the bed and stood up. 'I have only been here one night and you have already abused my privacy. I shall leave tomorrow morning, and you will return to me my entire twelve thousand dollars. And I will not accept a cheque.'

Ryan gave a soft chuckle. 'I do not like to insult a beautiful woman. But you are not being very intelligent this evening, Madame Achar. Perhaps the *I Ching* has misled you?'

'Get out of my room. Get out now, or I shall ring the bell.'

He stood up and moved towards the door. 'If you're worried that I shall go to the police, Madame, you are wrong. Unlike Dr Childs, I am not an informer. Neither am I indiscreet.'

'Why should you want to go to the police, Mr Ryan?'

'Please, Señora,' – this time Ryan spoke in Spanish – 'I think this game has gone on long enough. You are here, incognita, in a foreign country, surrounded by a gang of sadistic murderers who will almost certainly become more of a liability to you than a source of protection.'

She stood very still in front of him.

Ryan continued, brutally: 'Nor do I suppose your money's going to last forever. From what I heard, your old man didn't have much time to loot the national coffers before Gallo and his bearded boys came marching into Montecristo to proclaim their Revolution.'

'You know nothing! The General was not unprepared. He was never unprepared.'

'Your husband's forces collapsed almost overnight, Señora. You and the general escaped on virtually the last plane to leave for Miami.'

She laughed. 'You conceited idiot! There were two planes. I and the General flew out in one. The other just carried money. Eleven tons of it.'

'Monopoly money – or greenbacks?'

She frowned. 'Monopoly?'

'How hard was it? Suitcases of local escudos, with your husband's head on them?'

'No, Mr Ryan. Nearly four hundred million American dollars.' Her voice rang with boastful triumph.

'And how much is left? There must have been a few people to pay off. And Miami's a good place for big spenders.'

'Don't worry – there is enough.' She laughed again, savagely this time. 'So you hope to be able to dip your dirty hands even further into General Ramon's bank account? Goodnight, Señor Ryan. And I shall expect the return of my money by tomorrow lunchtime.'

'So be it, Señora. Providing you leave my premises immediately afterwards.' He turned and opened the door. 'By the way, it won't be the General's money I shall be dipping my dirty hands into. It will be yours. The General is dead, remember?' He closed the door softly behind him and returned to his study.

* * *

Next day, once again, Madame Achar did not appear for the early morning exercises or for any of the treatment sessions. Ryan glanced during the coffee break into the drawing-room, but she was not there either.

He had taken from the safe the plain buff packet which contained $12,000 in one-hundred bills. The chance that the money might be forged had occurred to him; but he knew enough about counterfeit money to make a simple test. Every US bill is printed with the distance between the serial number and the margin differing by a fraction of a millimetre. The same distance only repeats itself exactly on the plates at varying intervals of several hundred bills.

Madame Achar's original payment to him was made up conveniently into three sets of unbroken sequences. With the help of a powerful magnifying glass and a pair of dividers, Ryan had carried out random tests on two of these sequences, and had decided that if they were forgeries only a trained US Treasury official would be able to spot them. On the other hand, he decided that even if they were genuine – and he was fairly certain they were – this did not necessarily make Madame Achar an honest woman. But honest or not, she might still provide Ryan with some nefarious entertainment over the next few months.

His plan was still a tentative one: but on no account must it be rushed. As far as Madame Achar was concerned, Ryan would behave like the gentleman he almost was.

He delayed until 11.45 – five minutes before the gong summoned his self-denying clients to what passed for lunch – then headed towards Madame Achar's room. He knocked, but there was no answer. He knocked again, louder, then tried the handle. The door was locked.

He returned to his office and rang the bell. Miss McKinley appeared. 'Has Madame Achar gone out?'

'I haven't seen her since this morning, sir. She was making a call – from the public phone-box.'

'How was she dressed?'

'In a gown and slippers, sir.'

Ryan nodded. 'Her door's locked and she's not answering it.'

'Do you want me to use the pass-key, sir?'

Ryan looked at his watch. The meal would last barely a quarter of an hour. 'We'll give her till twelve-fifteen. If she hasn't appeared by then, meet me back here and we'll try her again.'

Exactly half an hour later his assistant reappeared in the office. 'There has still been no sign of her, sir.'

'Very well. You have the pass-key?'

She nodded; and he led the way back to Madame Achar's room. He knocked, again without answer; then stood aside while Miss McKinley unlocked the door.

Ryan noticed at once that the maid had obviously not been able to get in either. The Chinese housecoat lay crumpled on the carpet; the chair by the dressing-table had been knocked over, and a glass lay shattered near the door. Madame Achar was on the bed, half covered by the quilt, her head on her naked arm; she was breathing heavily. One breast was exposed. It was a small, rounded breast, perfectly formed.

Miss McKinley noticed other things. There was an empty bottle of five-star brandy lying partly hidden under the drapes of the bed. She grabbed Madame Achar's wrist and began taking her pulse; then leant down and smelt her breath.

'She is drunk.' Without looking at Ryan she lifted the woman's head and slapped her hard across each cheek. Madame Achar's head lolled sideways, and a trickle of saliva hung suspended from the corner of her mouth down to the pillow.

The Scotswoman slapped her again. This time Madame Achar made a choking sound, but her eyes did not open. Ryan looked down at her with distaste. He disliked having his house-rules flouted: and he was particularly intolerant of attractive women who exposed themselves to physical indignity.

Miss McKinley said: 'I think she's taken something, sir. But her one night's sedation could not be dangerous.'

'Not even with a whole bottle of brandy?'

'I agree that if she had drunk the whole bottle, that would be dangerous in itself. But we don't know that the bottle was full.'

'And she might have had other drugs with her when she arrived,' Ryan said. He swore inaudibly. This was just the kind of sordid complication which he loathed: not only did it threaten to bring doctors prying into his establishment, but it could easily lead to the Coroner's Court, and to stories in the press.

While McKinley was still bending over the bed, he began

hunting quickly round the room, looking through the bottles on the dressing-table, then in the medicine-cupboard in the bathroom. He found a plastic phial containing one hundred ten-milligram tablets of Valium; but it was nearly full. There was also a tin of Senecot, and a card of oral contraceptives, out of which he noticed that the last pill had been taken yesterday.

But what worried him was a second phial of pills, this time almost empty and marked with the trade-name *Abstem*.

His search was interrupted by Miss McKinley. 'She's showing signs of coming round, sir. I'm going to get the amyl-nitrate.'

'Is that wise?'

'Would you prefer that I called the hospital?'

He nodded. 'At all costs we must keep this thing quiet. Just one thing,' he added, as she reached the door, 'she was taking these.' He held up the phial of Abstem. 'If she had taken one, Miss McKinley, and *then* drunk a whole bottle of brandy—?'

'She would be dead, sir. But there'd be evidence of vomiting.'

'She's a nice refined lady,' he said, glancing at the half-naked figure on the bed: 'She'd have made it at least to the bathroom?'

'Not if she was falling into a coma, sir. I must get the amyl-nitrate.'

Ryan took advantage of Miss McKinley's absence to make a thorough search of Madame Achar's belongings. They were remarkable for their almost total anonymity. Apart from the essentials of expensive make-up, and a wardrobe containing rather more than most women find necessary in the clinical confines of a health-farm, the only items which caught his attention were a dozen packs of throw-away paper knickers, and four more bottles of five-star brandy at the back of a cupboard.

Just before Miss McKinley returned, he strolled again to the bed and pulled back the quilt and top sheet. Madame Achar lay sprawled out, one hand drooping between her thighs. Only her mouth – which was loose and wet, without lipstick, pressed against the pillow – betrayed her age. From the rest of her body, Ryan would have put her at no more than thirty.

At the same moment he noticed a damp stain on the sheet under her hips. 'You drunken dago slut,' he said quietly, and pulled the sheets back over her, just as his assistant reappeared.

Miss McKinley had the ampoule ready in her hand. She propped Madame Achar's head up on the pillow, then broke the glass tube under the woman's nose. Ryan caught the quick acid whiff, and saw Madame Achar's colour turn mauve: her body twitched and her eyes opened wide; the irises almost disappeared and became two black buttons that stared vacantly across the room; then she began to retch.

The Scotswoman said quickly, 'Leave this to me, sir. She will be all right now.'

As Ryan was leaving, he noticed the copy of the *I Ching* lying on a table by the door. Underneath it were a couple of maps. He picked up all three and returned to his study where he fixed himself a strong drink. Then, while he ate a light lunch, he looked at the maps.

The first was the standard Ordnance Survey of Oxfordshire and Gloucestershire. The nearest village to The Hermitage was marked with a red ring in one corner: but what puzzled Ryan was that the map did not mark the main road from London, by which he knew she had arrived by hired car. It could only mean that during her stay she was interested in excursions into the surrounding countryside – which seemed hardly compatible with a secretive woman desperate for privacy.

One other thing troubled him, though he had absolutely no evidence to link it with Madame Achar. In the centre of the map was a yellow blotch of bare wasteland, much of which he knew to be the property of the Ministry of Defence. Near the edge of this lay the village of Rushdale – only a few miles away from the Experimental Research Centre, although this was not marked on the survey.

A second map was of the Caribbean and covered the north coasts of Panama, Colombia and Venezuela, reaching up to Jamaica, the Dominican Republic and Puerto Rico. There were several arrows and rings, all in pencil, and all along the northern tip of Colombia where it jutted up just north of Maracaibo in Venezuela.

Ryan folded both maps away inside the *I Ching*. Perhaps they meant something, perhaps nothing. But what immediately intrigued him was why this rich international widow, who had spent most of her exiled life in Miami and Madrid, should suddenly decide to settle in England. If she merely wanted to be treated for alcoholism, why didn't she go to one of those ritzy little homes where they put you to sleep with a hypodermic needle, and fed you pills like sweets to a child.

That left the obscure Dr Lopez – the PhD graduate of three leading world universities – the disclosure of whose name had led to a quack psychiatrist being crucified on his drawing-room floor.

Ryan looked at his watch, made a quick decision, lifted the outside telephone and dialled a local number.

CHAPTER TWO

The Night Callers

At 7.30 that evening Ryan went round to the garage and got into his midnight-blue Aston Martin Lagonda. He had left Madame Achar in the care of Miss McKinley, who had assured him that by next morning his patient would be suffering from nothing worse than a massive hangover.

The autumn evening was dark enough for him to switch on his lights; but he became aware of the other car when he was a hundred yards past the gates.

For the first four miles it was a small winding road which allowed for no speed, no overtaking. He had slowed enough to see that it was a Ford Cortina with two men inside. He couldn't read the number-plate, or see their faces: though he could imagine them as oily scum from the back-alleys of Montecristo who had hiked their way up through the bloody ranks of General Ramon's Secret Police, then fled the vengeance of Gallo's 'Bearded Revolution'. Their job now was to look after the needs of his widow – whatever those were.

He had reached the A40 from Oxford to the West and leered into the mirror. A Cortina versus a Lagonda was a pitiful match: but he must give them a good run for their money – or rather, Madame Achar's money. On no account must he allow them to miss him at the turning.

They came up behind, their headlights on full-beam, obviously trying to dazzle him and so prevent him from reading their number-plate.

He flicked his indicator obligingly to the left, pulled slowly out and turned west towards Cheltenham. The motorway had drawn off most of the traffic and at this hour the road was clear. He waited to make sure that his pursuers were comfortably behind him, then pressed his foot gently down and heard the strong steady hum of the engine and the rhythmic click of the automatic gears changing up, as the road came racing towards him in the long white arc of the headlamps, and the cat's-eyes swept out of the night like a continuous curving burst of tracer-bullets.

The needle on the speedometer dial had crept round to between 100 and 110 m.p.h. He took the familiar bend under the elms with the controlled howl of tyres, then straightened up for the two-mile stretch into Burford.

The Cortina's lights had vanished. Ahead, there was still no traffic. He pressed his foot to the floor, glimpsed the needle as it edged past the 140 mark; then fifty seconds later allowed the power-brakes to press him forward against the seat-belt. The sign for BURFORD flashed past. He slowed down further, as the grey stone houses rose under the headlamps.

He now had two simple choices. He must have at least a ninety-second lead on the Cortina, and he hardly thought that a pair of Latin hoodlums would have taken a crash-course in the highways and byways of the Cotswolds. If he wanted to make sure of losing them, he could turn down into the old part of the village, then take the cross-country road to Stow-on-the-Wold, with its infinite number of side-turnings where he could either double back or lie low.

But he didn't want to lose them. He passed the turning down into the village. There was some traffic now, in front and behind, and at first he was unable to distinguish the Cortina's lights. A quarter of a mile beyond the village a big car moved up behind him, flashed him twice, swerved round him and pulled up ahead of him. It was a Jaguar with two men inside. Ryan stopped behind it, took out a cigarette and lit it from the dashboard lighter.

The passenger door of the car in front opened. The man got out and strolled back towards the Lagonda. Ryan flicked a switch, and his window slid down. The man put his head in and said, 'Evenin' Colonel. Giving this lovely toy of yours a bit of exercise, are you? You're not on one of those autobahns now, y'know.'

'Sorry, Sergeant, I'm getting careless. How long have you been following me?'

As he spoke, he saw the Cortina race past in a spray of loose grit. 'You ought to follow those lads,' he added. 'They've been keeping up with me for the last ten miles.'

The police sergeant ignored him. 'Know what speed you were

doing back there? We clocked you at over sixty through the town. One of these days, Mr Ryan, somebody's dog's going to get killed.'

'What are you going to do? Book me for careless driving? – for not looking in my mirror?'

The policeman sighed. 'You're bending the rules, Mr Ryan. Don't make me bend them too. This is the last warning I'm giving you. The law's made for everyone, even you.'

Ryan said, 'Cut the crap, Sergeant. There are bigger fish out tonight than me. Or rather, a couple of sprats that might lead you to a big fish. But remember, I'm not a grass. I don't know anything about it. Just the number. VJJ 280R – grey Cortina, probably hired, and probably with a couple of dagos in it. They may be armed, so watch yourselves.'

'When was this?'

Ryan leant back and drew on his cigarette. 'They passed us about a minute ago. If you put your foot down you might still catch them. But they're following me, remember – so they may be in a lay-by, or may try doubling back.'

The sergeant hesitated. 'I just hope you're not having me on, Mr Ryan. Because if you are, I'll put you in my report – and this time it won't get lost in our pay review files. Where are you heading?'

'La Reserve. Dinner for two – strictly stag. I'll try and get in front of those boys and lead them there, then we'll see what happens. It's a cul-de-sac, so if they're at all bright they won't follow me to the door. Only don't stamp around in your big boots and upset the other guests.' He flicked the switch and the window slid shut.

He did not wait for the sergeant to get back into the Jaguar, but pulled out in front of it and drove away fast. It was only six miles to the lane leading to the restaurant. After two miles he saw the Cortina drawn up without lights on the verge. He slowed gradually to the statutory seventy m.p.h., giving the other car plenty of time to catch up.

He had its lights once again in his mirror by the time he reached the turning to the restaurant. It was on his right, in front of an awkward bend, and he had to pull into the centre lane and stop, to make sure there was no on-coming traffic. Then he shot across onto the bumpy surface of the single track leading to La Reserve. The Cortina passed behind him, slowly enough for its occupants not to have missed him.

Ryan had enjoyed the escapade, and was almost sorry it was over. The police would no doubt pick his pursuers up, probably on some technicality such as carrying offensive weapons. Still, the brief excitement had given him an appetite.

He parked the Lagonda outside the renovated Elizabethan house, and walked between the coaching-lamps into a low bar with dimpled windows and bent beams hung with mugs and stirrups. Although *Michelin* had consistently ignored the place, the main English gastronomic guides continued to rate it one of the best restaurants in the region. The room was packed with the usual saloon bar crowd of the county breed. Ryan felt reassured. Among all these hairy tweeds and chequered trousers, a couple of Latin monkeys would stick out like B-movie heavies at the Lord Mayor's banquet. He himself, both worldly and chameleon-like, fitted round them like a well-made glove.

With polite skill he evaded the hearty welcomes from the bar, and made his way to a table behind the inglenook.

His guest was a man of undistinguished appearance, a small prune-like face, leather patches at the elbows, and some obscure regimental tie knotted too tightly round his thin neck. He looked like some retired Civil Servant – which was what he was, more or less.

Ryan sat down. 'Sorry, Miles, I'm a few minutes late.'

'I was a few minutes early. What are you having?'

'Teacher's and water.' Ryan noticed that his guest had hardly touched his half of bitter.

He watched his guest disappear into the crowd along the bar, and reflected that it was a piece of good fortune that he so loathed the little man's wife. Otherwise, he would probably have visited him that evening at his cottage just five miles away, in a remote area where he would have been dangerously vulnerable. Here he felt safe – at least, until he stepped outside and got into his car. He had no weapons, besides his hands and feet: and was now counting on the efficiency of the local police.

While Miles was still getting his drink, Ryan got up and made his way past the bar, out again through the front door. It was a damp black night, and it took him a few seconds to adjust to the dark.

There were about two dozen cars parked under the trees,

but no sign of a grey Cortina. For a moment he felt a frustrating sense of anticlimax. He hadn't come here looking for trouble, but when a couple of strangers threw it in his lap, he liked to be able to throw it back, with a vengeance.

He returned to his guest. 'Now listen, Miles. I didn't say much on the phone. I don't trust phones. And what I've got to say is entirely between you and me. For tonight you're back at your old desk.' He took a deep drink. 'I've got a problem.'

'Yes, you do seem to have got yourself into a bit of a jam, Hugh. The trouble is, you've no hard – *really hard* – evidence to go on. Certainly not enough to justify your going to the authorities – even assuming that your friends in the police car do pick them up. As for the immediate problem of your safety,' he added, removing a fishbone from his teeth, 'I should have thought *you* were the expert on that, not me.'

'Yes, I know,' Ryan said patiently. 'I'm not asking for your help. I want information. Why here? Why England? Why my place? What was wrong with Madrid or Paris or Miami?'

'Perhaps she got tired of them – or they got tired of her.' The little man's eyes had brightened with his third glass of wine. 'When all's said and done, Britain is still a very hospitable country. We have a tradition of offering asylum to political exiles which I have often felt goes far beyond the bounds of moral rectitude, even plain common sense. What is worse, we don't always seem to mind if our guests occasionally indulge in a little political activity. Providing there's no rough stuff, of course. The French and Spanish, even the Americans, are much tougher.'

'I thought they mostly cracked down on left-wing groups – Reds under the bed, and so on? In the States, anyway?'

Miles Merton gave a thin smile and this time there was a hint of patronage in his voice: 'You have a somewhat naive view of the Ramonista Movement, Hugh.'

'I'm not a political genius, for Christ's sake, but I thought most Latin American politics boiled down to pretty much the same thing. A gangster general seizes power, rules with the help of an army of hired assassins and torturers, and gets his hand in the till for the last time before he's flung out on his ear. The only difference with Ramon, as I see it, is that his career was livened up with a couple of glamorous sex-pots – the first of whom, at least, seems to have had some political impact on his country. And the second one – who is known as La Vuelva and who I've got sleeping off a bloody great hangover at my Farm – seems to have illusions that she can tread the same path.' He paused. 'Or does she?'

'I have no idea. I haven't had the pleasure of meeting the lady. You have the advantage over me here, Hugh.'

Ryan drank some wine. 'Listen, Miles, you're not in the Department now, and I'm not one of your dips. I want a straight answer. You weren't just picking your nose when you were on the Caribbean Desk. Exactly what do *you* know about the late General Ramon and his outfit?'

The little man made a careful incision in his fish, paused, then licked his lips.

'I don't want to disappoint you, but I've been out of touch for a long time. And I was pulled off the desk a couple months after Gallo got in.'

'Quite,' said Ryan. 'But you *were* on the desk while Ramon was in power.'

Miles took a slice of sole which he seemed to sip rather than eat; he said nothing. Ryan went on:

'You told me I had a pretty simple view of Ramon. All right, enlighten me. I'm not buying you this dinner for nothing, you know.'

The civil servant cleared his throat. 'You were asking why his widow has come here. And you remarked, quite correctly, that the French, Spanish and American authorities dislike left-wing exiles in their midst. Ramon may have been a thorough-going Fascist, but in his heyday he also enjoyed a great deal of left-wing support, particularly among the poor. He was a scoundrel but he wasn't a fool. He played it all ways. He oiled up to the big industrialists and landowners on one hand, and paid court to the lower orders by nationalizing the small hold-ings and businesses that couldn't fight back. It was the middle classes who felt the squeeze – as well as the wretched intelli-gentsia, of course. But those sort of people don't make good revolutionaries – and anyway, Ramon had a huge standing army, not to mention his police, which he kept fat and happy by printing more and more money, until inflation was running at nearly four hundred per cent per annum. But that wasn't what brought him down. It took the bishops to do that.' He gave a little smile. 'In the end Ramon went too far. He tried to introduce a programme of nationwide birth control. And then, my God, he tried to legalize abortion! Ironically, they were the only "liberal" measures he ever went for. And they ruined him. The Church saw to that. The one lot you don't upset in those parts is the Church.'

'How does Gallo make out with them?'

'I told you, Hugh, I was moved from the desk. I only know what I read in the papers. And Gallo runs a very tight ship. Our Embassy in Montecristo was closed a year after he came to power, when he broke off diplomatic relations with everyone except the Soviet block and the Third World. It's more or less a closed country. Tourism's dried up completely, and the few journalists who do get in are either hard-line Communists, or the odd so-called "neutrals" – usually bloody French or Scandinavians, who manage to find something encouraging about a country where not only the brothels have been shut down, but also the bars, and even most of the cafés.'

'Sounds a lovely place.' Ryan sat chewing his rare steak. 'You've no idea what the opposition might be?' he added. 'How many political prisoners, for instance?'

'Ten – fifteen thousand. Mostly from the middle classes and the intelligentsia. By and large, the same wretches who got it in the neck under Ramon.'

'The only difference being that Gallo's got Moscow behind him, and Ramon didn't?'

'Precisely. I know it's confusing, but if you know anything about modern Latin American politics, you'll realize that it makes some sort of unholy sense.'

Ryan paused. 'When I suggested to the woman yesterday that one of her henchmen might have Communist leanings, she laughed in my face.'

'That's not surprising. As I've tried to explain, Hugh, the Ramonista Movement has always been a broad church. Which in their case means, quite literally, that their right hand does not know what their left hand is doing.'

Ryan ordered coffee and brandy, and when the waiter had gone said, 'Ever heard of someone called Dr Lopez?'

Miles gave a chuckle, like toast being scraped. 'Which *Doctor* Lopez? You might as well ask if I know a *Doctor* Smith!'

Ryan did not smile. 'I told you about him earlier. Only this Dr Smith was enough to get a posh head-shrinker tortured to death in the middle of Mayfair.'

'Lopez is almost certainly not his real name. Anyway, it means nothing to me.'

'What about that stuff she told me about him being a PhD – Harvard, LSE, Berlin? Doesn't that mean anything? Apart from the fact that she might have been dropping me a hint? Or perhaps she was just over-excited and got careless?'

Miles sat frowning into his brandy. 'There must be thousands of Latin American students who have studied in Europe since Ramon fell.'

'You mean, thousands of Ramon's exiled followers?'

The other hesitated. 'More like a few hundred, perhaps.'

'Harvard and London, yes,' Ryan said, 'but Berlin – that's a bit off the beaten track, isn't it?'

The other nodded, still without looking up. 'But she didn't say whether it was East or West?'

'No. She evaded the question. I think she was getting rattled by that time. Her nerves aren't good. If I'd leaned on her, I might perhaps have broken her there and then.'

'You might have saved yourself a lot of trouble.'

'I seem to have enough trouble as it is.' Ryan lapsed into silence.

His guest ran a thumb-nail slowly along the ridge of the tablecloth. 'You've heard, of course, of "Pedro"?' he said at last. 'The press have described him as the most wanted man in the world – and probably, for once, they're not exaggerating. His real name is believed to be Frago de Sanchez – son of a lawyer from Sao Paulo, Brazil. Nothing much else is known about his background, except that he left home in his early twenties and travelled widely in Europe.

'He's believed to have spent some time in the Soviet Union. But rumour has it that he moved too far left even for the Soviets, and got flung out. From then on he seems to have flirted with the way-out Palestinian lot – Black September, and so forth. And West German Security are convinced that he was tied up at one time with the Baader-Meinhof mob.'

'God, a real death-and-glory boy! Kill anyone, bomb anything, tear down society, just for the hell of it. I wonder what his mother thinks of him?'

'The fact is, Hugh, he's damned clever. He seems to have used any number of aliases and to have been remarkably successful with forged documents. But he also left a paperchase of clues all over the Middle East and Western Europe. The Israelis were the first to get on him, after he blew up that airliner in Rome, but it was the French who came closest to picking him up. If you remember, he killed a Lebanese banker on a Paris street in broad daylight, was chased into a flat by two detectives, shot them both stone-dead, then vanished like a puff of smoke. But again he left enough material in that flat for French Intelligence to build up a pretty good picture of him.

'That was just over a year ago. Since then he's been lying pretty low. There was a scare a few months back when the Swiss had to blockade St Moritz while the Shah was on a skiing holiday, after the rumour got around that Pedro had been spotted in the town. But nothing came of it.'

'You sound pretty certain that Pedro and Dr Lopez are one and the same. Why?'

Miles Merton drained his brandy. 'Do you mind if I have another of these?'

'As many as you like.' Ryan effortlessly caught the waiter's eye, at the same time glancing quickly, thoroughly, round the room. The scene was quiet, passive, deeply English. He asked again. 'How does your Pedro come to be Dr Lopez, Miles?'

The other man waited until his second brandy had arrived. 'You do understand, Hugh,' he said finally, 'that what I'm going to tell you is only surmise. No more than smoke-room tittletattle. I was up in town a couple of weeks ago and was talking with a few old boys in the Department. You remember that incident some months ago when the police raided a flat near the West London Air Terminal and found a big cache of arms under the bathroom floor? Russian stuff mostly, fairly sophisticated, believed to have come in through Libya. It was put down as an IRA job at the time – a big splash in the press which dried up pretty quickly when there were no arrests.'

'What was the Irish connection?'

'The landlady said the tenants had Irish accents.' The little man smiled: 'You can't blame the police – it was an obvious conclusion.'

'Who's blaming the police? And what's all that got to do with Pedro?'

'Only that he was staying in the flat for a couple of months before the raid. Again, it seems he left a lot of clues lying around.'

'Such as?'

'Finger-prints all over the place. They were even on the guns. But more extraordinary, they found a whole stack of cuttings from French newspapers, all describing the double murder in Paris. It was again as though he were challenging the police to catch him. Turning international terrorism into a bloody great game,' he added, with uncharacteristic venom.

Ryan sat at ease, smoking a cigarette: then suddenly – 'Do you know anything about the Rushdale Research place near here?'

Miles Merton jerked upright in his chair and stared at Ryan. 'What on earth made you think of that?'

Ryan touched the side of his nose. 'Just a smell. The old instinct, you know.'

'Hugh, don't make things difficult for me.'

'Come on. We both signed that piece of bloody bumf – we're on the same side, for Christ sake!' He leaned forward: 'So don't play funny buggers with me, Miles. What do you know about Rushdale?'

'It's not my area. You must know that. It's strictly domestic – nothing to do with my lot. I just know the name.' He paused. 'What do *you* know about it, Hugh?'

'Nothing. Except I once heard they were trying to cure the common cold there, God bless 'em.' He grinned. 'Miles, what the hell's this Pedro person got to do with this bloody woman, La Vuelva?'

'Yes – well –' Miles had brought his head up and his eyes were focusing brightly now – 'you'd think that someone like Pedro would keep a few secrets.' He seemed relieved at being spared any further questions about the Rushdale Experimental Research Centre. 'Well, one of the things they found in his Paris flat was the photograph of a woman. It was signed in Spanish – no name, just *"To the Soul of my Heart"*.'

Ryan nodded: '*"A mi alma de corazon"*. How very touching. I suppose you're going to tell me he had her sign a whole set of her photos so that he could leave one at every last place he jumped off from? Did you see the picture yourself?'

'No. The French police were a little slow on the uptake. It

was only after the raid on the London flat, when our boys pooled their stuff through Interpol, that the penny dropped. Among the other things Pedro left in his London pad were two pages of another magazine, found at the bottom of a drawer. This time it was in Spanish – a two-page spread taken seven years ago, showing La Vuelva and the late General Ramon at their villa outside Madrid.'

'No signed copies this time?' Ryan smiled and drank some brandy. 'A pretty tenuous connection, Miles. I knew a fellow – bloody great bastard, was once a professional wrestler – who used to collect photographs of Marilyn Monroe. He had two suitcases full of them – just about every photograph of her ever taken.'

'I see. Does he still have them?'

Ryan laughed. 'No. He died – burst appendix. But it doesn't stop your friend Pedro collecting pin-ups of La Vuelva.' He lit a cigarette and smoked for some time as though his guest did not exist. At last, casually, he said, 'Tell me, what was Pedro's pad in Kensington like?'

'Oh, usual rabbit warren – a corridor of bedsitters, immersion-heater, posters of Ché Guevara on the walls.'

'Hardly the style you'd expect of the young escort of the Widow Vuelva?' Ryan stroked his jaw and grinned.

'We must not forget,' the other said, 'that the whole premise is purely circumstantial.'

Ryan chuckled: 'You're a cagey old devil, aren't you, Miles? I bet you've never told a fib in your life. And you couldn't make up a story like this, even if you tried. There's just one thing that bothers me.'

'Yes?' The little man sounded slightly worried.

'We can assume that Pedro has a fair amount of money. He wouldn't have been able to vanish always if he hadn't – and stay vanished, with at least three international police forces on his tail.'

'What are you suggesting, Hugh?'

'Just that you hardly expect to find a character like that dossing down with a couple of Irish hoods in bedsitter-land.'

'So where would you expect to find him?'

'Nothing wrong with a penthouse in Mayfair, is there?'

The man simpered into his glass. 'Maybe that would have

conflicted with his social conscience? But of course, with that sort of person you're up against a totally alien species.'

Ryan nodded. 'All right, Pedro's a nut-case. But the person I can't make out is La Vuelva. I mean, I know she's a rich, good-looking woman with a volatile personality. But that doesn't explain how she apparently still holds such enormous political sway over her people. I had always thought Latin-American countries are run by men and men only. The women are usually there only to cook and wash and open their legs. La Vuelva must be some sort of bloody female guru!'

'Not so much a guru, old man. More a product of tradition. The people think of her as being of the blood of their hero, Ramon. You might say it was a kind of *machismo* by proxy. She's also got what remains of her husband's fortune, of course, and that commands quite a lot of clout.'

'Enough to finance her come-back on the Island?' said Ryan.

'Now steady on – I didn't say that,' his guest said quickly. 'After all, you know more about the woman than I do.'

Ryan decided to change the subject. 'How old is Pedro?'

'In his mid-thirties, I believe.'

'Any pics of him?'

'Nothing that's any good. There was one photograph taken in Beirut, but it's very blurred – just shows a short dark man with round features and sunglasses. Could be anyone.'

'Nothing else you picked up from your old scouts round the Club fire?'

'Only that I got the impression that the trail's gone cold. Which is to say, Pedro's simply vanished again.'

'You sure they're not on to La Vuelva, alias Madame Achar?'

'I certainly didn't hear any mention of her.'

'And nothing to tie her or Pedro up with the Childs killing?'

'As I told you, Hugh, I was last in town two weeks ago. All I know about the murder – apart from what you've told me this evening – is what I read in the papers.'

Ryan turned and called for the bill. He paid in cash, leaving a handsome tip. 'By the way, Miles. Any idea of the size of Gallo's standing army – roughly, that is?'

His guest looked surprised. 'Roughly? It's supposed to be around eighty thousand – which is pretty big for a population of only six million.'

'But they're not all regulars?'

'Oh no. At least two-thirds are conscripts. They have three years' conscription on the Island, you know.'

'I didn't. But how many troops has Gallo got acting as Soviet understudies out in Africa?'

The little man still looked surprised. 'There's no exact figure. But I've heard it's between fifty and sixty thousand – probably nearer sixty. They reinforced them a couple of months ago – to make up for all the losses they were taking in the Bush, apparently. They were ferrying them across the Atlantic from the Island in a whole armada of freighters, as well as those giant Soviet transport planes.'

'So you might say,' Ryan put in, 'that at least from a military point of view, Gallo's Island is pretty well defenceless?'

'Hugh, just what are you getting at?'

Ryan ignored the question. 'Any idea whether he's using his crack troops in Africa? Or is he pumping in a lot of Blacks and mestizos to keep up the fraternal image among his African brothers?'

The little man gave a sour chuckle. 'I can't answer that for sure. But I can make a damn good guess. Those central Americans aren't exactly renowned for their fighting prowess, as you no doubt know. And from what I've heard, the Africans aren't taking all that kindly to them. Apparently, in some places they've been nicknamed the new white conquistadores.'

Ryan folded his napkin and stood up. 'Thank you, Miles. I've enjoyed our evening – it's been very informative. Come and see me at the Farm some time and we'll have a few jars, *à deux*. I might even stand you a free sauna and a going-over from one of my best girls.'

They reached the bar where Ryan turned and wrung his guest's hand in a smooth painful grip. 'Hasta luego, compañero! – as the good Dr Gallo would say. And if you hear anything else, just give me a tinkle.'

'Mind how you go, Hugh. And remember, if this woman you've got staying with you is the person we think she is, you could be putting yourself at serious risk. You mentioned yourself the case of the Mayfair doctor—' He broke off and glanced quickly round the now almost deserted bar.

'Cheer up,' said Ryan: 'I'm not so old that I get some dago tart to put the frighteners on me. I'll survive.' He watched the

43

little man slip away to the toilets; then turned towards the front door.

There were only a few cars left on the forecourt. Ryan peered through the dark and was satisfied that the Cortina was not among them. Nor was a police car, for that matter.

The Lagonda was the last car parked under the trees. It was very dark here and it took him a couple of seconds to select the keys. He got in, relaxed in the deep leather bucket-seats, flicked on the lights and started the engine. As he waited for it to come fully alive he saw his guest appear at the door of the restaurant: a small lonely figure in a long overcoat, moving slowly, head bowed, as though sniffing his way through the dark in the opposite direction.

Poor sod, Ryan thought, as he slipped the car into 'drive': no pleasures in store for you tonight, chum – just that damp little stone cottage with its herbaceous borders and pristine bookshelves full of the Folio Society; and your foolish old spouse lolling in front of the electric fire with a toothglass of gin and the *Reader's Digest*.

Ryan swung the Lagonda round and headed for the lane, without waiting to see the little man get into his own car. He felt relaxed but tired. He just hoped that Madame Achar had stayed tucked up in bed, to spare him any further excitement until the morning.

During the drive he turned on the car radio and caught the end of a local news-bulletin. There had been a serious rail-crash on the main Western line, not far from Woodstock. The night express had been derailed at high-speed and at least three carriages had been wrecked. There was still no report of casualties, although it was feared these were high.

Ryan switched off. He had no interest or compassion for the victims of either natural or man-made disasters. He had his own troubles to worry about.

He arrived back at the Farm without incident. For a moment as he parked the car, then let himself into the darkened house and along the still corridors, he considered how he might ravish the lovely La Vuelva while she still lay hungover and helpless. But once at his desk he assumed the air of a professional man:

he had ethics and responsibilities. He also had a problem on his hands which was going to require some degree of skill, nerve, and self-control.

He drank a malt whisky, then dialled the local police station and asked for Sergeant Dexter. He was told the man was out; but after giving his name he was put through at once to the night duty officer. Ryan had expected that the incident with the Cortina would have figured prominently on the evening's log, and was surprised, even angered, to learn that the officer knew nothing of any Cortina or of any hired car with two aliens having been apprehended by Sergeant Dexter or by anyone else. He added, by way of explanation, that earlier in the evening the entire station-force had been called to a serious rail-crash outside Oxford.

Ryan managed to say something polite, then hung up. He felt vaguely cheated. It was not so much the annoyance of having lost the two men in the Cortina as the humiliating thought that the sergeant might not have taken him seriously.

He had just reached into the desk for the bottle of malt, when he felt a delicate pressure on his shoulder. Fingers touched his cheek, as light as a moth. His body was alert, tensed; but he did not at once turn, or indeed make any movement at all. He remembered later being surprised that there was no smell – no trace of scent or tobacco. Ryan was fastidious about smells, particularly those of women: he preferred an uncertain, even obnoxious, smell to no smell at all. A woman with no smell was a neuter, a dish without salt or savour.

Cautiously, he brought out the bottle and poured himself a glass, lifted it to his lips and said, 'It's well past your bedtime. I should be angry with you.' His big hand closed round her small cold fingers. 'I didn't hear you come in, I've known very few people – besides myself – who could move as quietly as you. But then perhaps I'm tired. I've had a busy day.'

His hand squeezed hers, feeling it flinch like a trapped bird. He heard her voice, hoarse, reluctant: 'How did you know it was me?'

'After a time, Madame, one tends to have an instinct for these things.' He jerked forward, twisted round in his chair, and sat smiling brightly up at her. She looked smaller than he remembered her, frail, her shoulders slightly slumped under her loose Chinese-dragoned housecoat; and her neat oval face looked down at him with huge black eyes and bloodless lips. Her hair was pulled back against her scalp and shone in the light from the desk-lamp like rusted metal. He began to laugh, quietly, almost tenderly. 'Should I break all the rules and offer you a drink?'

'You saw me today. You came into my room.' It was not a question, and the words were stated without malice or rebuke; they were spoken in that same low voice that now had something dreamy about it: yet it was not the voice of someone who is drugged or drunk.

'Madame, you did a very foolish thing today. I don't wish to inquire too closely into the reasons, except to tell you that if this had happened in the case of any of my normal clients, I would have had to ask them to leave.'

'Since you have ordered me to leave anyway, does it matter?' her voice had taken on a tone of tired arrogance.

Ryan stood up, went over to the safe in the back of the hi-fi speaker, swung the little door open, removed the plain paper packet and returned to the desk. 'Here – you may count them. They have not been touched. I have not even deducted anything for your two nights' stay.'

Her hand took the packet and let it slap back on to the desk-top. 'Mr Ryan, I must ask you to forgive me. Certain things have been very difficult for me. You understand – a little perhaps?'

Ryan had been smiling all the time while she spoke. He was standing very close to her; he could see the regular movement of her breathing under the flaming silk, and it occurred to him that it was like the breathing of someone in a deep sleep. He said, 'What do you want, Madame?'

Her fingers, easily, without ceremony, untied the housecoat and let the sides fall open. She was as naked as Ryan had seen her that morning. His hand closed round her tiny wrist and he drew her gently aside and down onto the long-haired white rug. He did not speak; nor did he bother to lock the door, or even turn out the light. He was supremely confident, and she yielded to him at once and totally.

'Don't you want your money?' he said; and when she did not answer he got up, took the package off the desk, walked naked with it to the corner and replaced it in the safe, then turned to look at her. She was lying on her side on the rug like a diminutive Venus, eyes closed.

He was not sure whether she were asleep or not. His feet made no sound as he returned across the room and began to dress from his pile of clothes on the sofa. These he had left neatly folded, while he now noticed that her housecoat lay in a crumpled heap of silk where she had let it fall.

He stepped round her and lifted the outside phone on the desk; paused to watch if the faint *ping*! disturbed her, but her eyelids did not even flicker. Then he again dialled the local police. 'Duty Sergeant,' he said softly: 'Hugh Ryan of The Hermitage. Is Sergeant Dexter back yet?' Pause. 'Then I'll speak to Inspector Prentice.'

'You will replace the telephone.' Her voice was sharp and controlled, more confident than he had ever heard it. He had not even heard her stand up; and her nakedness somehow in no way detracted from her air of authority. He heard a voice crackle near his ear. 'Inspector Prentice is not on duty tonight. Can I help you?'

The woman's eyes had not moved from his face. 'Replace the telephone,' she repeated.

He looked straight at her and spoke into the mouthpiece: 'Will you tell Sergeant Dexter that Mr Ryan will get in touch with him tomorrow' – and he laid the receiver in its cradle. 'You would be more impressive if you put on your coat,' he added, and was relieved to see some colour appear in her cheeks.

'You told me you are not an informer,' she said, 'and now you are ringing the police. To tell them what? What do you have to tell them, Ryan?' – her voice was no longer steady – 'You have nothing to tell them. Nothing!'

Ryan sat down behind the desk. The movement seemed to disconcert her; she began to turn, then, conscious of his stare, backed away towards the sofa and retrieved her housecoat. Her cheeks flushed again as she drew the silk cord tightly round her waist and knotted it.

'I intended to inquire, Madame, after two of your compatriots.' And he recounted to her the events earlier in the evening with the two men in the Ford Cortina. She seemed neither surprised nor concerned. 'Now let's be frank with each other, Madame Achar. I'm prepared to be frank if you are. Why were those two men following me?'

She said nothing. Ryan tried again. 'Why did you get drunk today?' Still nothing.

'All right.' He spoke patiently: 'Tell me what you know about the Rushdale Research Centre near here?' He pronounced the name carefully, and watched the dull closed look that came over her face. It infuriated him; for like all satisfied lovers in the immediacy of their conquests, he wanted compliance, not blank resistance.

'You've got a map of this whole area' – his voice had taken on its soft threatening tone – 'and you're in cahoots with some lunatic little bastard from your part of the world who likes running around with a gang of psychopathic killers from the Middle East, Germany, Ireland – you name it! You ought to keep your sights on the right target, Señora.' He came towards her as he spoke: 'Don't fuck up with a lot of spoilt middle-class punks who can't make up their minds who they want to kill, or what governments they want to overthrow, just as long as they've got enough guns and plastique, and the newspapers are giving them front-page treatment.' He paused, came forward and took her hand. 'Don't be a fool, Señora. You can hire one of those international psychopaths any hour of the day. Drop him. He's playing games with you.'

He winced with annoyance as the intercom rasped on his desk, and the green light winked at him, denoting urgency. This time she did not interrupt him. He pressed down the switch and heard Miss McKinley's measured voice: 'Sir, there are two police officers to see you. They say it's a matter of some importance.'

Ryan glanced at La Vuelva and made a quick, enigmatic motion with his thumb. 'I'll see them in here in three minutes, Miss McKinley.' He snapped off the intercom and said, looking at the half-dressed woman, 'Go back immediately to your room. Don't argue. I have no more idea of what this is about than you do. That is my word. You will have to believe it.'

She was still pale, her expression mute; and her only gesture was to pull the housecoat more tightly round her, as she moved towards the door.

Ryan got two more glasses out of the desk cupboard, refilled his own, and waited. They knocked and came in together. The first was Dexter, who had failed to book him a few hours earlier for speeding through Burford. 'Mr Ryan – this is Detective Sergeant Sharp.'

Ryan nodded, without standing up. The second man was in plain-clothes. His ash-blond hair lay close to his scalp like feathers, and his eyes were grey and ageless, with pale smudges of eyebrows. His voice was toneless, without a trace of accent, of class or origin. 'Mr Ryan, you'll excuse us for calling on you so late. But as we explained to your secretary, we're here on a matter of some urgency.'

Ryan picked up the bottle of malt whisky and pushed two glasses across the desk towards them. Neither of them moved. Ryan grinned. 'What's the matter, gentlemen? Scared I'll report you for drinking on duty?'

Sharp said, 'We don't have time to waste, Mr Ryan. I'd like you to get your coat and come with us.'

'You're joking.' Ryan sat back and sipped his malt. 'Got a warrant?'

'This is not an order, Mr Ryan. It's a request.'

'To hell with you, Sharp,' Ryan said pleasantly. 'I don't mind old Dexter stomping about the place in his big boots, but a sleuth from the SB could get me a bad name, if it got out. So what's so bloody important that it won't wait till morning?'

'You know a man called Miles Merton,' the detective said; it was not a question, but a statement of fact. Ryan did not bother to answer. He drank his whisky and waited.

'You had dinner with him tonight, Mr Ryan.'

'Go on, you're doing well.' He lifted his glass to them both.

'When did you last see him?' Sharp said.

Ryan grinned again, but without humour. 'Come on, you know as well as I do. You wouldn't be here if you didn't.'

The detective's mouth tightened; when he spoke he seemed scarcely to move his lips. 'You had dinner with him tonight at a place about twelve miles from here, called La Reserve. What time did you leave there, Mr Ryan?'

'Around 11.30.' A doubt had crossed Ryan's mind. 'If you knew I went there, you must have checked the time I left.' He looked at Dexter. 'What's all this about, sergeant?'

It was Sharp who answered: 'Did you leave at the same time as Mr Merton?'

'Not precisely.'

'What does that mean?'

'It means he went to have a pee, or something. We both left in our own cars.' Ryan leant forward, his jaw muscles growing hard. 'Now what is all this? What's happened to Miles Merton?'

Sharp spoke as though he had not heard the question. 'You came straight back here?'

'That's right.'

'You can prove that?'

'I might be able to. But not before you've answered my question. What's happened to Merton?'

'He's dead,' the detective said. 'He died of multiple fractures of the skull about an hour and a half ago. He was found in his car by one of the diners. It was still parked outside the restaurant.'

There was silence. Ryan drained his glass, then nodded. 'Dexter, your chum from Special Branch is obviously rather greener than I thought.' He was still looking at the uniformed sergeant while he jabbed his thumb in the direction of the blond detective. 'You know my form. If I wanted to knock off some frail old pensioner from the Civil Service, I'd hardly do it practically in front of a dining room full of witnesses. And I certainly wouldn't go in for multiple injuries. One would be quite enough.'

The sergeant gave an official frown, but did not reply. Sharp said, 'What makes you think I'm Special Branch, Mr Ryan?'

'I've got a nose for you, that's all.'

'That's not good enough.'

'So what's the SB doing sniffing round an obscure murder in a country lane? It's not your manor, anyway, Sharp. A common murder case is strictly for the County boys. Unless there's a lot more to it that I don't know.'

'How long had you known Merton, Mr Ryan?'

'About fifteen years, on and off.'

'So you knew the sort of work he was engaged in?'

'Had been,' Ryan corrected him. 'He was retired – poor devil.' He turned to the uniformed sergeant. 'Did you pass on my tip, Dexter? About those two foreign jokers following me to the restaurant in a grey Cortina?'

The sergeant sat forward, staring at his feet. 'I mentioned it, Mr Ryan. But as you may have heard, there's been a very serious train-crash between Woodstock and Oxford. Every available man in the County has been called in to help.'

'But you were called off? To help the Special Branch investigate a murder?' Ryan looked hard at each of them. 'None of that adds up, gentlemen. So perhaps, if you still want my co-operation, you'll tell me what really *is* happening?'

'Perhaps you'll tell us first, Mr Ryan, why you thought these two men were following you?' Sharp said.

'I think they may have been interested in one of my clients, detective-sergeant. But before I go any further, you'll have to get me on a rack in front of your chiefs. I'm like a doctor or a solicitor, see. Professional confidence.'

There was a pause. 'When did you last crack a safe, Ryan?'

Ryan shook his head. 'Now you're being impertinent, detective-sergeant.'

'I've seen your record.'

'Then if you've done your homework properly, you'll know that the last job I was alleged to have done was over thirty years ago. And you'd also know that two very important people squared the judge. So be careful you don't make any rash accusations, Sharp. Dexter here will be my witness.'

Sharp nodded; he looked bored. 'All right, Ryan, let's hear what you know about the Rushdale Experimental Research Centre.'

Ryan concealed his surprise, although the question was not entirely unexpected. 'If you think Merton had anything to do with it, I can tell you I'm pretty certain he didn't. He knew as much about it as I do. It belongs to the Ministry of Defence – supposed to be top-secret, and as far as the public is concerned they specialize in anti-biotics. And as far as people like you and I are concerned, Sharp, they're building up a stock-pile of germ-warfare capable of wiping out most of mankind. Right?'

The detective stood up and said, 'I think I'll have that drink now, Mr Ryan.' He came forward and took both glasses off the desk, handed one to Dexter, and sat down again. 'I'd better tell you that somebody broke into Rushdale earlier this evening. They cut the wire, shot the dogs with silencers, short-circuited the alarm system, killed two guards, and broke into the high-security laboratory centre.'

'Some security,' said Ryan. 'Were there any other guards?'

'No.'

'How were they killed?'

'Strangled with steel wire.'

Ryan nodded. 'Almost as subtle as battering an old man to death with a blunt instrument. But I still don't see what all this has got to do with me – or with Miles Merton.'

'Perhaps not.' The detective gave him a dull smile. 'A lot of funny things have been happening this evening, Mr Ryan. Let's take them one by one. First – you report to the sergeant here that you're being tailed to a restaurant by two foreigners in a hired car. Then you go to the restaurant and have dinner with a gentleman who used to work for Intelligence. About the time you leave the restaurant some person or persons kill him.

'In the meantime, a couple of hours earlier, two other things happen. First, the concrete stanchion of a road-bridge over the railway near Oxford collapses just as the Inter-City from Worcester is going under it. Three carriages are wrecked, and one totally flattened. Every available policeman in the area is called in to help. And while this is all going on, somebody breaks into Rushdale. What's your opinion of that timetable, Mr Ryan?'

'Very professional. What exactly did they take?'

The detective sat turning his glass between his fingers as though it were a chalice. 'We don't know exactly,' he said at last. Ryan knew that the man was probably lying; yet he hardly expected him to say anything else. Then, as though the detective had anticipated his thoughts, he added: 'This is all under plain wrappers, you understand, Mr Ryan. I don't have to remind you that you're still bound by the Official Secrets Act – even if you did sign it nearly forty years ago.'

Ryan chuckled. 'The Act doesn't prevent me making a few guesses. Were you called down here before or after the train-crash?'

Detective-Sergeant Sharp took his time answering. 'We are working on the theory – and it's only a theory, mind – that the break-in at Rushdale and the crash are somehow connected. Probably to create a police diversion. Again, this is entirely off the record – but our forensic people are examining the wreckage of the collapsed bridge, and their provisional opinion is that it was brought down by some sort of explosion – probably triggered off by the train.

'What doesn't fit in – and why we're talking to you – is the murder of Miles Merton. You told the sergeant here that you were being followed, and that you thought they were foreigners and might be armed. I'm asking you again, Mr Ryan – can you elaborate on that?'

Ryan gave himself another drink. Christ, he thought, either they push me, or I push myself, to the limit. And why? To protect that arrogant bitch whom he'd just seduced on the carpet, and who kept a wardrobe full of throwaway paper knickers, and ordered indiscreet underlings to be crucified – all for some power-struggle in a far-away island in the Caribbean. Was it worth it? Ryan's perverse craving for adventure and malicious disregard for the rules of law told him that perhaps it was.

He put down his glass. 'I told you, I thought they might be connected with one of my clients. We get all sorts here. I try not to discriminate, and I don't ask questions – unless the client doesn't pay. And if one of them, for some reason, decides to turn nasty and put a couple of heavies on to me, I usually know how to look after myself. I also don't like running to the police. Still, because I'm a law-abiding citizen, I just thought I'd drop a word to the sergeant here.'

'That was very helpful of you, Mr Ryan. Unfortunately, I'm not entirely satisfied. I want to know more about those clients of yours – and you can forget your precious professional ethics. This is serious. I also want to know in detail what you talked about tonight with Miles Merton. There are certain statements we would like you to make – in confidence. We'd like you to do that in Oxford.'

'Why can't I make them here?'

'I'm sorry. I'm not empowered to act on my own. This has to go higher up.'

'How high?'

'If necessary, to the top.'

Ryan finished his drink and stood up. 'I'll meet you at Oxford Central.'

'We'll drive you.'

'I prefer to drive myself.'

'Why?'

'To convince myself that I'm not yet under arrest. Besides, I don't want one of my insomniac old dowagers snooping through their chintz curtains and seeing the boss driven away in a squad-car. I've got a reputation to protect.' He held out his hand.

Sharp hesitated. 'May I make an observation, Mr Ryan? You've led an interesting life. And so far you seem to have been pretty lucky. But don't push that luck. One man – a friend of yours – has been murdered tonight. It is not impossible that he was murdered because of you. Now, are you sure you wouldn't prefer a lift with us into Oxford?'

Ryan smiled. 'I'll see you both at the station in about forty-five minutes. But you never know, I might even overtake you.'

His smile was not returned.

Ryan scribbled a note to Miss McKinley to tell her that he would either see her or ring her in the morning. He had no idea how long he would be 'staying' in Oxford, but he packed an overnight bag, just in case. From his window he saw the police car drive away; it was an unmarked Rover. Still, Dexter's chequered-cap stood out like a flag, and Ryan could imagine the gossip next morning over the carrot juice and under the hairdriers. It was just a matter of whether Madame Achar got to hear of it, and what deductions she would draw.

The garage was unlocked. As he walked towards it, he lit a cigarette and sucked in a lungful of smoke to clear his head. After the wine, brandy, and three stiff whiskies, he was reminded of his age: his mind tended to grow sluggish at this hour. He didn't know who would be waiting for him in Oxford: but he was going to need all his wits about him, not only to satisfy his interrogators, but also himself.

He got into the car and as he switched on the engine, listening to its slow pleasing growl, he breathed out the smoke and sniffed. Above the smell of expensive leather, and through the taste of the cigarette – Ryan smoked only the strongest brand, and to hell with HM Government's Health Warning – he thought for a moment he detected the whiff of cheap scent. His mind went back to when he had last had female company in the car, and remembered that Finnish masseuse. He scarcely thought of Madame Achar as he eased the long car out through the doors.

The events of the evening made no sense. He wondered if they made sense to that blond sleuth, Sharp. The Special Branch would have sent him down as soon as they received news of the break-in at Rushdale; but that could not have been earlier than the death of Miles Merton. And was he right to suppose that the murderer, or murderers, had mistaken old Miles for himself? If not, what on earth had the poor sod known, or said, or done to cost him his life?

As Ryan drove past the lodge and out of the gates, he checked, instinctively, for a glimpse of that grey Cortina. But the drive, and the narrow road beyond, were empty.

He had smoked half his cigarette and, as was his habit, stubbed it out before it turned sour: and again caught that hint of scent. He wrinkled his nose and frowned. He hated cheap scent; he also remembered that the Finnish girl never wore any.

He glanced in the mirror and saw a pair of eyes. At the same moment he felt warm breath on the back of his neck. A voice said, 'You will please to keep driving as I say, Mr Ryan.' It was a low indifferent voice, with a strong accent, and it spoke as though reciting a line it had learnt by heart.

Ryan's only emotion was a dull rage at his own stupidity and carelessness. He felt like a poker-player who has picked up a good hand, then at the crucial moment drops all his cards for everyone to see. He said nothing; he needed every second in which to think. He wondered how far ahead the police car would be now: and what the hell these two monkeys – he could sense the second man, rather than see him – had done with their own car? He assumed that they'd decided to kip down in the Lagonda and wait until he used it again. If it hadn't been for Sharp they'd have had a long wait – but then if they were professionals they'd be trained to wait, just as they'd be trained to kill.

It was now about half a mile to the A40 – along the same quiet, twisting road that he had followed twice already this evening. He had unobtrusively brought down his speed, at the same time shifting his weight forward and slightly sideways, so as to get a better view in the mirror. He saw the same oily black eyes above high sallow cheekbones. But he could not make out the second man without turning his head. The one directly behind must have anticipated him, for just as Ryan was about to glance casually round, he felt a ring of steel touch the nape of his neck, nudging upwards into the muscles just below the cranium. The hand that held it was very steady, even with the swaying of the car.

He drove on, still without saying anything; rounded a bend where the offside wheels hissed through a trough of mud. It would have to be here or on the main road, at high speed. He was fairly sure they'd make him drive fast – fast enough for it to be dangerous for him to try anything.

There was just one other chance that occurred to him.

Dexter and Sharp had an almost fifteen-minute start – which must make them more than a third of the way to Oxford by now. But it was just possible that if he broke every rule of the road, he might catch up with them. But then that would depend on which direction his two passengers made him take when he reached the main road.

He moved his left foot onto the brake pedal, tensed his right on the accelerator, and gently eased his neck back against the firm muzzle of the gun. The eyes in the mirror watched him with their unblinking stare.

Ryan had decided to credit the man with being serious, at least with a gun. But just how serious remained to be seen – in about two seconds from now.

The last bend before the A40 swung into the high beam of the headlamps, and Ryan moved the fingers of his left hand off the wheel – slowly, relaxed – touched the stubby gear-lever next to his thigh, and changed smoothly out of 'drive', down to second. The engine hummed, as his hand dropped down by the left side of his seat. His fingers felt the small steel handle, closed round it, and in the next split-second he carried out four deliberate actions. His right foot rammed the accelerator flat against the floor; his left hand wrenched up the lever at the side of his seat, and in the same moment he hurled his whole weight backwards so that the bucket-seat slid into an almost reclining position; while his left foot stamped down with all his force on the brake-pedal.

Several things happened at once. The violent acceleration of the Lagonda's 5.3 litre V-8 engine threw the man with the gun back into the rear seat, while the sudden braking catapulted him forward again, his gun-hand temporarily immobilized in a struggle to regain his balance, as his body dived across Ryan's head and shoulders. Ryan stabbed at him with each hand, fingers stiffened as hard as wood. He knew anatomy as well as any surgeon, and he struck at the man's groin and one of his kidneys. The scream was muted by the howl of the engine and the long lurching swish as the car skidded sideways to a halt and stood rocking like a motor-boat in a swell.

Ryan felt the dead weight of the man's body sinking, with obscene intimacy, against his own, while the convulsed groin lay pressed for a moment against his face. He heard the scream dying into a choking sound somewhere near his knees. He knew that the gun had dropped to the floor. And in that long instant of repose which always follows sudden violence, he was again aware, vividly this time, of the smell of scent, thick and cloying, as sweet as honey; then he felt the man's body slide sideways and heard him vomiting against the door.

The entire sequence of events had lasted perhaps three seconds – which was probably a couple of seconds too long. What happened now, under the refracted glow of the headlamps, proceeded with the dim unreality of things seen in slow motion.

Ryan had no time to grope for the gun. Instead, he twisted round on the horizontal seat and peered up into the back of the car. He saw two rows of big square teeth under a bandit moustache and a pair of hands with knuckles the size of golf-balls. There were rings on the fingers, winking with paste diamonds, and he felt the tension and fury rising like bile in his throat as he breathed in the stench of scented vomit that was defiling his magnificent car. The huge teeth moved closer, until they were almost above him, opening wider as though taunting him with silent laughter.

Ryan struck out, upwards, two fingers forming a double prong that aimed at the eyes; but before he felt the impact there was a violent explosion. It seemed to come from inside his head; while a great pool of light spread over his left eye and his whole body felt like water flowing down into more water, his senses growing dull, his mind soft and silly as a child's. Then the water closed round him, black and cold, and he floated into sleep.

CHAPTER THREE

The Set-Up

The room was small and chilly, with a one-bar electric fire set into the wall. The only furniture were two deal-chairs, a standard lamp and an iron-framed bed, set high off the floor like a hospital bed. Ryan was lying on the bed with one arm crooked behind his head, the wrist clamped to the frame with a pair of handcuffs. They had removed his jacket and shoes, and thrown a blanket over him. His head felt several times its normal size, and when he moved it he could feel the dried blood flaking off his cheek and temple. His left eye had closed up and there was a towel under his head that had soaked up a big patch of blood which had also dried.

Through the one small window, grimy and uncurtained, was daylight. They had also taken his watch. With his free hand he touched his jaw and felt only a slight stubble. It was a thing they often forgot in this game. You could keep a prisoner unconscious, drugged or beaten up, so that he wouldn't know what time of day it was, or how long he'd been there. Except that one's beard gave it all away.

His immediate sensation, besides the cold and the pain in his head, was that he wanted to urinate. He twisted his head and inspected the handcuffs. They were regulation make with a square lock which he thought he might be able to manage, given a needle, a hairpin, and about half an hour. He tried his trouser pockets under the blanket. They were empty. He wondered what they'd done with the Lagonda. For a few moments the thought worried him perhaps more than anything else. If that bastard with the gun had been as badly hurt as he hoped, he didn't much like the idea of the big-toothed ape driving it even a few yards. On the other hand, it was not the sort of car you could leave abandoned in the middle of the night on a lonely road.

He looked again at the window. The view was not revealing:

the corner of a dirty brick wall and what looked like the roof of a shed or warehouse. One thing both puzzled and encouraged him. They'd beaten a harmless old man like Miles Merton to death, yet had done nothing worse to himself than give him a black eye and handcuff him to a bed.

He sat up as far as his manacled hand would allow and yelled, 'Nurse!'

Almost immediately he heard footsteps outside, the sound of a cheap lock being turned, and a short plump young man came in, wearing a Levi suit, T-shirt, and blue-tinted glasses. His hair was black and thick, and from his complexion Ryan guessed he had Latin blood.

Ryan grinned lopsidedly at him. 'I want a bottle. I've got to do wee-wee.'

The young man said, 'You will find it at the first door on the left.' He had a soft, pleasant voice, with that same cosmopolitan accent which Ryan now associated, like a far-off memory, with Madame Achar.

The young man had reached the bed and now took from his pocket a small object shaped like the key to a sardine-tin. He stepped up to Ryan and unlocked the handcuffs in a movement which left no doubt that he was experienced in these matters. As Ryan sat up, he saw a small automatic pistol pointing at him.

'Where are my shoes?'

'You don't need shoes.'

'It's bloody cold in here. Is this how you always treat your guests?'

'Please, if you want to use the toilet, go now.'

The gun followed Ryan to the door and along a drab, featureless passage to the second door on the left. 'Do not lock it, please,' the young man said behind him. This time there was a hint of apology in his voice.

Inside was just a lavatory, a roll of paper on the floor and a closed window of frosted glass. Not the least possible weapon – not even a chain, just a handle. He thought of opening the cistern and detaching the rod from the ballcock: but if they had wanted to kill him, they would have done so already.

The young man was waiting outside. Ryan said, 'I'd like a drink and something to eat. And I mean something serious to drink.'

The other nodded. 'That can be arranged. But I regret that

you will have to return to your room and stay handcuffed to the bed.'

Ryan grinned again as he walked past. 'Not taking any chances, are you, sonny boy? Don't even feel safe with a .32? I'm flattered. I must be at least twice your age.'

'You have caused me a great deal of trouble,' the young man said, as he followed Ryan into the bedroom.

Ryan rounded on him. '*I* caused *you* trouble! After some sly little punk creeps up behind me in the middle of the night and sticks a gun in the back of my neck? What did you expect me to do – kiss him?'

The young man motioned him on to the bed and deftly snapped the cuffs back on, using only his free hand, while the gun still pointed at Ryan's belly. 'I'll get sandwiches and some whisky. And I ask you, please, Ryan, not to play any games. We are serious people.'

Ryan peered at him through his good eye. 'Señor Fraga de Sanchez. Tell me about your latest revolutionary fantasy. Or rather what happened to the last one? Did you get bored with your playmates from that nutty Kraut gang they bust a few years back? Or with those poor bastard Palestinians they wiped out in Beirut? I even heard you were fooling around with the IRA? Rather a come-down for you, I should have thought? I mean, you're an international celebrity, Señor Sanchez. Or would you prefer me to call you "Dr Lopez"? Or better still, your more popular title, "Pedro"?'

The young man came towards him and struck him across the mouth with the gun-barrel. Ryan felt the foresight tear his lip and tasted the blood against his gums. The pain was less than his surprise. He had expected his captor to be a man who would at least enjoy a vigorous debate, even if it might include an element of abuse. Crude personal violence was something Ryan had not anticipated so early on.

The young man was now smiling down at him. 'Your moral and political judgements do not trouble me, Señor Ryan. But I would advise you, please, to be more respectful. You are an older man, yes, but you are no longer the boss – the man who speaks with money that he has made out of the vanity of rich parasites.' He smiled again. 'It seems, Señor Ryan, that our opinion of each other is – how would you say?'

'I'd say, Pedro, that perhaps we just aren't cut out for each other.' Yet there was a perverse streak in Ryan which could not help admiring the sheer audacity and scale of Pedro's apparent achievements. 'Get me the sandwiches and whisky, will you?'

The young man nodded and went out, locking the door behind him. He must have given some orders to someone, for he returned almost at once, sighed and sat down primly on one of the chairs. 'May I say, Señor Ryan, that I am not displeased with you. I did not expect you to be polite – that would have been a sign of weakness. No, you are a brave man. You behaved last night with great courage and initiative. But then, of course, you are an expert in these matters.'

'Do you want me on your payroll?'

The young man held up his hand. Ryan noticed that it was soft and well-kept, like a woman's. 'Please, I do not believe in hasty decisions.'

Ryan suddenly went into Spanish: 'Why did you kill Señor Merton?'

'I had reasons,' the other replied, also in Spanish. 'I do not kill for pleasure.'

'Does that go for your friends who nail people down on to carpets?'

The young man ignored the remark. He took out a packet of cigarettes and, without moving the gun from his right hand, which was now pointing at Ryan's head, skilfully tapped a cigarette into his mouth and snapped a gold lighter to it. 'Let us just say that if it had not been for your meeting last night with your friend, he might still be alive.'

'You had no reason to have Merton killed. He was no threat to you.'

Pedro breathed smoke slowly through his nostrils. 'Why did you meet him last night, Señor Ryan?'

'Why shouldn't I? We were old friends. We were also neighbours.'

'But you knew that Señor Merton was an important member of your British Intelligence Service?'

'He used to be. Until last night he was on an index-linked pension. He hasn't worked for the Service for years.' He was speaking English again, his temper beginning to rise for the first time.

Fraga de Sanchez sat watching him through his blue-tinted

glasses. 'Your assumption is incorrect,' he said. 'Intelligence officers are like your politicians and judges. They only retire when they are forced to. Your friend Señor Merton was still actively engaged in work which was becoming embarrassing to me and my friends.'

'Meaning your lady-friend who calls herself Madame Achar?'

The young man's features hardened: but he pulled at his cigarette and said nothing.

'She's not in good shape, Pedro. She's as jumpy as a virgin at her first dance. She's also hitting the bottle. What was old Ivor Childs treating her for?'

'Señor Ryan, you take terrible risks.' Pedro's voice was as gentle as falling leaves. 'What happened to the doctor should have been a lesson to any sensible person. Instead, you tried to intimidate your client. Not satisfied with that, you arranged a confidential meeting with a senior Intelligence officer who specialized in the affairs of Central America. What did you discuss at that meeting, Señor Ryan?'

'Will you believe me if I tell you?'

This time Pedro's body was tensed back against the straight chair. 'These decisions were not taken by me.'

'All right. I told Merton that I knew about La Vuelva. And he told me all about you, and of your possible connection with the good lady. Okay?'

'That is not quite all, Señor Ryan. On your way to meet Señor Merton, you stopped and talked to the police.'

'I was stopped *by* the police.'

'Why?'

'Exceeding the speed limit. Satisfied?'

'Not entirely.' Pedro stopped only to stub out his half-smoked cigarette and light himself a fresh one. Ryan noticed that for someone who smoked so much his teeth were surprisingly white. 'Did you perhaps tell them that you were being followed?' he added.

'Yes. I thought they were a couple of joy-riders trying to out-gun me. I don't like dangerous drivers – they kill people – and that's a stupid way to die.'

'I agree with you.'

'As it was, the police didn't act. They were too busy clearing up the mess after an express train had run off the rails. That was a nice touch, Pedro. Set off an explosive charge under the bridge and smash up three carriages. Then get every police force in the area called out. So you and your boys had that small road through the village of Rushdale entirely to yourselves.'

Pedro sat smoking calmly for several moments; then he stood up and stared at a point just above Ryan's head. 'How did you hear about this railway accident?' he said at last.

'On my car-radio back from the restaurant.'

'I also heard it on the radio but there was no mention last night of a bridge being blown up. So how did you hear about it, Señor Ryan?'

'Get me that whisky, you bastard.'

'When you have answered my question.'

'A couple of cops called on me late last night. They told me.'

'Why did they question you?'

'Because I'd had dinner with Miles Merton. And because the whole bloody evening looked to them like a set-up.'

'Did they talk about anything else, besides the death of Señor Merton?'

'You know bloody well what else they talked about. Though they didn't say exactly what it was you stole. Perhaps they weren't sure. But you're sure, aren't you, Pedro? Quite a coup. You must be very proud of yourself. Why don't you tell *me*?'

Pedro relaxed and looked at the ceiling, the gun still steady in his hand. 'It is beautiful,' he said softly. 'So terrible, yet so beautifully simple.' He brought his head forward slowly and smiled. 'We took a lot of things, but that was only to confuse the authorities. The only important ones were six small capsules' – he demonstrated their size between the thumb and forefinger of his free hand. 'Have you ever dreamt of the ultimate weapon, Señor Ryan? The equivalent of a nuclear bomb that destroys the insects but not the plant?'

Ryan lay listening, saying nothing. Pedro went on:

'You have heard of Lassa fever? It is one of the most virulent killers in the Tropics, and there are few cures. But at that nice little place in Rushdale they've come up with a few refinements. Not only has the disease been made more intense, but they've added to it a form of chronic shingles, combined with a nervous complaint that turns the skin into a scaly crust. A crust that resembles almost exactly the skin of a snake. You will admit that it would be a neither pleasant nor dignified way to die?'

Ryan felt an involuntary nausea. 'Have you got these cartridges with you?'

'No. But I know where they are.'

'And how much damage would one of them do?'

'It would destroy perhaps a town – or a whole army. Of course, it would depend how it was used, and which way the wind was blowing.'

Ryan said: 'The Rushdale Centre's a top-security Government establishment. How did you get in?' As he spoke, he wondered why Pedro had even bothered to answer his question about the fever in the first place: unless it was just another example of the young terrorist pushing his luck.

'It was not difficult. The security was lamentable. Even the alarm system was out-of-date. You British are so complacent, so confident. It is comic. You have lost your power, your glorious Empire, even your money. Now you run around the world with your begging bowls, yet you still think you are so superior – and so safe. One day you will wake up and find you are wrong.'

'Roll on the Revolution,' Ryan said cheerfully. 'But I don't suppose a few dozen passengers killed on that train are going to make much difference, one way or the other. Or even old Miles Merton, dead or alive, for that matter.'

The young man had picked up the carrier-bag and now handed him a bottle of Scotch and some plastic-packed sandwiches. He stood just out of reach of Ryan's free arm, and with the gun still pointing accurately at his head twisted the cap off the bottle with his teeth and handed it to him. Ryan drank deeply from the neck. The liquid seared his bruised gums like iodine, but the warmth in his throat and gut braced his cold cramped limbs.

Pedro removed the bottle, but left the sandwiches lying on the bed. He sat down again. 'You don't like us, do you, Señor Ryan?'

Ryan lay back with the taste of whisky still burning in his mouth, and smiled at the ceiling. 'Oh I love you. I just adore you. You world revolutionaries are a wonderful mob. You're all so concerned with the destinies of mankind – with all those starving millions being washed away by floods and potbellied with drought and crushed by earthquakes. I'm surprised you don't all break down and go round weeping and moaning, and covering yourselves in sackcloth and ashes.'

Pedro spoke without emotion: 'We are not sentimentalists, Señor Ryan. We are realists. One does not eradicate the injustices and indignities of humanity by writing letters to the newspapers and making speeches in your parliaments or in supporting your so-called free institutions which are based on greed and selfishness and corruption, and, above all, on the inherited power of a small elite.'

Ryan wanted to yawn, but it would have been painful. He listened to the young man's soft pleasant voice, steady and fluent: 'Your fine liberal ideals – what do they achieve against poverty, injustice, disease?'

This time Ryan brought his head up and managed to give a cracked laugh: 'Certainly not much against a good dose of "snake-fever"! But since the stuff's never been tested – under natural conditions, that is – you'll be doing the boffins a big favour, Pedro. Like the Yanks did when they dropped those two lollipops on Hiroshima and Nagasaki. Just think – if they hadn't done that, nobody would have really known what the results would be. Scientists are like politicians – they hate theories. They like practical results.'

Pedro stood up, and without removing his cigarette came across the room and brought the butt of his pistol down on the damaged side of Ryan's head. For a moment Ryan thought he heard himself scream, then unconsciousness came over him again.

The first thing he remembered was that he had not touched the sandwiches; yet he was no longer hungry.

Nor was he any longer cold. He was still in bed, but in a much narrower one this time, with a sheet drawn up under his chin and tucked tightly down round his shoulders. The bed was also vibrating, to the regular rhythm of a loud pulsating roar that came from all round.

His mind adjusted slowly. He was wearing pyjamas, and there was a bandage on the side of his head, and his left eye was still closed. There was also a foul-smelling antiseptic smeared across his upper lip.

From the seat at his side a face peered down at him. It was a young, chubby face and it had blue-tinted glasses. The mouth gave a faint smile, which Ryan did not acknowledge. He was aware that there were other passengers aboard but he lacked the energy to count them. He lay back and stared dreamily at the red metal plaque with white letters, EMERGENCY EXIT – PULL LEVER TO THE RIGHT. His hands lay at his side, held by the strap, his fingers limp and heavy.

He felt drowsy; his mouth was dry; and above the sticky smell of the antiseptic he became conscious of the after-taste of Pentathol. As one whose profession included the dispensing of soporifics of varying strength and specious legality, Ryan had a natural dread of all drugs. Yet at the moment he felt no emotion whatever. He had been kidnapped at gun-point, pistol-whipped and slugged unconscious by a political epileptic, shot full of dope and put aboard a private aircraft. Yet he was not surprised: he was not even excited – merely ready to be excited.

He felt the bed rock and the popping pains in his ears as the plane began to go down: a couple of bumps, a screech, then a howl as the airscrews were reversed. They slowed to a halt, the engines died, a door opened somewhere near him, and he felt the clean rush of air. His bed lifted quite gently; swayed and began to move forward, tilting down feet-first, and he found himself looking up at a heavy sky.

A man's broad back under a beret moved in front of him. They carried him across the tarmac, through a modern shed with posters on the wall – colour photographs of caravans and of children bathing, and advertisements for hire-car firms. There was no visible Customs or Immigration formalities. He was carried straight through, outside again, to where the stretcher was slid into the back of a Citroen DS Safari. Fraga de Sanchez, alias Pedro, climbed in beside him, while two men got into the front.

They started off, very fast. Through the windows he was beginning to get his bearings. The country was flat and featureless, except for stone walls and the occasional bungalow with a neat little garden. At one bend he glimpsed rocks and a dark, unwelcoming sea. The few trees were bare, but the fields were still green, and he thought – with a sudden awakening of consciousness – of his native Ireland.

They reached the edge of a town. It had the same grey-stone fronts, often with pretty little porches, with names like 'Mon Repos', 'Beau Rivage', and 'Que Sera Sera'. They turned into a square where he could feel the tyres drumming on cobbles. It was called Marais Square, and underneath was written La Place Marais. He caught a glimpse of a pub; a hideous granite church; a sweet shop advertising Benson and Hedges and the *News of the World*.

From the corner of his eye he saw Pedro sitting in the seat beside him, smoking a cigarette. He was paying no attention to Ryan. And Ryan knew that there is one serious disadvantage in doping a man: his captors can never control exactly when he is going to regain consciousness.

In front, the driver and his companion in the beret were facing out ahead. They were now driving down the High Street, subtitled 'La Grande Rue'. There seemed to be few people about, and Ryan guessed by the light that it was early morning. He licked the stubble on his upper lip, avoiding the antiseptic, and calculated that it must be Sunday.

They were going downhill now, between high stone walls and a glimpse of bigger houses behind trees. Unless they had passed only through the outskirts of the town it was scarcely larger than an extended village; and since it lay so near an airport, he reasoned that it must be either very remote, or be the main town – in which case he must assume he was on an island. An island whose street names were written in both English and French. He still felt dazed, but at least he was making progress.

The road had flattened out and they were now driving along the bleak coast. His good eye – its lid still drooping for the benefit of Señor Sanchez – now glimpsed across the sea a dim, grey coastline. Probably France. He was now fairly certain where he was.

A few minutes later they left the road and began bouncing along a track inland. After about a quarter of a mile they stopped outside what looked like a decrepit farmstead: a huddle of single-storey sheds, and a grim little house with its curtains drawn.

Ryan was still feigning half-consciousness as they carried him out, into a corridor and up a flight of wooden stairs, into a room lit with a single naked light from the ceiling. As they did so he heard a mutter of voices below, then the sound of the car being driven away.

They had laid the stretcher down on some kind of sofa. Pedro had come in, and with him the broad man with the beret. The strap across the blanket was undone, and Ryan remembered that he had seen no sign of a gun since he had recovered consciousness on the plane. He thought, Pedro should be easy: but his companion looked bigger, solider, probably more muscle than brain. Yet for the moment Ryan had no idea of his own strength; and if he was to take the big man first, there was always the risk that Pedro might be armed, as he had been in London – if it *had* been London. Pedro was not a lad to take chances.

The problem was academic, but in his present state it exercised Ryan's mental energies just a fraction too long. He felt the sheet and blanket pulled back, his right arm lifted and the sleeve rolled up above the elbow. His reaction was too slow. As he moved his left hand, it was grabbed by the wrist and he saw Pedro's blue glasses bending over him, and in the next second felt the quick dull ache as the needle went skilfully into the vein.

Here we go again, he thought: Roughhouse Ryan, the grey-haired Glory Boy from the Bog, ex-SS and Brigade of Guards, now flat on his back and weak as a suckling babe, being put out for the count for the third time in less than two days, and without even a whimper. Yet despite that nasty taste swelling up in his mouth, the sensation was exhilarating, almost ecstatic, as the room became blurred, then faded into total darkness.

His return to consciousness, as well as his sense of time, were now sharper, more concentrated. He had the distinct feeling of having been out for, at most, only a few hours. The room was in darkness, except for two dull strips of daylight from behind the drawn curtains. From under the door was also a bar of artificial light which lay across the room to his right. He began to observe this with some interest – if only because it seemed the one feature of interest in the room. It was not precisely a single bar of light, but broken at intervals, regularly spaced by two shadows, each about three inches wide and a foot apart. It took Ryan several seconds to realize what they meant. Someone was standing outside the door.

He lay for a few minutes testing his reflexes. He was still not sure that when the moment came his muscles would not betray him. Then slowly, without any sound, he slid out from under the tight sheet, and very carefully rested his bare feet on the wooden floor. The slightest creak would give him away. The house was as quiet as a church.

He stood up; swayed for a second and felt a surge of nausea. He sat down again. He needed a weapon – but what? Unless he risked drawing the curtains, it was going to be difficult to find one, at least without risking some noise. Apart from the sofa on which he was sitting, the room appeared to have no furniture.

He sat exercising his arms and fingers for perhaps a minute; then let out a low moan and sunk his face in his hands. His next moan was louder, more agonized; and as he lifted his head he saw one of the shadows shift under the door. He paused. Both shadows were still again. Then, in a moment of inspiration, he called very clearly in Spanish, 'Help me! Please, for the love of the Mother of God, help me!'

He blinked as the room filled with light. The door had opened and a man was coming towards him. From the shape of his silhouette Ryan guessed that he was the one with the beret who had come in the car. The man stopped a few feet from him. He said nothing. Ryan sank his head back in his hands and moaned again.

The man growled in Spanish, 'What is it?'

'I am sick,' Ryan told him, also in Spanish; and through the chinks in his fingers he could just make out, with his good eye, the gun in the man's hand. It was pointing at the floor.

The man took another step forward. The gun was only three feet from Ryan's shoulder now.

Ryan's body jack-knifed off the stretcher and the heel of his right hand slammed upwards, hitting the man's upper lip and punching the nose up into his forehead. He heard the crunch of bone and cartilage, while his left hand came down in a chopping blow, smashing into the carotid artery. He had just time to catch the weight of the man's body as it sagged forward, almost without bending at the knees. The fingers remained locked round the gun until it hit the floor. Ryan laid him out on the stretcher, felt his pulse, picked up the gun and went over to the open door. As he reached it he heard a car drawing up outside: doors slammed, another door opened downstairs, there was the sound of voices. Quickly, silently, he closed the door – which had no lock – and switched on the overhead light.

He now examined the gun. It was medium-sized, not too heavy; but it puzzled him, because he had never seen its precise make before. He had been out of this game for a long time, but he still reckoned he knew most hand-weapons on the market. At first it looked like a scaled-up copy of the German Walther PPK: a 9mm double-action semi-automatic, just over six inches long and weighing about one and a half pounds. Then he saw the Cyrillic lettering above the handle. It was a Russian Makarov, known by the Soviets as a PM – the standard side-arm of the Red Army and its adjuncts. Not the kind of weapon you'd expect to find on the Channel Islands: but in these unusual circumstances it made sense. Even if Moscow wasn't overtly backing Pedro and his lunatic fringe, Russian hardware would be the most likely to pass into their hands.

Ryan spent several vital seconds examining the gun. It was as well that he did so. It had an externally mounted slide-stop, which was simple enough; but what almost fooled him was that the safety-catch pushed up on to 'safe' and down to 'fire', which was the exact opposite to the Walther. For a few more seconds he stood practising the feel of the weapon, noting from the size of the box-clip that it would hold eight rounds, and from its weight that it was fully loaded; then, still in his bare feet, he turned again towards the door.

Outside he could again hear the voices downstairs, louder this time. One of them was a woman's. Ryan could not make out the language they were speaking until he was halfway down the stairs. He moved swiftly.

The voices came from behind a closed door at the end of the downstairs passage. They were speaking French. One was a man's, quiet, monotonous, interrupted at rapid intervals by the woman's. Even in French, which Ryan had not heard her speak before, the voice was unmistakable: sharp, impatient, with that rarefied elegance of one who has moved only in the best circles. La Vuelva spoke like a woman who, unable to settle her hotel bill, chooses to blame the manager rather than seek his indulgence.

Ryan reached the door and stood listening. He heard her say: 'Revolutions cannot be arranged to a schedule. They must depend on a thousand circumstances. And if the circumstances are propitious, it is the time to strike.'

The man politely interrupted her: 'But one must have time to make the necessary preparations. For example, there is this Englishman you are trying to recruit. Supposing people come looking for him? He is an important man – he has many friends.

Important friends, from what you say. And then, supposing he does not co-operate? Or worse, supposing he pretends to, then betrays us? You have told me that he is a hard man – that he is clever and dangerous.'

La Vuelva said, 'That is precisely why I require his services. Men like him can be bought. I shall buy him.'

There was a pause. Ryan heard the clink of a glass; then the man spoke: 'But supposing he does not trust us? He has already been ill-treated by those gorillas of Sanchez's. Maybe he is too angry to co-operate.'

'If he becomes angry at such small things, then he is of no use to me. It will be a good test. He knows we are serious. At this stage he will not expect us to treat him like one of our own. He has plenty of experience in these matters. He knows the rules.'

'Perhaps he prefers his comfortable life in England? Perhaps he is too old for these escapades?'

'Then we shall have to kill him.'

Another silence. The man broke it: 'How long do you think he will sleep?'

'Not long. He will be ready for us soon.'

Ryan opened the door. 'Bonjour. Or should I say bon soir? They have taken my watch.' He walked across the room and sat down in a lumpy armchair facing them both. It was a small room with a log-fire and three chairs. On a low rough table between them there stood, impeccably absurd, a bottle of Dom Perignon. Outside the single window it was getting dark.

Ryan smiled and shook his head. 'That's naughty of you, Madame,' he said in English. 'We both know that alcohol is not good for you.'

The two of them were drinking the champagne out of kitchen glasses; the man's was full and La Vuelva's almost empty. They sat with the glasses held rigidly in front of them. La Vuelva was wearing a simple skirt and her hair was loose and her face cleaned of all make-up; but her fine eyes were clear and showed no sign of inebriation, even surprise.

She looked at Ryan – in his crumpled pyjamas, with his sticky swollen mouth and puffed black eye – with an expression of mild curiosity, as though he were a total stranger who had stumbled in after an accident. Ryan also detected a degree of personal hostility towards himself – a symptom which he recognized well as the wretched feminine guilt which follows an impetuous act of fornication. He decided it was not something he would commit again – at least, not without considerable encouragement.

La Vuelva's companion was a lean tall man with short, steel-grey hair and the sort of narrow beard which had once been fashionable among the existentialists. He wore a white polo-necked sweater and narrow cord trousers tucked into high leather boots, and was sucking at a long curved meerschaum. His fine-boned features suggested a man of intellect; but Ryan also detected a distinctly military air.

Ryan said cheerfully, 'Aren't you going to offer me a drink?'

The man replied, in perfect English, 'How did you get out of your room?' He was pretending not to have noticed the gun, which Ryan had resting on his knee, pointing casually between himself and La Vuelva.

'I walked out. What did you expect me to do? – come down on all fours?'

For a moment he thought he saw a smile beginning on La Vuelva's pale lips. The man said, 'What has happened to the gentleman upstairs?'

'I killed him,' Ryan said, and La Vuelva's smile froze, as her tongue flicked out and licked her upper lip. There was silence.

'I see,' the man said at last, this time in French, and drew on his pipe. 'You know where we are, do you, Monsieur Ryan?'

'Alderney, isn't it? You call it Aurigny. Population about two thousand, including a couple of part-time policemen. But I don't suppose either of them have any more experience of murder than the Archbishop of Canterbury. Although, of course, I would plead self-defence.'

'You will know too,' the man said, 'that we are still under the jurisdiction of Great Britain. To have killed a man, here, could be extremely embarrassing for all of us – especially you.'

Ryan grinned. 'Madame here was saying just now that I know the rules. You know them too. You must have known that sooner or later I was going to hit back.'

La Vuelva now spoke for the first time. She spoke in English. 'You know you could be killed too? There are more of us, for a start.'

'Sure,' said Ryan, and tapped the gun against his knee. 'But I've always liked playing against the odds.'

La Vuelva emptied her glass of champagne and leant over to pour herself another.

'Don't I get that drink too?' Ryan asked again, in French.

The man said, 'There is a glass in the cupboard behind you.' Ryan guessed, from his cultured accent, that he was French, and of good birth.

'You get it,' he said. 'And if I don't like the way you do it, I'll use this' – he lifted up the Makarov off his knee and aimed the front blade-sight at the man's legs. 'I won't kill you – I'll just make it so you don't walk again.' He rubbed his finger along the stout three-inch barrel. 'A Walther PPK, isn't it?' – he nodded to himself, smiling – 'my favourite toy, this used to be.'

Ryan had taken possession of the Makarov as a simple precaution. He did not really believe that having gone to such pains as to bring him this far, they would be extravagant enough to kill him. But this assumed that he was dealing with rational people. La Vuelva was obviously a neurotic megalomaniac and Pedro a psychopath; and Ryan already knew – from what he had heard outside the door – that if he put one foot wrong, he would stand little chance, unarmed. In any case, there was always the advantage of testing them, and the ruse with the safety-catch might just be enough.

His suspicions were confirmed when the man with the beard looked at the gun with detached amusement. Ryan said, 'I don't feel like champagne. Whisky – if you've got it.'

The man moved past him and Ryan watched him leaning down, opening the cupboard. He glanced at La Vuelva. Her face was white; and he winked his good eye at her. The man stood up and took two steps back towards Ryan. He held an unopened bottle of Johnny Walker in one hand, a glass in the other.

'Pour it half-full and leave it on the floor,' Ryan said, and pointed the gun at the man's left kneecap. If they were going to try anything, this would be the moment. But the man courteously obeyed his instructions, then returned to his chair. La Vuelva took a long drink of champagne; and Ryan reached down for his whisky. As he did so, he heard the sound of another car. He brought the gun up suddenly, as the man reached out sideways. 'Hold it,' he said softly.

'I only intend to turn on the light,' the other said. Ryan

nodded, and the man switched on the lamp on a side-table. Ryan heard the front door open. He spoke quickly, again in French.

'If your visitors try anything, I shall not hesitate to shoot Madame here. I shall shoot her through the head. You will make that perfectly understood.' He finished speaking just as the door opened. He did not turn, did not move, except to level the sights at La Vuelva's mouth.

There were two of them. The Frenchman gave a sharp order, in an undertone which Ryan had some difficulty in recognizing as French or Spanish; but it had the desired effect.

They came in, cat-footed, keeping their distance from Ryan as they stepped into the middle of the room and stopped in front of the fire. One was Pedro; the other was the huge square man whose hideous white teeth had confronted Ryan from the back of the Lagonda. Ryan gave them both a momentary glance, but his gun did not waver from La Vuelva's face.

In at least one sense the sight of the massive, square-toothed thug, with a neck as thick as his head, and the biggest hands that Ryan could remember ever having seen, was reassuring. It meant that the number of heavies at the disposal of La Vuelva and Pedro would seem to be limited. Ryan guessed that his companion from the Lagonda was still *hors de combat*, if not worse; while a second bodyguard lay on the sofa upstairs with a broken neck. Ryan calculated that if he ever got level with this great brute in front of the fireplace the others might find their resources getting a bit thin on the ground.

They provided him with his opportunity sooner than he had expected. At first no one moved. La Vuelva was still very pale, not even drinking her champagne. The Frenchman sat relaxed. After a moment Pedro said, 'You will not object if I get out a packet of cigarettes, Señor Ryan?'

'Just keep your hands from your pockets.' Ryan's eyes swivelled for a second from La Vuelva to the soft pear-shaped face behind its blue-tinted glasses – a face which for some time now had decorated most of the police stations of the Western world. 'And tell your friend here to do the same,' Ryan added, in Spanish, for the benefit of the the bodyguard.

Pedro smiled. 'You think you'll kill anyone with that gun, Señor Ryan?' He nodded at the Makarov in Ryan's hand: and like the Frenchman a moment earlier, he sounded amused. At the same moment, as though acting from some pre-arranged plan, the Frenchman said, also in Spanish: 'Our friend claims he is very familiar with a Walther PPK. But he should not point it at people while the safety-catch is on.'

Even while he was speaking the bodyguard moved. He moved with the speed and agility of an acrobat. The distance between him and Ryan was about five feet. He had covered at least half this when the first 9mm bullet hit him. Ryan fired twice. The first shot stopped the man's huge body in mid-air, puncturing his jacket against his stomach and slamming him backwards so that the back of his head collided like a club against the mantelpiece. The second bullet blew a hole in his throat the size of a saucer.

Through the shattering noise, La Vuelva's scream cut like a knife. Ryan had the gun aimed again at the centre of her face. 'Shut up, you bitch!' he shouted in English, above the slumping crash as the big man's body collapsed half into the grate. One of his enormous hands, with their cheap rings, twitched at his side. Blood was pumping out into the hearth. Ryan looked at Pedro, who had not moved. He then turned to the Frenchman:

'That was a stupid mistake. Next time I'll shoot you as well. Now, are we all going to be sensible? You've taken the trouble to get me here – so isn't it about time we decided to talk seriously? Two of your gorillas are dead.' He glanced at the fireplace where the big man's hand now lay motionless. 'I've got a gun, and I know how to use it. I wouldn't be much damn use to you if I didn't.'

La Vuelva broke in: 'For the love of God, get rid of him!' She was not looking at Ryan but at the huge hunched body in the fireplace. There was already the smell of clothes beginning to singe.

Ryan leered at her. 'Feeling squeamish, are you? I should have thought that with your experience you'd have had a stronger stomach. Pedro, you and your French friend will please empty your pockets. You, Pedro, first.' His gun was still pointing at La Vuelva.

Pedro held out his manicured hands in a gesture of taunting irony. 'I am not armed, Señor Ryan. Nor is my friend here. Will you take my word for it? Or do you wish to search us both?'

'I suppose sooner or later we're going to have to start trusting each other, Pedro.' Still holding the gun steadily against his knee, Ryan leant forward, picked up his glass of whisky from the floor and drank half of it in a gulp. He replaced it and sat back. 'I think the dramatics have gone far enough. You will now do me the favour of explaining what this charade is all about?' He turned to the Frenchman. 'You will begin, Monsieur, by introducing yourself.'

The man sucked at his meerschaum, and found that it had gone out. He hesitated, as though deciding whether to risk reaching for a match. Ryan anticipated him, and with his free hand threw him a lighter. The Frenchman took his time getting the pipe going again.

Finally he spoke, with an air of false pomposity: 'My name is Commandant Jacques Moulins, formerly with the Tenth Parachute Regiment, the Army of France.'

Ryan drank more whisky. 'Very well. We will now start at the beginning.' He turned to La Vuelva. 'Madame, why did you come to my establishment in the first place? Who recommended me to you? Dr Childs perhaps?'

It was Pedro who answered: 'The late Dr Childs was merely being consulted by Madame for a minor complaint. It was I, Señor Ryan, who decided upon your establishment. You have, as you will certainly not deny, a wide reputation. From my various inquiries you appeared to be an interesting man. I therefore decided to kill two birds, as you say in English, with one stone.'

'You also had Childs murdered.'

Pedro ignored the remark. 'I recommended Señora to your establishment in order that she might first take a rest, and then, perhaps, sooner or later, you would not only make her acquaintance, but even gain her confidence. As it happens, it appears that you acted not only impetuously but with impertinent haste.'

Ryan noticed a flush rise across La Vuelva's pale features; but she said nothing: merely poured herself another glass of Dom Perignon. The handsome bottle was almost empty.

'So what went wrong, Pedro? It's not like you to panic just because some quack mentions your pseudonym on the telephone. Or maybe you were just getting fed up not slaughtering people. The Rushdale Research Centre must have seemed very tempting. I'm surprised nobody thought of it before.'

He drained his glass and went on: 'But for all your daring, Pedro, you've made one mistake – not necessarily a fatal one, but not good for someone of your experience. If there's one weak link in your plan, it's not me. It's our honoured lady-host over there – the widow of General Ramon, and apparently still the revered figurehead of the poor toiling masses in that Island of hers in the Caribbean.'

La Vuelva had gone pale again, but was still silent. Ryan said: 'She's close to cracking-up, Pedro. The day before you broke into Rushdale and set your goons on to me, she deliberately knocked herself out with a bottle of brandy. Do you really think she's ready to assume the ultimate mantle of the People's Saviour – the Great Liberator who come to sweep away the shackles of Dr Gallo and his bearded Moscow puppets?'

La Vuelva sat very still while Pedro frowned, with the palms of his plump hands turned upwards. 'It will do you no good, Mr Ryan, to insult the Señora. The penalties among us for that kind of insubordination are severe.'

'So what am I supposed to do? Crawl on my belly and beg her forgiveness? Just remember, Pedro, I'm not one of your toadies – or hers. Not yet, anyway. Until I got hold of this gun, I was a prisoner. But now I'm giving the orders. I've already killed two of your goons. And I promise you, I'll do the same to the rest of you – Madame here included – unless you cooperate with me completely. I don't imagine any of us has much time. So let's start now. Talk, Pedro.'

But first – to spare La Vuelva's sensibilities – there was the task of removing the body from in front of the fire. It was too heavy even for the combined strength of Pedro and Commandant Moulins. Ryan was reluctant to put the Makarov away, but decided that he could not hold the three of them perpetually at gun-point.

Commandant Moulins fetched some old newspapers, which they used to sop up most of the blood; then the three men lugged the massive body upright, wrapping more newspaper round its throat and belly. The weight was enormous, and it was with great difficulty that they manoeuvred the corpse up the stairs and laid it out on the floor of the little room, still swaddled in newspaper, next to the first bodyguard who lay rigid on the sofa. Ryan noticed that the second man's eyes were open, and the newspaper round his throat had fallen away to reveal a wide wound, dark and glistening, like the belly of a gutted fish.

Before they left Ryan took one final precaution. He removed

the dead man's gun – a .44 Magnum, with the serial number erased: a villainous weapon, with a kick like a mule's and the power to blow a hole in a brick wall.

Downstairs again, he stuck both guns into the sides of his armchair. 'If we're going to talk business, I suggest we dispense with the armoury. But that doesn't mean to say I'm not prepared to use it, if necessary.'

Commandant Moulins replied in French: 'If you'll excuse me, Monsieur Ryan – but your behaviour over the past couple of days has hardly been above suspicion. First, there were your two contacts with the police, then your meeting with the secret agent, Monsieur Merton. We were left with no alternative but to bring you here – with the minimum of force – to find out where your sympathies lie.'

'My sympathies! You French have got a nice cynical sense of the ridiculous, haven't you?' Ryan picked up the bottle of whisky and poured himself another glassful. 'Which reminds me – I haven't eaten anything since my dinner with that so-called secret agent. Which one of you plays the servant round here, now that your heavy mob are no more?'

Pedro smiled. 'You can go hungry for a little longer, Señor Ryan. I hear that whisky is quite nourishing.'

Ryan looked at La Vuelva. 'If your two boy-friends want to argue, Madame, that's their business. But they're wasting my time, and yours. And my guess is that at this moment your time's a lot shorter than mine. I can still make a lot of trouble for all of you. As for myself, I've had as much trouble as I can take.'

There was a pause. Pedro was again standing in front of the fireplace, his smooth young face inscrutable behind his blue lenses; while La Vuelva, her glass empty, looked bored. Moulins spoke first.

'As I said, I am a commandant, formerly of the French Army. My association with Madame and with Señor Sanchez here are of no importance to you. You have asked why you have been brought here. The answer is simple. Madame had been having certain troubles with her resident visas in France and Spain. She came to England in need of relaxation. But she was also anxious to contact a reliable recruit for her plans. As Señor Sanchez has said, your record is not unknown, and Madame hoped to make contact with you. But your own behaviour, and certain other circumstances, made it necessary for her to act with more haste. And I must admit, Monsieur Ryan, that your conduct over the last couple of days, though costly, has not been disappointing. Despite your age,' he added, with a note of relish.

Ryan ignored him. Moulins ignited his pipe. 'But since you asked us to be frank, I would say that you have other qualifications necessary to the success of our proposed operation. Your military record indicates that you have no political ambitions, and that your heroism during the last war was largely inspired by money. Secondly, you have a wide experience of the Caribbean and you speak fluent Spanish. Thirdly, in matters which concern our operation, you are unlikely to have been approached or suborned by any other faction. Finally – and I will be perfectly honest here – you are expendable.'

Ryan sipped his whisky and waited. He wondered what qualities this French ex-major himself possessed to merit the confidence of La Vuelva.

It was La Vuelva who now spoke. She spoke in Spanish, quietly, yet for the first time she made it clear that she was in total command. No longer was she a rich widow used to indulging herself in the playpens of the Western world: there was now a defiance, a concealed determination and will in her manner, as though she were already rehearsing her future role as the Supreme Lady President, who, like Maximilian-Maria-Isodore de Robespierre, would wake up in the morning with a whim which by afternoon would be law.

'It is my avowed intention to overthrow the odious tyrannical regime of Fulgencio Gallo,' she began. 'I will overthrow it and install in its place a government of liberation under the Movement of my late husband, General Ramon.'

Ryan chuckled quietly. 'I mean no disrespect, Señora,' he replied in Spanish, 'but from what you told me yourself, the last time Ramon left the Island it was with a plane-load of US dollars. I don't suppose the starving masses under Gallo are going to thank him much for that.'

'I am not interested in your cheap opinions.' Her voice was still controlled, but her eyes were furious. The memory of her dead husband was obviously more potent than the more recent memory of her little session with Ryan on the carpet of his study.

Pedro broke in: 'This is no time to quarrel about history. It is the future which concerns us.'

Ryan shrugged. 'I don't give a damn about the history or

the future of your beloved Island. But I am curious. I'm curious to know why the world's number one left-wing terrorist should be so keen to gang up with a right-wing outfit like the Ramonista Movement?'

For a moment La Vuelva watched him in silence. Commandant Moulins was tamping fresh tobacco into his pipe, and Pedro had lit another cigarette. She spoke at last: 'Señor Sanchez's motives are of no concern to you, Señor Ryan. It should be enough for you to know that he is a master of subversion and guerrilla warfare.'

'But apart from the thrills, what does he hope to get out of it?'

La Vuelva did not reply. Ryan pressed her further: 'Well, perhaps you'll tell me what *I'm* going to get out of it?'

'You will enjoy the honour and glory of liberating my country.'

'You will also,' said Pedro, 'receive money for your services.'

'How much?'

La Vuelva's reply was crisp, business-like. 'That will be decided when we have discussed the basic plans.'

'Fine. I like to know who I'm going to be shooting at. Also, I haven't eaten for two days.'

Commandant Moulins stood up. 'First you will hand over those two pistols. Then you shall eat. Afterwards we will talk.'

They talked long into the night. Ryan had almost finished the bottle of whisky, while La Vuelva continued to drink champagne. Pedro and Commandant Moulins drank nothing.

Finally the Frenchman, who had cast himself as chief military spokesman, sat back, smoking his enormous pipe. 'Well, Monsieur Ryan, what is your professional opinion?'

'I wouldn't put a bet on it.'

La Vuelva, slightly flushed, said in French: 'I am not interested in your skills as a gambler. I am interested in the fruits of your experience – of your ability to infiltrate an enemy and turn them against themselves.' She paused to light one of her black cheroots. 'Commandant Moulins has detailed to you our plans. I would now like your serious opinion.'

Ryan said, without irony: 'Less than 150 men to capture a country of some six million people. Those aren't good odds.'

Moulins broke in: 'When Napoleon escaped from Elba,

he landed at Nice with thirty men. By the time he reached Grenoble he had three thousand. And when he marched into Paris he was again in command of an entire army.'

Pedro said: 'Lenin and Mao did even better. Although it took them rather longer.'

Ryan smiled over his whisky. 'You also ought to remember what Karl Marx said – that history repeats itself, but the second time as farce.'

'La Vuelva waved her hand impatiently. 'We are not discussing after-dinner philosophy. What else disturbs you?'

'All the equipment, except the PT-boats, is Soviet stuff. Why?'

'My dear Colonel Ryan' – Commandant Moulins blew smoke lazily at the ceiling – 'the reason is a simple matter of logic and logistics. Gallo's Army and Police are supplied entirely by the Russians. We will be carrying sufficient ammunition for at least seventy-two hours. By that time we will have captured enough weapons and ammunition to last for weeks, perhaps months. As I have already emphasized, it is my considered opinion that we shall quickly attract wide support from the population, many of whom will rally to the name of General Ramon's widow.' He gave a small, reverential nod in the direction of La Vuelva.

'I should add,' the Frenchman went on, 'that besides among the poorer classes, General Ramon was particularly popular with the junior ranks of the military, whose pay he quadrupled during his rule. While Gallo's so-called People's Army is less privileged, and a lot less content.'

Ryan turned to Pedro. 'One thing still puzzles me. It's your role in all this. What's in it for you? Is it just for the hell of making a revolution and stirring the shit? Because that's how you get your kicks, isn't it, Pedro? With some people its booze, or drugs, or little boys, or laying whores. With you it's spilling blood.'

The young man's mouth showed a sudden petulance, which he dissembled with a smile. Moulins interrupted them:

'Gentlemen, please! We are discussing matters of practical importance.' He turned to Ryan: 'As I have said, I have been designated temporary commander of the operation. As soon as the attack commences, it is proposed that you should assume overall control. This will not be merely in a military capacity. We will be depending upon your skills and ingenuity in all clandestine activities against the Gallo regime.'

Ryan looked at each of them in turn. 'You take a hell of a lot for granted! You're prepared to risk this entire operation to a total stranger whom you kidnap at gunpoint, then keep for two days drugged and chained up like a dangerous criminal. Why?'

It was La Vuelva who answered, with that note of disdainful authority which Ryan had heard at his first meeting with her. 'Do not concern yourself with our methods, Monsieur Ryan. You will be well rewarded. On the other hand, if I have even the smallest doubt as to your loyalty, I shall not hesitate to have you eliminated. Meanwhile, I have decided that you are the man I need.'

Ryan finished his whisky, sat back and smiled at her. 'You talk of loyalty and efficiency, Madame. I prefer to talk about money. I want your cheque before I leave. And I don't want a retainer, or a sweetener, or whatever you like to call it. I want front-money – which means the lot. And I shall want confirmation that it's been paid into my Swiss bank account before I commit myself any further.'

'What are you asking?' La Vuelva said, as though the question were routine.

'A quarter of a million dollars.'

'That is absurd.'

'No more absurd than this operation you're planning against Gallo. And how much have you invested in that? One million? – five million? – ten? As for me, the only way you're going to get me is by offering me so much that I can't turn it down – even if I never live to spend it.' He paused. 'A quarter of a million dollars, Madame. Take it or leave it.'

None of the other three moved. The only sound was the slight crackle of Moulins' pipe. Le Vuelva broke the silence. 'We will be in St Malo tomorrow for a few hours. There will be no time to clear a cheque.'

'Then I shall mail it to Geneva and telex them, with the number of my account, from Colombia.'

Pedro was smiling again. Ryan looked steadily at him: and for a moment his self-confidence faltered. For he remembered that this pampered bourgeois kid had an appetite for violence that went far beyond rational tactics. What was more, he had amply proved that he had both the nerve and the skill to satisfy that appetite. It was no doubt he, and not La Vuelva, who had thought up the plan to raid the Rushdale Experimental Research Centre and carry off its deadly produce. Earlier in the evening La Vuelva had assured Ryan that the poison would be merely a deterrent – the ultimate threat, in case the operation went wrong. But Ryan wondered how powerful her influence really was over Pedro. Or, for that matter, his over her.

Ryan now considered her, sitting here quietly holding her champagne glass – a woman whose only ambition was to overthrow one of the most ferocious Marxist states on earth. For all her poise and elegance and barely concealed fanaticism, he could still not understand what attracted her to Pedro – unless it were a perverse blood-lust, a love of danger that bordered on a death-wish.

But Ryan was already determined not to be distracted by La Vuelva's enigmatic relationships. For the moment – providing he was paid – he would go along with what was required of him and concentrate on the practical matters at hand. He turned to Moulins: 'A freighter from St Malo to Madeira seems a pretty odd means of travel these days?'

'It is necessary,' the Frenchman replied, 'to avoid unnecessary scrutiny. That is one of the advantages of bringing you here to Alderney. Even a sophisticated country like Great Britain has loopholes in its immigration procedures. The Channel Islands are one. Although they are technically British, there are also almost no formalities for going to France. Most of the ports along the French coast here do not even have a proper Customs post. And travellers from the Channel Islands are allowed to visit France for twenty-four hours without a passport.'

'There are always half a dozen ways of getting out of any country illegally,' Ryan observed. 'But why Madeira? I thought it was a pimple sticking out in the Atlantic where retired English gentlefolk sit around drinking tea and waiting for the next cruise-ship to come in so they can make up a new bridge party?'

The Frenchman smiled patiently. 'Precisely. Only we shall not be arriving to play bridge. Also, Funchal – the island's main town – has an international airport. Security there is lax. And they fly planes to the Caribbean.'

'Well, that may take care of us,' said Ryan, 'but what about young Pedro here? I mean, even the wildest Portuguese revolutionary might have a few qualms at having *him* around. I hear that even the Russians chucked him out.' He shook his head. 'It must get lonely, being unwanted.'

The young man's fat cheeks flushed below his tinted glasses. 'I shall be making my own travel arrangements.'

Ryan picked up the empty bottle at his feet and held it out to Moulins. 'Have you got another of these?' And he glanced at La Vuelva, who looked at him enviously. Ryan grinned at her and waited until Moulins had brought him a second bottle, then filled his glass. 'We may not need papers for St Malo tomorrow, but what about Madeira – and afterwards?'

Moulins replied: 'You will receive new papers in France, Monsieur Ryan.'

Emboldened by the whisky, Ryan said, 'Commandant, since I'm to be you commanding officer, I object to being addressed as "Monsieur", "Señor" or plain "Mister".'

La Vuelva said promptly: 'I am aware that you were only a major in the British Army at the end of the war. But to satisfy your future status with us, I shall reinstate you with your previous German rank of full colonel.'

Ryan gave a laconic bow. 'In that case, Madame, I should be given something decent to wear.'

La Vuelva gave a nod. Commandant Moulins stood up and beckoned to Ryan who followed him outside and upstairs, into another sparsely furnished bedroom where a set of smart city clothes were folded over a chair. There was also an expensive suitcase, obviously not new, with several labels stuck over it, from the best hotels in North America and around the Caribbean.

'You will find everything you require here, mon Colonel. The toilet and bathroom are down the passage on your left.' The Frenchman saluted and withdrew.

Ryan tried the door: no lock. First he examined the pockets of the jacket on the chair. In one was a British passport – again not new – in the name of ROBERT BROAKES, Business Executive. Inside were a few European entry and exit stamps, and a visa for Colombia, valid for twenty-eight days. He also found a sealskin wallet with a number of credit cards, British and International driving licences, five hundred French francs, and nearly two thousand dollars in twenty and fifty-dollar bills.

The suitcase contained several tropical suits and short-sleeved shirts; a pair of Gucci shoes; sober tie; monogrammed silk pyjamas; and a shirt from Jermyn Street to go with the suit. He tried on some of the clothes and found they fitted perfectly. Whatever the crudity of La Vuelva's henchmen, there must be someone in her outfit who had both taste and subtlety. As a final touch they had given him the latest issue of the *Economist* and *Investor's Chronicle*.

He stood in the middle of the room, clenching and unclenching his fists. He felt humiliated and furious. For the first time he realized the full implications of the events of the last forty-eight hours. It was now quite clear that his role in this operation had been prepared well in advance. From the very beginning he had been set up. He had been used.

He grabbed his new leather toilet-case, together with a pair of ivory-backed hair brushes, and marched along to the bathroom where he paused in some dismay, inspecting his appearance in the mirror. His battered face was hardly that of a prosperous well-travelled English businessman; and even after he had painfully shaved his bruised cheek and around his cut lip, the effect was not prepossessing.

He climbed into bed exhausted; yet lay awake for some time, wondering if La Vuelva's sexual appetite would require further gratification that night, and whether this time he should take the initiative. It was something he contemplated with a certain trepidation. However volatile and unpredictable her character, she was a woman now cast as a future leader, perhaps even as a despot; and whatever her private vagaries might be, he judged her character, in its present mood, to be strong enough to resist them. If he were wrong, his prospects could be gravely jeopardized.

He chose the safe option and went to sleep.

He woke late to find that Pedro was gone. Ryan was given no explanation; nor did he seek one. A straight answer would have been unlikely. Pedro had his own way of doing things.

They had an early lunch, prepared by Moulins; locked up the house, with its two corpses upstairs, then drove in the hired Citroen to the airport. Moulins carried a tartan grip-bag and black attaché case, while La Vuelva sported three pieces in white leather. She had discarded her plain skirt and reverted to her cosmopolitan style: loose-woven oatmeal coat belted over a matching dress, high heels, white scarf, and her enormous dark glasses.

Ryan was aware that they made a conspicuous trio; on the other hand, Alderney is a resort that is used to well-heeled foreign visitors. How long it would take for someone to call at that lonely farmhouse, and discover its gruesome contents, was another matter.

The airport was a small shed where formalities were as perfunctory as at a bus-station. There were only about half a dozen other passengers, all of whom looked like English day-trippers laden with duty-free goods. Moulins had charge of the tickets. While they waited for the 2.30 plane, there was a certain awkward atmosphere between the three of them, like strangers on a train.

The plane came in on time – a three-prop Islander, with a capacity for fourteen and no toilet. Once airborne, they were spared conversation by the noise.

Fifteen minutes later they landed in St Helier, Jersey, where the airport was larger and busier than Alderney. The first thing Ryan saw was a newspaper rack containing the London nationals. He bought a copy of each. The banner headlines all carried variations on the same story: TERRORIST 'PEDRO' BELIEVED TO BE IN BRITAIN – OXFORD RAIL HORROR LINKED TO 'PEDRO' THE KILLER, IRA CONNECTION SUSPECTED.

Pedro's one blurred photograph appeared in tabloids and heavies alike, showing those plump anonymous features shaded by dark glasses. But of the Rushdale Experimental Research Centre there was no mention; and Ryan was mildly mortified to find nothing about himself, nor was there any reference to La Vuelva. And poor old Miles Merton merited only an inside paragraph, reporting that the police were still searching for the killer.

The failure to mention the break-in at Rushdale could only confirm Pedro's diagnosis; that the authorities were afraid to spread a national panic. This official silence did not surprise Ryan; but he was certain that international Security would be on total alert. Every airport, railway terminal, and sea-port in Western Europe would be watched twenty-four hours a day; and every piece of luggage searched for those six capsules of snake-fever.

As soon as he entered the transit-hall his fears were confirmed. A rigorous check was going on – something almost unheard-of in the Channel Islands. But they were not scrutinizing passports, only luggage. Two officials were doing this with an expertise which suggested they were not local men.

Ryan saw the passengers' luggage being wheeled away from the plane – again, something quite exceptional on such a brief stop-over en route for France. And Ryan thought sardonically of Commandant Moulins' suave assurance that all countries have their immigration loopholes.

He stood in line, just in front of La Vuelva and the Frenchman, who both behaved as though they had never seen him before. It was his turn next. The official said, 'Is this your only luggage, sir?'

The man sorted thoroughly through Ryan's new suitcase, seemed satisfied, then peered at his face. 'Had an accident, sir?'

'That's right. Some damn fool didn't stop at the lights.'

'You want to be careful, sir. Thank you. Have a pleasant journey.'

While the man was speaking, Ryan could see the second official going through La Vuelva's three expensive cases. He did it swiftly, without embarrassment. Ryan could not see if he found any packets of paper panties, but the man did lift out three jars of a proprietary brand of marmalade, each with a label from Jackson, of Piccadilly. He replaced them without comment.

The first man had moved on from Ryan and had now turned his attention to Commandant Moulins' briefcase; and again Ryan saw him take out three more jars of exclusive condiment, this time from Fortnum and Mason. He stood examining them for a moment, then the Frenchman said something which was evidently a joke, since the man gave a faint official smile and replaced the jars in the briefcase.

Ryan waited until La Vuelva and the Frenchman had started back towards the plane. They had still not given him even a glance. Then he saw their luggage being reloaded on to the trolley outside. It had all been very neatly done. Pedro himself couldn't have bettered them.

Ryan was almost the last to board the plane, and sat near the back this time, away from the other two. But he had the impression that they were aware of his every movement, measuring his every thought. There had been no metal-detectors at the airport, and he wondered if Commandant Moulins was armed.

Thirty minutes later they began to bank down over the network of St Malo, with its sprawling yacht-basin with white pleasure-craft, and the docks tucked away behind the little peninsula surrounded by the ancient ramparts enclosing the Old Town. From the size of the ships at berth, Ryan guessed that it must be a shallow harbour, and that the freighter – on which they were due to sail that night – would not be a comfortable one in which to cross the Bay of Biscay in autumn.

This time the airport had a control-tower, a bar and restaurant. The CRS man who checked their passports looked bored; but as they waited again for their luggage to arrive, Ryan noticed a short man in a blue raincoat standing in the corner of the hall. He seemed to be looking at no one in particular, but Ryan recognized a weary watchfulness which betrayed him at once. He was good, but not the best: in his profession, to stand about doing nothing, while looking convincing about it, is one of the most difficult tricks of all. But he wasn't looking for Ryan, or La Vuelva, or Commandant Moulins. He was looking for a pear-cheeked young Latin American who had murdered two of his police colleagues in Paris.

Customs formalities were swift. Ryan was amused at the obsequious air with which the official smiled at La Vuelva and tactfully avoided chalking her suitcases, let alone asking her to open them. Ryan and Moulins' inspection was almost equally casual.

Once past the gate La Vuelva and the Frenchman became almost affable. At her suggestion they went into the bar where La Vuelva offered Ryan a drink. He accepted politely, noticing that she chose for herself only a Campari, while Moulins drank Vichy water.

The ship, the *Santa Teresa* – registered under the Panamanian flag – was due to sail at nine p.m., and embarkation was at seven, two hours earlier. La Vuelva suggested they went to the Hotel Central – the grandest in town – standing within the old walls. The idea appealed to Ryan because it would give him ample opportunity in which to bring up again the small matter of a cheque for a quarter of a million dollars.

When they arrived La Vuelva led them to the bar, where this time she ordered champagne. Ryan stuck to whisky. After his first glass he broached the subject directly. 'Madame, I have done many dangerous, even reckless, things in my life, but rarely for nothing. And then, never from choice. As I made clear last night, I am not sailing until I am paid.'

For several seconds she stared at him through the smoke from her little black cigar, while Moulins looked both uneasy and angry. Suddenly she laughed. 'Colonel, you are an audacious scoundrel. But I like you. At least you are not afraid to speak your mind, even to me.' She opened her bag and took out a long stout cheque-book, issued by one of the most exclusive banks in France. 'How do you wish me to make it out?' she asked. He told her. She produced a slim gold pen, wrote in a flowing hand, signed, tore the cheque out and passed it across the table.

Ryan examined it carefully, and noted with some misgiving that it was signed *Isobel Achar*. Otherwise it seemed in order. He then called the waiter and asked for some notepaper and an envelope. While he was writing the instructions to his own bank in Geneva, La Vuelva ordered a fresh bottle of champagne. The act of signing away $250,000 seemed to have meant as much to her as paying the bar bill.

Ryan excused himself and went to Reception where he mailed the letter, together with the cheque, to Switzerland. When he returned to the bar, he found La Vuelva and Moulins in huddled conversation. They broke off as soon as he appeared. He sat down. La Vuelva said, 'Now you are committed, Colonel Ryan. If you change your mind and go back on your word, I shall consider it treason and will deal with you accordingly.' She did not sound entirely sober.

'Madame, I shall consider myself committed only when I receive the telex confirming that your cheque has been cleared.'

Commandant Moulins sat forward, grey-faced. 'You will apologize to Madame, Colonel Ryan! How dare you doubt the honour of her word!'

'Oh shut up,' Ryan said in English. 'Have something proper to drink.' Moulins was still on Vichy water. To Ryan's surprise, La Vuelva seemed more amused than injured.

'Tell me, Colonel,' she said, 'you have made it plain that you are not an idealist, nor a political thinker. However, you must have realized that our operation will have profound political implications?'

'With respect, Madame, from what I've heard of your late

husband's regime, he surrounded himself – like most of your flashy Latin American dictators – with a gang of parasites whose main function was to appear on parade in gorgeous uniforms covered in salad. When it comes to this operation, Madame, I want fighting men, hard experienced men who've seen battle and don't crap in their trousers the first time they hear a shot. And Latin America hasn't had a real battle – let alone a war – for at least half a century.'

She drank some champagne. When she spoke, she enunciated each word with careful precision. 'It will be your duty, Colonel, to make sure that my officers and men are fully trained. They are not all professional soldiers – but every one of them is a patriot. Above all, they are not afraid of being killed.'

'I don't want them killed, I want them killing the enemy. Which brings me to one last point. What about Gallo's friends in the Kremlin? Just supposing our operation looks like being successful – are the Soviets going to pass by on the other side?'

'The Soviets! – what can they do!' And she gave a joyless laugh. 'They have no troops on the Island – only a few hundred so-called technical advisers. And when our operation ignites a national uprising, there will be no Soviet armour to roll into Montecristo, as it did into Budapest and Prague. Dr Gallo exists at the end of a very long life-line. It will not be so difficult to cut that line.'

Soon after they left for an early dinner at a restaurant which La Vuelva chose called the Duchesse Anne where fish was the speciality. Ryan guessed that she kept a careful watch on her figure, which did not prevent her ordering more wine.

The meal was not an easy one. La Vuelva sat very erect, saying little, while her eyes, usually so fine, began to take on a dull, slightly crooked look. Commandant Moulins was little help either. Despite his soldierly appearance, he maintained a respect for his employer that bordered on the abject. He felt obliged to address every remark to her personally, and since she rarely replied, except in monosyllables, the conversation tended to flag.

Ryan himself became increasingly curious about the Frenchman's past, but was wary of seeming too inquisitive. Commandant Moulins was obviously an intensely proud man; and Ryan already suspected that he owed his present circumstances to some disastrous, even shameful, episode in his military career. That was the trouble with the French Army, he thought: they were too fond of meddling in politics.

Towards the end of the meal, in a desperate attempt to touch on a lively topic, he mentioned Pedro. He turned to La Vuelva and asked casually, 'Is he joining us on the boat tonight?'

'As he told you, he has made other arrangements.'

Commandant Moulins said suddenly, 'What is your opinion of Señor Fraga de Sanchez, Colonel?'

'Much the same as most other people's I should think. He's clever. He's brave. He's also mad.'

'Mad?' La Vuelva repeated. 'Explain yourself, Colonel.'

Ryan drained down his wine. He said: 'A young man from a faraway continent comes to Europe and starts mayhem with a handful of organizations to which he has no national or natural allegiance. I don't say he actually enjoys killing and maiming people – but he might find life a lot duller if he couldn't. For him terrorism is a sport.'

'You think Señor Sanchez is a psychopath?' said La Vuelva.

'I'm not a doctor. I'd just say he was a suitable case for treatment.'

'He has his uses,' Moulins said dryly. 'Like you.'

CHAPTER FOUR

The Point of No Return

It was nearly eight o'clock when they took the taxi to the docks. There were few lights on the *Santa Teresa*. As Ryan expected, she was not a large ship, nor was she imposing – a graceless oblong hulk standing high out of the water, its white-painted flanks turned a brownish-grey with blotches of seeping rust. Although it was barely an hour before the scheduled sailing time, there seemed to be little activity aboard.

As Moulins paid off the taxi Ryan whispered to him, out of ear-shot of La Vuelva: 'Won't our President-to-be look a bit out of place on a filthy Panamanian tramp? Ladies like her go by air – first class.'

The Frenchman replied stiffly: 'International airports are very public places, and Madame is a very public person. Besides, people still take sea-trips, you know. And Madame is not adverse to dressing like a common woman – providing it is in a good cause.'

Nine o'clock passed and they had still not sailed. Ryan decided on a stroll round the ship. As he left the cabin he looked at the lock on the door. It did not look strong, although anyone wishing to search his belongings would certainly be disappointed.

He left the door unlocked and walked down a narrow gangway lined with pipes, like huge distended entrails. The ship smelt of hot iron and engine-oil. He met only one person – a dark-skinned sailor who passed him without even a nod – before he reached the deck. He walked round the ship half a dozen times, then went in search of the wardroom, and a bar. He did not see La Vuelva or the Frenchman again that night.

Just after eleven he heard the rattle of the anchor-chain, and twenty minutes later they sailed. He undressed, squeezed himself into the bunk, and slept surprisingly well.

*

The morning was foul and the sea heavy, under a veil of rain and dark rolling clouds. Ryan had difficulty dressing, and had to use both hands to steady himself along the gangway, up the narrow steel steps and along to the wardroom. It was empty except for a man with a beard and tabs on his white shoulders.

He nodded at Ryan, without speaking. The bar was open. Ryan ordered a muddy black coffee and a shot of brandy. He drank three of each, then ordered breakfast. There seemed to be no menu. After a long wait he was brought a couple of eggs fried in oil, and a roll without butter.

The movement of the ship was now pronounced. Ryan's coffee cup slid off the table and smashed on the floor. He did not manage to finish the eggs. He returned to the bar, bought a quart-bottle of Johnny Walker, and started back towards his cabin.

At the corner of the gangway he collided with Commandant Moulins. The Frenchman smelt of after-shave. 'Good morning, Colonel. I trust you slept well?'

'Thank you. How is Madame?'

'Still asleep. This weather does not agree with her.'

'Do me a favour, Commandant. Get her off the drink.'

The Frenchman stared over Ryan's shoulder. When he spoke, his voice was cold and cautious. 'As a fellow military man, Colonel, you will know that it is not easy to give orders to one's supreme commander.'

'Shit. You mean to tell me, you've never once questioned the wisdom of your superiors? You're not at St Cyr now, you know. Where we're going there aren't going to be any clean mess-halls and fancy uniforms and bugles and prancing horses. We're going to war, Commandant. And whether we win or lose, it's going to be a dirty little war.'

'Are you insinuating, Colonel, that I am not prepared to fight a war?'

'I don't know, Commandant. I don't know anything about you. I just see a man who should, at your age, and with your presumed abilities, have made it at least to colonel, if not higher. But then, the French Army have always assumed they knew better than their politicians. Perhaps it was a pity the politicians proved, in the end, too strong for you – or perhaps too clever?'

The Frenchman said nothing; his expression was grim and mute. Ryan continued: 'I may see you in the wardroom for lunch. By the way, are there any other passengers, besides us?'

'No.'

Ryan nodded and headed for the steel stairway. He made another six clumsy rounds of the deck, at the end of which his eyes were stinging and his face raw with wind and salt. Back in his cabin he lay down, drank a medicinal dose of whisky, and slept.

He lunched with Commandant Moulins in the wardroom, at a table apart from the ship's officers. These were a sullen lot, separated by the language barrier from Ryan and the Frenchman who had no wish to let on that they spoke Spanish. When the meal was over and the tables had been cleared, the two of them stayed on and played chess. Once Ryan inquired after La Vuelva, and was told that she was still in her cabin.

On their second game, Ryan said, 'You and I, Commandant – we're going to have to have a little talk.'

'Yes?'

'I insist that I know my men – particularly my officers. I want to know more about you – everything about you.'

The Frenchman drew back his lips over his half-drunk coffee. 'You will be disappointed, Colonel. It is not a sensational story. I was merely involved, some years ago, in an attempt to kill de Gaulle. It was a fiasco, like all the others. I was able to get away to Sicily, then to Rome, and later Madrid, where I met Madame. Does that satisfy you?'

'You are not a crack shot, Commandant?'

'I am not a bad shot.'

'But you prefer to delegate that sort of thing to others? Just as in this operation you're happy to be the middle-man – you have the ear of La Vuelva, but you accept me as your commanding officer. You will transmit my orders to whatever riff-raff La Vuelva has lined up on that beach in Colombia, but you will conveniently avoid any ultimate responsibility. Perhaps that's why you never made it higher than commandant?'

The Frenchman's face had grown stiff and his knuckles white round his coffee cup. 'Perhaps,' he said at last, 'I should also tell you that I won the Medaille Militaire at Dien Bien Phu. That was while you, Colonel, were making money out of sauna baths and diets for rich women. You have no right to criticize me. You do not know what it was like in those last two weeks in that valley – with twelve thousand dead, whom we could not bury, and the last parachute reinforcements falling behind the Viet-Minh lines. No one can have any idea. No one.' His voice had sunk to a whisper, and Ryan noticed, with some misgiving, a nerve tugging at the edge of the man's eye.

There was a pause, broken by the monotonous roar of wind and sea. The Frenchman made no move to lay out another game of chess. Ryan said: 'The operation we're heading for won't be quite as glorious, but it may be just as bloody – on a smaller scale. It may also end just as badly. Why are you doing it, Commandant? You don't look the mercenary-type. And you don't look like one of La Vuelva's political disciples. What are you?'

Moulins gave a short harsh laugh. 'You're wrong. I am a mercenary. I'm also a soldier. But what can a soldier do without an army? I fight for whoever pays me. Like you.'

Ryan nodded. 'There are worse ways of making one's fortune. Not many, but some. How much *is* she paying you?'

The Frenchman tasted his coffee, which was now cold. 'That is an impertinent question. I decline to answer it.' He stood up. 'We shall meet for dinner, perhaps?'

Ryan nodded, and the two of them returned to their cabins.

Ryan took a salt-water shower, then dozed on his bunk till eight. When he returned to the wardroom for dinner, La Vuelva again did not appear.

Between his regular prowls round the wind-swept deck, Ryan spent his time wedged in his narrow bunk against the queasy heave and pitch of the ship, treating his stomach with a diet of coarse Spanish brandy.

He felt suspended between reality and responsibility – his senses numbed, his emotions detached and relaxed.

His original diagnosis of the situation still seemed valid. If they had gone to these lengths to recruit him, they would not eliminate him now. Nor did the crude violence of his initial treatment at their hands greatly trouble him: they were crude, violent people, and Ryan's own experience of the Caribbean had taught him that even in the highest political circles you do not expect subtlety. Whether they had killed poor Miles Merton in order to silence him, or merely to prove to Ryan that they were serious, was something upon which he could only speculate.

If there was one thing that did worry him, it was the fate of his Lagonda; as well as a nagging concern about how – back at The Hermitage – they would treat his unexplained disappearance. But then the ineffably competent Miss McKinley would have the establishment under control: and it was even with some chagrin that Ryan realized that his absence would mean little or nothing to the smooth clinical process of removing several pounds of surplus cellulite fat from the buttocks and thighs of his affluent clientele. In fact, he had made himself professionally so efficient as to have become dispensable.

The few doubts he did have usually came at night, in the small dead hours when the creaking and groaning of his tiny cabin seemed even louder than the boom of the sea outside. These doubts did not so much centre on the operation itself as on its leader. In La Vuelva Ryan thought he recognized the type: a rich, spoilt South American slut – clothes a little too chic, voice a little too shrill; who always travelled first-class and treated the stewards and hostesses like dirt.

But with this woman there was something else. As well as her immense wealth, she still obviously had power, and an appetite for even greater power. Yet beneath that well-bred exterior, purchased by money and sustained by toadies and sycophants, lay a dangerously vulnerable, neurotic creature striving desperately to live up to the memory of her dead husband. A coarse lonely woman with a weakness for drink, for casual sex, and probably for gratuitous violence.

And it was to this woman that Ryan had been hoaxed, forced, and finally bribed to entrust his very existence.

On the third night he was lying in the hot humming darkness when he became aware that the sheet and blankets had been pulled down below his waist, and that two sets of cool fingertips were touching his belly and thigh: that his pyjama trousers had been pealed down to his knees, and that his erect penis was being softly, skilfully licked and sucked by some invisible creature in the dark.

His first reaction, beyond his physical response, was suspicion. He had not locked the door, and now reached down and felt the smooth face over his groin, the hair hanging loose over his fingers. His heart was beating hard. He took her face in his hands and pulled it towards him, kissing her aggressively on the mouth. Her body came down towards him. She was wearing only a thin nightdress. He pulled it up to above her breasts, and dragged her body against his, wedging it underneath him in the narrow bunk. She said nothing. He entered her gently, but she was already moist and let out a shrill moan; and together their bodies moved to the throbbing vibration of the ship.

Three times she screamed, and Ryan feared – even above the roar of the sea – that Commandant Moulins, in the next cabin, must hear. Five minutes later they lay still, and he could feel the pain in his back where her fingernails had scraped deep into the skin.

He felt pleasantly exhausted, still keeping the weight off her with his elbows, kissing the lobes of her ear and the corners of her mouth. She suddenly kicked away the sheet and blankets and slid to the floor. He felt he ought to say something but at the same time wanted her to speak first. She said nothing. He heard the faint rustle of her nightdress in the dark, then the door opened and closed behind her.

He lay for some moments, sated but not at ease. And again he realized that this was hardly the kind of relationship he should have chosen with his future Supreme Commander. Either he was to be a casual stud – which certainly flattered him, considering his age – or he was to carry out a specified military operation. But liaison like this was likely to have only two results. He might become indispensable to La Vuelva, in which case he would find himself playing a surrogate General Ramon; or she would tire of him, and that could easily mean a bullet in the neck.

Above all, he liked to be master of events, particularly in matters of sex. La Vuelva had recruited him, by a series of eccentric and brutal means; and was now indulging herself with his body as though he had no choice in the matter. His pride was hurt; while all his professional instincts warned him against becoming further involved.

For the next two days he did not see her; and at night he lay awake, uneasily expecting another visit.

Next day they docked at Funchal. On the quay-side Ryan saw a large hoarding in English, advertising tea-bags.

They left the ship last, separately, with La Vuelva and Commandant Moulins taking the lead: the Frenchman in his white polo-necked sweater, she in a smart fawn suit. There were no problems with the officials: the young man who examined Ryan's new passport smiled and wished him a happy stay in Madeira. He ignored his black eye and cut lip.

Outside the dock a large car was waiting. Ryan got into the front, with La Vuelva and Commandant Moulins in the back. The Frenchman gave a brisk order in Portuguese to the driver, who skirted the town, along the coast-road towards the airport.

The plane was a twin-jet Executive, with tables set between the seats, and an air of spacious extravagance. When Ryan inquired what the fuel consumption was Moulins assured him that the plane carried enough to reach the Caribbean and land anywhere it pleased.

They both sat near the front, with La Vuelva alone at the back. They did not see the pilot or navigator. The jets gave a low howl; they turned, lined up for the take-off, and with a long smooth scream were airborne. Ryan dozed off.

Four hours later he saw the sprinkle of lights below him and fastened his belt. The Jamaican authorities were all white-teethed and white-shirted, gleaming with hospitality at the arrival of a private jet.

They went to the bar, where Ryan was relieved to see La Vuelva share a bottle of mineral water with the Frenchman. Ryan drank Scotch. Their conversation was oblique, with no suggestion of conspiracy. La Vuelva hardly joined in.

It was nearly midnight when their connecting flight was called – commercial this time, Colombia Air, destination Bogota. There were only a couple of other first-class passengers: the usual dark, well-fed figures in business suits with rings on their fingers and a contented look which took for granted the instant attention of the stewardesses. There was mock caviar, pâté de fois gras, and a not very good champagne. Ryan again asked for whisky. He noted that La Vuelva was not drinking.

The dawn was coming up as they circled in over Bogota: a tall narrow city which looked from the air like a long graveyard, its skyscrapers jutting up from a high ridge between dim, rolling mountains.

There seemed to be only one official on duty at the airport – a man in uniform with a gun, and sleep-dirt in his eyes. He glanced at their visas and stamped them, then waved the three of them through. Outside, a long black American limousine was waiting, with a chauffeur in cap and leggings standing at the kerb. They were driven away through miles of steaming shantytown into the neon-lit splendour of the new city. The hotel was a heavy edifice, whose marble exterior dated from the twenties. Inside was the deep-carpeted, air-conditioned luxury of any modern first-class hotel in the world.

While La Vuelva and Commandant Moulins were checking in, Ryan confirmed that the hotel had an international telex. He also knew that Bogota was six hours behind Geneva, which gave him a comfortable hour in which to settle in and have breakfast while his Swiss bankers finished their lunches.

She and Moulins had disappeared when he reached Reception and checked in under his new alias as Robert Broakes. While the boy carried his case to the lift, he bought the morning papers from the lobby kiosk. They were all in Spanish – the two American papers, from Panama, only arrived in the evening – and he glanced through blaring headlines in which the Government congratulated itself on a new highway, an irrigation works, a dam in the south of the country. The rest of them were devoted to sport. There was almost no foreign news.

Looking out of the picture-window of his room Ryan had no sensation of being in a strange city, except for a slight giddiness caused by the fact that this was the highest capital city in the world – standing at 8,700 feet above sea-level. The weather was grey, and cloud hid the tops of the surrounding mountains like clumps of fungi. The streets below were wide, moving with modern traffic, the buildings tall and uniform, like rows of upturned mouth-organs.

After a shower, shave, and an American breakfast, he rode down again to the lobby. There was piped music and a stream of short, sleek-haired men with briefcases who paid no attention to him. He was just another ordinary well-dressed gringo tourist.

He went to the telex bureau and sent his message to Geneva, identifying himself only by the seven-figure number of his secret account. He had already informed the bank, in his covering letter from St Malo, that they were to address any messages to his new name of Broakes.

The reply came twelve minutes later. His numbered account had been credited with US $250,000 – minus the usual charges, and what the Swiss so charmingly call 'negative interest'.

Feeling braced and relaxed, he went to the bar. It was empty except for a slim long-legged Negro whose shiny complexion matched his charcoal silk suit. He was wearing wrap-around mirror-glasses that reflected the orange juice he was drinking. He seemed not to notice Ryan.

Ryan himself drank a couple of whisky-sours, then sauntered back into the lobby and stood for some time looking into a souvenir shop, full of hideous Indian artifacts. When he turned, he saw the Negro in the middle of the lobby, lighting a cigarette. Ryan was still aware of that slight giddiness; and he now felt a quick surge of adrenalin.

He began to walk towards the entrance. As he passed the Negro, the man flicked his cigarette into a marble box of sand. His inscrutable glasses made it impossible to tell whether he were watching Ryan or not. Ryan walked on, out through the revolving doors.

A tepid rain was falling. Along the pavements umbrellas were sprouting like mushrooms; but few people seemed to be hurrying or seeking shelter. The poorer women were bent double under black shawls, their teeth stained blood-red with betel-juice.

Ryan soon found that the effort of walking left him slightly breathless: a combination of alcohol and altitude. He turned into a cheap supermarket, mostly full of Indians and mestizos; made several rounds of the poorly-stocked shelves, and saw the tall Negro waiting near the entrance. Either the man was new to this game, or was deliberately waiting for Ryan to make the first move.

Ryan walked out again into the rain. At the corner he turned into a narrow street where a gang of children were playing some complicated game on the pavement. He continued another few hundred yards, between steep ugly tenement blocks, paused at a cigarette kiosk, bought a packet of king-size filter-tips and a box of cheap wax matches. He put the cigarettes in his pocket, kept the matches in his right hand, swung round and lifted both fists, one aimed at the Negro's jaw, the other at his belly. In the same moment the Negro also raised both hands, in a defensive stance, moving with the speed and grace of a dancer, or a boxer.

Ryan said, 'All right, hold it! Who are you? And don't play dumb – you've been following me for the past half-hour. Just about the worst tail-job I ever saw.'

'Name's Jones,' the Negro said, in a rich Southern accent. 'You're Ryan, ain't yah? That's an Irish name, if ah'm right?' He grinned. 'That makes us kinda brothers – both Celts. Me, ah'm from an ole Welsh family – Robert Jones, o' Mississippi, in the USA. When mah daddy first saw me, he said, "Son, you're a lil' on the dark side!"' He grinned again, and Ryan found himself staring at a distorted double image of himself in the pair of mirror lenses. The Negro added: 'Shall we stroll up the block and have a drink?'

'I think it's time we did. But no tricks – I'm not in the mood.'

'Ah'm a peaceable man, Mr' – he hesitated – 'Mr Broakes. Or maybe ah should be callin' you Colonel?'

'Please yourself. But what the hell was all that play for just now? Trying to pretend you're some kind of spook? Because if you are, forget it. You wouldn't make grade one.'

The Negro shook his head, looking serious now. 'I just wanted to see how good you were. Sometimes you can tail a guy for a whole day and he don't notice.'

'You must have rated me pretty low, Mr Jones.' They were walking together now towards the end of the street. 'Anyway, let's have that quiet drink, and then you're going to tell me exactly what your game is.'

They stepped into a shabby little café with a marble-topped counter and youths playing pin-table machines. Ryan ordered a rum-and-Coke. The Negro chose plain Coke. 'You wanna go easy on the booze when you first get up here,' he said. 'At this height it can take you kinda funny. Me, ah'm strictly TT. Don't get me wrong, though. I got nothin' against booze. Just that ah got a bad gut.'

When the mestizo waiter had put down their drinks, Ryan said, 'I take it you're working for the Company?'

The Negro gave a shout of laughter and smacked both hands down on the counter. 'Shit, man, ah should take that as an insult! You better get this straight – you and me, we're on the same side. All that CIA crap – forget it! Hell, ah got a certain pride.'

'So what's it all about, Jones?'

'You can call me No-Entry – No-Entry Jones, that's what everyone calls me.'

'So?'

'I got the name back in Vietnam. Used to fly spotter-planes. One day ah took a round through the floor and up mah asshole – wasn't wearing a groin-protector. It came out through my stomach. I managed to get the plane down, then passed out. When ah comes to in the hospital ah had a whole lot o' puzzled medics round me. They'd stitched up the exit-wound in mah gut, but goddam it! they just couldn't find no entry-wound. After that, the name No-Entry stuck. Major Robert No-Entry Jones, US Army, Purple Heart, and an honourable discharge, all on account of one Commie bullet up the ass.'

'Do you still fly planes, Major?'

'When ah'm paid to.'

'Is someone paying you now?'

'They might be. Ah'm a good pilot, Colonel. And mah services don't come cheap.'

'Still on spotter-planes?'

'Maybe.'

'What sort?'

'L-19. She's tied up with string, but if she gets a bullet through her, you just tape it over with Elastoplast. She's a good plane.'

Ryan frowned. 'Nobody mentioned any aircraft to me.'

'Well, mah little bird-dog would hardly rate as a strike-plane, Colonel. She's even got wing-mirrors for spottin' them lil' MiGs! No, ah'm strictly reconnaissance.'

'You mind telling me who for?'

No-Entry Jones rubbed his smooth dark jaw. 'At a guess, ah'd say the same people as you.'

'So why the hell not call me up at the hotel in a civilized way, instead of all this amateur play-acting round the back-streets?'

The Negro tapped his long dark fingers on the counter, as though practising a silent rhythm. 'Just let's say, ah don't trust people that easy. You don't know who might be hangin' round that hotel. Anyway, ah was actin' under orders – told to contact you in a quiet street where there'd be no hassle.'

'I'm not a particularly trusting person either,' said Ryan. 'Any reason why I should think you're on the level?'

'Well, ah know both your names, for a start. And I knew what you look like, and when you were checkin' into the hotel.'

'A government agent could know that too.'

The Negro shook his head. 'Hell, ah'm strictly free-lance. After that razzmadazz out in South-East Asia, you don't catch me workin' for any government no more.'

'And you don't think the people you're working for now might turn out to be Government?'

No-Entry Jones showed his very white teeth. 'Man, the moment they become a government, ah take my cheque and vanish! Ah'm a simple guy. I got no big ambitions.'

'Have you had a down-payment?'

The Negro looked suddenly solemn. 'Let's say, I don't work for nothing.'

They sat for a moment in silence, listening to the banging and shouting of the young men at the pin-tables. 'You still haven't told me why you picked me up,' Ryan said at last.

The Negro leant forward, his pink palms turned upwards. 'You know what it's all about, Colonel Ryan. You and ah, we're gonna do what those boys in the CIA, and about half a dozen other governments, have wanted to do for ten years. We're gonna waste Gallo guy – he and his whole shitty regime!'

Ryan nodded. 'What's your motivation, Major? – apart from the money, of course. Political? I thought Gallo was supposed to be on the side of the under-dog – the champion of the poor and oppressed, the victims of gringo Imperialism?'

No-Entry Jones gave a slow chuckle. 'Don't give me no crap about politics. Politics is like the three-card trick. Unless you're the dealer, you don't win. You talk about motivation? Hell, man, ah got one motivation in this game, and one only. A nice stack o' greenbacks in some friendly bank. Same as you, ah guess, Colonel?'

Ryan shrugged; he preferred to change the subject. 'Have you met the woman yet?'

No-Entry Jones shook his head. 'I deal exclusively through a guy called Captain Rodriguez. He operated out o' Caracas. Used to be in General Ramon's Special Police on the Island. Between him and Gallo's boys, ah'd say that poor bloody country don't have much of a choice.'

'Have you met a man called Pedro?' Ryan said; and this time the Negro looked puzzled, and shook his head. 'You may know him as Dr Lopez? Or Fraga de Sanchez? Young fellow, rather fat, wears blue shades. Believes in world revolution. Sort of boy who would put Trotsky into the Goldwater Fan Club.'

'He sounds like too much trouble for me. I believe in keepin' mah nose clean. More you know, more likely you run into shit. I just stick to flyin' planes.'

'Have you flown over the Island yet?'

'Twice. Ah'm gonna be flyin' over it a third time – with you. I was the man that marked out the invasion beach.'

'And no opposition?'

'Nothin'. I came in real low, at sunrise, and there wasn't a darned movin' thing down there. Gallo's a confident sonofabitch. After that State Department got too yeller to beat their meat no more in the Caribbean, he's not expectin' trouble – not from the outside, anyways.'

'I just hope you're right. How's our security, by the way?'

'How d'you mean? You not on again about those spooks from Langley, Virginia, are you? Because you'd be wastin' your time. Those boys had their claws taken out a long while back.'

'I still wouldn't underestimate them. Anyway, why are you so sore against the CIA?'

'Ah'm not sore at 'em. I just think they're dumb. Most of 'em are so goddam dumb they can't find their asses with both hands.'

'What about local security? I mean, the woman may have found a nice quiet training-spot close to nowhere, and she may have greased the right palms, but you're still not going to tell me that you can get over a hundred men training for two weeks with modern Soviet weapons, and six PT-boats, and nobody's going to notice and not start passing the word around?'

No-Entry relaxed, with his elbows on the counter. 'Man, you gotta appreciate a country like this. We're not in Up-State New York or lil'ole England, now, y'know. Here you hire a private army like you hire a TV. 'Course, ah'm talkin' about the fat-cats who run the coffee plantations and don't pay no tax, and have bank accounts in Europe. They believe in real protection – and ah don't mean a couple o' hard numbers with pockets bulgin' in the wrong places. Oh no – those boys ride round in bullet-proof Caddies and have a few Browning fifty-mils stuck up on their roof-tops, with maybe a couple o' hundred men on the payroll.' He shook his head. 'No, the lady's chosen her spot pretty well. We won't get bothered – and if we are, we got more than enough hardware to look after ourselves. Probably the biggest danger up there is snakes. The whole goddam area is crawlin' with the lil' bastards.'

He noticed Ryan wince, and gave his low chuckle. 'Do ah divine you're not partial to serpents, Colonel?'

'I am not. There are only two things I'm really frightened of in this life, Major – middle-aged ladies with the seventeen-year itch, and snakes.'

'Well, you're sure goin' to the right spot in the Guajira Peninsula! I wouldn't say nothin' disrespectful of our lady employer, but as for snakes – oh shit! I once met a man stayin' on the tenth floor of the biggest hotel in Caracas, and he found a snake four feet long curled round the john. No one ever did find out how the thing got up there.'

There was a pause. A dwarf in rolled-up jeans and a faded denim shirt had stopped by their table and stood grinning up at them. He had a huge head and both his arms ended in rounded stumps. No-Entry snapped something at him and the creature sidled away, proffering his amputated limbs to a table with men playing dominoes.

Jones got up. 'Let's get out o' here. We'll go round the block, then back to the hotel. We split there – it's better that way.'

'So there *is* a security problem?' said Ryan.

No-Entry made no comment. They walked down to the corner and turned into a bright gaudy street that reminded Ryan of Tottenham Court Road: cheap cafés, cut-rate shops, hideous modern furniture stores, hoardings for patent medicines and mineral water.

'One thing puzzles me, No-Entry. You say you've flown sorties over the Island? If you flew from the Guajira Peninsula, that makes it by my reckoning a round-trip of over six hundred miles. And an L-19's no bigger than a sports-car.'

'Sure. But this baby's fitted with two ferry-tanks – extra hundred gallons.'

Ryan nodded. 'So, when do we leave?'

'By train up to Barranquilla at seven this evenin'. We ride first-class, take our own food, and plenty to drink. And we don't sleep – not unless we wanna get ripped off down to our underpants. In Barranquilla a jeep picks us up and drives us out to the camp. Then we take off in the afternoon, and we'll be over the Island toward evenin'.'

'Do we land?'

The Negro showed his white teeth. 'Not me, soldier. Not

till ah got the whole force behind me. I believe in playin' safe.'

'Are you sure our friend Gallo hasn't got a string of the latest radar stations all round his coast?'

'If he does, we'll be flyin' under 'em. Skimmin' the waves, we will. I jus' hope the weather's good. That Caribbean can get mighty frisky at this time o' year. Okay. Ah'll see you at the station at six-forty-five this evenin'. Good day, Colonel. Nice meetin' you.'

The train looked at least fifty years old, with carriages which reminded Ryan of long gypsy caravans, covered in gaudy flaking paint, and a funnel like a huge black ice-cream cone. No-Entry did not arrive until five minutes before departure. He had changed into a blue tracksuit and was carrying a rucksack.

The first-class compartment had an ancient, dilapidated charm: lamps with red shades and gold tassels, and a lot of brass and polished mahogany. Their fellow passengers were two surly-faced men in crumpled business suits, each smoking a foul-smelling cigar. Ryan had bought a bottle of Scotch from the hotel bar, and a couple of tortillas and a loaf of bread from a cantina on his way to the station, as well as a carton of his favourite cigarettes.

The journey was slow and uncomfortable, the train swaying and clanking for the first few hours down through the mountains, stopping at every station. In the dark Ryan could see no more than a few guttering oil-lamps and dirt-platforms crowded with Indians burdened with great sacks of belongings, like refugees in the aftermath of war. At one stop a couple of nuns joined them and immediately began counting their rosaries to an interminable, muttered litany. They broke off only to give Ryan a disapproving look each time he got out the whisky bottle.

Towards midnight they made a long stop at the town of Medellin, which was near the end of the mountains. Here the engine took on more water and logs. It was another three hundred and fifty miles to Barranquilla.

As the dawn came up, with the darkness rising like smoke off the empty brown plain, Ryan gazed out at a melancholy landscape lying under a leaden sky: patches of thorny vegetation; mules, mud-huts, the occasional run-down factory, and narrow roads that meandered off, wet and shiny, towards a distant rim of ash-grey mountains.

At some time in the early morning the muttering nuns mercifully got out, at a little stone town dominated by a huge church, its elaborate belfry mouldering with age. A young man and a fat pasty-faced girl got on and they immediately began to argue, in rapid high-pitched Spanish. The two men in the dark suits were again smoking cigars. Ryan rarely travelled by train, but he had retained a certain romantic notion about long railway journeys: yet this one filled him with nothing but boredom and discomfort. The noise made conversation almost impossible; and anyway, he was reluctant to converse with No-Entry, in case one of their fellow-passengers spoke English.

The sun was breaking through, in a yellow glare which brought with it a clammy humidity mixed with the acrid stench of burning wood-smoke from the engine. They reached Cartagena, on the coast, shortly before noon; but the sea brought no fresh breezes, only a muggy salt-smell which seemed to increase the humidity.

Ryan's whole body felt damp and dirty; the sweat began to collect in the corners of his eyes and on his upper lip, and his mouth tasted of stale whisky. Once they had started again, he swayed along to the first-class toilet where he waited in a queue for twenty minutes. When he got inside he almost retched: the place was splashed and stinking, with no toilet-seat, no paper; and when he tried the tap on the basin it coughed a couple of times and spat out a huge cockroach.

He got back to their compartment to find that they were already drawing into the outskirts of Barranquilla: the usual sprawl of shanties, then modern buildings with concrete walls already blotched with damp; several churches, and the refreshing glimpse of a leafy square. Beyond, in the harbour, Ryan could see the masts and gantries of ships.

He and No-Entry climbed out into the sticky heat. Outside the station, under a row of dusty palms, an open jeep was waiting with a sleek-haired young man at the wheel, wearing loose olive-green combat fatigues. He said nothing as No-Entry got in beside him, with Ryan in the back; then drove off at a furious speed, weaving perilously between the traffic which consisted mostly of antique American sedans. The slip-stream was warm and moist, and brought Ryan no comfort.

Near the centre of the town he saw something which made him shudder. They had pulled up behind a big ramshackle truck. As the driver swerved to overtake it, Ryan saw what he thought at first was a large spring-coil rolling out from under the truck's rear-wheels. It took him a moment before he realized, with a visceral stab of horror, that it was a snake.

They drove through the last of the shanty-towns, bouncing along a road that seemed to be made up of an odd combination of mud and dust; then crossed a wide breakwater over the bay to reach a bridge where a couple of motorcycle police flagged them down, each carrying the statutory machine-pistol.

Their young driver said something which Ryan did not catch, then showed them a piece of typed paper bearing an official stamp. The police saluted and stood back.

Beyond the bridge the jeep entered a sandy wasteland with the sea breaking with slow, grey waves on their left. The villages they passed were no more than huddled shacks, often built from tin cans and corrugated iron. Indian families squatted outside, watching them pass with lethargic button-black eyes. After the town of Guajira – the last stop on the main road before the Venezualan frontier – they turned left on to a track almost indiscernible from the scrub and sand-dunes. The young man had switched on to four-wheel drive, but for most of the next thirty miles they were doing less than twenty kilometres an hour.

'What's the accommodation like?' Ryan shouted, with an edge of sarcasm.

'Nice and primitive!' No-Entry grinned over his shoulder. 'Real Club Méditerranée! Huts for officers. Other ranks sleep under the sky.'

'How's the swimming?'

'Not recommended. Sharks – barracuda – every friend you can think of.'

They bumped over a rusty bridge spanning a filthy culvert, and drove slowly between more dunes that opened suddenly on to a long white beach fringed with palms which looked like broken parasols, and rolls of tumbleweed, reminding Ryan of barbed-wire. The scene was spoiled by a dozen huts constructed round bamboo frames with flat roofs and canvas flaps for doors. Several groups of men, in shabby miscellaneous uniforms, were idling around, a few of them stoking up a barbecue. None appeared to be armed.

In the distance Ryan saw the L-19, looking like a fragile silver bird perched on long thin legs. He turned to No-Entry Jones: 'What time do we take off?'

'Jus' as soon as you're ready, Colonel. You'll want a wash and shave, ah guess – though it'll be in sea-water, if you don't mind that?'

It was a long time since Ryan had enjoyed a spartan existence. He was quite looking forward once again to the rigours of military discipline. For at least two weeks he would be going without booze, eating frugally, waking with the sun, and taking command of a hundred and fifty men whom he was determined to lick into fighting order, however short time might be.

The first sight of his troops did not impress him. Most were dressed in baggy, sweat-stained jungle-fatigues like the driver of the jeep; others wore smarter leopard-spotted or tiger-striped combat uniforms with floppy jungle-hats. Some were bare-headed, despite the noon-sun, while a few wore peaked green forage-caps; and at least two sat sprawled under sombreros. It was impossible to tell which were officers, as none wore any insignia.

Ryan felt irritated, as well as slightly absurd in his crumpled city-suit and Gucci shoes. Yet the men showed little interest in him, as he and No-Entry tramped past, heading for the officer's hut.

'Where are the landing-craft, Major?'

The Negro gestured ahead. 'In a lil' lagoon 'bout two miles up. Real smart. Surrounded most o' the way by palms, so they're pretty well hidden 'cept from low-flyin' aircraft.'

They had reached the last of the canvas huts and turned right, climbing a sand-dune into a palm grove which sheltered a rusty Nissen shed. Inside, the air was hot and fetid, with insects pinging monotonously against the wire mesh over the curved windows. There were four camp-beds, with just a blanket on them.

No-Entry pointed to a big metal tank attached to a hose with a tap. 'That there's your ablutions, Colonel. When you wanna crap, you do it outside. Long way from the Hilton, afraid.'

Ryan undressed, showered and shaved in the tepid salt-water; then realized that he still had nothing to wear but Mr Broakes' clothes. He was just dressing when he became aware of a tall figure watching him from the door. He swung round.

The man straightened up and gave a casual salute. He was young, with long black hair, black Indian eyes, and the profile of a Castilian nobleman. He spoke in Spanish: 'I am Corporal Fisco, Señor Coronel.' He used the word 'cabo' for his own rank. 'I wish to welcome you.'

Ryan nodded without enthusiasm. 'Who is the senior officer here – after myself?'

'You want Capitano Rodriguez, Coronel. Only he will not see you until he has finished sleeping.' The young man yawned and stretched like a cat.

'Cabo Fisco, you will wake the capitano at once and tell him that I am leaving on a reconnaissance flight with Comandante Jones. I wish to speak to the capitano first. And stand to attention when you address me!'

The young man brought his boots together and saluted. 'Señor Coronel!' And he was gone. No-Entry Jones came in a moment later.

'I see you been and met young Cabo Fisco, Colonel?' The Negro shook his head. 'That kid's nuts – real wild. What you call gun-happy. He's not a bad kid – he jus' likes to kill. It don't matter to him whether it's Man, beast, fish or fowl – just as long as it's livin' and moves.'

Ryan made no reply. He followed No-Entry out into the palmgrove where they stopped at a large canvas sheet pegged down into the sand and sagging in the middle. The Negro pulled out the pegs on one side, to reveal the corner of a pit, six feet deep, its walls also lined with canvas, and stacked with well-oiled Kalashnikov AK-47 assault-rifles, their short barrels and scythe-like magazines each lying between layers of waterproof paper. Ryan also saw a couple of 105mm recoilless antitank rifles, and – even more gratifying – a number of single-tube, portable 122mm rocket-launchers, each with a range of up to eight miles. Their ammunition was piled up in neat racks, like Indian clubs.

He turned to No-Entry: 'I want a full inventory of this stuff, Major. Particularly the ammunition. What about communications – radios, I mean.'

'All the PT-boats have R/Ts, UHF, VHF an' short-wave. I guess that aspect's all sewn up to your satisfaction, Colonel.'

Ryan nodded doubtfully as he led the way back from under the trees. 'And I want a full list of the men, and their officers. By the way, have you come up against a Frenchman called Moulins yet?'

'Not to date,' said No-Entry. 'He's adjutant to the Señora, ah understand? But ah don' work in those high circles. I jus' drive the plane – so ah can give the rest o' you the low-down on what's waitin' for you the other side.' He paused, while Ryan wiped the sweat from his face and neck. 'So how d'you figure it all, Colonel?'

'Too early to say. I don't altogether trust Soviet equipment, but from what I've seen it looks like the right stuff. It's a pity we haven't got any armour, though. And it looks as if I'm going to have to spend every waking hour working on those troops back there. Where's that Capitano Rodriguez, by the way? – the one you said was your pay-master and superior? And why does a US major take orders from an exiled captain in an army that doesn't exist?'

The Negro smiled and shook his head: 'Man, you really get bugged by rank, don't you? It's just that the Señora don' want any US personnel officially in on this operation. You and this Frenchman, you're the only foreigners we admit to. Me – ah don' exist.'

'What's this Rodriguez like?'

'A real gen-u-ine sonofabitch. And not strictly a soldier. He's a cop – and a political cop at that. Works as a sidekick for one of the Señora's chief right-hand men, a certain General Romolo. An even bigger sonofabitch.' He nodded down the beach. 'Rodriguez's over there now, by the barbecue.'

Together they walked back over the hot sand, and No-Entry introduced Ryan to a short stout man in khaki shorts and a leopard-spotted tunic hanging loose over his belly. He was sweating and needed a shave. Ryan waited for him to salute. When he didn't, Ryan told him: 'I am Colonel Ryan, your superior officer during this operation. I am relying on you, Capitano, to see that all my orders are carried out and to take full responsibility whenever I'm away.'

The man's small eyes looked at him with a surly contempt. It was clear that, as a former officer in Ramon's Secret Police, he resented being given orders, particularly by a foreigner.

'While I am gone this afternoon,' Ryan went on, 'you will take your men on target-practice. AK-47's, on semi-automatic. I want five rounds in the inner three circles of a bull's-eye within a hundred feet. Those men that fail I want reported to me on my return. Understand, Capitano?'

The man drew in his stomach and gave a slow salute.

'And get a shave. Any man or officer I catch unshaven after six in the morning will be disciplined.'

Captain Rodriguez saluted again, with obvious reluctance; and as Ryan walked away among the groups of indolent soldiers – many of whom he noticed were mestizo, mulatto, even deep-Black – he felt an urge to throw in his hand and get clear of this make-shift mob of bums and desperados who were supposed not only to overthrow the Gallo regime, but spit in the eye of the Kremlin too.

He turned to No-Entry. 'Right, let's get flying, Major. I need some fresh air.'

Clear of the huts and walking back towards the little plane, Ryan added: 'By the way, what's the code-name for this operation – if it has one?'

'*Belladonna*,' the Negro replied. 'Kinda suitable, in view of the Señora's appearance. Judging by her photos, that is. Ah've not had the privilege of meetin' the good lady yet, y'understand.'

Ryan shrugged. 'Highly suitable – particularly as Belladonna's also a poison. Used to be very popular in the last century among wives who wanted to knock off their husbands.'

No-Entry was still chuckling when they reached the plane. Ryan climbed into the navigation seat, while the Negro adjusted his sunglasses, fiddled with the few controls, then started the engine with a roar that shattered the silence of the beach.

Ryan could see that he was a meticulous pilot: he checked oil-pressures, hydraulics, flaps, fuel-feed, then edged the plane out on to the firm sand, just above the shore-line. He kept her for a couple of minutes rocking on her brakes, while the engine heated, then sprang her forward. Within forty yards they were airborne.

Ryan found the narrow metal-frame seat too narrow for his shoulders. He edged open the side-window and felt the rush of cool air. In front of him, No-Entry Jones's dark slender fingers moved over the controls with the delicacy of a surgeon. The plane turned at right-angles and the beach passed below them, with the flat scrub-land behind, and the grey-green ocean ahead, heaving under the low misty sky like the skin of some vast reptile.

Looking over No-Entry's shoulder, Ryan saw that the magnetic compass was set almost exactly due-north. In the pocket of the seat in front of him he found a large-scale cloth-bound map, which showed the whole expanse of the Caribbean, from the long southerly coast reaching east from the bulge of Honduras, along the slither of Panama, to Colombia and Venezuela. The course that No-Entry Jones was following would take them across the broadest, deepest stretch of the Caribbean, to Haiti and the Dominican Republic. From here it was a short north-easterly hop to the southern-most extremity of the Island.

Ryan unfolded the whole of the map and studied it as it lay juddering on his knees. Even at this scale, the southern part of the Island showed no towns, no roads, no names of any beach. The closest point of civilization appeared to be a place called Carrudas, on the eastern seaboard, lying on the main road north to the Island's second largest city, Santiago y Maria, which was situated inland, mid-way between the invasion beach which No-Entry had selected, and the capital, Montecristo.

After nearly two hours' flying they came in sight of the distant green coast of Haiti and the grey smudge of Port au Prince. No-Entry banked sharply to the left, and over his shoulder Ryan was relieved to see the needle of the compass swing due-west. Haiti was not the most reassuring country to fly over: for even No-Entry's skill could not rule out engine-trouble, and the L-19 was certainly past its prime.

The thin cloud, which had lain over the sea since they had left the Guajira Peninsula, was now melting into brilliant blue. Below them the land had vanished, and No-Entry was turning north again, over the deep indigo veins of the Windward Passage.

The motion of the plane was steady, monotonous, and Ryan found himself dozing off. He was woken abruptly by a shout from No-Entry: 'Colonel! We should be in sight o' the Island in about ten minutes! You'll find the camera an' binoculars under yo' seat.'

As Ryan reached down, he happened to glance over No-Entry's shoulder and saw that the fuel-gauge was touching 'empty'. With a touch of panic, he pointed this out to the Negro, who twisted his head round and grinned: 'You flyin' this plane, or me, Colonel?' He turned back, and flicked a switch on the narrow dashboard. 'Reserve ferry-tanks. No sweat – ah believe in lookin' after mah passengers!'

But even as he spoke, Ryan heard the humour go out of his voice. The needle on the fuel-gauge had not moved. No-Entry snapped the switch several more times, but without effect; then muttered something inaudible.

Far ahead, along the rim of the sky, Ryan could just make out the greenish blur of land, and far beyond that the white teeth of mountains. He guessed that the coast was between fifteen and twenty miles away.

A moment later the engine gave two loud coughs, a final shuddering roar, and died. Through the sudden stillness, broken only by the hum of the slipstream, No-Entry yelled: 'The filthy, mother-fuckin' slit-eyed spicks!' Despite his fury, his hands were fondling the controls with their usual gentle agility.

Ryan leant forward, staring helplessly. 'What's happened?'

'What's happened is precisely fuckin' this,' No-Entry cried: 'Those spick mother-fuckers back at the camp didn't fill the ferry-tanks.'

'Why the hell not?' And as Ryan spoke, he saw the luminous green arrow of the altimeter sliding slowly back round the dial – 4,000, 3,800, 3,500 and still falling.

'Could be they took the gas into Barranquilla and made some bread.' No-Entry paused, and Ryan felt the floor dip under them like a lift going down.

'But there could be another reason,' the Negro added. 'That big bastard Rodriguez didn't take exactly kindly to bein' outranked by you, Colonel.' He shook his head and made a quick adjustment to the flaps.

Ryan saw that their air-speed was down to less than eighty knots. 'So you think he deliberately fixed it so we wouldn't get back?'

'We'll get back,' No-Entry said. 'These lil' bird-dogs float down like feathers, even when they're wounded. We should just about make the beach. It's a goddam miracle we're this close.'

'Why not try for Jamaica? At least we can count on a friendly reception.'

The Negro shook his head. 'Not a hope. Let's jus' pray to the Lord that we can make the Island.'

They were losing height more rapidly now. Ryan lifted the binoculars and saw the shore suddenly very close and coming up to meet them – a long curve of gleaming sand, dissolving into a dark network of mangrove swamp that seemed to reach back for miles.

They were coming down fast now, and through the glasses he saw a thin chalk-white road running parallel to the beach, about two miles inland beyond the mangroves. No sign of any dug-outs, bunkers, barracks. A no-man's land.

No-Entry had been bringing the little plane in like a glider: the prop turning on its own momentum against the slip-stream, and the Negro wiggling the wings so as to give him some control against the flaps.

Ryan had never been in a crash-landing before. He was not so much scared, as intrigued by the technique and skill with which No-Entry was handling the plane.

He brought them down, skimming a couple of dunes, and just managed to keep the nose up, before the wheels hit the beach. When it happened, they did no more than jump, swerve, and slide to a halt, while the whole plane tipped forward and its nose sank into the sand.

No-Entry unstrapped himself and gave a loud sigh in the stillness. 'Okay, Colonel, you can change your pants now, only take it easy. Ah'm gettin' out first.' He slid open his door and jumped down. As he did so, the little plane rocked back on to its tail.

Ryan got out and stood examining the propeller. It did not look damaged. Then he peered up and down the beach. Nothing moved through the heavy haze. He turned and saw No-Entry coming round the side of the plane, carrying a dip-stick. The Negro shrugged. 'Jus' givin' those bastards the benefit o' the doubt. Could be there's a fault in the fuel-switch.'

He spent a couple of minutes undoing a flap in the side of the plane behind Ryan's seat; knelt over with a stick; then straightened up. 'Dry as a nun's pussy.' He looked mournfully at Ryan. 'This is a well-policed country, Colonel. If Gallo's the boy they say he is, he'll have his fuzz here within the hour.

So what do we do? Sit tight and wait for 'em? Or make tracks inland and try to hole up some place till the invasion comes?'

'No. We play innocent. We bum a lift to the nearest city and I give myself up as a DBS – Distressed British Subject. We were on a joy-ride and we ran out of fuel. And we've got the plane to prove it.'

'Yeah, but what about me?'

'You're black. That should give you a head-start with Gallo's boys.'

The Negro said nothing. Ryan added: 'If a private plane crash-lands, the first thing the crew does is go for help. Your papers are in order, aren't they?'

'Yeah, maybe they're in order. But ah still don't like you and me fraternizing wi' the Opposition.'

'That's not what we're going to do,' said Ryan. 'I told you – we play dumb. We give ourselves up, show our papers, and rely on the munificent hospitality of a Gallo's People's Democracy.'

There was a long silence. The heat – even in the late afternoon – was stifling: and the sea gave off a diamond-white brilliance that was making Ryan's eyeballs ache. He peeled off his jacket and could feel the sand warm through his shoes. He got into the shade of the plane and began to light one of his last cigarettes, then leant against the fuselage; but even here the metal was growing too hot to touch.

He was furious with No-Entry. If the Negro's only job was to fly the plane, the least he could have done was make sure it was fully fuelled. Ryan was already determined to trust his luck with the local authorities – and if necessary with Gallo's dreaded Security Police, known as SACA. As for No-Entry, he was prepared, quite ruthlessly, to deny any knowledge of his pilot's origins.

'You've got a radio on this plane?'

''Course ah got a radio. But if ah use it here, ah might as well call the local fuzz direct.'

Ryan sank down on the sand and tried to think things out. 'We're in this together, Major,' he said at last. 'Somebody may have spotted us coming in. On the other hand, if this spot is as empty as it looks, they may not. So let's try and make it inland.'

No-Entry nodded glumly. 'Jus' one thing, Colonel – you ain't got a gun, have you? Because we gotta be legit out here. But ah guess we also better get rid of that camera and those glasses.'

Ryan climbed back into the plane and ripped the film out of the camera, exposed it, then buried camera, film, and binoculars at a reasonable distance from the plane.

When he returned, he felt dejected. 'Let's go. From what I saw from the air, there's a road about a couple of miles back from here beyond the swamp.' He climbed again into the cockpit and collected the large-scale map; made sure it had no telltale markings to indicate their route; then folded it inside his jacket, which he was carrying over his arm.

Then together they began to trudge up the sand towards the mangrove swamp.

CHAPTER FIVE

The Island

The soles of Ryan's expensive shoes were now burning his feet; and in the hot stagnant stillness his shirt was soaked against his back and he could feel the sweat itching between his buttocks and down the backs of his legs.

Beyond the beach they began to clamber carefully through clumps of cacti higher than themselves – weird green statues armed with razor-sharp spikes. No-Entry had broken off a palm-frond and began swishing it lazily about him.

After about a hundred yards they reached the edge of the mangroves. At first they looked surprisingly verdant and inviting after the scorching beach and the villainous cacti. They were soon to realize they were wrong. The mangroves sprouted from a bed of damp leprous moss out of which their roots twisted upwards under their thick leaves like shards of half-buried bones. The whole swamp seemed to be severed with a network of narrow paths, many of them a maze of blind alleys.

No-Entry was setting the pace, swishing the palm-frond about him, beating the branches on both sides as he moved slowly forward choosing his steps with care. Ryan soon found that the moss under foot was no more than a thin spongy carpet that sagged and squelched under his weight, his ridiculous shoes sinking to above the ankles. And as they moved deeper in, the moss began to burst round them with bubbles of black stinking water, like some evil pus breaking through the skin of the swamp.

No-Entry was now beating the ground, as well as the mangroves. Ryan asked him what he was doing.

'Scarin' away the snakes.'

The mangroves were now reaching above their shoulders and there was no sign of them coming to an end. Ryan had said he thought the road ran about two miles parallel with the beach; but he knew that distances from the air are deceptive.

It was also impossible to calculate, with any accuracy, their rate of progress.

He would have paid a lot for a glass of whisky at this moment, if only to drive off the stench of the swamp-gas.

They squelched on until at last the sun began to lose its heat; and suddenly they touched firm ground. They had reached a high ridge studded with more cacti and rocks; and after several hundred yards of steep climbing they came to the road. Their trousers were soaked black to the hips, their bodies sweating and stinking.

The road was no more than a track of powdery dust which bore no traces of either footprints or wheel-tracks. No-Entry turned, his face behind his dark glasses brown and shiny like varnished wood. 'What do you think, Colonel? You still wanna walk?'

'I don't want to sit here and die of thirst, Major Jones. Let's keep going.' It was nearly six o'clock, but the heat was still clammy and oppressive.

They now started down the long white road, which seemed to lead interminably to nowhere. Ryan was now feeling the first real pangs of thirst, and was angry that they had not taken the basic precaution of bringing water on the plane. He looked at the surrounding landscape, but except for an occasional palm or cacti it was the same parched colour as the road.

Along the horizon rose the snow-tipped mountains of the Hiarra. Their distance was unreal, and when he looked more closely he could see that some of the highest mountains were flat-topped cones smudged with smoke. This chain of volcanoes, he remembered, was called the Sierra Hiarra, and stretched north up the spine of the Island, to just above the capital, Montecristo, which had several times in its history been destroyed by eruptions. It was country, he concluded, blessed by neither God nor Man: with a history racked not only by political upheavals and atrocities, but also by the violent tantrums of Nature.

They had been going for nearly two hours since leaving the beach – resting only at brief intervals – when No-Entry Jones suddenly stopped and stood pointing to above the volcanoes. A thin white streak was crawling across the darkening sky, needlesharp at the front and spreading out behind in wisps of cloud. 'Goddam plane,' he said, in little more than a whisper. 'Pan-Am or Jamaican Airlines – probably headin' for Kingston. Jus' think, Colonel – all those nice people up there in their drip-dry shirts an' light-weight suits, with the air-hostesses slinkin' up and down the aisle with trays o' dry martinis and bourbon-on-the-rocks.'

'I'd settle for a large carafe of iced water.'

The plane's white airstream had almost disappeared now, the wisps of cloud dissipating themselves into the smoke from the volcanoes. No-Entry shook his head. 'Looks like we may be in the shit, Colonel. No plane at that height's gonna spot us two lil' people down here. Y'know, ah'll be right glad to see Gallo's boys turn up and take us in.'

Ryan trudged on in silence a few paces behind No-Entry. Their shadows were growing long and the sun hung low over the green sea, and the air became fresh, almost cool. The mountains now seemed very close, their flanks the colour of rust, and ribbed with long purple lava-flows that reached down from the snow-line to just above the plain.

They had walked several miles along the road and the only living creatures they had seen were a couple of lizards. Then No-Entry turned. 'That map you got – it shows a place called Carrudas? About fifteen miles from where we landed?'

'That's right.' Ryan watched the still shadows of the cacti growing longer, blacker. Then he spoke, quite casually. 'You were in a pretty big hurry to get me away from the camp at Guajira, weren't you, Major? You'd have done better to have given the plane a thorough check-out and flown over tomorrow. What was so pressing?'

'Weather, mainly. As ah said, this sea blows up quick and funny. Unless the weather's real still and sluggish, you can get storms come up in minutes, and planes disappear and boats sink.'

'The weather was the only reason?'

'Sure. This afternoon was perfect flyin' conditions.'

There was a long silence. 'What were you doing before you got in on this junket, Major?' Ryan said at last. 'Were you regular?'

'Yes an' no. After Veetnam ah did a spell as a disc-jockey in Miami, but ah got bored bein' served last in every bar, or told the joint was closed. When mah guts got healed ah went back to Indo-China, but not to the front-line. I chose Laos. Nice and peaceful, then. I was co-pilot for an outfit called Air America. Ever heard of it?'

'Tell me.'

'Used to be the only registered civil airline in the world that carried no passengers. Its motto was, "We fly anywhere – drop anythin'." Mostly it was rice, to the mountain tribesmen. Sometimes, ah guess, it was other things. We didn't ask. We collected five hundred a week, no tax, so why make problems?'

'Then what happened?'

'I got in with some bad boys, and we tried the biggest heist in history – one point five billion in greenbacks. Five tons o' the stuff. It was the end o' the war. They was shiftin' all the loose change out o' Nam before the final curtain. We hijacked one of the planes.'

'Just like that? So why aren't you basking on a yacht somewhere out there in the blue? Or did something go wrong?'

No-Entry laughed – a strange rippling sound in the evening stillness 'Yeah, it went wrong. We finished up in *North* Veetnam. I only got out last year.'

For some time the only sound was the scuffing of their feet on the dusty road. Ryan said at last, 'And how do the authorities feel about you back home? I mean, they not only lost the bloody war out there, but – if I'm to believe you – it seems they also lost one thousand, five hundred million dollars – and to the enemy at that. They can't be too happy about you, Major. And you still say you got an honourable discharge?'

'They never did prove it. Officially, I was posted missing. And the plane just disappeared. Ah'm still a US citizen, and ah've got a passport to prove it.' He hesitated. 'Matter o' fact, Colonel, I got two passports – both for real. You might say, ah'm jus' one o' Nature's born bet hedgers. Fact is, mah job as a freelance pilot takes me all kinds o' places and 'mong all kinds o' people. In some o' those places a US passport is like a ringside ticket to Madison Square Gardens. In others it's like walkin' round with a dose of syph. I jus' like to be flexible.'

'And the second passport?' said Ryan.

'Puerto Rican. That's for when ah go slummin'.'

Ryan gave a long slow nod. 'With your record, Major Jones, I'd say you needed half a dozen passports. It must also give your former employers in the CIA a pretty good hold over you. Nobody likes living the rest of their lives with a criminal charge hanging over them. Believe me, I know.'

The Negro slowed his step. 'Excuse me, Colonel. I thought we'd been over this territory before, when we first met? I told you then, and I'm telling you now – I don't work for any government, or any government agency. I'm self-employed.'

'That's just it. But you say you're also employed by Señora La Vuelva and her gang.'

The Negro had halted. His dark face was grave in the fading light. 'Just what does that mean, Colonel? I'm stupid – I didn't get the kind of schooling you white boys got.'

'You know what I'm talking about. You used to fly for the CIA in South-East Asia – and don't give me all that innocent crap about the Yanks not being interested in this Island anymore. They're like the Russkies – they're interested in everything, everybody, everywhere.'

No-Entry let his breath out in a low hiss. 'So you figure that if ah once worked for the Company back in Asia, ah'm still on the payroll? You're crazy, Colonel. You're also wrong.'

'You know what they say about Intelligence work? It's like the Communist Party and the Catholic Church. Once you're in, you're booked for the duration.'

No-Entry nodded. 'Well, that makes two of us. From what ah heard, Colonel, you were in much the same racket in World War Two. In fact, you were pretty big.'

'I was in a different league. I was a double-agent. But I also worked for myself.'

'Are you suggesting I might be double too?' The Negro's hands hung loosely at his sides, curling into fists, his feet widely spaced. 'You've got a dirty mind, Colonel.'

'Dirty and suspicious. This afternoon we've hardly arrived at the camp at Guajira when you insist we fuck off in that bloody little string bag of a plane, and hey-presto! – we run out of petrol, do a beautiful landing, and are stuck like a pair of rabbits in the middle of a cut cornfield. And after a bit, I get to wondering if you and I are playing the same game. I mean, I'm wondering if the cards are marked.'

The Negro opened his fists and gave a sudden shout of laughter, shattering the silence round them. 'Man, you really are crazy! First you say ah work for the Company – now you think ah work for that bearded bum, Gallo? And what do you suppose ah'd get out o' *him*? A few million People's Democratic escudos? And what would ah do with 'em? – use 'em to wipe mah ass for the next twenty years?' His face became serious again. 'Colonel, we're two lonely people out in a very lonely place. Haven't we got enough trouble, without fighting each other?'

Ryan relaxed. 'All right. I apologize. But I had to be sure.' Solemnly they shook hands in the empty darkness. 'So you're strictly freelance – in it just for yourself, and for the money? Like me. But how did you get involved in the first place?'

'That bum Rodriguez hired me, in Mexico City. He said he had a good outfit goin' – and that the person behind it was someone who was guaranteed to lead a revolution against Gallo. He made it all sound mighty tempting.

'Anyway, ah wasn't going to argue. As ah said, ah don't give a goddam about politics – or a sweet fuck if this dirty little Island is run by a bearded thug with a hot-line to Moscow, or by a rich bitch like La Vuelva and her so-called Ramonista Movement. Jus' so long as ah get paid. Okay?'

'Okay.'

They began to walk again. 'One last thing,' said Ryan. 'When we get picked up, we've got to have some sort of story ready. You're my hired pilot out of Barranquilla and we were making for Jamaica when we had to put down here. I'm just an English businessman holidaying in Colombia. You know that much – and that's all you know.'

He looked up. No-Entry's hand had closed round Ryan's wrist. 'Hey, wait a minute!' – his hold tightened – 'hear somethin'?'

They had both stopped again, listening. At first Ryan thought it was the sound of wind, or sea, or perhaps a swarm of insects. He swung round. Two pricks of light had appeared on the dark flat horizon behind them. 'Here we go,' said No-Entry. 'Do we lie low, or stop them? You're the boss.'

'We stay put. It doesn't matter if they're friendly or not – we get them to take us to the nearest authorities. There we tell our story. How's your Spanish?'

'It works.'

'Don't let it work too hard. Leave the talking to me. If we're too fluent, they'll get suspicious. They'll be suspicious anyway, but we don't want to encourage them.'

'Sorry, Colonel, but ah gotta speak Spanish. On this ride, ah'm a Puerto Rican.' And he tapped the top pocket of his tracksuit.

'Well, just as long as you make it convincing,' said Ryan.

They waited another few minutes, in silence. The noise behind them had risen to a steady growl. They stood and watched the lights approach. It was a medium-sized truck with a canvas hood over the rear, all painted drab green. The headlamps were dipped and they could not see how many people were in the cabin. They moved into the middle of the road and Ryan waved his jacket.

The truck let out two shattering honks and its lights came on full-beam, dazzling them both. It was doing about twenty miles an hour, its engine rising to a crescendo, and for several seconds Ryan thought that they would have to jump aside or be run down. Then it braked noisily and a voice shouted at them. Ryan walked towards it, and the truck stopped. A grisled mestizo head above a grey vest peered down at him from the high cabin window. Behind him was a man in olive-green uniform with a soft peaked cap. The mestizo said in Spanish: 'Who are you? What are you doing here?' He glanced beside him at the man in uniform, then added, 'You know this is a prohibited zone?'

'You go Carrudas?' Ryan asked, in halting Spanish.

The man shouted again, above the throb of the engine: 'What are you doing here?'

Ryan replied with a preposterous charade of waving his arms in the motion of a plane landing. 'We go Jamaica! Aeroplano kaput!' – he crouched down, his outstretched hands almost touching the ground. 'Polizia!' – and he pointed to the road ahead.

The driver was talking again to the man in uniform. The other nodded, opened his door and climbed down. 'Documents,' he said, coming towards them. He had a fierce Spanish face. Ryan took out his new British passport and handed it to him. No-Entry Jones did the same with his, issued by the Government of Puerto Rico. The soldier stood studying them both, frowning.

'Habla ingles?' Ryan asked.

The man looked at him and shook his head. 'Here is prohibited.' Then he jerked his thumb towards the back of the truck. He did not give the passports back. 'Accompany us!' He followed them both round and unhitched the tailboard, watching carefully as they both climbed aboard; then slammed the tailboard shut, leaving Ryan and No-Entry in total darkness. A moment later the truck started.

Ryan got out a packet of cigarettes and offered one to No-Entry, who shook his head. 'I don't smoke. I got no vices, Colonel.' He spoke without humour.

Ryan sat back against the hard wall of the truck. There seemed to be nothing in the back except themselves; but there was a strong smell of coffee.

They drove for three-quarters of an hour. After about half of this the road became smoother and several times they slowed down, as though for other traffic. Ryan crawled to the back and looked through the canvas flaps.

It was quite dark now, and they were driving through a small town with a little square with white houses and a row of arcades hung with guttering lamps. Otherwise there were no lights, no sign of any people, although it was barely seven-thirty in the evening: an hour when the pavements of most Caribbean towns are at their most crowded. Once a car drove past – a dusty grey, hump-backed Moskvitch with four men inside.

The truck passed round a square with more arcades, mimosa trees and a dry stone fountain. There was also a plinth with what looked like a pair of amputated bronze boots – the relic of some hero of the Island's history, some great liberator turned tyrant? A slogan had been neatly sprayed onto the base with a red aerosol: VV LA REVOLUCION!

The truck swung sideways, slowed to walking pace, and Ryan had a glimpse of a sentry standing beside an open gate under a bunch of red flags. He heard voices – harsh shouts in the dark, and the distant blaring of some martial song on a gramophone or radio. The truck stopped and the canvas flaps were stripped back. A torch shone in their faces and a voice asked them in Spanish to step down.

They were in what looked like a low barrack-square with under-powered electric lights in each corner. The men wore the same green uniforms as the man in the truck. They looked very young, and their long hair stuck out from under their soft peaked caps. Several had scrawny black beards. Ryan noticed them enviously eyeing his filter-tipped cigarette.

After a long wait in a corridor, guarded by two armed men, he and No-Entry were led into a large white-washed room, lit by a strip of bluish neon which fizzed and blinked from the ceiling. On the wall was a framed photograph of President Fulgencio Gallo, his black beard almost covering the open neck of his khaki jacket. Two red banners were draped round the frame, and formed the only decoration in the room. There was a row of steel-backed chairs along one wall, facing a cheap wooden table. Behind it sat two men.

One was a mestizo with broad flat nostrils and a mouthful of metal teeth. The man beside him looked scarcely out of his teens; a sleek handsome youth with large eyes and tabs on his shoulders. There was an old-fashioned telephone at his elbow, while in front of him lay Ryan's and No-Entry's passports. He spoke polite, rather pedantic English with a slight American accent: 'I am Captain Monica, of Field Intelligence for the Carrudas area. It is necessary that I ask you some questions. Will you please explain why you are here?'

Ryan said: 'If you don't mind, Captain, first I'd like a glass of water.'

'Certainly.' The boy turned to the mestizo and muttered an order, and the man rose and loped away through a side-door. No one spoke until he returned, bringing two mugs and a plastic canteen. Both men at the table watched as Ryan and No-Entry drank greedily until the canteen was empty.

Ryan got out his American cigarettes and offered them to the two men. They both hesitated, the mestizo looking at the young captain as though awaiting his decision. The officer finally accepted – out of curiosity, Ryan thought, as well as a guilty desire. 'Thank you. We have not seen American cigarettes for nearly ten years – since the Americans imposed their embargo on us.'

He lit the cigarette and puffed at it tentatively. 'Now, you will answer my question, please, Mister' – he glanced down at Ryan's passport, 'Brox.'

'Well, my friend here, Mr Jones, was flying me to Jamaica from Barranquilla, in Colombia, when we ran out of fuel and only just managed to make a crash-landing. Your friends in the truck fortunately came by and picked us up.'

There was a pause. When he spoke, the young man seemed almost embarrassed. 'You are no doubt aware that Jamaica is some distance from the direct route between Colombia and the Island?'

Ryan shrugged. 'We had trouble with the compass. It's easy to get lost in those little planes. The nearest other place we might have been able to land was Haiti – and quite frankly, Captain, I've heard a few nasty stories about that country. We decided we'd get more hospitality from you.'

The young man gave a little nod. 'I understand. But you also must understand that we have to be very careful in this country. Socialism has many enemies, and here we are surrounded by enemies. It is necessary to be vigilant at all times.' He paused again. 'Your passport, Mister Broakes, says that you are a business executive. Do you have business interests in Colombia or Jamaica?'

'Neither. I'm supposed to be on holiday – in Barranquilla. But you know what we Capitalists are! We're like you soldiers – always on duty.' He smiled, and to his relief the captain smiled back.

'How long have you been on holiday, Mr Broakes?'

Ryan knew what the other was thinking. He had no suntan, and the side of his face still bore the puffed bluish traces of his recent pistol-whipping, while the cut over his eye was obviously only a few days old. 'I'd only just arrived. Then I got this damn call from Jamaica.' He smiled again, but this time it was not returned. The young officer was looking at him with a steady stare.

'You have had an accident on your holiday?'

'Yes. One of those crazy Colombian taxi-drivers. I was lucky it wasn't worse.'

Captain Monica now turned to No-Entry's passport. 'Mr Jones' – his eyes looked slowly up at No-Entry, and for a moment Ryan thought he detected in them an expression of incipient contempt for the black skin – 'you are a citizen of Puerto Rico, and you have a residence visa for Mexico? What where you doing in Colombia?'

Ryan noted that the officer had made no effort to address No-Entry in Spanish, and the Negro replied in his deepest drawl: 'Workin'. I take work wherever ah can get it, Capt'n.'

'You speak English like an American. You do not, perhaps,

also work in the United States? I hear that there are many immigrants from your country?'

No-Entry gave him a wide grin. 'Well, ah'll tell you somethin', Capt'n. I actually *em*igrated from the US of A. If you was a professional pilot and had my skin, where would you choose to work – Puerto Rico, or Yazu, Mississippi?' He paused, and with perfect timing his face grew serious again. 'You people are lucky here. You got free.'

The young man nodded ambiguously. Just then the telephone rang on the table. Captain Monica answered it, in rapid Spanish: 'I know, I have them both here.' Ryan was careful to look as though he did not understand. 'Their papers seem to be in order. But look for the plane. And make a thorough search of the area.'

He broke off and looked up at Ryan. 'How far did you land from where you were picked up?'

'We'd been walking for about two hours. It's on the beach – I'd say about fifteen kilometres from where the truck stopped.

Captain Monica spoke again into the phone: 'Try Zones Eight to Ten.' He looked again at Ryan: 'What exact type of plane?' Ryan told him; and the Captain's next words were not reassuring: 'L-19, American military spy-plane. Two-seater. Used mostly for low reconnaissance operations. Check the fuel capacity.' He sat listening for a moment, then said: 'Very good. Yes. Yes. Thank you, Compañero. Saludos!'

He put down the phone and stubbed out his cigarette. Ryan quickly offered him another, but he shook his head. 'Gentlemen, you will both be staying here tonight. We will discuss your situation again tomorrow.'

Ryan's face assumed an expression of bogus anxiety. 'Captain, I must remind you that I have colleagues who are expecting me in Jamaica. I was due there nearly three hours ago. I also promised to telephone my wife in Barranquilla as soon as I arrived. Unless I contact them, they'll start sending out search-parties for us – and I particularly don't want to have people worrying on my account more than is absolutely necessary.'

'I understand. But I regret that we have no facilities here to contact either Jamaica or Colombia.'

'Can't you send a telegram, or radio them?'

The captain hesitated. 'I am sorry, Mr Broakes. But first there are certain matters which must be clarified.'

'You mean, you're holding us incommunicado?' This time

Ryan simulated a righteous anger. 'Then I demand that you contact whichever foreign embassies in your capital represent the interests of Great Britain and Puerto Rico.'

Captain Monica shook his head. 'At this hour the only Western Missions in Montecristo will be closed. But that is another matter which we will discuss tomorrow.' The young man's voice was suddenly hard, official. 'Mr Broakes, you are staying in which hotel in Barranquilla?'

Ryan thought rapidly. He knew nothing of the city except its profile of dirty shacks, a few skyscrapers, and a glimpse of the port. 'We're staying with friends in a villa just outside.'

'In what area is that?'

'Oh, some Spanish name – I forget it now. We only arrived yesterday.'

'And who are these friends who have this villa?'

'An American couple. The man's a business colleague. He's got a damn pretty wife, I tell you.' And again he smiled at the young man without effect.

'Perhaps Mr Jones knows where you are staying?'

The captain's eyes moved again towards No-Entry, who nodded and said:

'Sure. Bajo de Caja – nice place! About the only place where you can swim along that whole goddam coast – and it's got good fishin', even a golf course.'

'I am happy that you are able to afford such pleasures, Mr Jones. I do not expect that such luxuries are available to the local population.' Captain Monica looked slowly back at Ryan, and his eyes now seemed many years older than his face. 'You will understand, Mr Broakes, that I am obliged to make certain investigations into your story.' He paused. 'When were you last in England?'

Ryan glanced across at his passport, still lying closed on the table in front of Captain Monica. It would contain his Colombian entry-stamp, dated only yesterday; but it had not been stamped in either Jersey or St Malo. And he was not sure about Funchal. Madeira would have sounded a conveniently innocent spot in which to have started his winter holiday; but he remembered again that he did not have a suntan, and decided to play safe. 'Two days ago.' He gave a deferential smile. 'I'm afraid I don't seem to have got off to a very good start, do I? First a car accident, then a forced landing.'

'You have certainly not been fortunate, Mr Broakes.' The

young man rather pointedly took out a packet of local cigarettes, lit one, then leant over and whispered something to the mestizo beside him, who merely nodded. He turned again to No-Entry.

'How long had you been in Colombia, Mr Jones?'

'It's all there in my passport,' No-Entry said easily. 'Eleven days.'

'And what had you been doing for the nine days before you met Mr Broakes?'

'Havin' mahself a ball, Capt'n. Sunshine, cheap booze, plenty o' flesh on the beach. You ought to try it sometime – Colombia's a fine place!'

'I do not like Fascist countries. But we are diverting from the central matter. Where were you staying during your visit?'

'Bogota, Medullin, Barranquilla – but mostly Bajo de Caja. That's where the action is, Capt'n, sir! And that's where I ran into Mr Broakes here.'

'You said "action", Mister Jones? You did not perhaps, during your stay in Bajo de Caja, hear any stories, any reports, of soldiers training in the area?'

The Negro wrinkled his smooth brow for a moment, then gave a peal of laughter: 'D'you mean, did ah see a whole gang o' CIA spooks trainin' on the beach? Hell no! I meant girls, Capt'n – and ah tell you, out there they come in every size and shape an' colour. And ah'm not choosy! As for the men, all ah seen is the usual bunch o' Yankee tourists in Bermuda shorts, practisin' their bum golf-shots and payin' through the nose to try and catch a barracuda.'

Captain Monica nodded, murmured again to the mestizo, and stood up. 'Gentlemen, you will now be shown to your quarters. Food will be brought to you, and you can sleep.'

'Does that mean we're under arrest?' said Ryan.

'It means that you are under temporary detention until further investigations are made. Good evening, gentlemen.' The captain collected up both passports, saluted and walked smartly out of the room, while the mestizo stood up too and jerked his thumb at the side-door.

Ryan and No-Entry walked in front of him, out into a dim corridor, down a flight of concrete steps, and were shown into two separate rooms. As Ryan's door closed, he heard the lock turn.

*

The room was not exactly a cell. There was a high window with glass reinforced with wire-mesh, a camp-bed, table and chair, and a door leading into a second, windowless room with a lavatory and a basin with a single tap and a towel. It was more like the temporary quarters of an officer on manoeuvres.

The first thing Ryan did was to relieve himself; he then took off his shirt and vest and filled the basin from a trickle of rusty water from the tap. He had begun to sluice down his face and shoulders and the back of his neck, washing off the dust and dried sweat, when he found himself swaying. He grabbed the side of the basin and steadied himself, placing one hand against the concrete wall. There was no mirror.

He had touched no alcohol since leaving the train at noon: yet his immediate sensation was that of being drunk. Then he noticed two things. The water in the basin had begun to slop from one side to the other; and the towel was gently swaying from its nail.

The next instant he heard a low grumbling, like a distant artillery barrage. This was followed by other sounds, closer, louder – a crashing and bumping of metal and wood, then shouts from all round, rising to yells of panic. The next moment the light went out. The whole room was shuddering, and every loose object was either rattling or jumping or had fallen to the floor.

It went on for twenty seconds, then there was a dead hush, broken by more shouts, then the howl of a siren. Ryan, who was used to all manner of danger, stood in the dark, half-naked, fascinated and terrified.

He was creeping across the room on all fours when he felt the second tremor. This time it came with a roar like an express train racing towards and past him at less than a few feet.

The whole room was rocking; his eyes and nostrils were clogged with dust; and he could hear the sound of concrete being split open. The siren cut out, and he felt the iron bed edging against his legs. The yelling outside grew louder, and continued well after the earth had grown still again.

He finally picked himself up, groped about for his clothes, carried them to the bed and dressed sitting down, ready to throw himself to the floor at the next quake.

He heard the lock turn and a hurricane lamp glared into the room. A voice in Spanish yelled: 'Out! Immediately!' Ryan could not see the man. He ran for the door, into the corridor and up the concrete steps. At the top there were men running in all directions: some had torches, others were just bumping into each other in the dark. Nobody seemed to be giving any orders.

Ryan reached the square, where – surprisingly – the floodlights were on. He heard several engines start, saw the headlamps of trucks light up and begin to move towards the gates. He ran with them.

There was a smell of dust everywhere, which grew stronger when he reached the street. Under the moving lights he saw that several of the darkened white houses and arcades had collapsed; others were sagging, cracked open, leaning into the street as though they had been pummelled by giant hammers. Nobody seemed to be running out of them. The only movement came from the panic-stricken militia.

Ryan looked around for No-Entry Jones – not because he was greatly concerned for the Negro's welfare, but because he needed an ally. But there was no sign of No-Entry, or of Captain Monica. Trucks were roaring past him now, with the choking stench of dust and the fumes of low-grade Soviet petrol. Several of them had their tailboards still down, crowded with troops. One of them had slowed down at the gates, and Ryan grabbed at the back and hauled himself aboard. No one around seemed to take the least notice of him.

The only lights in the rubble-clogged streets were the careering white beams of the trucks' headlamps, in which the dust rose and swirled like smoke. On the edge of the town came a thundering roar and a massive gong boomed through the darkness. Several of the men round him wailed and sank their faces into their hands, even made the Sign of the Cross. From the muttered cries around him, Ryan gathered that the church tower had collapsed. It was the first indication that the revolutionary zeal of the Island's people might not be so pervasive after all, nor the loyalty of its militia to Gallo's regime quite as firm as young Captain Monica's manner had suggested.

Ryan was trying to work out an immediate plan. Technically he had not escaped from custody, since he had neither been formally arrested nor charged: but whether these niceties of law would be appreciated or respected on the Island was another matter.

He could not tell in which direction they were driving. Instead, he considered the implications of Captain Monica's last words, before he had dismissed them both. Why had he questioned No-Entry about possible military manoeuvres along the coast near Barranquilla? For it is one of the basic rules in interrogation that you do not disclose what you already know. Either Captain Monica was very inexperienced, or the authorities behind him – advised by their Moscow-trained technicians – had heard rumours about La Vuelva's plans.

He was again wondering about what had happened to No-Entry, when the floor of the truck tipped up almost at right angles, the engine howled, there was a crash and grinding of metal, and the darkness was full of screams of pain, bodies toppling over each other as they were heaped up against the side of the canvas hood which was now lying where the floor had been.

Ryan was lucky. Because he had been at the back of the truck, he was able to grab the tailboard and break his fall. The engine had stopped. There was a strong smell of petrol, and the yelling now subsided to moans and cries for help.

A man was lying across him, his leg bent at an ugly angle, and Ryan could feel his warm blood seeping over his own trousers and into his expensive shoes. He moved to disengage himself, careful not to disturb the man's shattered leg, and his hand closed round the metal stock of an assault-rifle. The strap must have broken or come unclipped from the man's belt: it came free in Ryan's hand.

The confusion around him was still total, while the stench of petrol was becoming ominous. Holding the assault-rifle in one hand, he clambered up over the tailboard, leapt into the darkness and fell painfully into a pile of rocks and rubble. The headlamps of the truck had gone out; but behind him other pairs of lights were bouncing towards him. He stumbled over the rubble and reached soft earth.

The next truck behind had come to a halt. Ryan began to crawl forward on his hands and knees, feeling in the dark the mechanism of the gun – which he guessed was an AK-47 – until he was well-hidden under some bushes.

A siren wailed, and a flashing red light came racing down the road, causing the following trucks to pull over. A second siren started, and this time a blue light appeared. In the swaying beam Ryan could just make out what had happened. At first he had thought the truck must have hit a rock and gone over into the ditch; then he saw, with horror, that a long black crevice, like an enormous wound in the earth's surface, had opened down the whole side of the road.

The other trucks, police car and ambulance had slowed to a crawl; but Ryan was still able to rely on their lights to see where he was going. He seemed to be in an orange-grove. He began running, dodging, crouching between the trees, keeping well in the shadows. It was a technique he knew well, though the last time he had practised it had been over a generation ago.

It was almost 9.15, and behind him he saw the glow of fires back in the town. He still had no idea where he was – although he still had his map – and knew that his options were severely limited. He might find a hacienda, or a lonely peasant house, and either hope that the people were not Government sympathizers, or hold them at gunpoint, and perhaps steal some truck or jalopy. What he really needed was a boat.

He was still heading into the orange-grove when a loud whisper reached him out of the dark. His hands tightened round the AK-47, his thumb felt for the safety-catch and slipped it off, as the voice whispered again, 'What is happening, Companero?'

'Who are you?' Ryan growled back in Spanish.

'I am Coronel Macho de Rivera. What unit are you from?'

It was too dark for them to see each other properly: all Ryan could make out was a man of about his own build, with broad epaulettes and a peaked cap with some gold braid. He did not seem to be armed, unless he had a concealed hand-gun.

'I am Field Security, Coronel,' Ryan replied. 'Two foreigners have been apprehended in the area under suspicious circumstances. They were being interrogated when the earthquake occurred. In the confusion, it appears they have escaped. We believe they may have got aboard one of the forward trucks. Now, tell me what you're doing here, Coronel?'

The man was either suffering from slight shock, or was so impressed by Ryan's air of authority that he replied simply, 'My villa is just down the road. Fortunately, my family is in Montecristo.'

Ryan made some suitable remark of comradely thanks, then added, 'I am obliged to ask for your credentials, Coronel.'

The colonel recovered some of his dignity. 'I am not in the habit of submitting to random checks, even by Security. You will identify yourself first.'

Ryan was aware that even in the darkness his smart Western suit – blood-spattered from the injured man in the truck and mud-caked from the swamp, together with the fact that he was holding a Kalashnikov assault-rifle – must have looked odd, even in the aftermath of an earthquake.

Colonel Macho de Rivera was obviously beginning to think so too. 'I request again that you prove your identity Companero! You will also drop your gun.' As he spoke, he made the one mistake that Ryan had been waiting for: he drew a heavy automatic from a holster under his tunic.

Ryan kicked the colonel's knee-cap from under him, and as the heavy body toppled forward he swung the skeleton-butt of the AK-47 into the man's face. He went down with a thud, dropping the pistol on to the ground.

Ryan made sure that the colonel was senseless – and would remain so for some time – then dragged him into the cover of the orange-trees, where he rapidly removed his uniform: the long, smock-like tunic and flared riding breeches, above high calf-skin boots, in the Russian style; and retrieved the pistol and peaked cap.

When he was fully dressed as Colonel Macho de Rivera he was pleased that the uniform, particularly the boots, fitted him reasonably well; and the inside pocket of the tunic bulged with a promising wad of documents.

He then performed the awkward task of dressing the unconscious colonel in his own clothes – noticing, with a twinge of conscience, that the man was wearing a truss. His grey hair was also not dissimilar from his own, while the face had become temporarily unrecognizable from the blow with the gun-butt. Then he examined the heavy automatic – a Soviet 9mm Stechkin, fully loaded with twenty rounds – and returned it to the holster under his tunic.

With luck the orange-grove might be part of an estate attached to Colonel Macho de Rivera's villa. For even under this ruthlessly egalitarian regime, senior Army officers would no doubt be granted the privileges of an elite, if only in order to purchase their loyalty. Ryan now turned in the direction from which the colonel had appeared, hoping to reach the temporary sanctuary of the man's villa.

A moment later he saw the building. It was in total darkness: the only sign of life, the terrified yelping of a dog. Ryan's eyes were now becoming accustomed to the dark, which was broken by the moving beams of heavy vehicles on the read and by the flames from the town which were growing brighter.

There was no garage, but he found a car parked under a lean-to roof. It was a black Skoda. He extracted a large bunch of keys from his tunic pocket, and after fiddling with several of the smaller ones opened the door on the driver's side. He groped for the interior light, decided to risk turning it on, and spent a moment examining Colonel Macho de Rivera's documents.

They were impressive. Apart from his Party membership card, in its stiff red cover with the emblem of a red-and-black star bracketed by two maize-leaves, there were his identity papers, and several safe-conducts, not only for the Prohibited Zone round Carrudas – including the proposed landing beach to the south – but also for the area north, including the road inland to Santiago y Maria. There was also a petrol allowance for two hundred litres a month.

Ryan switched on the ignition, checked the fuel-gauge – which registered half full – practised using the awkward Czech gears, turned the lights on to full-beam, and drove slowly, carefully, round the front of the villa, across the forecourt and down a narrow track between the orange-groves. He met the road after a couple of hundred yards.

Here he saw an empty sentry-box and a lowered bar with a luminous red disc and the word PARADA! – *Stop!* The place was deserted. He got out and swung the bar up. No alarm sounded. The road on either side, for as far as he could see, appeared undisturbed by the earthquake. He climbed back in.

He now had a crucial decision to make. He guessed from the stars that the colonel's villa lay to the south of the town, on the road back to the beach. Should he risk heading north, through the chaos of Carrudas – where he might always be stopped, despite the confusion, and his false identity revealed – and continue towards Santiago y Maria and the capital, Montecristo? Or should he try to make it back down the coast to the stranded L-19? For there was always that radio on the plane: and he calculated that in the panic caused by the earthquake he might be able to get a message through to the camp at Guajira, and hope that his new comrades-in-arms had enough initiative to send one of the PT-boats, or even a second light aircraft to get him out.

It was a long chance. Yet if it didn't come off he knew the best he could expect would be to spend perhaps the rest of his life in one of Gallo's over-crowded jails: but, more likely, to be put up against a wall and shot without ceremony.

Just after sunrise an Avianca private jet put down on the small runway of Barranquilla airport. Since it was an internal flight from Bogota, there were no Customs or Immigration formalities. Instead, a black Mercedes 450 drove out and stopped next to the plane's door. A woman and two men stepped out and got into the back of the car. Their luggage was unloaded by the pilot and navigator, and put in the back of the Mercedes by the chauffeur. They then drove swiftly to a side-gate and headed towards the centre of the city.

The car drew up outside the most exclusive hotel, El Prado, which had not yet been tainted by universal modernization. Its façade, behind tall palms, was white and baroque, its floors marble; there were slow fans instead of air-conditioning, an iron cage of a lift; no piped music, and huge baths on pedestals in all the bathrooms.

The woman was dressed in a white trouser-suit with a red scarf over her head, and large dark glasses. The man who accompanied her into the hotel was tall, in jodhpurs and riding-boots. They both looked like typical paid-up members of the cosmopolitan polo-set.

The third member of the party was a hefty little man with stiff oily hair. He was wearing a black suit and also dark glasses, and remained slightly apart from the other two, while the tall man handed over their passports and signed in. Two porters, in white mess-jackets, carried their luggage to the service-lift; and an elderly hotel retainer bowed and showed them to their three separate suites.

The three of them had risen early and were tired. While

their manner downstairs had seemed relaxed, they were all in a state of excitement and uncertainty. They had heard the first rumours in Bogota before leaving, and just had them confirmed on the car-radio in from the airport. Colombian news bulletins were not the most reliable, even for Central America, but in this instance, since there were no political implications, they could be considered reasonably trustworthy. There had been a violent earthquake in the centre of the Island – judged at between 7 and 8 of the Richter Scale. Also, several volcanoes – some of which had been thought to be dormant – had become active overnight. One of these was the notorious Monte Xatu, dominating the capital, Montecristo, which it had twice destroyed in recent history.

At midnight President Fulgencio Gallo had declared a National Emergency. His speech on the radio and television had announced that his Revolutionary Army, working in solidarity with the people, would soon have the situation under control – adding, rather unnecessarily, that they did not require 'the fat hand of the United States, stuffed with dollars, to help them'.

The first thing that La Vuelva did, after the porter had laid out her luggage and left, was to undress and go into the shower cubicle, where she noticed with distaste a couple of cockroaches curled up near the drain. She then made two telephone calls: the first to Room Service, ordering a flask of vodka martini. The second was to Suite 212 – on the same floor as her own – asking that the French gentleman join her.

Commandant Moulins bowed and kissed her hand. 'Madame, it is still too early for the morning papers. But the radio continues to carry the same news. Jamaica confirms the reports from Montecristo. According to the French Consulate there, the earthquake appears to have been one of the most severe in the Caribbean area for many years. The damage along the east coast of the Island is said to be extensive.'

'Have you called the base-camp at Guajira?'

'I have instructed General Romolo to do that. He has ordered an immediate alert.' The Frenchman paused. 'He was anticipating your wishes, Madame.'

'Does the general think that I am incapable of giving my own orders?' La Vuelva took off her dark glasses and the edges of her mouth grew tight. 'He talked to that buffoon, Rodriguez, I suppose?'

The Frenchman nodded. 'Unfortunately, Madame, he had some other news to report. It appears that our friend, the English colonel, together with his American pilot, have disappeared. They left yesterday afternoon on a reconnaissance sortie over the invasion beach, and have failed to return. There has been no news from them – neither from Jamaica, Santa Domingo, nor Port au Prince.'

There was a light tap on the door and a waiter came in with a silver flask on a tray, and one glass. He bowed as he set it down on a side-table, then retired backwards out of the door. La Vuelva poured the glass full, and sipped it.

The Frenchman looked uneasy. 'With due respect, Madame, is it not a little early for such refreshment?'

'Shut up, Jacques. How do you know it is not iced water?' She had turned away from Moulins, so that he could not see she had gone very pale and that her hand holding the glass was shaking. 'In any case, it is none of your business.' She paused, gazing out at the balcony. 'You have not told me yet how it happened.'

'Madame, I only know what Capitaine Rodriguez told me on the telephone. He said merely that the colonel's plane has been missing since yesterday evening. It had fuel for only six hours.'

'Did the pilot send a radio message?'

'It appears not, Madame.'

This time she turned and looked at him. 'Then he must have crashed on the Island.' She stood with her small hands clenched at her sides, her face rigid and dry eyed. The Frenchman hesitated. 'Madame, permit me to make a comment.'

'Well?'

'Capitaine Rodriguez is of the opinion that the Englishman may have defected to the enemy.' He paused, watching as she poured herself another martini. 'The theory is plausible,' he added. 'Colonel Ryan has received full payment in advance. And he would no doubt be amply rewarded by Gallo if he were now to inform him of our precise plans.'

'Is that your personal opinion, Commandant? Or are you just quoting Rodriguez?'

The Frenchman shifted and looked at the floor. 'I am merely expressing a possible explanation for the colonel's disappearance, Madame.'

'You and Rodriguez, you are both jealous of Colonel Ryan. And you are no doubt glad he is gone.'

The commandant flushed. 'With respect, Madame, that is untrue. But I admit that Capitaine Rodriguez is a very suspicious man.'

'Rodriguez is a brute. He knows how to kill, but he does not know how to think. If the Englishman had tried to give himself up to the enemy, they would not believe him. They would shoot him. But Colonel Ryan is not a fool. I would not have chosen him if he were.' She drank some more martini, while the Frenchman remained standing dutifully in front of her. 'So it appears, Commandant, that you are now commander-in-chief. And what is to be your first move?'

Moulins spoke judiciously. 'I think we should definitely wait until we have more detailed information about events on the Island. We know that their Army is already seriously depleted, and if the disaster is as great as has been reported, the country will be in great confusion. In such a situation, the Army will be the main – perhaps the only – means of restoring order. That gives us a clear advantage. Gallo will be hard-pressed to combat an invasion and – at the same time – a natural catastrophe. On the other hand, our own forces are unprepared. We are relying on at least two week's extensive training.'

La Vuelva did not answer at once. 'Obviously the men are not trained to full capacity. But you have just said that Gallo's remaining Army is itself not ready to withstand an attack. This earthquake is not only *un coup de nature* – it is also an act of God. And if God is on our side, we must respond. I suggest we attack.'

'Those are fine words, Madame. But God will not command those landing-craft – he will not discipline our men to fire at the right time.'

La Vuelva banged her glass down on the marble table beside her. 'Perhaps, Commandant, even if you have no confidence in God, or in my men, you will at least have some confidence in me? I am giving the orders. You and Capitaine Rodriguez will have the troops and their equipment ready by noon. And I want General Romolo to monitor every radio broadcast, to read every available newspaper, and to telephone every reliable foreign embassy in Bogota, to verify what is happening on the Island.'

The Frenchman nodded gravely. He was inured to hasty and impulsive instructions: to the whims and vagaries of a High Command whose judgement he instinctively distrusted, but which discipline had steeled him to obey without question. He bowed his head. 'Madame, we cannot reach the invasion-beach before tomorrow night. Dawn would be the best time to make a landing.'

'You will strike at the very first opportunity, while there is still chaos on the Island.' He saluted and left the room.

La Vuelva appeared on the beach at Guajira twice that day, dressed in a tight-fitting khaki uniform under a jaunty peaked cap. The first occasion was to make a short address to the men, who had been assembled under the hot sun and stood in ranks of three, bearing their miscellaneous arms.

She spoke to them briefly, in a shrill passionate voice, calling upon them to remember the soul of her dead husband, and to recall the honour and traditions of the Island; and – in conclusion – telling them never to surrender: death was more glorious than defeat, and Gallo was no more than a vulgar prostitute of the Kremlin. The troops cheered long and loudly.

Her second appearance was in mid-afternoon, when again she was cheered; but this time she did not speak to the men. Instead, she conferred for some time with Commandant Moulins, and with his second-in-command, Capitano Rodriguez, who had shaved for the occasion and was wearing a clean uniform.

La Vuelva now had an air of quiet dignity, like a self-proclaimed leader who, of a sudden, finds herself a leader of men. After consulting with the two officers, she had concluded by ordering that the men must be ready, with all their weapons, and the landing-craft made ship-shape, by seven o'clock that evening. She had overruled Moulins' objections to an evening attack: time was of the essence – and the men must be prepared for every eventuality.

She left them with the words: 'You will be opposed by a so-called People's Army which enjoys no confidence from the people. They are an army of oppression. They are not prepared to fight a force of liberation. What they have learnt, they have learnt second-hand, from the Russians, and the Russians have never been our Island's friends. They are distant barbarous foreigners – impostors. We must root them out, destroy them. You are to be the destroyers. Do your duty. Your country awaits you!'

Afterwards, in the shabby Nissen, she demanded from Commandant Moulins a glass of cognac. He obliged her, with evident reluctance; then she lay down on one of the bunks and asked for a resumé of the latest radio bulletins.

These had not changed. The situation on the Island was desperate. The earthquake, combined with the eruption of several volcanoes, had destroyed much of the central plain, and a thirty-foot tidal wave had ravaged the east coast, south of Montecristo. Meanwhile, the capital was still menaced by the dormant volcano, Monte Xatu.

Out on the beach, La Vuelva's troops appeared little moved by the plight of their fellow countrymen on the Island. They were restive, excited. Commandant Moulins had mustered them together again during the afternoon. They came to a total of one hundred and thirty-eight men, with twelve officers. The disappearance of Ryan had caused him no distress: he had been secretly irritated at having his command passed over in such an arbitrary and eccentric fashion, and was also envious of the apparent interest that La Vuelva showed in this elderly ex-Nazi colonel.

What did worry him was the loss of the L-19, the only aircraft at their disposal. When he had asked La Vuelva if there was any news of it, she had disparagingly referred him to General Romolo. This was the short, thick man who had arrived with them both from Bogota, and whose tight black suit was already damp under the armpits and crotch, his crocodile-shoes stained with salt and sand. His face behind dark-glasses was secretive, with a large blue chin that could never look freshly shaved. He informed Moulins, with an expressive shrug, that there was no news of the plane, or of the English colonel.

Commandant Moulins was used to conflicts of command, but he expected his position to be at least precise. He had grudgingly accepted Ryan as his military superior; yet this so-called General Romolo was no more than a former State-licensed gangster under Ramon, and was no doubt hoping that La Vuelva would help him snatch back his old position of power.

The Frenchman was not happy about Romolo; but when he pressed La Vuelva she replied, 'The general is my political adviser. He was in the Police Secretariat of my late husband's Cabinet. He is a useful man. If you have any problems of discipline among the men, report them directly to the general. He will deal with them without delay.'

Even to a man of Moulins' experience, this seemed an extraordinarily capricious order: for in the few hours left to them, he saw little point in disciplining men, and perhaps having a few of them shot by Romolo, *pour encourager les autres*.

He felt a spasm of despair. And as the glaring sun flashed off the sea like a knife between his eyes, and beat down on his head as though a steel band were being twisted round his scalp, he remembered another situation – of heat, confusion, a handful of ill-equipped troops, exhausted and without proper orders, while the hordes of little men in their solar-topees, armed with bamboo-poles stuffed with high-explosive, came charging up the hill, blasting through the wire, blowing bugles and dying like flies, at a ratio of ten-to-one to the legionnaires. But at least they had fought like tigers, and died like true men.

What made this present business so miserable was that it threatened to be such a puny affair. Dien Bien Phu had at least entered the glorious folklore of France. This little excursion would, at best, merit a contemptuous footnote in the history books, then probably be forgotten. But the commandant had sworn his allegiance to La Vuelva: he had given her his trust and taken her money. He was not a man to run shy now.

He began to round up the other officers and delegate various duties. The PT-boats were to be brought out of the shelter of the lagoon and their engines fully serviced. Each was to be mounted with a 105mm recoilless rifle, and would carry two of the portable 122mm rocket launchers. Moulins checked the ammunition and calculated that, in a fierce fight – and providing the men held their fire to a minimum – it could not last more than a few hours. The same went for the half a dozen .50 Brownings and the AK-47's.

He wondered what Colonel Ryan had made of the situation, and could only conclude that he had not had the time to examine the ammunition bunker in any detail before leaving on his disastrous flight. What dismayed the Frenchman most was that two of the anti-tank rifles were already rusty and jammed. He called Rodriguez and ordered his best ballistics man to get the things working again within the hour. He finally checked all radios and their batteries, and found these to be working.

But his surprises were not over. La Vuelva had disappeared into the Nissen hut and was asleep. Commandant Moulins' bottle of brandy was on the floor beside her, half-empty. He hid it in his locker, and went out again, only to be told that one of the PT-boats had fouled its propeller at the entrance to the lagoon. Wearily, he gave orders for it to be repaired without delay, then checked the fuel and water supplies.

There was enough diesel-oil to get them to the Island, but certainly not enough to get them off again; and the water and rations, he calculated, would last them, at most, two days.

He saw the squat black figure of General Romolo watching from the shade of one of the palm trees. The Frenchman marched up to him and described to him the state of the PT-boat and the two anti-tank guns.

The general puffed sanguinely at a cigar. 'I am not a military man or a technician. My duties are political. Do you have any complaints about the men's conduct?'

'Do you, General?'

Romolo showed his yellow teeth. 'I am observing, Commandant. I am observing both men and officers. Is it your opinion, as the commanding officer, that the men responsible should be punished?'

'There's no time to discipline them. I had been given to believe that we had two weeks to train these men. Instead, we have barely half a day.'

'Then you must continue to make the best of that half-day, Commandant.' They saluted, and Moulins walked away.

He spent the next two exhausting hours checking that every man had systematically stripped, cleaned and reassembled his rifle several times; supervised the unfouling of the PT-boat's propeller, the loading of ammunition, the fixing of the heavy guns and rocket-launchers, and, above all, the repairing of the two vital anti-tank guns.

He wondered how Ryan would have acted. Maybe he would have shot half a dozen men out of hand. And maybe he would have been right. But Ryan was gone now, to whatever hell had taken him. And perhaps he was better off.

Moulins had no fear of defeat, provided it was defeat with honour. Defeat through incompetence would be intolerable. For a moment he was greatly tempted to take comfort from his bottle of brandy in the Nissen hut. And it occurred to him, with sour rage, that La Vuelva was hardly at this moment showing her mettle as a great national leader.

By midday Task Force *Belladonna* had at least the appearance of some order. The men had been herded into platoons, and Moulins had retired to one of the canvas huts to brief the officers. They already had No-Entry Jones's two reconnaissance reports, with photographs, of the proposed landing zone. The whole area appeared deserted, and the Negro had reported no sign of coast-guards or enemy patrols. Just the road leading directly north.

A lush green coastline, with a long tropical beach. Isolated. Placid. The perfect spot. But as Moulins studied the photographs he felt a shameful sense of inadequacy. He knew that all depended on surprise: that it would only need one heavy machine-gun to slaughter the whole force even before they got off the beach. And he remembered Ryan's words on the boat to Madeira: that the operation might be just as bloody, and end just as badly, as Dien Bien Phu – only without the glory, or the dignity.

Commandant Moulins' last act on earth might be to preside over a small, pitiful military disaster.

When Ryan reached the road, he found that the decision as to which direction to take had been made for him. From the north, towards the town, a long swerving convoy of trucks was bearing down on him. He could see by the drivers' faces that they were terrified. A Russian jeep with four men in it had been forced on to the side of the road, almost colliding with Ryan's Skoda, which was still in the entrance of Colonel Macho de Rivera's driveway.

Ryan took a calculated risk. He rolled down the window and shouted: 'What are you running away from?'

The men in the jeep saw his uniform and the red pennant on the car. One of them saluted and yelled back, '*Aguaje, mi Coronel! Tremblor de tierra!*' The man seemed too frightened to salute, just gesticulated back at the road behind him.

Ryan understood the second phrase, but the word *'Aguaje'* puzzled him for a moment. It must have something to do with *agua*, water, and water was about the last thing Ryan had seen since leaving the swamp. The jeep had begun to career away, tucking itself perilously in between two six-wheeled trucks, when he realized.

Lord God Almighty! he thought. That was all these poor bastards needed. The shell of the barracks had been strong enough to resist both tremors, but the danger was not over yet. Even if they were several miles from the epicentre of the quake, and there were no more to come, there was still another, perhaps more devastating peril in store for them. He knew that there were two essential rules about an earthquake. You got out of your house and tried to reach an open space; but if you were near the sea or a large lake, the last thing you should do was make for the shore.

Unless the man in the jeep had been merely mouthing a panic-stricken rumour, he had been trying to tell Ryan that there was a tidal-wave coming up behind them.

Ryan backed further into the driveway and consulted one of the maps from the Skoda's glove-compartment. The road out of Carrudas was only about one kilometre from the sea. He would have to wait until the convoy had passed, then chance his luck and follow them south, where he would try to reach the L-19 and raise someone on the plane's short-wave radio. Failing that, he might find some fishing village on the way, and either by force or money get hold of a boat. He had found in the colonel's wallet a wad of 100-escudo notes. Although he had no idea of the exchange rate, he guessed that a half-starved fisherman would probably not turn him down.

The convoy ahead was weaving chaotically through the rubble. Some way outside the town they passed a little white church which had collapsed into the road like a piece of smashed porcelain. Ryan guessed that Carrudas must have been an entirely military town, for he had so far seen no ordinary civilians, either among the dead or the fleeing.

After about two miles the convoy stopped. Ryan drove slowly up behind it, halted a few yards from the last truck, and called out, 'Who is in command here?'

A thin young man with a single tab on his shoulder stepped

forward smartly. 'I am, mi Coronel!'

'Why do you stop?'

'We have orders to re-group outside the town, mi Coronel.'

'Where are you from?' Ryan was careful not to address the young man by any rank, since he was still ignorant of the Island's military insignia.

'We come from Llaja de Zancha, mi Coronel. There has been much damage. Many of our comrades have been killed or injured.'

Ryan saw more men moving cautiously into the Skoda's headlamps. They looked bewildered and scared, but Ryan also detected a general expression of relief at the sight of a senior officer. He turned to the first young man. 'What is your name?'

'Teniente Orlaro, mi Coronel.'

Ryan nodded. He noticed that the lieutenant carried no weapon. 'What is the total strength of this convoy, Teniente?'

'We have eight trucks, and two half-tracks, mi Coronel.'

'And how many men?'

'Thirty-seven, I think, mi Coronel.'

Ryan squared his legs and stared at the row of bewildered faces before him. 'Teniente, what are your precise orders?'

'To remove the vehicles, mi Coronel, as far as possible from the disaster zone, in case there are more tremors. They will then be utilized for relief-work.'

'So why do you stop?'

The young man hesitated and his eyes dropped. 'Forgive me, mi Coronel, but I have two brothers in the garrison left in Carrudas. I had decided to wait, and if there are no more tremors, I will return to help.'

'You have acted from personal motives, Teniente. You have disobeyed orders.'

The boy's face had gone pale under the headlamps as Ryan went on: 'I am now in command. This convoy will continue south, where you will await further instructions.' And again he noticed that the other men looked relieved at the sound of his words: it was clear that their only wish was to get as far away from Carrudas as possible.

'Get back to your places!' he yelled, and was just turning to open the Skoda's door when the young lieutenant stepped up to him.

'I omitted to inform you, mi Coronel. We have a prisoner.'

'Prisoner?'

'We picked him up near the barracks in Carrudas. He has a broken arm.'

'What sort of prisoner?'

'He says he is from Puerto Rico, mi Coronel. I have been instructed to guard him until he can be fully interrogated.'

'Where is he?' Ryan instinctively touched the bulge of the holster under his tunic.

The young man led him past the rear truck and pulled open the flaps on the one ahead. Ryan peered into the darkness of the truck, as the lieutenant turned on a torch. The whites of No-Entry Jones's eyes stared back at him. The Negro's woolly hair and blue track-suit were ashen with dust; one wrist was tied behind him, his ankles were lashed together with wire, and his boots had been removed.

Ryan turned calmly to the lieutenant. 'Who gave orders to have him tied up, Teniente? The man is injured.'

'He is a foreigner, mi Coronel,' the boy said innocently. 'And we are told that all foreigners who come here without papers are spies and enemies of the Republic.'

'He is also black. He may be seeking refuge from White Imperialism. Have the man untied and return him his boots. I will take responsibility. You will see that the convoy is moving in thirty seconds.'

He turned and got back into the Skoda; and they began to move again, very slowly. Ryan guessed that they were hindered by the speed of the two half-tracks.

His immediate plan remained uncertain. But of one thing he *was* sure. If he could once free No-Entry and get inside one of those half-tracks, he would at least have a sporting chance – even if it did mean eliminating a whole platoon in the process.

Commandant Moulins had ordered that the embarkation of Task-Force *Belladonna* would take place at 7.00 p.m. local time.

The crossing, barring accidents, should take them between twenty-six and twenty-eight hours, which would give them at least an hour's darkness after landing. Yet the plan was still against the Frenchman's rules of war: a major attack or invasion should always be launched in the small hours before dawn.

In the late afternoon, when he calculated that La Vuelva would be awake, he visited her in the Nissen hut. She was sitting up on the camp-bed, her hands clasped to her knees, staring in front of her. The bottle of brandy stood between her slim boots, almost empty now.

She looked up at him, the muscles round her mouth taut, her eyes hidden again behind her dark glasses. He knew from experience that she was not drunk, nor was she quite sober. 'Is everything in order, mon Colonel?' Her French was careful, controlled.

'I would like to discuss certain matters with you, Madame.'

She nodded stiffly, but did not reply.

'Since I have your complete confidence, it is only correct that I repay you with my complete honesty. Firstly, Madame, the men are not merely untrained, they are lamentable. They simply do not understand these new Russian weapons. Secondly, they do not respect their officers – and what is worse, what officers they have do not respect them. It is my opinion that the whole operation amounts to a suicide venture.'

Her head straightened. 'Do you have any further comments, Commandant?'

'Unfortunately I do, Madame. I accept that Capitaine Rodriguez's suspicions about Colonel Ryan may be mistaken. But even if the colonel is not a traitor, there is always the possibility that his reconnaissance plane was shot down over the Island and that he has been captured. What guarantee do we have, in such a case, that he will not tell all?'

She took a packet of black cheroots from her pocket and slowly lit one. 'You have *my* guarantee, Commandant. Colonel Ryan is a loyal officer. He will tell nothing.' Her voice carried the clear implication that she did not think quite the same of Moulins. 'But we must not be pessimistic,' she added briskly. 'Ill luck has deprived us of the colonel and the plane. Good luck has given us a traumatic, national disaster on the Island. If we do not attack now, our best chance is lost.'

The Frenchman knew it was useless to argue. But he was a dutiful man: he saluted and began to turn, when La Vuelva called after him:

'You see that suitcase over there?'

Moulins nodded towards the pile of expensive luggage in the corner.

She drew on her cigarette. 'And where is your luggage, Commandant?'

'In my room, Madame.'

'You have not, of course, unpacked your three jars of marmalade from London?'

'No' – he hesitated – 'you instructed me not to.'

'Because they are still our most valuable asset.' She sat forward on the bed, elbows now on her knees, and her mouth moved into a smile. 'Does that alter your attitude?'

The Frenchman remained standing, his mouth drying up and his face growing white. 'It is not war, Madame. It is a kind of madness. Supposing' – his voice was feeble but angry – 'supposing these germs are used? Do you have any idea what would happen?'

'Yes. Many people will die. You are used to seeing men die, Commandant. That is one of the things I am paying you for.'

'I did not understand that it would be this kind of war.'

La Vuelva leaned down and uncorked the bottle of brandy. 'What kind of war do you want it to be, mon élégant Monsieur? You are not still dreaming of the heroics of Austerlitz or Verdun? You are not even fighting for your country this time.' She lifted the bottle to her lips.

'You are fighting for me, Commandant Moulins. And you will fight, if necessary, with all the means at my disposal.'

He saluted again and walked into the twilight, mindless of the platoons of men around him – still lethargically stripping and assembling their guns – and trudged the quarter of a mile to where the palms hid the PT-boats. His thoughts were mercifully dulled by the heat. He had a job to do.

The lagoon on which the boats lay was not so much a shell of blue water as a stagnant pond on which the flat-topped boats floated like basking whales. He yelled some orders, and a couple of officers slouched up to his side. One of them was Captain Rodriguez.

Moulins addressed him in his pedantic Spanish. 'We leave in exactly thirty minutes, Capitano. Is everything in order?'

'It is,' Rodriguez replied; and observed the tired, parched lines round the Frenchman's eyes.

'Start the engines, Capitano. I want the boats lined up along the beach in fifteen minutes.' Moulins noted, with sullen satisfaction, that all the guns, ammunition and supplies had been loaded aboard. A couple of men lit hurricane-lamps. He watched as each engine was started, and listened to the roar of diesels as the first boat began to move towards the mouth of the lagoon. Another engine chattered and failed to fire.

'Get over there, Capitano!' And he waited while the heavy figure of Rodriguez loped round the lagoon to the inert PT-boat. There was a pause; then a prolonged chunting of the engine, before it died; and then a scream, followed by another – a choking cry of agony and terror.

Moulins ran round the lagoon. In the half-light he saw a man writhing at the bottom of the last boat, just behind the engine hatch. The screaming kept up. It was Captain Rodriguez. At first the Frenchman thought he was trying to remove his jacket; then he saw what looked like a rubber tyre wrapped round his neck.

The tyre moved, squirmed, made to crawl down the man's back, then a diamond-head jerked sideways into his arm. The man was howling and thrashing about like a maddened bull.

Moulins saw, with a gasp of horror, that the reticulated jaws were buried deep in Rodriguez's stout upper arm; and that the man was bleeding from two puncture marks in his throat. The snake seemed to have got its fangs caught in the material of his tunic and was twisting its silvery-grey body around in a hideous rhythm with its victim. In the next second it slipped over the side into the dark water and was gone.

The Frenchman leapt aboard and turned the captain's face over. It was mauve, with the eyelids twitching, while the whole body rolled and arched like some obscene gymnast. This continued for several seconds, gradually subsiding until Rodriguez lay shivering in spasms on the deck-boards. Moulins moved helplessly over him.

It took the man nearly ten minutes to die – during which Moulins learnt, to his fury, that the first-aid kits on board each boat contained no snake-bite serum. He had the body removed and hastily buried under the sand-dunes.

None of the soldiers showed any emotion. Moulins could not decide whether this was a good omen or not. Either his troops were a band of barbarians or they were so hardened to the sight of death that they feared its prospect as just another act of Providence.

Eighteen minutes later – only three minutes behind schedule

– all six PT-boats were drawn up along the beach, with their flaps down in the shallow water, awaiting embarkation. Rodriguez's rank had been assumed by Cabo Fisco, whom Moulins had promoted temporary acting second-in-command. To the Frenchman's eye, the young corporal seemed exceptionally keen and alert, as well as being undeniably adept in weaponry.

The embarkation was less speedy and efficient than Moulins would have liked. When it was complete he boarded the leading boat. Cabo Fisco went in the second.

The last people to appear on the beach, besides the three radio operators and a couple of guards, were General Romolo and La Vuelva. Under the bobbing beams of the ship's lights, Romolo kissed her hand, then boarded the first boat, climbing into the forward wheel-house to join Moulins and the helmsman, who was also chief navigator.

La Vuelva stayed on the beach: a small, frail figure in her khaki suit, hair blowing slightly in the evening breeze. She raised both arms, waited for the cheers to subside, then spoke. 'Men, God go with you! I go with you as far as this beach. But I shall follow. And together we shall march in triumph to the liberation of our country!'

They cheered again, and went on cheering, as she walked slowly, steadily up the sand into the darkness. Then Moulins gave the order and the engines started.

Mexicana's once-weekly flight from Mexico City to the Island – the only airline in the non-Communist world to operate such flights – was ten minutes out from Montecristo's Simon Bolivar Airport.

The pilot had just announced that they were coming into land when those over the port-wing observed a curious phenomenon. Far below they saw what looked like a row of clumsy fireworks, some giving off a vivid purple gas, others showers of sparks, and some that bubbled and boiled over, in long creeping tides of orange flame.

The plane's wings shuddered with the heat-waves, and the pilot quickly gained height. Beneath, the volcanoes were now bursting in a continuous necklace of juddering bright light. The passengers craned over, fascinated, but also becoming apprehensive.

One such passenger was a Dr Lopez, a chubby smooth-cheeked young man wearing rimless bi-focals which matched the photograph in his Dutch passport. He was anxious, not for his own safety, but that the eruptions should prevent their landing and so frustrate, even destroy, his well-laid plans. He disguised his worries by opening a paperback of Sartre's philosophical essays, translated into Spanish.

The plane landed late, but without trouble. Dr Lopez collected his luggage and limped through Customs and Immigration, where the officials pretended not to notice that he had a club-foot. Outside the terminal there were no taxis, and he boarded one of the old Leyland buses that had been sold to the Island some years before.

He sat at the back and looked out at the dark drab suburbs. Usually at this hour the city was almost deserted, except for a few couples returning from the cinemas, which showed a stale diet of Soviet and East European films. But tonight news of the earthquake and the erupting volcanoes had spread a mute panic throughout the capital. Most of the cafés and bars, even restaurants, had been closed under the regime's anti-bourgeois decrees, so there were no public places in which to meet and talk, except on street corners and in the squares – and even this, although not officially proscribed, was frowned upon by the authorities 'in the interests of public order'.

Tonight was different. On his ride in from the airport Dr Lopez saw street after street, all dimly lit, jammed with static crowds listening to transistor radios. He also noted the extra Security patrols, known disrespectfully as '*Cobras*' – short for 'Comandos Barbudos', or 'Bearded Commandos' – because of their black beards, dark goggles, red and green helmets, Soviet machine-pistols and camouflaged jeeps – howling down the centre of the streets, sirens blaring, lights flashing.

Tonight however the crowds treated them with indifference. What concentrated all their attention and fear was the great black mass of Monte Xatu, rising above the city like some pyramid of death.

There was still a total news blackout on the earthquake, but those with radios could pick up Jamaica and Santo Domingo, even Miami; and the fact that the reports were confused and vague only increased the rumours, which were now running wild. At the Hotel Nacional, where young Miguel Lopez finally descended, they were exchanged, embellished and distorted by the few taxi-drivers and hotel-touts who were still allowed to operate.

Up in his room Dr Lopez lifted the telephone and asked for a number known to less than a dozen people in the whole Island: a secret bleep-code which would rouse the subscriber wherever he was, twenty-four hours a day.

In this case the recipient was a certain Brigadier Gavra, the Chief Intelligence Officer of SACA – those grim custodians of the People's Security who preferred to be known by their official title, 'The Society for Action Against Aggression'.

Dr Lopez was one of the few people in the world who knew that Brigadier Gavra was a secret but fanatical supporter of the Ramonista Movement: and that during the years of Gallo's regime he had worked, tirelessly and subtly, to establish a network of cells within both the Police and the Army, which would be able to seize the levers of power the moment the counter-revolution began.

In the craft of subversion and security the brigadier was an expert. Each of the cells which he had created consisted of only three men, no one of whom knew the names of the other two. Gavra's own identity, as leader of this conspiracy, was known in turn only to Dr Miguel Lopez, otherwise Señor Fraga de Sanchez, alias Pedro.

The two men's relationship was a curious one, which did not relate to the normal rules and mores of current political thinking. Both Pedro and Brigadier Gavra saw the political spectrum in the shape of a horseshoe – a magnet to which the extremes of Right and Left were attracted by mutual forces.

For the stiff, autocratic and devious Gavra, young Pedro represented both his exact opposite, as well as his mirror-image in reverse. To Gavra the Ramonista Movement – even deprived of its crudely charismatic leader – incorporated all the virtues of a Socialist New Order: the destruction of the Church, the landowners, the affluent middle classes and, above all, of the vulgar little bearded brutes who had turned the Island into a Moscow-wired Soviet state.

In Pedro, Brigadier Gavra recognized not so much a political guru as a superb technician in the trade of terrorism and political murder: a political aesthete for whom violence and revolution was an art-form in its own right.

Pedro's telephone call to the brigadier was couched in a few innocuous phrases concerning the International Social Welfare Programme for the Progressive Countries – for which Gavra had been appointed co-ordinating secretary. He agreed, briefly, to meet Dr Lopez that night.

By the standards of most citizens on the Island, Brigadier Gavra lived in patrician style. He had the use of an air-conditioned Russian limousine to drive him from SACA headquarters to his residence outside the capital; a magnificent Spanish mansion which had once been the resort of a string of former dictators, and which later, under President Ramon, had been turned – as a democratic gesture – into a municipal golf-club whose membership had been restricted to the top ranks of the military, police and high society.

The household was now composed of the brigadier, five mestizo menservants, and four bodyguards. Gavra knew that they all spied on him; but he accepted this as normal.

It was 11.10 p.m. when he received the bleep from control, requesting him to ring Room 218 at the Hotel Nacional. He made the call from his SACA office, aware that several tapes of it would be available in a matter of minutes for the scrutiny of those whose duty it was to keep vigil over their superiors. Brigadier Gavra often felt that an organization like SACA, constructed on the near-perfect model of the Soviet Secret Police, could best be compared to a snake which eats its own tail. It was merely a question of how long the digestive processes lasted, before exhausting themselves or killing the creature off.

An hour and a quarter later Gavra was sitting in the back of his Volga saloon, with the electrically-operated windows rolled down against the hot night air. His chauffeur and bodyguard had retired to the house. The car was parked on the gravel driveway, close to the open-air swimming-pool. The brigadier smoked a couple of cigars and waited.

The taxi was an old Mercedes-diesel that came clanking and wheezing up the drive, its engine drowning the scream of cicadas. Gavra watched Pedro pay off the driver, then move with his heavy limp towards the big Russian car. He opened the rear door without a word and climbed in, folding his alpaca raincoat across his lap.

The sky was black and starless, except to the west, high above the horizon, where they could just see the dull rhythmic glow of Monte Xatu, its central crater burning in the night like the end of Gavra's cigar.

The brigadier hardly glanced at his companion. However much he might admire the young man's skills and cunning, he found it impossible not to feel a certain covert revulsion in his presence. It was nothing political or moral – rather an instinctive awareness, like the obverse of sex appeal. Tonight even Pedro's grotesque built-up black boot – although Gavra knew the club-foot was false – only increased the older man's dislike for his young clandestine partner.

Gavra spoke first. 'You arrived without trouble?'

'No trouble. Only the earthquake and the eruptions have altered things. I shall have to request you, Brigadier, to use your radio to alert our comrades in the south. It should not be too dangerous,' he added smugly. 'The area is devastated – the authorities will be in total confusion and disarray.'

'You take a great deal for granted.' The brigadier sat smoking in silence. 'So what papers are you travelling under this time?'

'I am a Communist refugee from Brazil – now a student in Amsterdam – and I have a valid Dutch passport.'

Gavra nodded, still without looking at him. 'And why the club-foot? Another daring whim to attract attention?'

'Quite the contrary' – the young man smiled in the dark and lit a Gitane – 'I would have thought that a man in your position, Brigadier, would know all the rules and tricks. It seems you have not considered that most people – even officials – dislike looking a cripple in the eye.'

'Very clever. We must some day invite you to lecture to our cadet school for young officers. Now, what is the news?'

'The Señora ordered the invasion to proceed at 7.30 this evening.'

This time Gavra turned and stared at him. 'Was she mad – or drunk?'

'That is hardly respectful, Brigadier. My opinion is that she has acted with great flair. If she had waited the two weeks to complete the men's training, she would have lost the supreme advantage of this unexpected disaster. For if the radio reports are correct – and they are certainly trying to minimize the damage – it will take several days before order and communications can be restored.

'The landing will take place sometime tomorrow evening. By that time you should be able to mobilize an effective reception party. Then, if we proceed with our original plan and capture the radio station in Santiago y Maria, we should be able to create the right psychological climate for a partial if not general uprising.

'It is even possible,' he added, tapping his cigarette nonchalantly on to the carpet of the car, 'that an effective rumour could be spread – on the evidence of unnamed experts – to confirm that Monte Xatu is in imminent danger of exploding, and that the population of the capital should be evacuated. Such a situation would almost certainly paralyse all local authority.'

Gavra glanced up at the red glow in the sky. 'What do you know about volcanoes?'

'I studied geology for a short time back in Sao Paolo. Volcanologists have an old saying: "A volcano which is dormant is not necessarily extinct." The dormant ones are among the most to be feared. And Monte Xatu is still technically dormant.'

'It doesn't look dormant to me,' Gavra said impatiently. 'Come to the point.'

Pedro lit another cigarette. 'Just take it from me, Brigadier. Monte Xatu is a type of volcano which builds up intense pressure over many years. When that pressure reaches a certain point, blocked chimneys of the crater blow out like a champagne cork. What follows is not immediately molten lava, but a cloud of burning gas – what the French call a "nuée ardente", after the famous eruption of St Pelée in Martinique at the turn of the century. Then the cloud rolled down the mountain and destroyed the entire town. The only survivor was a murderer awaiting execution in the death-cell. The authorities had the good grace to reprieve him.'

'You are seriously suggesting the Xatu is capable of such an eruption?'

'It is possible. It is certainly plausible.'

'President Gallo and his friends will need more to convince them than the advice of an anonymous expert speaking over a pirate radio.'

The young man turned to him with his pleasant white smile. 'That is only a third line of attack, Brigadier. Or perhaps you would rather call it a diversion?'

'A third?'

'The first, of course, will be the assault on the beach south of Carrudas.'

'And the second?'

Pedro leant back in the deep leather seat and fondled his cigarette with soft fingers. 'The second is an ultimate weapon.' He drew calmly on his cigarette, then explained about the snake-fever capsules and their probable effect.

Gavra turned again and looked at the young man with disgust. 'I am committed to the return of the Ramonista Movement, and to the liberation of my country. That does not mean that I am prepared to poison half my people with this filth of yours.'

Pedro trod out his second cigarette on the carpet, using his club-foot this time. 'Let me give you a word of advice, Brigadier. In this game it is unwise to become sentimental. Wars and revolutions are not won by good intentions.'

'Don't instruct me in my profession!' Gavra said, with quiet fury. 'Just tell me the rest of the details.'

'There is only one other detail. It is a small misfortune, but it should not concern us greatly – not if the attack goes ahead on schedule. The English colonel – the one the Señora took a liking to in England, and whom she promoted as commander of the operation – disappeared yesterday afternoon, with his American pilot, while on a reconnaissance flight over the beachhead. Do you have any reports of their having crashed or landed here on the Island?'

'I have not. But as you know, all lines to the south have been cut by the earthquake.'

Pedro shifted his fat hips and simpered. 'Let us just hope that they are dead. As long as they do not end up in the hands of your organization. The English colonel is a hard man. But I understand that your own people are trained in some very persuasive techniques. I believe you even devised a few of them yourself?'

The brigadier made no comment.

Ryan's convoy reached the block-house at 11.20 that night. It stood facing the coast, at a junction with a single track which led off into the night towards the black mass of mountains.

He calculated, from their time and speed, that they must be within a couple of kilometres from the landing-beach and the crippled L-19. The main reason why he and No-Entry had missed the block-house building that afternoon was because its flat roof lay beneath the level of the mangroves. Even now, under the powerful headlights of the trucks – and the Skoda's spotlight – it was barely visible: a squat black hunk of concrete with naked slits and a fringe of barbed-wire which was almost indistinguishable from the mangrove roots.

Ryan saw its advantages at once. It would prove a formidable obstacle to anyone approaching either from the shore or from any direction inland. He got out of the Skoda and went round to find Lieutenant Orlaro. 'We stop here and await orders, Teniente.'

The young man had the same confused, cowed look. He glanced back up the road, as though expecting to see at any moment that roaring wall of water which would wash them all away.

'You will order the trucks to disperse inland,' Ryan continued. 'The half-tracks will remain here. So will the prisoner.' He did not wait for the lieutenant's reply, but walked over to the truck containing No-Entry.

The Negro was being guarded by a single man who did not seem to be armed. Ryan guessed that the earthquake must have caught them all either in the mess-room or their bunks. He ordered the man out, then climbed aboard. 'You all right?' he whispered.

No-Entry's teeth gleamed back at him. 'Y' know what that spick sonofabitch threatened to do to me – been threatenin' to do to me since they picked me up? He was goin' to break mah arm again. Kept callin' me a Black son of a whore – all the way here.'

'Keep your voice down.' All the truck motors had stopped now and the only sound was a muttering from outside. 'Is your arm really broken?' Ryan added.

'Jus' bruised but ah guess okay. I made out it was broken so as to get some sympathy! Can you get this wire off mah wrists? I wanna get down and have a crap.'

'You'll have to be a good boy and hold on for a moment. I'm getting rid of the trucks.' Ryan climbed back down and yelled: 'Teniente Orlaro – here!'

The young man came trotting round the front of the rear truck. Ryan guessed that he had been having some kind of unofficial discussion with his men. 'Why aren't you all moving? And salute when I talk to you!'

The lieutenant stiffened and brought his hand up with the fist-clenched salute.

'You said we were to await orders, mi Coronel.' And Ryan wondered quickly if the young man were perhaps more cunning than he looked. He said:

'Have you got any radios, Teniente?'

'Yes, but we cannot make contact. There is no reply from Carrudas or any of the other garrison posts.'

Ryan nodded. 'Right. Now move! You will leave the trucks dispersed at one hundred metre intervals up the track over there – the last one at a distance of no less than five kilometres from here.'

The lieutenant paused, then brought his clenched fist up again. 'I ask your pardon, mi Coronel – but you will not accompany us?'

'I am staying to interrogate the prisoner and examine the block-house. It may have a more powerful radio. Do not delay, Teniente. We are very near the sea here – another tidal-wave may still reach us.'

'But you, mi Coronel?'

Ryan leant out and gripped the young man's arm. 'I shall stay and do my duty, Teniente. You do yours!'

Lieutenant Orlaro saluted yet again, swung on his heel and began to shout orders. Ryan pondered on how long it would take him and his men to grow suspicious: or whether the events of the night, combined with the iron discipline of a People's Army, would render them docile to the strangest orders.

He then called for a pair of wire-cutters and ordered No-Entry's wrists and ankles to be released. At the same time, to show the troops that he intended to treat his prisoner seriously, he drew his Soviet 9mm pistol from under his tunic.

No-Entry came hopping towards him on the arm of a soldier, his face contorted with theatrical pain, Ryan motioned with the gun for him to sit down at the side of the road. Then he walked over to the half-tracks. They had stopped at the head of the convoy, and Lieutenant Orlaro was ordering the crew out. There were two to each vehicle, and they all wore the padded leather helmets with ear-flaps of tank-crews. All four saluted Ryan, and without a word climbed into the leading truck.

Ryan stood with his pistol at his side, waiting until the whole convoy had reversed and turned up the narrow track towards the mountains. They drove faster being no longer impeded by the two armoured vehicles ahead; and he watched their rear lights bouncing and flickering like fire-flies as they retreated into the night.

'Now what – you mother-fuckin' genius?' No-Entry said from below him.

'We check the half-tracks – make sure they've got enough hardware to cover the road both ways – then take a look at the block-house.' Ryan paused. 'Unless you can think of anythink more brilliant?'

'Jus' now ah can think o' something a lot more personally pressin'.' No-Entry disappeared into the darkness.

Ryan climbed into the first half-track. It was hot and cramped, with the bitter-sweet smell of Russian petrol. The headlamps and interior lights had been left on. The controls were relatively simple; but what interested him was the three guns.

There was a 105mm recoilless cannon on the front, with a shell in the breech, and a stack of about two dozen more clamped to the armoured wall. To the front and rear, a 12.7 heavy machine-gun, capable of firing six hundred rounds a minute, of which every twelfth round is an armour-piercing explosive shell that can blast through an inch of armour.

Ryan decided to back the second half-track down into the swamp next to the block-house. The first, he would turn round and position at the junction of the road, where its cannon and forward 12.7 would command the whole horizon to the north, towards Carrudas; while No-Entry could man the rear gun, in case there were any unsuspected arrivals from the south.

Twenty minutes later they were in position, ready. By any military standards it was a highly precarious position, and one that offered few options. They could hardly sit here for two weeks and wait for La Vuelva's invasion fleet; and the panic caused by the earthquake and tidal-wave could not last forever.

Their only real hope was still to try and make it in one

of the half-tracks back across the swamp to the L-19. Here Ryan planned to siphon out of one of the half-tracks enough of the low-octane Russian petrol to refuel the plane and get them at least to Jamaica.

He put the proposition to No-Entry who nodded and said, 'Fine, only we're gonna have to wait till first light. Ah'm not riskin' takin' off in the dark blind, with all 'em dunes around.'

'I just hope to hell first light doesn't come too late.' Ryan then led the way down the slimy slope towards the block-house. They both carried torches from the half-tracks, and made enough noise with their boots to waken anything that was alive in the building.

The double-doors had no locks. Each was made of a sheet of cast-iron as thick as a man's thumb, and was secured by huge bolts which required all their strength to open. The doors then rolled back with difficulty on rusted bearings.

Inside they were met by a vile stench of swamp and excrement and things that had been dead for a long time. The concrete ceiling was encrusted with insects and hung with bats, the floor littered with green cigar-butts. But there were no weapons.

They returned outside to the half-tracks which had been backed down into the mangroves; found the tool-kit and dismantled both heavy machine-guns. They also carried down to the block-house two one-litre cans of drinking water, together with the belts of 12.7 ammunition. Finally Ryan fetched the map-case from the Skoda, then backed the car over the edge so that it was half-buried by the mangroves.

After the air of the block-house, the stagnant night seemed fresh and clean. In the direction of the mountains Ryan could see the faint flicker of lights from the convoy.

'Right, we take turns sleeping over there. Two-hour shifts. Otherwise, there's nothing to do but wait.'

He did not say what they were waiting for. For the good reason that he did not know.

Darkness fell swiftly as the flotilla of long low boats moved out into the deeper waters off the Guajira Peninsula, north into the Caribbean.

In the leading boat, along with Commandant Moulins and General Romolo, was the man who, for the next twenty-five hours, was going to be the most important member of the expedition. He was the helmsman and chief navigator – a tall silent man with reddish-blond hair and an untidy beard. His incongruous appearance was matched by his name: Sebastian McIntyre Hausmann.

Conditions on board were not good. The forward portion, in front of each wheelhouse, was entirely full of arms and ammunition. Each boat carried roughly twenty men; but at least half the space in the open after-section, behind the wheelhouse, was taken up with food, water, light weapons, more ammunition, and medical supplies. There was scarcely room for the men to sit, let alone lie down; and the only latrine was a single plank set out of the stern, with a rope to hang on to.

For the first half-hour their spirits remained high; and despite the noise and stench of the diesels they sang and smoked and shouted endless anecdotes at one another about foul and improbable sexual escapades. They did not discuss politics, and there was almost no mention of the operation ahead.

Commandant Moulins had ordered the boats to steer in haphazard formation, at a minimum of five hundred metres' distance from one another, to avoid giving too obvious an impression of a convoy. They were still uncomfortably close to Venezuelan territorial waters, which lay in the jurisdiction of a relatively neutral regime whose leaders would be far from happy to be caught abetting the overthrow of a fellow-Caribbean country. The same hazard would arise when they neared Jamaica. However, La Vuelva had assured Moulins that the authorities in the Dominican Republic would be more accommodating. And as for Haiti, that wretched land could afford no regular patrol boats, and so presented little danger.

To conserve fuel they were doing only fifteen knots – although the powerful Perkins diesels were capable of up to forty. Then, after only eight miles they ran into a dense sea-fog. Moulins knew that the Caribbean is – at all times – an unpredictable and treacherous sea. Each boat carried the statutory warning lights and flares, but no fog-horn. The Frenchman ordered Hausmann, who was also in charge of the radio, to instruct the other boats to close in and proceed in pairs.

The greatest danger now was not so much a Venezuelan

patrol-boat picking them up as being run down by some dirty old freighter – especially if the captain and look-out were either drunk or asleep. There was also the risk of themselves running down one of the innumerable tiny fishing-craft which ply the Caribbean in all seasons, with no radar and no respect for international fishing limits.

The fog dampened the men's enthusiasm. The air was warm and clammy, and the steel walls and metal fittings of the boat were sweating. They had slowed to five knots, and Moulins found his eyes beginning to smart with the effort of staring into the thick darkness ahead.

He was thinking that their reduction in speed held one advantage: at this rate they would not make the landing-beach much before the small hours of the day after tomorrow. He had seriously considered disregarding La Vuelva's orders about an evening landing, but was deterred by the bulky, enigmatic presence of General Romolo.

After four hours the fog cleared. In its place came a heavy swell, and soon the boat was full of men groaning and heaving over the side.

The commandant gave instructions to break convoy.

It was well after dawn when they passed two hundred miles west of Jamaica across the Cayman Trench, on latitude 18. The silent Hausmann stood erect at the wheel, next to his charts and compass, his eyes a fierce steady blue under his reddish brows. Not once during the night had he stirred from his post, even to relieve himself; and he had refused all food and refreshment, except a drink from a thermos of black coffee.

Moulins, after consulting the charts with Hausmann, now gave the order to steer due east.

During the night they had passed a number of ships, including the fire-fly lights of fishing skiffs; but none had come close enough to threaten them, and the radio had picked up no awkward signals. For most of the time they had kept tuned in on the short-wave, to catch all the latest news bulletins from around the Caribbean.

The reports about the situation on the Island remained confused, since there were no resident Western journalists or friendly embassies to bear witness to the disaster; but from weather reports and seismological readings it seemed that there had been several quakes, as well as volcanic eruptions, and that a tidal-wave had swept along half the east coast, devastating whole towns. The death toll was believed to be running into thousands.

The Island's Radio Nacional Popular, from Montecristo, gave almost no details at all, but confined itself, with a measured sense of urgency, to repeated instructions to the population, in the interests of national security, to avoid all panic and the spreading of rumours. Each bulletin ended with the exhortation: 'The Government is in full control – the Army and Security Forces are at their posts – trust the People!' – and there followed the blare of canned martial music.

Towards dawn it was clear that the Island was in the grip of a major catastrophe. Moulins took heart from this, and for the first time was inclined to credit La Vuelva with an inspired tactical move.

But with daylight came a fresh danger. In the dark their straggling lights had attracted no attention; but now, under the huge rising sun, the boats would present a far more suspicious spectacle. They were all painted sea-grey, and flew Panamanian flags. La Vuelva's orders had been explicit: if they strayed into unfriendly waters and were intercepted, they were to use their maximum fire-power and sink the assailant.

Moulins himself had taken the extra precaution of stowing one of the 122mm rocket-launchers under a bunk in the wheelhouse. He glanced at it now, lying like a giant cigar-tube, and felt a disagreeable pang of conscience. It was not for the first time that he had fought in someone else's war, against someone else's enemy. But it was the first time that he had ever been asked to use Communist equipment.

But finally the heat became the greatest menace. The whole sky and sea seemed to be welded into one gigantic bowl of burning glass. Water was strictly rationed. The men sat slumped against crates of food and ammunition, their slovenly uniforms soaked dark with sweat, their mouths so parched that most of them did not even want to smoke.

Some time towards noon Commandant Moulins lay down on one of the bunks and tried to sleep. The rhythm of the diesels pounded through his aching body; yet he ordered them to increase speed, not so much in order to make up lost time as to get up a little breeze.

For him the one encouraging sight was the figure of Sebastian McIntyre Hausmann. His makeshift uniform – the colour of his tunic did not match that of his trousers – was as ragged as his beard. In normal circumstances Moulins would have put him on charge.

But these were not normal circumstances: and there was something about the man's gaunt, freckled face and his immutable expression, neither of which had altered a muscle since they had left Guajira, which secretly heartened Moulins in his lonely command. He considered himself a brave man. Yet not for the first time during the last twenty-four hours he found himself wishing for the company and cold self-confidence of Colonel Ryan.

At around six o'clock they passed south of the Grand Cayman – this time keeping well out of British jurisdiction – and were now headed north-by-north-east, steering a smooth course into the clear, still horizon. As they passed over latitude 80, Commandant Moulins noted that they were ninety minutes behind schedule.

CHAPTER SIX

First Blood

Ryan was feeling his age. This was the second night that he had not lain between sheets, and he could not sleep: his whole body taut, every sense alert to the smallest sound, the slightest movement.

But for many hours there was no movement, and the only sounds were the ticking and purring of insects from the swamp. The lights from the trucks up the road towards the mountains had gone out. It was still night, full of stars but with no moon. The perfect night for an ambush.

Twice – soon after they arrived, then towards midnight – he had tried tuning in the R/T in the half-track, but all he could get was a static crackle and occasional muddled words which had meant nothing to him.

Between shifts No-Entry Jones slept like a child. He slept on his back, his long legs sprawled out in the dust, his woolly head cradled by his elbow. Ryan had given him the AK-47 which he had taken from the man in the truck. Although the assault-rifle would be far more effective, Ryan preferred to keep the Stechkin 9mm for himself in order to preserve his role as Colonel Macho de Rivera for as long as possible.

It was in the small hours, just before sunrise, that he saw them coming.

No-Entry was still asleep, and it was almost the end of Ryan's shift. At first there were just two pricks of light moving down the road from the north. They moved unevenly, but were approaching fast, and Ryan guessed that they were motorcycles. The easiest target in the world – like shooting pheasants out of season.

He shook No-Entry awake and took up position behind the forward wheel of the half-track, while the Negro crouched down on the other side. The half-track was showing no lights. They heard the snarl of the engines for nearly a minute, the pair of headlamps wobbling on the dusty road, and not slowing until the powerful beams picked out the square camouflaged shape of the armoured vehicle, its slanting bonnet painted with the red-and-black starred emblem of the Island.

Both riders howled to a halt on either side of the road, their figures obscured in bright funnels of dust. Ryan took a step forward and waited. The two engines stopped, but the headlamps stayed on. Ryan heard the crunch of boots, and the snap of No-Entry's safety-catch.

He only saw the two men clearly when they were a few feet away. They were in black leather, black boots, white belts and sashes, and red and green helmets. Ryan turned on the torch in his left hand. The men's faces were invisible behind huge goggles and full black beards. The impression was both macabre and absurd. He still did not move.

Neither of them saluted. Instead, each had drawn a gun from his white holster. 'Quien es?' one of them shouted, and Ryan noted that he deliberately omitted the formal Spanish use of 'Usted'. 'Who are you?' he repeated; and they both stood with their goggles staring into Ryan's torch.

'I am Coronel Macho de Rivera. You will show respect to a senior officer.'

One of the beards opened in a grin. 'We show respect only to our own officers – mi Coronel' – and he spat deliberately in front of Ryan's boots.

The second man spoke: 'You have authority to be here?'

'And what cursed authority have *you* to be here?' Ryan said furiously.

The second man answered, more quietly this time, 'We have authority to be everywhere. As members of the Society for Action Against Aggression we must be vigilant at all times. Your papers, Coronel. And you will put away your pistol.'

Both men had brought up their guns in their gloved hands. Carefully, Ryan replaced the Stechkin in his tunic, but in the side pocket this time, and without putting it on to 'safety'. His torch did not move from the men's faces. Then, with his free hand, he took the documents from his inside pocket. The second man stepped forward and took them, turned and began to read under the light from the motorcycle headlamps. The first man kept his gun pointing at Ryan's stomach.

At least a minute passed. On the other side of the half-track,

No-Entry still waited, as still as a corpse. The second man turned back to Ryan. 'Your authorization to visit this zone is not counter-signed for tonight. Where is your special Security pass?'

Ryan decided to take the offensive. At least he now knew with whom he was dealing; and he guessed that, as in most totalitarian states, there would exist a bitter rivalry between the traditional military and the upstarts in the political police. His voice became angry again: 'So you want something in writing, do you? Don't you know there has been a national disaster? Yet you still spend your time looking at pieces of paper! What are you – bureaucrats?'

The first man's hand tightened round his gun. The second spoke: 'Security.'

'And how am I to know that? Any hoodlum can paint his helmet and get into fancy dress like you two. Where are your papers?'

Both men hesitated, then the second one lowered his gun a fraction and flicked from his top pocket a card in a celluloid holder. Ryan had time to glimpse a diagonal red and green stripe and the initials SACA – Sociedad de la Acción Contra Agresión. The man slipped it away again and said sourly, 'Satisfied now, Coronel?' He pronounced the rank as though it were a term of abuse.

Ryan decided to change tactics. He would either have to kill these two men – which perhaps he should have done in the first place, or somehow get them on his side. He nodded. 'Very well, companeros. Let us not waste time arguing. I have received orders to evacuate Carrudas and come as far south as possible. Is there any more news of the tidal-wave, by the way?' He sounded genuinely concerned.

'The tidal-wave did not reach Carrudas.'

The first man nodded at the half-track. 'Where are your men? Or did you evacuate the town alone – taking with you a valuable armoured vehicle?'

'They're up the road there' – Ryan pointed at the track towards the mountains – 'I decided to order the convoy as far away from the coast as possible.'

There was a pause. The two men seemed to be making up their minds – which gave Ryan time to make up his. 'Compañeros, I have answered your questions. Now answer mine.

Who ordered *you* down into this place?'

'We take our orders from the Society for Action Against Aggression,' the second man said. 'You do not require further answers.'

'Maybe not' – Ryan sounded cheerful – 'but it so happens I have some good friends in your Society. I would not like to make trouble for you. Which officer sent you?'

This time there was a longer pause. It was the second man who finally spoke; his voice was more subdued. 'We come on the authority of Brigadier Gavra.'

'For what purpose?'

For the first time the man sounded evasive. 'Our instructions are confidential. But we are to ensure that the zone remains empty. Even the military must not be here' – his voice was regaining confidence – 'which includes you and your men, Coronel. What other units are here?'

Ryan was thinking fast. He knew that if he and the convoy failed to return, it would certainly be reported within a few hours. And these two boys would remember Colonel Macho de Rivera, separated from his men on a lonely road with a half-track. Besides, it was also certain that most of the garrison must know the real colonel – while Ryan and No-Entry were themselves known to at least two men in the town: Captain Monica and his mestizo subaltern.

Ryan decided that he preferred to stay with the half-track, and fall back, if necessary, on the sanctuary of the stinking block-house where they would wait until dawn. He would now have to act accordingly.

The second man persisted: 'Are there any other units in this area?'

'I am not sure. There has been total confusion. But I think we are the only ones.'

The man nodded and jabbed his gun towards the road up to the mountains. 'Your evacuation orders are countermanded. You and your men are to return at once to Carrudas.'

Both men turned, and without reholstering their guns began striding back towards their motorcycles. Ryan slipped his hand down to his tunic pocket and shot the second man through the spine. The impact of the 9mm soft-nosed bullet hurled the body a full six feet, where it lay flat in the dust and did not move.

The sound of the explosion was still ringing out through the empty darkness as the other man whirled round and was hit by a short burst from No-Entry's AK-47. He stumbled backwards, fired once, wildly into the air, did a quick pirouette, then crumpled on his face in the dust and lay still. No-Entry came round the front of the half-track, clicking his tongue against his teeth. 'Good shooting, Colonel.'

Together they walked over to the bodies, made sure that both men were dead, then dragged them towards the mangroves.

Ryan's shot had blown an exit-wound the size of his fist in the second man's belly. There was surprisingly little blood, but when he unzipped the black leather jacket to remove any documents the man might be carrying, he saw a blue bubble of intestine swelling out through the torn shirt.

No-Entry wiped some blood off his hands and rinsed them in the dust from the road. 'You considered that it could be mighty handy if we dressed up as these two boys? I mean, might give us some kinda immunity – seein' they can pull rank on a full colonel?'

'Except for the holes in their jackets. Your one's got about as many as a colander. And I've an idea those beards are part of the uniform. Still, the bikes might come in useful.'

They pocketed the men's ID cards, identification bracelets, and a wad of documents; then went over next to the motorcycles and switched off the headlamps. They were two massive 900 cc Russian models, painted entirely black, except for the huge chromium double exhausts, and carrying no markings besides the number-plates, which were just two digits.

They wheeled both machines across the road, using Ryan's torch to guide them, down the bank past the second half-track, and parked them out of sight behind the block-house. Then they returned and kicked dust over the two patches of blood on the road. There was not much they could do about the wheel-marks.

No-Entry turned to Ryan. 'Now what?'

'As before. We wait. Only this time there'll be no sleeping. We'll sit it out in the half-tracks.'

Across the rim of the sea there was already a pale strip of light. It was just after 5.15 a.m. Ryan looked to the west, in the direction of the mountains, and saw no lights. It was always possible that young Lieutenant Orlaro would still be too scared to move: or perhaps the sound of shooting round here was so common, even at this hour, that it would arouse little interest.

Inside the half-track he switched on the dim map-light. While No-Entry kept a look-out through the narrow forward window Ryan examined in more detail the dead SACA men's documents. Most of them were routine stuff – special passes and travel documents headed with the black-and-red star and issued by Security Headquarters in Montecristo. There seemed to be no personal papers of any kind: nothing sentimental, no love-letters, no photographs of mothers or wives or children to tug at Ryan's conscience.

But one thing did interest him. It was a plain sealed manilla envelope. Inside was a single sheet of paper. It was typed, with no heading, no date, and was signed with the single word, 'Zorro', the Spanish for 'fox'.

Ryan read:

To the Commander of Task-Force *Belladonna*. Salutations! This is to confirm that the officer who brings you this is to be treated as a friend. He has been authorized by myself to mobilize all troops in the area in our struggle for independence and freedom. Other agents will be despatched during tonight and tomorrow to make further contact. They will identify themselves under the code-names Caballo, Marrano, Perro, Gato, Vaca, Campañol. These men can be totally trusted. They will bring with them re-enforcements. They have great authority and their word will not be questioned.

Fellow-Countrymen, have brave hearts! The Soul of General Ramon is with you! Death to the traitor Gallo! Deliverance is near! Long live the Free Republic! Long live the Ramonista Movement! Long live La Vuelva!

Ryan found that his hands were sweating as he read it. 'Jesus wept,' he said, and passed the paper to No-Entry. The Negro read it impassively, then he handed it back with a sad smile.

'Look like we gone and killed the wrong boys, Colonel.'

For several seconds they stared at each other in silence. Ryan was the first to speak. 'I think you may be right. No-Entry, we're now going to get down to some serious thinking. This letter comes from near the top – and from the inside. It means that if La Vuelva's got agents working in Gallo's Security Forces, then it looks as though she hasn't been whistling through her fanny after all. Maybe she *has* got a serious counter-revolutionary movement going for her. In which case, that crumby outfit on the beach back in Colombia is just the detonator – the spark to set the whole Island ablaze.

'And there's another thing,' he added: 'Why was that dead bastard carrying this letter down here *tonight*? The invasion's not scheduled for another two weeks.'

No-Entry looked at him, calmly. 'You're the commander-in-chief, I don' know nuthin' – 'cept how to drive a plane. And maybe shoot the wrong man. Didn't they brief you, Colonel?'

'Brief me – hell! They've been keeping their security as tight as a snake's arse-hole. About the only open thing they've done is pay me.' He peered at No-Entry through the dim light. 'Check the road – both directions.'

'Not a soul.' The Negro sat back on the narrow bucket-seat and again there was silence. It was getting light outside, but still no movement from any direction. The sun would be up in a few minutes and they would be visible to Lieutenant Orlaro's convoy.

'The way I see it,' Ryan said at last, 'we now have several new options. We've got this letter, and it doesn't say a damned thing about who brings it, except that he can be trusted. Now, let's assume the invasion is going to take place tonight or tomorrow morning. We don't know exactly how bad this earthquake has been, but our boys over in Colombia must have been following the news, and if Carrudas is anything to go by, then I'd say it was bloody bad. Which means that not only will all communications be cut, but the Army'll be up to its neck in salvage work.

'Now, our immediate problem is this. We've got a whole day to kill. We can stick it out here. Or in the block-house. Or we can take the initiative. That means we use this letter to contact all officers in the area. We mobilize what troops we can find, and hold the road against anyone coming from the north. And if they don't play friendly, we kill them.'

'It's a helluva risk, Colonel. But it's a helluva good'n!'

'You're going to stay here, Major, and hold the road. Meanwhile, I'm going to take one of the motorcycles and contact the young lieutenant up there with the convoy. If I'm not back in exactly thirty minutes, you're to take this half-track and find out what's happened.'

They nodded to each other. Then Ryan got out and walked

over to the mangroves where they had hidden the two machines.

The darkness ahead was total. The bright veil of stars ended at a black wall high above the horizon. Unless they were running into another sea-fog, this could only be the Sierra Hiarra.

For the last hour there had been no sign of a ship, not even a stray fishing-craft – just the lights of the other five PT-boats strung out behind them at broken intervals over a mile.

It was 8.45 p.m. Latitude 22. Water calm, heaving slowly, with a muggy smell of seaweed.

Sebastian McIntyre Hausmann switched on the depth-finder. Only three fathoms. Commandant Moulins had finished shaving round his narrow beard with a dry cut-throat razor. He drank some coffee from the Thermos flask, offered it to Hausmann, who shook his head, then filled his pipe, and went over to wake General Romolo.

The man rolled over on the bunk, coughed and sat up. His blue jowls had now sprouted a heavy bristle. He cleared his throat and spat through the open window of the cabin. 'Qué pasa?' he growled. His small raw eyes peered suspiciously at the Frenchman, then at Hausmann.

'We are approaching the beach, mi General.' Commandant Moulins looked into the back of the boat, where the men lay sprawled asleep like rows of dark sacks. 'Troops! Stand ready!' he yelled. There was a sluggish stirring from below. 'Attention! Immediately!' The men began shuffling to their feet, groping for their weapons. Moulins turned to Hausmann. 'What does the chart say?'

'Three kilometres, maybe less.'

'Try the radio again,' Moulins said: 'UHF.'

Hausmann's bony freckled hand moved from the wheel, and flicked a switch on the large elaborate transceiver, and turned a luminous dial. The first two wavelengths gave out only static; the third was alive, but silent.

Moulins moved over to the set, put a match to his pipe, picked up the microphone and said three times, 'Here is *Belladonna*.' Then: 'Entiene?'

For a few seconds the silence continued: then a voice, clear and calm: 'Entendo, *Belladonna*. What is your precise position?'

The Frenchman felt the quickening of his heart as he passed the microphone to Hausmann, who began reciting a complex list of bearings.

The voice continued: 'We will contact you again in five minutes.'

Commandant Moulins had again turned and was watching the men below assembling themselves in two rows, a couple of them each carrying a 122mm rocket, and another two manning one of the 105mm guns. He drew on his pipe, with excited satisfaction. Beside him, General Romolo had shunted himself to his feet and squared his thick shoulders under his tight black suit. 'Everything correct, Comandante?'

'Everything is excellent, mi General.' Moulins felt the clouds of doubt beginning to lift. He had never been sure that the radio would answer. Since arriving at Guajira the day before yesterday he had never believed in anything but failure. Now, suddenly, he had hope.

General Romolo was frowning. 'They did not identify themselves. Order the boats into line – on short-frequency, remember – and when the next call comes, demand the code-word. Meantime, slow down. Five knots. They may have heavy guns out there. It could be a trap.'

Hausmann cut the diesels, then transmitted the call for the convoy to close in. They stood in silence, watching the lights behind slowly drawing nearer, into rows of three, while Hausmann moved the wheel two degrees to the left.

Exactly five minutes later the UHF receiver crackled to life again. The first voice said: '*Belladonna*, do you hear me?'

This time, because his doubts and suspicions had been re-awakened by Romolo's remark, Moulins thought he noticed an odd inflection in the voice.

Romolo leant forward. 'Ask him for his code-name.'

Moulins said into the microphone: 'Identify yourself.'

'Mais bien sur, mon cher Commandant! Which would you prefer? – "Horse?" "Pig?" "Dog?" "Cow?" "Field-Mouse?" Or perhaps you would like something really important – like a "Fox"?'

For several seconds the Frenchman stood staring at the set in front of him. Except for the opening words, the rest had been spoken in English. A fluent, self-confident English, without any discernible accent.

Before he could reply, General Romolo grabbed the microphone from him. 'What in the Virgin's name is happening?' – then, into the mouth-piece: 'Identify yourself! Who are you?' His stout face had turned puce as he spoke and the veins in his neck stood out like dark worms.

The voice came back, in Spanish this time: 'Take your choice – I am Señor Broakes, or Task-Force Commander-in-Chief, Colonel Ryan.'

General Romolo let out a low obscenity, and without switching off the set turned to Moulins. 'The Englishman! This is all crazy. Somebody is playing the comedy with us!'

'Let me speak to him, mi General.' He took the microphone again and said, in his quiet careful English: 'Can you provide proof of your identity? But quickly – it is dangerous to keep this wavelength open too long.'

This time a laugh came back: 'Commandant, you can keep it open as long as you like! We're all friends here. Still smoking that damned great pipe of yours?'

'Very well, mon Colonel' – the Frenchman was holding the microphone very tightly – 'what is the precise situation?'

Ryan's voice came back again in English – to Romolo's growing irritation, since he spoke only Spanish. 'I've got about a battalion of men here. They're taking orders like lambs. So I don't even need your lot – they're probably worse than useless, anyway. But I do need your guns, particularly the heavy stuff.'

'I understand.' Moulins turned to Romolo. 'It is the English colonel, mi General. He claims to have a battalion at his command and that there will be no resistance.'

The general just nodded. Moulins spoke again over the air: 'If you assure us that it is safe, we will keep this wavelength open until we strike the beach.' He replaced the microphone without switching off the set.

'How has it happened?' said Romolo; he sounded furious. 'How does the man come to have five hundred of Gallo's troops at his command? It is impossible! It is a trap. We must withdraw at once.'

'If it were a trap,' Moulins said, 'he would not have identified himself. And what about all those code-names? Are they genuine?'

The general had begun to sweat. He was now thoroughly bewildered, as well as angry. He did not answer Moulins; nor did he repeat the order to withdraw.

The Frenchman turned to Hausmann. 'How many fathoms now?'

'Less than two.'

'Call the other boats.'

Ahead, a couple of lights flashed on. They seemed very close. Without being able to see the beach itself, Moulins ordered full-speed from all six boats.

Hausmann sank in the throttle and the diesels howled, the floor of the wheel-house lifting a good ten degrees as the whole boat roared forward, its prow raised several feet out of the waves, until it was thrusting ahead at 40 knots, with only its crews and the back of the stern left in the shallow water. The noise was colossal.

Thirty seconds later they hit the beach. Hausmann had braced himself against the wheel, but Moulins and Romolo were thrown forward in an untidy huddle, banging their heads against the windows. Hausmann cut the engines. In the sudden quiet the Frenchman yelled, 'Disembark! And hold your fire!' Before he went over the side he remembered to knock out his pipe, and to retrieve the long single-tube rocket from under the bunk.

Wading ashore, he felt confused rather than excited or scared: and as a soldier he hated confusion. But he was also aware that so far things might be going just a little too well.

There were half a dozen men waiting for them on the beach, all in uniform, all armed. Ryan was not among them. A young man stepped forward and said, 'I am Teniente Orlaro. I am instructed to accompany you and your men to the coronel.'

As he spoke, Moulins caught the stench of the swamp from the man's uniform, and again he was assaulted by doubt. Why hadn't Ryan been here to meet them himself? All the Frenchman's instincts warned him that Romolo might have been right after all: it was a trap. Yet his sense of discipline told him there was no way back. Ryan was his commander, and it was Ryan's voice he had heard on the UHF: of that he was sure. It was just a matter of which side Ryan was now on.

The long high corridors had been stripped of their carpets; the folding ormolu doors were chipped and flaking; the elaborate mouldings on the ceiling had shed their gold-leaf like autumn trees. Protocol had not merely been dispensed with, it had been actively repudiated. The guards wore sloppy green fatigues and black beards. They stopped the visitor at every corner, always in pairs, examining his credentials carefully, suspiciously, like men who are not used to reading.

He finally reached a plain white door, like a door in a hospital. Above it was a red flashing light, and set into the wall an entry-phone. The guard lifted it, and for the first time since entering the building the visitor saw him come stiffly to attention. He mumbled a couple of words which the visitor did not catch, replaced the phone, and the light above the door turned green.

The door was opened by a big wide-shouldered man with thick, curly black hair and a square beard, and dressed in the same fatigues as the troops outside. In his mouth was a long fat green cigar. He nodded at the visitor, stood back and closed the door behind them both.

The room was furnished with a number of hard-backed chairs, a crowded desk, steel filing cabinet, framed photograph of Lenin, and a portrait of Bolivar. The man waved his visitor to one of the chairs, then stretched his long legs out behind the desk and spat out a leaf from his cigar. 'I have been waiting since before midnight. Well?'

'Things are proceeding excellently – exactly according to plan.'

The man behind the desk spoke without removing his cigar: 'You call an earthquake, a tidal-wave, the destruction of half a dozen towns, the death of many thousands of my compatriots – you call all that excellent and according to plan, Señor de Sanchez?'

His visitor sat forward with his elbows on his knees and blinked at the big man through his glasses. He had dispensed with his club-foot and bi-focals, and was again wearing his blue-shaded lenses.

'I am sorry, Comrade President – I phrased my statement most unfortunately. Of course, the tragedy that has befallen your country grieves me greatly—'

The big man behind the desk waved a hand at him and laughed: 'It grieves you about as much as the death of one cockroach! Please, hypocrisy is bad enough. Sentimental hypocrisy is beyond endurance. Now, what have you come to tell me?'

'I understand that lines of communications with the south are not good. But you will no doubt have heard, Comrade President, that the invasion-force, code-named *Belladonna*, landed four hours ago south of Carrudas? And I have heard from my own sources that although a number of local troops have defected, they are poorly armed and should provide you with no problem.'

'It has been reported to me that Carrudas is in ruins,' the President said. 'In a moment like this we cannot afford to have *any* troops defecting.'

'I understand from my contact that it is merely a battalion. When it is all over, they can be shown as an example to the others – yes?'

'They will be dealt with. Just as Brigadier Gavra and all the other vermin will be dealt with. But I cannot allow this charade to go on indefinitely. When does the Widow Ramon intend to arrive?'

The young man was silent. There was about him a sinister composure which the big man found unexpectedly disconcerting. Like all famous leaders, the Island's president was used to fawning and flattery, and although he mocked most of the traditions and panoplies of power, secretly he welcomed its instant gratification. This chubby young man in his blue glasses was very polite, almost demure: yet there was also a superiority about him, a concealed arrogance which seemed to imply not so much a rebuke as a sneer.

'When can I expect the widow to arrive?'

The young man slowly raised his head. 'You must understand, Comrade President, that she is quite clever. She is used to servants to do her work for her, but when it comes to organization, she is by no means stupid.'

'That is not what I asked. When does she plan to arrive?'

'She has not yet disclosed her exact plans. She will certainly be awaiting the results from the south.'

The big man turned and switched on a portable fan on the desk; then he ripped open the top three buttons of his tunic and began scratching a mat of black hair. His cigar was only half-burnt, but he picked a new one out of a large box among the papers in front of him, bit off the end, spat it over his shoulder, and crushed out the old one under his boot.

'I spent nearly ten years in those mountains in the south – living like a wild dog, fighting like a wild dog. And this Ramonista bitch thinks she can just walk into Montecristo and be greeted by the populace as if it was the return of the Virgin Mary?' His black eyes had grown bright and hot. 'Tell me, who does she have with her? Who are the brains and muscles behind this operation?'

'Until two days ago, Comrade President, the commander-in-chief was an old Englishman – one of the most famous spies of the last World War. But he disappeared the day before yesterday – he was on a flight over the beach to the south, and the plane never returned. He was the only serious soldier among them. The second-in-command after him is a Frenchman – an old Army man, very stiff and correct, but not impressive as a leader. The rest are riff-raff – exiles and Ramonista filth recruited from the bars and back-streets of Bogota, Caracas and Mexico City.

'Oh yes,' he added, 'and there is also a little fat fellow whom I have heard called General Romolo – though he is not a general in command of the operation.'

Gallo stiffened. 'Romolo? *General* Romolo? And did he sail with the invasion-force?'

The big man's shoulders began to heave with pleasure. 'Hijo de puta! For twenty years now I have prayed to get my hands on that pig – to be with him for just half an hour! He killed my brother-in-law and sent my sister his testicles, all nicely wrapped up with a greetings card – greetings from General Romolo, on behalf of his Special Police.' He sat for a moment stroking his thick black beard. 'Tell me something else, Sanchez. What makes this woman and her band of scum so confident? That old bastard Ramon is dead. And although there are people still foolish enough to believe in his Fascist legend, can that whore of a widow of his really turn that legend into practical power?'

His visitor was again silent. The president took the cigar from his mouth, leant back and put both feet on the desk. He was wearing rubber-soled combat-boots, Chinese People's Army issue. Everything about him, from his ideology to his costume, was borrowed from abroad. Only the green cigars were native to the Island.

He smoked and watched the young man and waited. He had discounted the other's silence as being due to nervousness, and was beginning to find it offensive.

Señor Fraga de Sanchez, alias Dr Miguel Lopez, and known to the world as Pedro, spoke at last, in a soft, passionless monotone:

'A week ago, before I left England, I and a couple of La Vuelva's gorillas broke into a secret scientific establishment in the country. The place is reputed to experiment, among other things, in the production of toxic bacilli to be used in germ-warfare. While inside, I was able to steal six small metal capsules – each no larger, and very similar, to a soda-bulb – from the top-security wing. These are supposed to contain a concentrated gas infected with something called "snake-fever".' He gave the president a brief but graphic description of the alleged symptoms of the disease and of its after-effects. Gallo listened so intently that he allowed his cigar to go out.

Pedro went on: 'I gave the six cartridges to La Vuelva, who successfully smuggled them into Colombia.' He lowered his eyes, with a little smile. 'It is those six capsules, Comrade President, which have made her so confident.'

President Gallo took his feet off the desk and leant forward. He had begun to sweat. 'You are crazy, Sanchez. You think these things are toys. You hand them out to that mad widow so that she can play games with them? What are you going to give her next? A suitcase of plutonium? And why do you come to tell me all this? To take pleasure in seeing me scared?'

'Please, Comrade President, permit me to finish. The widow Ramon and her confidants believe these capsules to be lethal. They believe that they will destroy your Army, and, in the last resort, much of your population.'

Pedro paused dramatically. The only sound was the humming of the fan.

'Comrade President, let me reassure you. I have too much respect for you, and for your people, either to lie to you, or to put you and them at such dreadful risk. You have my solemn and absolute promise that even if this so-called weapon *is* used, it will be without effect. But in the meantime, it will have served you well.'

'Just tell me how?' Gallo's face was savage and the sweat glistened in his beard.

Pedro evaded the question. 'Comrade President, I would suggest that you may underestimate the potential threat of this Ramon woman, La Vuelva, and that of her following. That you underestimate the powerful influence still exercised by the dead Ramon. His widow is merely the reincarnation of that influence – but none the less dangerous for that.'

Gallo leant forward, still holding his dead cigar. 'Continue.'

Pedro pressed his soft finger-tips together and looked Gallo in the eye. 'Let us both admit that during his reign Ramon enjoyed wide support among the common people. And they regarded La Vuelva as their goddess. It is regrettable, Comrade President, but I believe that many of them still do.'

Gallo sat very still. 'They are simple, primitive people. Yet I fight to educate them. And I will also fight to defend them.' He had thrown down his cigar and now sat chewing a pencil. 'For simple people nothing is so impressive as power. That was Ramon's greatest attraction. By the same token there is nothing so undignified as defeat.

'And for that very reason, I propose to allow this whore-widow, La Vuelva, to indulge her cheap fantasies for a few hours, even a few days.

'I shall allow her to consolidate her bridge-head on the beach, with whatever local support she can get, and I shall even allow her to march north. And when I have decided that the time is right, I shall surround her, trap her, take her. Then, under the full glare of publicity, I shall show her for what she is. A failure. A cheap jumped-up international whore who has challenged our Socialist State and been found wanting. I shall then let the people judge.'

Pedro wetted his lips. 'May I venture to make a suggestion, Comrade President?'

Gallo stared back at him, saying nothing. Pedro cleared his throat. 'Nature has just played a cruel trick on your people, in the form of this earthquake. But such a natural catastrophe can still be put to positive advantage. While your towns lie devastated, and your Army selflessly strives to repair the damage and rescue the survivors, La Vuelva and her Fascist gang are attempting, with outrageous opportunism, to overthrow your regime.' He paused, with a modest smile.

Gallo lit a fresh cigar. 'I am not interested in lectures, Sanchez. Just what is it you wish to say?'

'Only, Comrade President, that when you have successfully crushed this invasion, you will be able to capitalize on much international sympathy – not only from your friends, but from many countries which are not normally well-disposed to your political system.'

Gallo slammed his huge hairy fist down on the desk. 'What the hell do you mean, young man? That I need the sympathy of my enemies? Do you think I need their love and respect, any more than I need their dirty dollars in aid? While I sit back on my haunches with my front paws in the air, waiting to be fed like some tame dog?'

Pedro's face remained bland and immobile. 'May I make one last observation, Comrade President? Your Army, as we all know, is fully extended in helping the Liberation movement in Africa. This operation is a worthy one, Comrade President, and it is greatly appreciated by your powerful friends, the Soviet Union. But I know that it is not popular with all your own people. I do not blame them. As you have correctly said, there is much education still to be done.'

Gallo blew smoke at the ceiling, but said nothing. Pedro went on:

'That Ramon woman has chosen her moment well, Comrade President. Or perhaps, rather, fate has chosen it for her. A surprise attack on the Island at this moment could cause us much mischief. A mere handful of men hiding up in the Hiarra mountains, with La Vuelva as their prophet, could well tie up a large proportion of your remaining troops.

'You must know the odds as well as anyone. When you started your campaign against Ramon, you had only thirty men and two girls. It was a long, long journey, but already it is one of the great classics of modern history.'

Gallo nodded. 'I was patient, Sanchez – I bided my time. But this La Vuelva woman is too greedy, too ambitious. Not for her a ten-year guerrilla struggle in the mountains. She wants nothing more or less than a swift and easy victory.' He leant forward again, measuring Pedro with his bright black stare. 'And that is precisely what I intend to give her – temporarily. There is nothing so sobering to an invading army as a false dawn.'

He suddenly smiled. 'Sanchez, you interest me. Tell me something. Why do you do it? Not for any love of me or my people – not because anyone pays you – not because you want to step into my boots, or anyone else's boots for that matter. You are not an idealist. You are a professional. But why do you do it? What do you want?'

'I wish to destroy the Capitalist system, Comrade President. I wish to destroy the rich, well-fed, powerful arrogance of the Western world. My opinions are perhaps old-fashioned, in these days of so-called *détente*, but I believe in the absolute destruction of existing society. I do not believe in change, in gradual reform – they are euphemisms for compromise, for doing nothing. The modern world moves too fast for such sophisms. Two thirds of the world do not have enough to eat, while the other third has too much. That is wrong.

'But how can such a wrong be made good? Even your own experiment in Socialism is constantly in peril. You lie too close to America. You are ever at the mercy of foreign reactionaries who wish to get their hands on your coffee, your tobacco – the staple luxuries of the West. In this case, it is La Vuelva and her cheap gang of desperadoes.'

Gallo stood up. 'We will see, Sanchez. We will see.' He came round the desk and shouted an order. The door was opened at once.

'One last thing,' he added, as Pedro prepared to leave. 'You and I, we have both taken many risks in our lives. But you take risks for their own sake. I do not distrust your sincerity, but you are like a gambler who plays more for the skill of the game than for money.

'I am more practical. That is why I am more powerful. When I take a risk, it is always a calculated risk, with a concrete objective in view. If I let La Vuelva march north, I shall do so for one reason. I will learn who my friends are, and who are my enemies. Salutations, Sanchez! And thank you for the information about the bacilli. I shall remember it.'

He did not shake hands.

The news of the invasion did not reach General Pallas, Commander of the Southern Zone, until nearly two hours after the PT-boat had hit the beach.

It was not until after midnight – more than three hours after the invasion – that he was able to establish a telephone-link with High Command in Montecristo. He received his orders direct from President Gallo himself: he was to abandon Carrudas, leaving only a skeleton-force to continue the salvage-work, take what armour was still in working order, and fall back north to Santiago y Maria. Here he was to take up positions outside the town and wait for reinforcements.

The general did not question these orders. He had no precise idea of how large the invasion force was, or what kind of weapons and equipment it carried. The situation on the Island was chaotic, and Pallas, never a bold or adventurous man, had heard that much of the Southern Zone was defecting to the enemy. He was glad to get into his staff-car and set off on the shattered, flooded, road north.

Behind him there followed, at a grindingly slow pace, an entire armoured column, including Soviet-built heavy T54 tanks, lighter T34s, a number of half-tracks and APCs, and a convoy of jeeps and troop-carrying trucks.

They left Carrudas shortly after two a.m., and hoped to be in Santiago y Maria by mid-day.

Colonel Ryan had met up with Task-Force *Belladonna* on the road beyond the mangroves, parallel with the beach. The half-track and the original convoy of trucks from Carrudas were with him; together with a mixed force of men and officers who had joined him over the last thirty-six hours before the invasion.

At first Ryan had been able to convince them of his authority as Colonel Macho de Rivera; but later, knowing that the pretence could not last much longer, he had relied entirely upon the letter from SACA.

Meanwhile, he had established a forward position in the derelict block-house, commanded by No-Entry, and bristling with fire-power. But all had now depended on how reliable that letter from SACA proved to be: and whether it really predicted a premature invasion.

Ryan, who had an innate faith in luck, decided to risk waiting until the following night. If Operation *Belladonna* had not struck by then, he would revert to his original plan. He and No-Entry had gone back and found the L-19 on that first morning, and refuelled it from the half-track. The Negro had made no complaint about not flying out there and then;

he had worked efficiently, in silence, respecting Ryan's nerve, while privately thinking him as crazy as a drunken polecat on Hallowe'en.

During that long hot first day more men had appeared on the road from Carrudas: but in ragged groups, mostly on foot this time, some without weapons, all without orders. Their only aim was to escape the havoc in the town, and the danger of more tremors. Their officers were all well below Ryan's assumed rank, which they did not question; and all proved utterly compliant to his command.

But by nightfall other, more senior men began to arrive – mostly by jeep, some by car. This time it was clear, as soon as Ryan produced the letter, that most of them were either already aware of its contents, or were at least in some way privy to the conspiracy. That night three officers came to him and identified themselves by the code-names 'Dog', 'Cow', and 'Fieldmouse' all mentioned by the mysterious SACA official who signed himself 'Zorro', the 'Fox'.

They did not even ask Ryan for his own credentials, apart from the letter, which apparently invested him with all the power and sanctity of La Vuelva's personal representative, and so ensured him of their unquestioning loyalty.

By the second day he had assembled a makeshift but adequate fighting battalion. He had been advised that a few of the officers might not be wholly reliable: either reluctant to commit themselves, or still faithful to President Gallo's Road to Socialism. These Ryan had temporarily confined to a camp on the beach beyond the mangroves opposite the block-house.

As soon as the invasion force was safely off the landing zone, and drawn up in platoons on the road, Ryan and Commandant Moulins held a long consultation. General Romolo, whose authority had been visibly reduced by the condition of his suit – now sodden and stinking after wading through the swamp – was excluded from the conference on the grounds that he was a policeman, not a tactician.

Ryan's plan was audacious but simple. Its essence was speed. He had seen from the map that there was a small road inland which by-passed Carrudas at the foot of the mountains. He proposed to take the two motor-cycles and a number of Russian-made jeeps, together with half the 105s and 122s from the block-house, and race north, round the ruined town, to cut off the road up to Santiago y Maria.

Moulins was to stay behind with the rest of the troops, the half-tracks and all the equipment. If they were unable to keep up radio-contact, the motor-cycles would be used for communication.

Ryan had had only a few hours in which to determine the varying virtues of the troops who had defected to his command. Although he could not be sure of them all, he had an instinct for the reliable, just as he did for the faint-hearted. He picked his men with care, often preferring the local troops to those from the landing-craft. In all cases he made certain that they had a healthy hatred for Fulgencio Gallo and all his works.

In the small hours he set out with a total of thirty men – including No-Entry Jones, Sebastian McIntyre Hausmann, and the wild young Cabo Fisco – in a convoy of eight jeeps, each one armed with a recoilless rifle and a rocket-launcher. Ryan rode in the first jeep, with No-Entry driving, while the two motor-cycles took up the rear.

There was no movement on the road, no traffic of any kind. As they made the detour round Carrudas they could see fires still burning in the town. Here the road became little more than a rough single track, but once inland Ryan's jeep set the pace, driving fast, even dangerously, since he knew that every minute counted.

Exactly seven hours and ten minutes after the invasion, Ryan's strike-force reached the fork that rejoined the coast road north to Santiago y Maria. It was again deserted in both directions. He called a halt and gave this orders.

The sun was coming up on Ryan's fourth day on the Island. He had eaten only combat-rations, and a little fruit; and slept in snatches of no more than a couple of hours at a time; and while he had been able to shave with Moulins' razor, he had not taken off his clothes since stripping Colonel Macho de Rivera of his uniform in the orange-groves outside Carrudas.

He was now lying in the long pampas grass, on a rocky shelf overlooking the fork with the coast road from Carrudas. The sun flashed off the sea, two miles away, with a grey glare. From time to time he sipped the tepid brackish water from his belt-canteen and scanned the horizon through a pair of powerful Russian binoculars. The road both north and south was still empty.

He had left Hausmann – who had been recommended

to him by Moulins – in charge of four men down at the junction with the main road. They had with them one jeep and were armed only with AK-47s. The rest of the force, together with all the heavy guns and rockets, was deployed along the rocky ridge some thirty feet above the junction; while the other seven jeeps and two motor-cycles had been left up the narrow track inland, out of sight of the road.

The position on the ridge had been well-chosen: it commanded a wide view in all three directions, while providing perfect cover.

Ryan had spread the men out in groups of four, over a distance of about fifty yards. The flank facing south towards Carrudas was commanded by Cabo Fisco – whom Ryan had again selected on the recommendation of Moulins, but with some misgivings this time. The boy seemed both too nonchalant and too excitable for Ryan's liking: but in the heat of battle such characteristics were preferable to caution or timidity.

He himself commanded the northern flank, where he most anticipated an attack. With him was No-Entry, in charge of the radio: one man with a recoilless rifle, another with a rocket; while Ryan was manning a 12.7 heavy machine-gun dismantled from the second half-track. Beside him lay a long belt of ammunition, coiled up like the gleaming spine of a deep-sea fish.

They had now been here for nearly three hours. The heat was beginning to rise, thick and sticky, out of the pampas grass, reflected off the bare rocks like oven plates. Several of the men had stripped off their tunics, even their shirts, and had tied handkerchiefs round their foreheads. Ryan did not object: their bedraggled, abandoned appearance seemed somehow in keeping with their mission.

As for himself, as he watched the sun climb higher and felt the sweat stinging his eyelids and soaking into the ridge of red-and-gold braid round the high collar of his Soviet-style tunic, he wished he too could tear off his uniform: but he feared that it might detract from his authority – or at least the appearance of authority.

Just after 10 a.m. No-Entry received a radio message from Commandant Moulins, at base-camp in the stinking blockhouse, informing them that there had still been no counter-attack against the invading force or the battalion of defectors.

This worried Ryan for two contradictory reasons. He could

not understand why Gallo was not using his Air Force. Unless the earthquake had disrupted or even destroyed every airfield, the dictator's first move – now that it was light – would be to dispatch at least reconnaissance planes; then, when he had their positions plotted, he could send in his air-strikes, complete with Russian air-to-ground missiles.

Ryan – like all soldiers who had been schooled in the arts of clandestine warfare – had a natural aversion to air-power. It seemed a mean, unimaginative, scientific way of fighting a war. You sat up there in your perspex bubble, guided by electronics, your weapons aimed by computer: and even while your victims were being shredded and roasted below, you were already far away, watching the radar, tuning in for the next invisible target.

At 10.25 a.m. they picked up another radio message, this time from Santiago y Maria. It was not even in code – just a simple call-signal to a convoy which was moving north from Carrudas towards Ryan's group.

The reply came back so clearly that the convoy could not have been more than a few miles away. It reported that one of their heavy T-54 tanks had broken down. Santiago y Maria answered with an order to bulldoze it off the road and make full speed ahead, irrespective of breakdowns.

Ryan turned to No-Entry. 'Stay on that wavelength.' As he spoke, he took the mouthpiece and spoke into it in Spanish: 'What is your exact position, and what are your orders?' – adding the call-signal which Santiago y Maria had used while addressing the convoy.

The reply came at once, without questions. The convoy was acting under the orders of the local Commander-in-Chief, General Pallas, that all surviving heavy armour from Carrudas was to withdraw north, in the defence of Santiago y Maria.

Ryan thanked them and went off the air. He knew their position and he had no intention of allowing them to pinpoint his.

As he turned from the radio he saw the tall, black-haired figure of Cabo Fisco dodging between the rocks towards them. The young man flung himself down in the grass beside him. 'Tanks! A whole sacred line of them! Big ones – T-54s' – he waved his long arm towards the road below, in the direction south – 'coming this way!'

Ryan nodded. 'I know. I've just spoken to them. But you

hold your fire. I want those boys on our side.'

Cabo Fisco gave him a sly white grin. 'And if they are not willing to come on our side? What then, Coronel?'

'Return to your position, Cabo, and await my orders.'

'God go with you,' the young man replied, and raised his fist in a mock Communist salute, then weaved his way back, his head down below the high grass and parapet of rocks.

A moment later Ryan heard the tanks: that familiar slow screaming clatter, with the engines whining and roaring as the tracks scrabbled to keep a level course on the loose dusty road. He raised the binoculars and adjusted them to the distance – just under a mile.

The big T-54s were out in front, with their hatches open, a couple of crewmen standing up in each, behind a heavy mounted machine-gun. The men in the first two turrets were not wearing the usual leather helmets with ear-flaps, but instead seemed to be taking the air, avoiding the heat and fumes inside. They were not ready for fighting: and they were not expecting to fight.

Yet as Ryan watched them come on, at no more than ten miles an hour, he was puzzled. The column did not look as though it were fleeing in disarray or panic. It was either regrouping or making an orderly withdrawal. But why?

It could only be that Gallo was pursuing a devious and dangerous strategy. For whatever else the man might be, he was certainly not a coward. Like Ryan, he would enjoy the challenge of ingenuity and adventure, rather than the tactics of formal warfare. In order to lure his enemy into the centre of the Island, he was withdrawing his armour north. What he did not know was that he now risked that armour.

Ryan watched the long pall of dust rising like a yellow smoke-screen along the bleached horizon. The column must have stretched back at least a mile. On and on it came, with a pounding and rumbling that rose to a slow crescendo through the still hot air, until Ryan could feel the beat of the massive engines through the vibrating rock under him, and smell the dust and exhaust-fumes, as he now turned the binoculars on to Sebastian McIntyre Hausmann and his four men below.

Through the glasses he watched the blond-bearded Hausmann get out of the jeep and begin to stroll down the middle of the road, straight into the path of the leading T-54. When the two were no more than fifty feet from each other, Hausmann raised his hand for the tank to halt. Ryan heard the pitch of the engine change.

He signalled to the man beside him, who tuned in the radio's UHF to the column's wavelength. A voice came on, ordering all vehicles to halt.

Hausmann had reached the first T-54 and was now talking to the two crewmen in the hatch. Then the radio came on again: 'Capitano, I am being ordered to leave the main road and to take the short-cut via Benisalem to Santiago y Maria. The officer says he is acting on the authority of SACA.'

A voice came back, brisk, self-confident – a young voice that Ryan and No-Entry recognized, even over the muted crackle of the UHF: 'This is Capitano Monica to all troops. The column will proceed as ordered. Disregard all instructions, except those from General Pallas and myself. And detain this officer for questioning.'

What happened next was very swift, as though part of a well-rehearsed operation. The six men in the three leading tanks leapt down and surrounded Hausmann; while two more from inside each tank bobbed up in their place, manning the heavy machine-guns in the turrets.

Hausmann grabbed at his AK-47, just as three of the men thrust hand-guns to his head. A fourth removed his machine-pistol, and a fifth stood back and kicked him in the groin. Ryan watched his long body twist round and lie writhing in the dust, his knees drawn up level with his beard.

Ryan leant out and took the R/T transmitter. He said, 'Capitano Monica, it requires no courage to kick a man in the *cojones*. Your column is fully covered. If you attempt to break out, we shall destroy each of your vehicles one by one. Your T-54s are too heavy for the mangrove swamp. They will sink. If you try and turn round on this side of the road, you will be in our direct line of fire. I await your decision.'

There was a crackle of static, then Captain Monica's voice: 'Who are you? On whose orders are you acting?' He still sounded calm, but there was now a note of hesitation. Ryan guessed that he could not believe the rebel force had penetrated this far north.

He answered slowly and deliberately: 'I am acting on the direct authority of SACA headquarters in Montecristo. The man you have so brutally assaulted carries a letter to prove this. I give you exactly sixty seconds to read the letter and comply with its contents.'

He next instructed the man beside him to aim the long silver tube of the 122mm rocket at the third tank in the column. He wanted to avoid killing Hausmann, who still lay hunched on all fours, vomiting in the dust.

Captain Monica's voice came back, issuing rapid orders to search the man, and Ryan watched through the glasses as they found the letter. As they did so, Captain Monica's slim figure appeared in the turret of the third tank. He jumped down, walked towards the group round Hausmann – whose inert body was still being covered by three guns – read the letter, then turned and said something to the crew of the first tank.

He was still speaking when the hot sluggish air was shattered by the shrieking roar of gunfire. It came from about fifty feet away, to Ryan's right, and for a few seconds it deadened his ear-drums. On the road below he saw Captain Monica leap backwards, as though he had been given a tremendous jerk from behind. His body slammed against the leading tank, then sagged down with his head caught among the heavy runners of the tracks.

Ryan swore foully. He and No-Entry looked in the direction of Cabo Fisco. The young man lay splayed out behind his smoking 12.7 machine-gun, grinning. 'The mad bastard,' Ryan muttered: 'they'll have our positions in a couple of minutes!' He glanced at No-Entry and nodded: 'All right, let them have it! You take the men – I'll get the third tank. And careful you don't hit that poor sod Hausmann.' Then he yelled the order to fire, in Spanish.

Once more the air burst round him like a paper bag. No-Entry's fire was economical and accurate: his own 12.7mm ripped through the bodies of the men below, tearing their limbs, exploding into the hull of the leading tank with a whining clang and splashes of bluish-green sparks, as the metal casing shredded off the shells like strips of banana peel.

The man beside Ryan lined up the sights of the long, light rocket-launcher, aiming just below the turret of the third tank, close to where the spare drums of fuel were strapped to the side. As he pulled the trigger Ryan felt the hot roar of flame over his shoulder, with a low ear-cracking howl, and a white-streak that arced elegantly down towards the road, ending in a shuddering crack.

The tank juddered, then appeared to leap into the air, its steel hull crumpled, its turret lifted off, then the whole thing disappeared into a boiling mass of orange flame, swelling up like a giant cauliflower under a blanket of oily black smoke.

Ryan could see the other turrets slamming shut. The man beside him had the R/T still tuned in, but no further orders came through. On Ryan's orders the man swiftly reloaded the 122mm rocket-launcher, careful not to burn himself on the searing hot metal. He now aimed at the sixth tank and hit it in the middle of its tracks. This time it lurched over, but did not explode.

The entire contingent now opened up together. Ryan was relieved – as well as slightly dismayed – at the eagerness with which they applied themselves to the task of killing their own countrymen. He could even hear them shouting and laughing as they watched the results of their fire, with the 105s and 12.7s drilling into the steel frames below, slicing down the crews as they tried to flee through the turrets before the fuel-tanks exploded.

Ryan had difficulty ordering them to hold their fire; and had to send No-Entry in person to curb the enthusiasm of Cabo Fisco. When it was all over he spoke into the R/T: 'This is Coronel Macho de Rivera. Your commander, Capitano Monica, has been foolish enough to disregard my orders. If you refuse to obey these orders and turn off the road, we will continue to destroy your entire column.'

As he finished speaking, No-Entry's dark fingers gripped his wrist, while his other hand pointed down at the road. The turret of the fourth T-54 in the line – still almost completely hidden by the smoke from the third tank – had begun to move, its long deadly gun swivelling upwards, pointing almost exactly at Ryan's position. He guessed that they had some special heat-seeking device that could track down the 122s.

The man with the rocket-launcher fired a fraction of a second before the gunner in the tank. The two explosions were simultaneous.

Ryan felt the earth disappear beneath him; the sun went dark, and his face and body were pummelled and lashed by flying earth and shards of rock. At first he could not breathe.

There was blood on his face and hands, and he could hear a whimpering close by.

Instinctively he reached out and felt a body lying across his ankles. No-Entry was huddled over the remains of the radio-set, scarcely breathing, while the rock and pampas under him were wet with blood. The man with the rocket-launcher was dead.

Ryan muttered half to himself in English: 'If that's what they want, that's what they're going to get.' He climbed to his feet and stumbled, still half-dazed, down the line of troops to his right, towards the flank held by Cabo Fisco. The men here were armed with more 122s. He shouted in Spanish, 'Take out every other tank in the line! Aim for the tracks or the fuel-tanks' – he broke off, with a spasm of coughing – 'and make it quick – before they get a fix on our position!'

Cabo Fisco looked up from his gun, leering brightly. 'You see how I killed that bastard officer, mi Coronel?'

Ryan blinked down at him, controlling his temper. If the young man had held his fire, as he had been ordered to, there might still have been a chance to bluff their way out and avoid this butchery. He said, 'I'll deal with you later, Cabo.'

But his words were lost in the roar of one of the rockets, followed a second later by another – then the double crack and boom as the first and fifth tanks went up in balls of flame.

He dodged back under the rocks, where the men had opened up again with an unbroken barrage of fire, smashing the bodies of the tank-crews as they struggled up out of the hatches, and tried to leap to safety. He reached No-Entry and rolled him gently on to his back. The Negro was half-conscious, bleeding heavily from the head. Ryan bathed it with water from his canteen, then tied the wound up with a handkerchief. The shell must have exploded a few feet below them.

He lifted the binoculars, which had somehow escaped damage, and examined the scene below. It was almost entirely blotted out by smoke and dust. At least six tanks were now on fire, and several others had been crippled; while the ones further back in the column were trying to shunt themselves round and head off the road towards the mountains.

But the going was bad, broken up by small precipices and shoulders of rock, impassable even for a T-54. Several of the smaller tanks and half-tracks were trying to break out through the swamp, but the two rockets on Cabo Fisco's flank were keeping up a deadly fire, picking off every other vehicle one by one, as Ryan had ordered.

It was a massacre. The smell of roasting flesh now reached him, cloying and bitter sweet, clinging to his nostrils and bringing up the bile in his throat. He looked round and saw Sebastian McIntyre Hausmann limping up towards him between the rocks. His face was taut with pain. For a moment Ryan had forgotten both him and his colleagues in the jeep below.

For some reason the tank crews also seemed to have forgotten them, or at least had done nothing to try and stop them. The jeep, as well as the two valuable motor-cycles, had been able to retreat, and were now parked under the rocks, out of the line of fire from the column. Ryan ordered Hausmann to fetch a first-aid kit and see to No-Entry's head.

The fight had been going on for less than ten minutes when Ryan noticed a man running out of the smoke towards them. He was waving a piece of white cloth. Through the binoculars Ryan saw that it was his underpants.

'Hold your fire!' Ryan yelled – but it was hopeless against the appalling din. He had to run down the line on both sides, ordering the men individually to stop shooting.

By a happy chance the man with the underpants was not hit, and was able to reach the head of the column, next to the first burnt-out tank, where he now stood waving his pitiful flag of truce and shouting frantically. Ryan could just make out the words, 'Rendamos! Sin condiciones!' Without showing his head Ryan shouted back, 'Tell all the crews to dismount! Any tank that moves will be instantly destroyed! Entiene?'

'Entendo!' the man's voice came back – a thin cry above the crackle of flames, almost inaudible to Ryan's numbed eardrums.

During the next sixty seconds at least a hundred men climbed down and began walking slowly towards the rocks, most of them with their hands on their heads. Ryan turned and called to his own men: 'I am going down to talk to them. You will cover me, but under no circumstances are you to fire unless I give you the signal – which will be a raised arm.'

He stood up, wiping the dust and No-Entry's blood from his face and tunic; and with the Stechkin 9mm pistol in his hand climbed down the rocks to where Hausmann, in one of the jeeps, was bathing No-Entry's wounds. Despite his own damaged groin, and with his face still white with pain, Hausmann had carried the Negro the whole way down, unhelped.

Ryan thanked him, then said: 'You didn't by any chance get the letter back?'

Hausmann shook his head. He spoke with difficulty, wincing with every word: 'I gave it to that officer. There won't be much left of it now.'

Ryan turned, scowling. There would be time enough to settle accounts with young Cabo Fisco. The boy might be brave and passionately motivated, but Ryan knew there was no one so menacing to any disciplined unit as a trigger-happy soldier.

He reached the head of the burning column, and for a moment nearly vomited with the smell. The troops looked exhausted, terrified. Several of them saluted uneasily when they saw his uniform. He returned their salutes and called: 'Who is now in command?'

Several of them replied, 'Capitano Monica, mi Coronel!'

'The Capitano is dead. Who is next in rank?'

A burly man with a black beard stepped forward. 'I am, mi Coronel. Teniente Martinez, at your disposal.'

Ryan looked at him dubiously, wondering if – as with the two SACA men on the motor-cycles – a beard were some political token worn by officers who had special status in the regime. 'My colleague here – the one your men attacked – handed Capitano Monica a letter. Unfortunately, that letter has been destroyed.' He nodded sideways, down at the charred and shrunken remains of Capitano Monica where they lay congealed between the blackened tracks of the leading tank.

'That letter,' he went on, 'was an official authorization from SACA headquarters in Montecristo. It endowed me with full command over the whole zone. My men will now join your column and replace those crews who have perished. You will then carry out my instructions without question. I order this column – those vehicles which are still able to move – to follow my jeeps to Santiago y Maria. And there is to be absolute radio silence.' As he finished speaking, his eyes moved from the bearded man, across the lines of dusty haggard faces in front of him. Almost all of them lowered their eyes in time to avoid his stare.

'Soldiers of the Republic!' he said, raising his voice now so that the whole column could hear: 'As you may know, during the night a landing was made by patriotic forces on the coast south of Carrudas. This landing is part of a consolidated plan to liberate the Island from the tyranny of Gallo and his Russian masters. The invasion is led by La Doña La Vuelva – beloved widow of the late President Ramon—' There was a slow murmur among the men; and Ryan guessed that even the younger ones were well versed in the Ramonista legend.

He raised his hand for quiet. 'We are the spearhead of La Vuelva's forces. Every man among you who joins us will join in one of the most glorious moments in your Island's history. But any man who stands aside will be against us, and will suffer the consequences. Choose now. Your country's future depends upon you.'

There was another, louder murmur across the massed ranks. Many of the men glanced nervously at one another, each waiting for the other to respond first. A few looked genuinely enthused; some even raised a small cheer, which was taken up by others: 'Viva La Vuelva! Abajo el Gallo!'

Ryan turned to the bearded lieutenant and looked hard at him, waiting for his reply. When none came, Ryan's hand tightened round his Stechkin.

The lieutenant spoke at last. 'With respect, many of our men have died on your orders. I therefore request that you prove your identity.'

At that moment Ryan was aware of the tall lean figure of Cabo Fisco at his side. The young man had slunk up without a sound and stood smiling insolently at the bearded lieutenant. He had left his 12.7 up on the ridge, and appeared – to Ryan's relief – to be unarmed. 'What the devil are you doing down here?' Ryan roared: 'Get back to your post!'

The young man put his head on one side and went on smiling. In the dead stillness the only sound was the faint crackle of flames. Cabo Fisco licked his lips and spat on the scorched hull of the leading tank, where the gob sizzled for a moment and was gone. 'Mi Coronel,' he said at last, 'it seems that the Teniente here questions your loyalty? We cannot afford such dissension in our ranks.'

'Who is in command here, Cabo? You or I?' This time Ryan's voice was menacingly low, and the smile went rigid on the young man's dark face.

'I ask pardon, mi Coronel. But in these times one must be vigilant. I request a favour.'

'So?'

'That for reasons of security, you permit me to ride in the same tank as the teniente.'

The bearded lieutenant squared his shoulders. 'Mi Coronel, I do not accept orders from inferior ranks. I will obey you, but you only.' The suspicion had gone from his voice, and his next words sounded anxious: 'You have my word, mi Coronel – on behalf of the troops here – that you can depend on us.'

Ryan nodded. 'I have given you my instructions, Teniente. Order the men to remount. Cabo, you will accompany me.'

As he walked away, with Cabo Fisco sauntering at his heels, Ryan felt an immense relief. It would have been no part of his plan to have had to massacre the whole remaining force where they stood. Besides, he needed their armour; he also needed their trained crews.

CHAPTER SEVEN

A Touch of Triumph

La Vuelva sat in her suite on the third floor of the Hotel Prado in Barranquilla, drinking champagne and listening to the radio.

She was alone, dressed only in a pair of narrow lace underpants. On the floor were two bottles – of the best vintage the hotel could provide. She had eaten a small salad for lunch, and was now feeling drowsy. Her initial excitement at the news that morning had been blighted by maudlin doubts. She hated being alone; above all, she hated having to wait alone.

Colonel Ryan was gone, stupidly lost in an aeroplane – drowned, crashed, perhaps even made prisoner on the Island. In which case they would have probably shot him by now. She felt enraged and bitter: she had paid him 250,000 US dollars, and now he was lost to her. Lost to the whole operation. Useless. She wondered how difficult it would be to block the cheque? She could cable her bank in Zurich, but it would be too late. And at any moment the telephone might ring: her man at the airport, telling her that the twin-engined Piper Comanche was waiting, ready to fly her to Santiago y Maria, or even to Montecristo itself.

Yet the same nagging thought kept returning. Her commander-in-chief was gone. Disappeared with some American Black, in a tiny plane made of paper, and she would never see him again. The possibility that he had cashed her cheque and then vanished – to Jamaica, or to some Mexican pleasure-palace – was too humiliating for her to contemplate.

She emptied the second bottle of champagne and drained the glass. The atmosphere in the room was clammy and oppressive. She opened the french-windows and let in the late afternoon breeze, which smelt of salt and fish and petrol-fumes. Outside, it was very noisy.

She stood up, stepped clumsily out of her pants, and went into the big tiled bathroom where she gave a start of horror.

In the bidet lay a spider the size of her hand. She hastily pulled on a silk housecoat and rang for room-service.

A young mulatto in a white uniform knocked and entered timidly. She shouted at him, wild-eyed, pointing towards the bathroom. He went nervously to the door; there was a pause while he gathered up a towel, then a series of smacks from his sandal. He came out again, grinning sheepishly and holding the rolled-up towel with both hands. 'It was a common spider, Señora. It was not dangerous.'

'Get it out of here!' She waited until the door had closed then rang down to the bar, ordered another bottle of champagne, called Reception and again asked if there were any messages. The answer was the same.

In a spasm of panic she flung herself down on the bed, pressing her knuckles between her teeth, and broke into silent tearless sobbing. She was interrupted by the waiter who arrived with the champagne in a silver ice-bucket.

He opened it carefully. She stood in front of him, holding out her glass while he poured it full. He was a handsome boy, with pure Spanish looks – large eyes under long lashes, and a high Castillian nose.

For a moment she thought of walking over and locking the door. She was drunk enough, and lonely enough. But she knew how these encounters always ended. He would be hot-blooded and inexperienced, reaching his climax long before her; then there would be the furtive business of getting dressed, the muttered false gallantries as she saw him out, and that night, in a cantina, the chattering and sniggering with his young friends.

She was a proud woman; and she told herself – without humour or humility – that she was about to inherit a country of over six million inhabitants. She must suppress her coarser emotions, and wait instead for that phone call.

She sat down again and began to drink the champagne; but this time it tasted sour and cheap. She was beginning to sweat, yet kept shivering in the muggy breeze from the windows; and she could not bear to go into the bathroom again to take a shower, even to relieve herself.

At six o'clock she tuned in to Radio Jamaica. Almost the entire news bulletin was devoted to the invasion of the Island the night before, together with the aftermath of the earthquake.

The reports were still very confused.

The only official source remained Radio Nacional de Montecristo, which had announced at noon that a state of emergency had been declared throughout the Island. Great play was made of Imperialist foreign forces attacking the country in its gravest hour of need, while thousands still lay buried in the rubble of their homes, and every soldier, every able-bodied adult had bravely volunteered to help.

It was in this critical hour that the counter-revolutionary forces, with shameful cowardice, had chosen to strike. 'Let the world judge!' the announcer roared; and added, rather lamely, that the United Nations would also be asked to judge.

La Vuelva, her mind muddled with wine, was still able to glean from the reports one strong impression. There had still been no official announcement – not even a hint – that the invasion-force had been destroyed, or even contained. And its code name, *Belladonna*, was not mentioned – which probably meant that no prisoners had yet been taken.

The newsreader promised that if there were any immediate developments the programme would be interrupted at once.

La Vuelva had to wait nearly two hours for such developments. A reggae-band was cut off in mid-bar; then a tense voice: 'We have just heard that Santiago y Maria, the Island's second largest city, has fallen to the rebel forces who invaded last night. We have this news direct from Radio Santiago y Maria, which – according to the rebel spokesman – was captured an hour ago after only sporadic fighting. All reports indicate that Fulgencio Gallo's regime may be on the point of collapse. Whole units of the People's Army are said to be defecting to the rebel cause.

'According to the rebel spokesman, the widow of the late General Ramon – who is known as La Vuelva – is expected on the Island imminently to lead the rebellion. Keep tuned to this station for further reports—'

Three minutes later the telephone rang. She snatched it up in a hand damp but steady. A man's voice said in Spanish, 'I have received instructions direct by radio from General Romolo. He has been in contact with your Commander-in-Chief, the Englishman, the Coronel Ryan—'

'Ryan?'

'Si, Señora. He has been in radio-contact with the Coronel

from Santiago y Maria. His troops have captured the city.'

'I know. I heard it on the radio. So he is alive?' Her last words were faint and slightly slurred.

'According to General Romolo' – the voice at the other end sounded disconcerted – 'the Coronel has contacted Commandente Moulins and they have joined forces. No resistance is reported.'

She steadied herself against the chair. Still holding the glass of champagne in her free hand, she took a gulp from it before sitting down; then said, in a quiet, rigid voice:

'I will fly to Santiago y Maria tonight.'

The man replied cautiously, 'If I may suggest, Señora—'

'You will address me as Doña Presidente.'

'Doña Presidente – if I may suggest, it would be both wiser and safer for you to arrive tomorrow – in the late morning. Gallo's Air Force is reported to be close to mutiny, but at this moment your troops still do not have control of the sky. To fly there tonight could be unnecessarily dangerous.'

'I am not afraid of danger.'

'Claro, Doña Presidente! But there is another reason. The Coronel Ryan will need time to prepare the populace for your arrival. I suggest that if you wish to make the maximum impact, you would do better to delay your departure until early tomorrow morning. If the weather conditions are good, the trip should last no more than three hours. I suggest I collect you at the hotel at 6 a.m. We can be in Santiago y Maria well before noon.'

'So be it. When you speak to General Romolo, convey to him my salutations to all who have taken part in this historic operation to liberate our country. Tell them that I and God go with them.'

She had deliberately not mentioned Ryan. His success had both sobered and thrilled her: yet in a perverse way it also exasperated her. She had waited so long for her return to triumph, and now she was in danger of having Ryan steal all the glory.

She replaced the phone and sat completely straight, not moving. She was thinking of Ryan. She thought of him without shame, without regret. He fascinated her, with a compulsion which she found both daunting and irritating. It was not so much his physical presence which attracted her, as his elusive strength – a strength which had now been translated into an apparently brilliant military victory. He seemed indestructible: and she realized, with some dismay, that he was the first man since her husband's death who had not bored her.

Ryan sat behind the open shutters, high above the crowds in the Plaza del Popolo. He was exhausted yet exhilarated, his mind and body impelled by the swift and bloody events of the day.

Now, as the grey tropical twilight fell over the square and the massed crowds below, his head was aching from the mighty din of bells – a hideous, clanging cacophony which had started nearly two hours ago and had continued, uninterrupted, from every belfry in the city. For exactly what purpose, Ryan still did not know. Some said it was to welcome the liberating forces; others, that it was to warn against the perils of the invasion; yet others, that it was a plea to the Almighty not to punish the Island with more earthquakes.

Since early afternoon every shop, and the few remaining cafés and restaurants, had been closed, locked and shuttered. Ryan had eaten some cheese and a hunk of smoked pork, which one of his officers had managed to scrounge from the kitchens of the Hotel Fenix; while someone else – a mournful man who had wept on his shoulder when Ryan had arrived on the steps of the Ayuntamiento – the City Hall – had brought him a pot of coffee and a bottle of white rum.

Racked with hunger and lack of sleep, maddened by the bells, and beset by a growing volume of problems and doubts, he had broken his own first rule of the campaign, and drunk half the bottle, laced with the foul muddy coffee.

He was seated behind the side-window on the top floor of the Ayuntamiento – a fine, Spanish-baroque edifice whose marble façade still bore the pitted wounds and scars of two centuries of revolutions, coups, civil wars.

For the moment he was alone. The door was guarded by two trusted young soldiers from the original Operation *Belladonna*: while other soldiers and officers, some of them from Guajira, others who had been tested and had proved themselves during the day, were posted throughout the building, on the stairs, at very door, in the busy hallway and on the steps outside.

The mayor and his staff had fled; so, too, had the general in command, with most of his officers. The problem now was not so much the consolidation of power as the need to restore normality to the city. Essential services had either been cut or suspended; even the lights down in the square had failed to come on. The telephone exchange had been sabotaged, but the radio-station had been taken almost intact. The most serious hazard was a breakdown in the water-supply, with its risk of epidemics, and the distribution of food.

Ryan knew that he could depend on a few hours – perhaps even a whole night – of initial euphoria, before law and order began to break down. Shops would be looted, liquor stores broken into; then would come the ugly, frenzied hour of reckoning and retribution.

He had already had a glimpse of this a couple of hours earlier, when the local SACA headquarters had been sacked and set on fire, with the help of the spare fuel tanks off one of the T-54s. Five men had been burnt to death, and two others – including one who had leaped out of a second floor window and smashed both his legs – had been hanged by their belts from two palm trees. Ryan could still see their Russian-style boots dangling and twitching, and their bloated tongues, like liver-sausages, lolling out over their black beards.

Ryan had been mildly disgusted, but not angered: he remembered that he was a mercenary: with no ties with the Island: no loyalty to it, no love for its people. He had been merely paid to do a job, and do it he would, if not with patriotic fervour, at least with diligence and a proper sense of of duty.

So far things had gone well – perhaps too well. His ragged army had entered the city from the direction of the mountains, taken the local garrison totally unawares and met with little resistance. Most of Gallo's troops, as he had calculated, were deployed on the road south, or engaged in salvage-work after the earthquake and tidal-wave – both of which had missed Santiago y Maria itself.

Ryan believed in good luck as an essential military requisite; while bad luck was something for which one had to compensate. Too much bad luck could destroy even the mightiest commander, as it had done with Napoleon at Waterloo. But too much good luck was another matter altogether. Ryan was not yet worried or suspicious of it; but he was conscious of it, like grit in one's shoe.

The people in the square below were now linking arms and singing. Ryan caught the obscene phrases of some ballad in which Gallo's name occurred in every verse. Others had set up a slow hand-clap and were chanting, 'Tomorrow we march on Montecristo! Death to the Moscow Puppet!'

There were few women or girls in the crowd. Most of them filled the windows and balconies round the square. Occasionally one of them would wave a handkerchief, or a red and green flag with the starred emblem of the Gallo regime cut out of the corner. But most were content to watch, silent and wary.

Ryan's own supporters, who formed the central mass below, were not an altogether encouraging sight. From time to time one of them would fire a pistol or a burst from an automatic rifle above the heads of the crowd, and send the old women scuttling back from the windows and off the balconies.

Ryan looked at his watch. In half an hour's time he had an appointment to receive a number of middle-ranking officials and civil servants who had either decided, or been obliged, to remain behind when his armoured column had broken into the city in mid-afternoon.

He had also arranged, an hour later, to meet with all local Army officers who had stayed, as well as with his own immediate staff. This was headed by No-Entry Jones, who – while they awaited the arrival of Commandant Moulins from the south – was the most senior officer after Ryan.

He had also picked the inscrutable Sebastian McIntyre Hausmann, together with six members of the tank crews who had all impressed him during the day with their enthusiasm and loyalty; and had retained, with some doubts, the services of Cabo Fisco, whose fervour, Ryan hoped, might compensate for his ill-discipline.

He had drunk all the coffee and half the rum when there was a knock on the door. He looked at his watch. The city officials were not due for another ten minutes. He tucked the rum bottle behind the curtain, stood up and called for them to enter. The tall mahogany door opened. No-Entry Jones stood just inside, dressed in a freshly-laundered uniform, his head bound up in a white bandage like a turban. There was something faintly comic about his appearance which Ryan hoped would not be contagious.

'Colonel, there's a young guy downstairs who claims he's a close friend o' yours. Won't give his name, but says it's important. And he ain't armed.'

'Show him up.'

No-Entry withdrew. A moment later Pedro came in. He was wearing rubber-soled mocassins and a bright blue suit that matched his blue-tinted glasses, and carried a briefcase.

'Felicitaciones, mi Coronel! Today you have written a page in the history books. Perhaps several pages.' He stood with his manicured hand held out. Ryan refused to take it.

'Hello, Pedro. And when did you come crawling back? In time to choose which way it goes, eh, before you jump?'

The young man sat down on a Louis Quinze sofa, crossed his legs and lit a French cigarette. 'I am sorry you do not understand, Colonel' – he now spoke in English, like Ryan – 'but whatever the fashionable theorists may say, revolutions do not come uniquely out of the barrel of a gun. What you and your colleagues have achieved in the last few days – particularly today – has been remarkable. But while you, Colonel, win all the glory and take all the prizes, there must be others who work in the background. There are many things still to be done – to prepare for La Vuelva's return, for instance.'

'Where is she now?'

'In her hotel in Barranquilla.' Pedro looked at his watch. 'Precisely forty minutes ago she received a telephone call from one of her agents in Colombia. This man also happens to work for me. He informs me that she plans to fly from Barranquilla early tomorrow morning to the military airfield outside here. I trust I can rely on you, Colonel, to see that all security measures are taken, and that full preparations are made for her arrival? She will speak, naturally, from the main balcony of this building. Her speech will be relayed over the radio, so that it can not only be heard throughout the Island, but by the whole world.'

He was interrupted by a huge howl from outside, drowning even the chaotic booming of bells. Ryan saw against the darkening sky the walls of the square lit up by burning torches and bonfires, around which a circle of men were leaping and dancing, holding on to each other's sashes or belts with one hand, waving their rifles in the air with the other. A voice was booming through a loudspeaker, the words echoing inarticulately off the houses. Then the chanting began again – this time with the steady beat of the words: 'Ra-Mon, La Vuel-Va!'

Pedro sat watching Ryan through a haze of cigarette smoke. 'The military perspective is a very narrow one, Colonel, while the scope and traditions of Latin American politics are very wide. May I be permitted to give you a piece of advice? Stick to military matters – that is where your talent lies, not in politics. If you try and involve yourself in the affairs of this Island, things will not end happily for you.'

Perhaps it was Ryan's empty stomach, his lack of sleep, or those bells: but for a second he had a mad urge to draw his Stechkin 9mm pistol and below a great hole in the plumb complacent body in front of him.

His jaw muscles stiffened. 'I am due in a few minutes to meet a delegation. Our aim is to draw up some plan to restore essential services and maintain law and order. But I don't suppose such details interest you? As you say, I am not concerned with your politics.

'You go and play whatever games you like. I shall attend to more mundane matters, like feeding the people, and seeing the sewers are working, and that the hospitals have electric light. I shall also try to win the war.' He nodded briskly. 'Now I have an appointment.'

Pedro did not move. 'Colonel, you have not asked me why I came here.'

'Why should I?'

'Because your time is valuable. So is mine.'

'Come to the point.'

'I have come to ask, Colonel, that a broadcast be made over the city radio. I have prepared the speech myself – it is quite short' – he had produced a sheet of paper from inside his jacket – 'though I do not propose to read it myself. My Brazilian accent, you understand? It would sound better coming from an official news-reader.' He stood up and handed the paper to Ryan.

It was a long typed text, full of technical details about the volcano, Monto Xatu. Ryan skimmed through it and gathered that it was a grave warning to the entire population of Montecristo, together with all outlying towns, that they were in imminent peril of being destroyed by burning gas which had been building up for days under the dormant crater.

He noted that there was no reference to the invasion, no mention of politics of any kind. He handed it back to Pedro. 'Is this authentic?'

'Of course not. I wrote it myself.'

'What guarantee do you have that anyone will take a blind bit of notice?'

'I have no guarantee. But as you know, several volcanoes have already erupted. And Monte Xatu has a terrible history. Besides, the people are ready to believe anything. Why should they not believe this?'

'And what's the purpose behind it? To spread gloom and despondency?'

The young man gave Ryan a half-sad, half-mocking smile. 'You are tired, Colonel, after your exertions.'

'Don't be impertinent.'

The smile remained on Pedro's smooth round features. 'The purpose is to have the capital evacuated. Drained of its life-blood, like Moscow before Napoleon.'

Another great howl came from the square below, and Ryan had to raise his voice: 'It is just that life-blood that we need! What chance do you think I would have stood today if it had not been for the collaboration of the local people? The officials and police would never have fled if they had thought the population was on their side. For Christ's sake, that's the whole point of having La Vuelva arrive tomorrow. So that we can provoke – in advance, if possible – a spontaneous uprising in the capital itself.'

Pedro put his head slightly to one side; his expression was serious again. 'Colonel, I fear that you do not understand the mood and sentiment of the Island's people.'

'I'm learning.'

'You do not understand that the people here – in the south – are poor, primitive. They are also very superstitious. It was from this area that Ramon drew his greatest support. His first wife, La Consuelita, came from this city, and the people still think of her as a saint. Many of them think the same of La Vuelva.

'But the people from Montecristo are different. They are better educated, more sophisticated, far more disciplined. They are also more prepared to listen to the Socialist doctrines of Gallo.'

Ryan nodded. 'I've always thought Socialism was a middle-class vice.'

Pedro ignored the remark. 'You would be making a serious mistake, Colonel, if you really believe you can take the capital with a single column of tanks and a few hundred ill-equipped troops. In Montecristo Gallo's Army and Police – above all, his Internal Security Troops, SACA – will stand and fight.'

'Maybe they will. Nor am I fool enough to risk taking on the hard-core of Gallo's Army in a deserted city where he'd have a free hand to wipe us out with superior weapons, and without the danger of harming the local population. Besides, I still believe we can draw support from that population. Gallo might have been a conquering hero once, but I certainly haven't got the impression that he's much loved any more.'

Pedro stood for a moment with his head tilted to one side, and waved the sheet of typed paper in front of him like a small fan. 'You forget one thing, Colonel. You forget that we have the ultimate weapon. We have enough poison bacilli with which to destroy Gallo's Army and Police five times over.'

There was a long pause, filled with the steady roaring and cheering and singing from outside: and again Ryan had an overwhelming urge to empty his pistol into the young man there and then. 'Where is it?' he said at last.

Pedro nodded at the briefcase on the floor. 'Do you want to see the stuff, Colonel?'

'How did you get hold of it?'

'I was given it – to give to you.'

'By La Vuelva?'

'But who else? She trusts me. She trusts us both.' He smiled. 'Do you want to have a look for yourself?' he repeated.

'I'll take your word for it,' Ryan said quietly. 'Do you know how to use it?'

'There should be no problems. A small time-bomb would be enough to destroy the casings. After that, it will simply be a matter of judging the direction of the wind.'

'And if the stuff blows back in our faces? What happens then, Pedro? Do we just lie down and watch our skins turn to scales, and die?'

'No, Colonel. You will take six of your best men, each with

a capsule wired to a stick of plastique, with a sufficient time-fuse, and send them into different areas of the capital. When they go off, your own troops need be nowhere near Montecristo.'

Ryan felt a sudden chill, although the room was still warm. He shivered. 'Leave them here, And also give me that radio text. I'll decide later whether it should go out or not.'

As he spoke he was aware that the noise from outside had changed. Instead of the singing and chanting, there again came that ugly swelling sound, louder this time, rising like a furious sea beneath the windows of the Ayuntamiento, swamping even the clang of church bells. Then a sharp rattle of gun-fire: screams; more shots, single ones this time; and the howl again, rising to a crescendo.

Ryan leant out between the shutters. Below, under the light of the torches and the bonfire, a broad space had been cleared in front of the steps. A number of troops were beating back the crowd with rifle-butts; while more troops, this time among the crowd, waved their rifles in the air and tried to press forward to break the cordon. In the space below the window lay three bodies. From what Ryan could see, they were all civilians.

He took out his Stechkin pistol, strode past Pedro and through the door, and ran towards the wide marble staircase, now lit by hurricane-lamps. He went down four steps at a time, waving the guards aside, reaching the mezzanine from where he saw a huge crowd gathered in the entrance hall. They swirled under the white glare of the lamps – some trying to get out, others fighting to get in.

Ryan noticed several men in dark suits, carrying briefcases, and obviously terrified. Through the entrance, between two stout marble pillars, there now appeared the ferocious face of Cabo Fisco; and behind him a gang of long-haired youths, some in grubby tunics, others in sweat-shirts, some bare to the waist with scarves knotted round their throats and tattered trousers rolled up to the knees. Some wore boots, some sandals, the rest had nothing on their feet at all.

They reminded Ryan of some awful animated painting of the French Revolution. With the time-table of history interrupted by this schism of national and political loyalties, the abscess, which had been growing in the body of the Island during the ten years of Gallo's bleak reign, had now burst:

and what Ryan was seeing was the pus flowing out, in the guise of this traditional and terrible mob.

He guessed at once what had happened. While he had been in closed session with Pedro the delegation of civic dignitaries had arrived. Ryan had no doubt that some, if not all, had thrown in their lot with the Gallo regime, or had at least passively complied with it. Cabo Fisco, who seemed to have already appointed himself unofficial witch-hunter for the rebellion, either knew the men by reputation or perhaps just by instinct. And men like Fisco did not believe in the balance of reasonable doubt.

Ryan reached the hallway a couple of seconds too late. The noise from the square was sliced by two bursts of machine-gun fire: and he saw the face of one of the civic officials disintegrate like a crushed fruit. Chips of marble flew off the pillars and balustrades up the stairs. More bullets flattened the dark suit of a second official who was knocked backwards, his spectacles falling off his nose as he sat down on the stairs, rolled over and died.

Ryan grabbed Cabo Fisco and spun him round, wrenching his long arm up behind his back until he yelled with pain. The young man was holding his AK-47 with his other arm, and now tried to swing it backwards, to hit Ryan over the head. Ryan held him locked with his left hand, raised the Stechkin and shot him at point-blank range through the back of the neck. He felt the boy's warm blood splash over his hand and face: the neck had been almost severed from the body. Ryan let him drop in an untidy heap at his feet, where he lay in a thick spreading pool that was almost black under the hurricane-lamps.

The rest of the gang had stopped in the doorway. Ryan shot the leading man in the stomach, and he went down screaming like a wounded dog. Only one of them made a move, swinging up his rifle from the waist, and Ryan shot his arm through at the elbow, where it dangled, blood-soaked and useless, in the sleeve of his olive-green shirt.

Ryan yelled: 'Drop all your guns!' They had already begun to back away, gaping, wide-eyed. There followed a clatter as they let their weapons fall on the steps.

Ryan blinked round him. He could feel Cabo Fisco's blood congealing in sticky trickles down his face and hands. His new colonel's tunic, with the red stars cut out of the epaulettes, was a mess. The three men in dark suits stared back at him, white-faced, shaking; one of them was muttering prayers over a crucifix.

Ryan nodded to them and gestured towards the stairs. This was not the time to offer condolences over their five dead colleagues. But at least he could offer them some rum before they got down to business.

Half-way up the stairs he met Pedro padding down. For all the young man's flair and audacity, there were clearly some situations which he preferred discreetly to avoid.

He stopped beside Ryan. 'Colonel,' he said softly in English, so the guards could not understand, 'I have left a copy of the broadcast and the six capsules on the desk in your room. Be careful with the capsules. It would be unfortunate if they fell into the wrong hands.'

'Don't tell me what to do! As for that poisonous shit up there, I'll decide what's done with it. And I alone. Now get out. Get out before I put a soft-nosed bullet through that psychotic brain of yours and do the whole world a service.'

Pedro shrugged, turned and walked on down the stairs. He did not look back and he did not hurry.

At 8.55 p.m. on the night following that of the invasion, President Fulgencio Gallo arrived at the National Radio and Television Centre in the modern grey-block suburb of Costelano, near the coast outside Montecristo.

As usual he rode in his old mud-coloured Land-Rover. It had been a present to him from a leading European ambassador during those first heady days after he had seized power from General Ramon, when he was still the bearded political pin-up boy of the Western world: particularly among the chic intelligentsia, in permanent need of a radical hero without too much blood on his hands.

In the early months of his reign, Gallo had seemed perfectly cast for such a role: the popular revolutionary who had purged his people of the base, corrupt and increasingly oppressive regime of Ramon and his gang, which had included the old general's second wife, La Vuelva.

But just as the experts and political analysts had never been able to decide whether Ramon himself had been a Fascist or a Socialist, so the same experts, who often advised Western governments, were still not agreed as to whether Gallo was a Marxist, Maoist, Agrarian Reformer, or red-blooded Stalinist.

It was indeed probable that Gallo himself did not know: or that he aspired to all four creeds at once, or alternatively, as the mood took him. He was a vainglorious and obstinate man; but he was not stupid, and in a crude immature way he was honest.

He had mortgaged his country's economy, his political independence, his own reputation to the whims and devices of the Kremlin. He had done it not only to buy insurance against the ring of potential enemies which surrounded the Island, but because he believed, with the unquestioning passion of a zealot, in the Soviet Socialist experiment. When tame critics inquired whether the Russian system of government was entirely appropriate to the needs of the Island, Gallo would slap his knee and say, 'My country has chosen its own Road to Socialism! The Soviet Union is simply supplying us with a means to travel that road.'

While Gallo believed in his life's mission – which happened to be inextricably tied up with the lives of six million of his compatriots – he was careless about his own personal security. Strangely, assassination did not worry him; he was a brave man, he was not frightened of death, and he saw the assassin's bullet or bomb as a further short-cut to immortality.

What he feared was disloyalty, treachery, a breaking of his own ranks. And deep inside him was a secret craving to be loved: to be respectable as well as respected, by all the nations and peoples of the world.

No one had ever asked their President and Revolutionary Leader why he still insisted on driving about in his old Land-Rover, which had no bullet-proof armour, not even self-sealing tyres. To his own Security men this vehicle was a constant grievance, even a source of panic; but Gallo clung to it perversely, because it was the last relic of that brief era, ten years ago, when he had enjoyed the favours and adulation of both East and West, as well as of the Third World.

He was like one of those tough but sentimental men who keep some special toy, carefully preserved, through their adult years. Gallo's Land-Rover was just such a toy.

The only protection he received was from the driver, who was armed with a hand-gun, and from his personal bodyguard who rode in the back with a machine-pistol; while two 'Cobra' outriders cleared the streets ahead with sirens, and a carload of plain-clothes police followed at a discreet distance.

The Radio and Television Centre was under heavy guard. Three companies of the crack Fifth Infantry – which had recently returned, much depleted, from Africa – were deployed around the main gate and other entrances; while inside, the civilian staff were pacing the hall with obvious agitation.

They had experienced many hundred of sessions with their president in front of the microphone and cameras, and knew that he always arrived with only a couple of minutes to spare. He would then speak for as long as he cared. He had once spoken for a total of nine hours, with two unscheduled breaks while he left the studio to relieve himself. But while his minions were used to his eccentric habits, they were never happy until they saw him step out of his Land-Rover, raising a clenched fist and biting off the end of a cigar.

Tonight he followed the same routine. He had memorized the few notes he had made on the back of an envelope, which was now in the button-down breast pocket of his tunic. In the other pocket he had five cigars, while his bodyguard kept an unopened box in reserve.

Except for the salutes, there were no formalities. Gallo led the way to the stairs – he never used lifts, which he despised as an indolent Western luxury – and reached the studio with thirty seconds to spare before the National Anthem went out.

As usual he refused any make-up, although tonight he looked pale and his eyes were puffed with tiredness. When his bodyguard – one of his closest confidantes – had discreetly remarked on it, Gallo replied, 'The people must see me as I am. I shall ask their pardon for my appearance, and tell them that in this hour of national crisis the Leader of the Revolution is the last man who can take time off to sleep.'

Sitting down on his familiar chair, under the tiny eye of the camera perched above him, he could see the programme controller and his assistant behind the sound-proofed window. The digital clock on the studio wall flicked to 9.00.

But instead of the first crashing bars of the National Anthem, Gallo saw a third man enter the glass-fronted cubicle opposite. He recognized a senior officer in his Security Forces. The man, who was in plain-clothes, was whispering intently to the controller.

Gallo stood up, strode to the door and entered the control-cabin. The officer had a thin grainy face behind dark glasses. 'Mi Presidente, I ask you to postpone your appearance for a quarter of an hour. This has just come in – from the Monitoring Service' – he handed Gallo a foolscap sheet of duplicated typing – 'ten minutes ago. It is from Radio Santiago y Maria.'

Gallo held the paper with both hands, turning his cigar round between his lips. 'So – tomorrow, before noon. I see.' His voice was quiet, almost with a note of pleasure.

'Mi Presidente, they must be crazy! Don't they know we have an Air Force? – one of the best in Latin America? Do they think our pilots will go running to join that ex-dancing girl and her scum from the south?'

Gallo crumpled the paper into his hip pocket. 'The broadcast said only that she will make her first public appearance tomorrow at noon in Santiago. There is no mention of her flying in.'

'Then she must be on the Island. In Santiago y Maria, or more likely in the mountains behind?'

'No,' said Gallo. 'I know that bitch – I understand her type and class too well. She will not risk her rich neck until she has smelt victory. Well, she will have smelt that victory this afternoon – even if it is a false victory. I also have other sources of information. La Vuelva will fly in either tonight or tomorrow morning.' He looked at the officer of Security. 'Have you communicated this information to anyone else?'

'No, mi Presidente.'

'See that the men at the Monitoring Service are held incommunicado. That goes for Rilla and Dominguin here' – he nodded at the two controllers – 'and make absolutely certain that our conversation is not repeated.'

The officer stared at him from behind his dark-glasses. Had his leader finally succumbed to fatigue and strain? 'Permit, mi Presidente – but that broadcast has already gone out. Half the Island will have heard it.'

'I know. But I want La Vuelva to land tomorrow on the Island. I want her to appear in Santiago y Maria. I shall be interested to see what reception she gets.' He turned to the controller: 'We will now continue.'

Twenty seconds later the light above the control-cabin turned red and President Fulencio Gallo was once again on the screen of the Island's single television network, as well as on Radio Nacional de Montecristo.

He crossed his legs, removed the cigar from his mouth, and began with his familiar, 'Companeros de la Revolution!' Yet those who saw him tonight, despite the acute drama of what he had to say, detected a weariness in his delivery. There were no endless platitudes about economic achievement and dubious collective harvests. Tonight their president was telling them about an invasion that had already swallowed, if not digested, a third of the Island.

Gallo was careful not to mention La Vuelva by name, or even the Ramonista Movement: but he did make it clear that in the next forty-eight hours – perhaps even sooner – the people would be called upon to come into the streets and show their true colours.

It was not one of Gallo's best speeches. It was also relatively short – only forty-two minutes. As he left the studio he was stopped by the same senior officer of Security. 'Mi Presidente, I have serious news. I did not wish to interrupt your broadcast – but this has just come in, again from the Monitoring Service.' He handed Gallo another sheet of duplicated paper.

The president read it, chewing the end of his fifth cigar. 'Was this being broadcast simultaneously with me?'

'Si, mi Presidente.'

Gallo gave a tired grin. 'Then it should be interesting to see which of us attracts the greatest audience – myself, who am here to save the people; or Monte Xatu, which we are told is here to destroy them.' He handed the paper back to the controller. 'Have this broadcast immediately on both the radio and television.'

The officer looked at him in astonishment. 'But this comes from the rebels, mi Presidente!'

'That's why I want it broadcast.' He slapped the man on the arm: 'You do not take me for a fool, do you? Remember – it is sometimes wise for the fox to run with the hunters. Goodnight, companeros!' He raised his clenched fist and marched out, down the stairs, where his bodyguard was waiting with the Land-Rover outside.

* * *

All evening Radio Santiago y Maria had been announcing the arrival tomorrow of La Vuelva. The news only increased the frenzied excitement of the crowds in the square – now re-named La Plaza de la Liberación.

These were the masses: the people baying for Freedom and Democracy. Ryan watched them cynically from the high window of his makeshift office, and reflected that if their gruesome passions, together with their numbers, could only be harnessed, he might have a chance of complete success.

Yet what he saw, under the flickering torch-light, was a rabble – an incoherent wastrel mob, howling outside his doors for the promised pleasure of usurping power and overthrowing the established order. For them freedom and democracy were words synonymous only with the portraits of Bolivar and Zapata in Government offices and on postage stamps.

For Ryan they meant almost as little: abstract virtues which provided him merely with the licence to lead his own life. But he had not been hired to lead the people to a new Eldorado. He was here to overthrow the Gallo regime. What happened after that was none of his business.

For the moment, his first duty was to restore the rule of law – another abstract for which, throughout his life, he had had little respect. If he had not been so exhausted he might have laughed. As it was he had talked to the surviving civic dignitaries, but they had proved a feeble trio, more in need of his help than able to help him.

He had then consulted his assembled officers, including those of the Army group who had remained behind. But here there had been little between the wild and the weak; there was either too much enthusiasm, as with the late Cabo Fisco, or the cringing indecision that characterized most of Gallo's officers who had changed sides.

Ryan was becoming increasingly impatient for the arrival of Commandant Moulins and his troops from the south. The Frenchman had been left behind, with the remains of the original force, in case Gallo tried a pincer-attack – perhaps even an airborne or amphibious landing – to cut off the southern zone of the Island. For Ryan knew, even at this hour of triumph, that any number of things could still happen; and in the event of a mass retreat, the PT-boats would be their only hope.

The airfield at Santiago y Maria had yielded a prize of five old MiG 21s, and two even older Tupolov transports; but the pilots had all fled; and there remained no one to handle them, except No-Entry Jones.

Five minutes after the conference with the officers had ended, Ryan was handed a message from the radio station. It read: '*A citizen calling himself Dr Miguel Lopez, who claimed to be acting on your orders, tonight requested a member of the radio staff to broadcast an urgent message concerning Monte Xatu. The broadcast went out at 2100 hours. Ends.*'

Ryan was furious, not so much at the fact that the false alert concerning the volcano had been broadcast without his final permission, as at himself, for not having shot down that vicious little sod while he'd still had the chance.

Instead he sat down and contemplated the six gun-metal capsules which Pedro had left on his desk; then he carefully picked each one up and tucked it behind the pelmet of the curtains.

Just after 1.00 a.m. he fell asleep, fully-clothed, with his boots still on, curled up on the Louis Quinze sofa. The church-bells had stopped at midnight, and he was able to sleep for two hours before the officer on guard woke him.

Commandant Moulins and his troops had arrived in the city.

Groggy and sore-eyed, Ryan sent out for coffee. The Frenchman was shown in – a slightly absurd figure in his polished black boots, flared khaki breeches, and a white turtle-neck sweater which he had obviously packed with some care among his kit before leaving. Around his beard he was carefully shaved and his short grey hair shone like moths' wings in the light of the hurricane-lamp.

'Good morning, Commandant.' Ryan handed him a cup of brown coffee smelling of burnt nutmeg.

'You've heard the news? La Vuelva's scheduled to arrive tomorrow morning. She'll be speaking from the balcony here at noon.'

The Frenchman stretched his legs and began filling his pipe. He spoke slowly, impersonally, as though addressing an audience of more than one: 'It would appear that things have gone remarkably well – so far, Colonel.'

Ryan yawned. 'You sound doubtful.'

'I was at Dien Bien Phu, remember?'

'I remember. But we're not fighting the Vietminh now, you know.'

'No, Colonel. But we are fighting a man who has learnt all his tricks of guerrilla warfare from that school.'

'What is your point, Commandant?'

The Frenchman re-crossed his legs and took a sip of coffee. 'My point, Colonel, is that I suspect Gallo of luring us into a trap. We would do far better to consolidate our position here in the south.'

'And wait for Gallo to consolidate himself too? He still has an air-force, remember.'

'Precisely. And you do not think it odd that he has not yet used it?'

For a moment Ryan was silent. He said at last, 'The Gallo regime is collapsing, Commandant. Meanwhile, until La Vuelva arrives, it is my duty – as her commanding officer – to draw whatever advantage I can from the military situation. And it is my considered judgement that the rest of the population will rise, as they have done here in Santiago y Maria. I would be criminally negligent if I held back at this stage. Some might even claim that I was a coward.'

The Frenchman sat sucking at his pipe. 'You are very confident, Colonel. Others might interpret your crime as being your decision to advance on the capital. You have not explained, for instance, why Gallo has so far put up only negligible resistance? In fact, he seems to have put up no resistance at all.'

Ryan ignored this last remark. He drank some coffee and said, 'What exact authority has La Vuelva? Does she have the power to overrule me?'

'She has the power to overrule all of us.'

'Very well. I state now, Commandant, that is is my resolved intention to march on Montecristo as soon as La Vuelva has established her presence here on the Island. If she opposes my decision, then I shall resign.'

'You would not leave the Island alive.'

Ryan grinned wearily. 'We shall see, Commandant. We shall see.'

CHAPTER EIGHT

The Widow Returns

The white and blue Piper Comanche came floating out of the cloudless sky at just after 10.30 a.m. It flew low, in a swooping, diagonal motion to avoid radar.

Whatever else Ryan thought of La Vuelva, he had to credit her with courage. He stood on the terrace of the small airport building, still dressed in his colonel's uniform of the People's Army with the regime's insignia removed, and watched the little plane flutter down and come riding round the empty tarmac.

High overhead No-Entry Jones also swept across the airport building, wiggling the wings of his solitary MiG 21. During the early hours he had mastered its controls and had been keeping a constant, lonely look-out since dawn.

Twenty feet away from the airport building, La Vuelva's plane slowed to a stop. Ryan and Moulins walked out to meet it. The door opened, a man in uniform jumped down, and a moment later La Vuelva appeared, dressed in quiet widow's black, exquisitely cut. She stepped up to Ryan and took his hand in a firm, small-boned grip. 'You have done well, Colonel. Very well.' Her voice betrayed not the least emotion, not a hint of intimacy.

He bowed and kissed two of her fingers. 'Your car awaits you, Doña Presidente. All preparations have been made. You will speak from the Ayuntamiento at noon. However, while I have done all I can to guarantee your security, I must emphasize that nothing in the present situation is secure.'

She made no remark until they had entered the large black car, chauffeured by one of the officers from the original invasion force, with a bodyguard in the front and back. There were no sirens, no flashing lights; and as yet no crowds, since the time and place of her arrival had been kept a close secret.

After a pause she lit one of her thin black cigars and spoke, in her elegant Spanish. 'What is your appraisal of the situation, Coronel?'

'It is mobile, Doña Presidente. I must speak frankly. All will depend upon the reception you receive at noon. If the people rally to you – and that includes the Army and the various police forces – then I consider we have a chance of success.'

'Only a chance?' Her face was pale behind the dark glasses. 'Why is there no one here to greet me?' she added, with a glance out at the empty waste of shanty-huts with their half-naked Indian children squatting in the dust, glancing big-eyed and indifferent as the cars passed.

'Doña Presidente, there will be plenty of people to greet you. But I must warn you again – things have moved so fast we have not yet been able to re-establish a stable situation. If there are enemies among the crowd, I cannot guarantee your complete safety.'

'Are you suggesting that I should cancel my speech?'

'Doña Presidente, your decisions from now on must be your own. I have, of course, my most reliable troops on duty, and we are taking every possible precaution.'

She sat back with her black-gloved hands folded in her lap. 'I have the backing of the people,' she said. 'They will ensure my safety.'

Ryan nodded, but said nothing.

They were now driving through the industrial suburbs of the city; small, cheap factories, built with Soviet aid; breeze-block tenements rising among ponds of dust, their walls sprouting lean-to shacks and chicken coops – the few mean concessions to free enterprise allowed under the Gallo regime.

To Ryan's relief, people were now beginning to appear on the streets. They were not so much enthusiastic as curious. They stood in their wretched clothes watching from under their sombreros, their dark faces revealing as little emotion as La Vuelva herself.

But as the cars approached the broad boulevards, with their palms and dead cafés, small cheering groups began to emerge; and by the time they entered the centre of the city, down the avenue that led to the Plaza de la Liberacion, there were crowds standing ten-deep on the pavements; and with an infectious enthusiasm that filled Ryan with both excitement and concern, the noise of the car's engine was drowned by their cheers and chants. At the entrance to the square his view was blocked by youths leaping on to the bonnet; others tried to drag the doors open, while groups of soldiers nervously beat them off with their rifle-butts.

They were fifty yards from the Ayuntiamiento when they were totally locked in by a shrieking mob. Ryan drew his pistol and forced the door open. The crowds were all round, howling and weeping with emotion, trying to fight past him to touch the woman whom they believed was about to bring them liberty.

A couple of soldiers with AK-47s were brutally beating back those nearest the car. Ryan saw the tall figure of Commandant Moulins struggling towards them. He himself was being forced back; as he put out his hand to fight off the crowds, he fired two shots in the air.

It was like the effect of Ephedrine on a choking asthmatic. The crush broke round him and the car was temporarily free.

He got back in and sat clasping La Vuelva's small gloved hand as the car nosed its way slowly up to the steps of the Ayuntamiento. As they got out a shield of weapons and sweaty uniforms closed over them like some evil-smelling umbrella.

Once past the door La Vuelva again appeared cool and relaxed. She allowed Moulins to kiss her hand, then Ryan led her up the three floors to where her rooms had already been prepared. He turned to her. 'Would you like to sleep a little? You have forty minutes before you are due to speak.'

'I am not tired.' She moved round the room like a cat inspecting new premises, but avoided going near the balcony.

'You have your speech prepared?' he said.

She looked at him disdainfully. 'I am not an amateur.'

Ryan bowed, kissed her hand again, and left her. He was relieved by her demeanour, but slightly troubled by the volatile crowd outside.

Downstairs he saw General Romolo entering the hallway. He was wearing a fresh black suit, and was surrounded by a dozen other men, similarly attired as though all in uniform. To Ryan they seemed to bring with them a stench of vicious privilege – of bribes and double-dealing, of the midnight knock, of naked cells and bright lights and rubber hoses.

He watched the general starting up the stairs, followed by his posse of short stout acolytes: and he wondered if they had been here throughout the whole decade of Gallo's rule, concealed in attics and cellars, to emerge now into the light of day, their eyes shielded by dark glasses, their suits mothballed like their bodies. Or was it more likely that for them a change of regime meant merely the changing of the photographs on their office walls?

Romolo and his men were now going to pay their respects to their new political mistress. A quarter of an hour later they had still not come down. Ryan decided to join them.

Security, he noted with satisfaction, was twice as rigorous as it had been last night. At least a hundred men were posted on the stairs and in the adjoining corridors.

When those outside La Vuelva's door saw him they came smartly to attention, smacking the skeleton-handled butts of their rifles. Ryan made a casual but interesting observation. Nowhere – neither among these troops nor anywhere in the crowds outside – was there a beard to be seen, although there had been plenty in evidence yesterday. For it is a lot easier, and a lot quicker, to shave a beard off than to grow one.

The door was opened by one of Romolo's henchmen. He stood aside and let Ryan in. As he did so, the room fell silent. La Vuelva had been talking on the sofa with the general. Both turned and stared at him from behind their dark glasses, without moving.

Ryan went over and kissed her hand yet again. 'You would not think it impertinent of me, Doña Presidente, if I was to stay while you deliver your speech?'

She nodded ambiguously. 'I regret that I cannot invite you to share the balcony with me. There are certain political considerations, certain conventions that have to be observed. It would be unfortunate at this stage of the Revolution if it were thought that the Ramonista Movement had to depend on foreigners for its leadership.' Her voice was steady and quite impersonal.

Ryan could not see the expression in her eyes; but he had already sensed her change of attitude towards him, and wondered if her last words had implied a deliberate snub, perhaps to impress General Romolo. Or whether she were merely asserting her new authority, magnified now by the trappings of imminent power. For the last thing she would want to be reminded of at this moment was that she had only recently been Ryan's client, under treatment for alcoholism, and later his floating bed mate.

He was determined to contain his annoyance; he steeled himself to smile down at her and said, with only a hint of irony:

'Of course, Doña Presidente!'

But his pride was not to be salvaged so easily. As he turned she added in the same clear voice, 'Coronel, please wait outside until I am due to speak. I have State business to discuss with these gentlemen – business of a confidential nature.'

'Of course, Doña Presidente,' he repeated, and walked with dignity from the room, watched by the dozen pairs of dark glasses.

There still remained fifteen minutes before the speech was scheduled to go out. He would pass the time making sure that the microphones and loudspeakers were in order, and that all arrangements had been made with the radio station. There was also the matter of the foreign press. Two chartered plane-loads of reporters and TV camera-men – one from Miami, another from Kingston – were expected at any moment.

Ryan would have liked to discuss with La Vuelva the most profitable way of handling them; but in his present mood he thought, What the hell? She could look after herself.

He reached the hallway just as No-Entry appeared, his lithe body zipped up in a silver-grey G-suit, his head still swathed in its turban of bandages. Behind him came Sebastian McIntyre Hausmann. Most of the officers around had put on clean uniforms and were freshly shaved; but Hausmann was conspicuously shabby and dishevelled, his reddish beard looking like a hunk of shredded wheat.

Ryan walked up to him, still smarting from his encounter with La Vuelva. 'Haven't you got any self-respect, man? By tonight you are going to be in the world's news. The least you can do is clean yourself up!'

Hausmann gave a broad shrug, but did not reply; and Ryan felt himself losing control. He was interrupted by No-Entry. 'The lady's got a mighty fine turnout – eh, Colonel? I damn near didn't get through from the airport.'

'It's a bloody mob. What I need from now on is an army – a decent army I can trust.'

The Negro smiled. 'They haven't done that badly so far, Colonel.'

'We'll see how well they make out when they start taking casualties.' Ryan glared again at Hausmann, but the man still appeared unmoved.

'And how is the Lady President?' No-Entry asked.

She's closeted upstairs with that General Romolo and his boys – apparently discussing "State secrets". Probably dividing up the spoils – before they've even got them – and arranging their Swiss bank accounts. They look a right gang of shits, I tell you. Revolutions in this part of the world may still be the stuff that dreams are made of – but they damn well don't lend themselves to ideals.'

'I guess you're right, Colonel. But then I never did believe in ideals – I just like to get my cheque at the end of the day.'

A moment later a great roar went up from outside, and a dozen loudspeakers began to blare out around the Plaza. Ryan waited until his watch said two minutes to mid-day, then walked back up to La Vuelva's room. The twelve black-suited men were now drawn up in two rows in front of the open french windows, just out of sight from the crowds. La Vuelva was out on the balcony, her hair shining in the sun. She lifted both arms and leaned forward, reaching out over the balustrade.

Below, at least fifty thousand faces were raised towards her. The noise was exhilarating, terrifying. She tried to speak, but even with the battery of loudspeakers her voice sounded shrill and feeble. The howling and cheering continued for three full minutes; and even when it subsided it left a febrile vacuum, an uneasy lull that might explode again at any moment.

'Compañeros!' she began – intentionally using Gallo's familiar form of address – 'Ten bitter years ago I promised you that I would return. Today I have kept my promise!'

The storm broke again, and for several more minutes she was unable to make herself heard. When she finally did, her voice was charged with increasing animation, rising even to passion – something that Ryan had not observed in her before.

It was not a particularly original speech, but it had a certain vulgar eloquence entirely appropriate to the occasion. She spoke for twenty minutes – about a third of which time was taken up with the cheering – and finished with the words, 'But the fight is not yet over. Much blood may yet have to be spilt. Let us ensure that it is not spilt in vain. But always remember – and I speak in the memory of my dear husband – that I am with you, every one of you, man, woman, and child. God go with you!'

This time the sound from the square reached the room with a physical force, and was sustained, as though by its own momentum, for over five minutes. Each time that it seemed about to slacken, a fresh roar of cheering would break loose, echoing round the tall square with the shattering boom of a tornado.

When it was at last spent – except for a few frenzied cries of 'Viva La Vuelva!' – she raised her arms in a final salute, wide above her head, then turned and came back into the room. Her cheeks were flushed, her eyes shining and dilated.

From either side came a patter of applause from General Romolo's henchmen. She walked between them as though in a trance, and was almost touching Ryan before she seemed even to notice him. She gave a little gasp and he could feel her breath on his cheek. For a moment he thought she was going to faint.

He reached out to steady her, and her whole body went rigid, then recoiled with a quick shudder. 'Don't touch me! You heard them outside? You heard the people – the true voice of the people – you heard them! So don't think I am just a poor piece of flesh and blood. If you think so, ask the people out there – ask *them* what I am!'

She swung round, with a mad glare in her eyes now, as she surveyed the double row of dark-suited men; then she looked at Romolo. 'Champagne. Where is the champagne?'

The General jerked his head forward like some glove-puppet. 'It shall be arranged – at once – Doña Presidente!'

Ryan stepped between her and Romolo and looked down. 'We celebrate when we get to Montecristo – not before. Do you want those people outside to follow you? Do you want to see Gallo and his regime swept away? Or do you want to rest by the wayside, and drink champagne?'

There was a moment of dead stillness, then Ryan felt the sting of her hand against his cheek. He did not move. She slapped him twice, hard. 'Who are you to speak to me like that?'

'I am your commander-in-chief. But if you want someone else' – he nodded at Romolo – 'I'm sure you'll find plenty of candidates.' He turned and walked to the door; and for a moment he sensed, even with his back turned, that she made an involuntary movement towards him, then checked herself.

He reached the corridor outside, strode past the lines of soldiers, down the stairs, back to the crowded excitement of the hallway. Sound-booms and television arc-lights had appeared, along with all the aggressive appendages of the world's press: unshaven men in expensive, casual clothes, with that expression of nonchalance mixed with a weary watchfulness which is the mark of their trade.

Several tried to reach him. Soldiers forced them back. There were arguments, shouts; an American voice called out, 'Colonel Ryan, can you make a statement?'

'Get one from La Vuelva!' Ryan yelled back. 'I'm a military man. I just win the battles.'

A flash-bulb flared in Ryan's face. As the light died, he found himself staring at a broad man with wavy blond hair, a button-nose and cleft chin like a hoof. Ryan stepped past him, and the man touched his sleeve. 'Colonel Ryan, I would like to speak with you for a moment. In private.'

There was a soft tone of command in the man's voice that made Ryan look at him a second time.

He wore a light gaberdine suit, cheap white shirt, no tie, and his teeth and nostrils were stained dark with nicotine. 'My name is Adam Arkov. I represent the Soviet Trade Mission to Montecristo.' He spoke in English, very quietly, with little accent.

Ryan laughed. 'You've got a bloody nerve! All right. I'll see you upstairs.'

There was a light tap on the door. He opened it and gestured to the two armed soldiers, who stood aside. Ryan closed the door and the two men shook hands. 'What can I do for you, Mr Arkov?'

'You can talk. We can both talk, discuss matters.' The Russian's English had a studied nicety which Ryan already found irritating. He waved the man to a chair and sat down himself on the sofa.

'What do you want to discuss, Mr Arkov?'

The Russian took out a packet of cigarettes, offered one to Ryan, who accepted; lit both and sat down again. They were oval gold-tipped cigarettes with the label 'Troika', in Cyrillic script, and tasted of black Balkan tobacco. The Russian said,

'There are certain matters of international diplomacy which might be of mutual interest to us both. But first allow me to congratulate you, Colonel Ryan. You appear to have achieved a magnificent victory – so far.'

'Has President Gallo sent you here? I mean, he couldn't come himself, so he sends one of his Soviet protectors?'

'That is not entirely correct, Colonel. I am acting on the initiative of my Embassy – not on that of the National People's Government. There are certain matters which need to be clarified.'

'Such as?'

'The Soviet Government is anxious to maintain the best possible relations with the Island. As you know, we have a heavy investment in this country – and the cause of many Black people in Africa also depends upon it.'

Ryan nodded. 'So you're worried that La Vuelva's popularity is going to get out of hand? That you're going to find all those troops suddenly withdrawn from Africa? And your Government's going to be able to do nothing but chew their fingernails?' He smiled.

'Tell me something, Mr Arkov. Is Gallo preparing to throw in the sponge? Or are your boys going to throw it in for him?'

'You are very direct, Colonel. As I have said, we wish only to have the best possible relations with the government in Montecristo.' He inhaled deeply. 'With whatever government in Montecristo.'

Ryan sat back and chuckled maliciously. 'What you really mean is, it's too far to send your cowboys in grey coats and T-54s over from Mother Russia? Too far to do another Budapest or Prague?'

'That is rather crude, do you not think, Colonel? But time is short. Let me come down to the facts of the matter. We estimate that the People's Democratic Republic of President Gallo is no longer stable. The Soviet Union, however, has no desire to interfere in the internal problems of a sovereign, fraternal state. If the people wish to replace their government, that is their affair not ours.

'On the other hand, the interest of a Great Power must be respected. All we desire is an assurance that the new government – if one is formed – will be sympathetic to the Soviet Socialist Republics.'

'Why don't you ask La Vuelva that?'

The Russian lit another gold-tipped cigarette, this time without offering one to Ryan. 'To be frank with you, Colonel, we believe that at this moment you are more important than La Vuelva. We believe that without you her success would be nothing. Without you, she cannot capture Montecristo.'

Ryan put his hand casually into his tunic pocket and touched the Stechkin 9mm. 'So I suggest your best course of action would be to kill me, Mr Arkov. Then – according to what you have just said – your Democratic People's Republic, under Gallo, and all his troops in Africa, would be safe.'

'Colonel Ryan, please! We are not barbarians. I, personally, feel no great enchantment for the Ramonista Movement. But I am obliged to admit that it is a popular movement. It commands the voice of the people. That is all that interests us.'

'Don't fuck around with me, Arkov. If you want a deal you can start by withdrawing your support from Gallo. He gets everything from you – guns, tanks, aircraft, plus your advisers. Cut him off and pull your advisers out. Tell him he's finished. Give him a nice big pension, and a dacha outside Moscow, and another by the Black Sea, and tell him to take up knitting.'

The Russian broke his cigarette in two, sat inspecting both parts for a moment, then lit a new one from the burning stub. He dropped the broken pieces into the ashtray at his elbow.

'You have been most obliging, Colonel. I trust I have not wasted your valuable time?' He stoood up. 'Perhaps you could arrange for me to speak with the Señora Ramon?'

When Ryan and the Russian reached the floor below, and had been admitted by the guards at the door, they found that General Romolo and his entourage had left.

La Vuelva was sitting alone in an armchair. Ryan saluted. 'Doña Presidente, you must excuse my intrusion. But I wish to introduce a representative of the Soviet Government.'

She nodded. 'Leave us. And give orders that on no account are we to be disturbed. I wish to speak to this gentleman privately.'

As Ryan withdrew he had the uneasy suspicion that Mr Adam Arkov had been expected all along.

* * *

President Fulgencio Gallo spent the rest of the hot sweaty afternoon in the concrete bunker under Command Headquarters of the People's Army in Montecristo.

Shortly after lunch, the unthinkable had happened. A group of workers at the city's main electricity plant had downed tools in sympathy with La Vuelva and only half of them had been rounded up and forced to continue work. The rest had gone underground, or had otherwise vanished.

La Vuelva's speech had been well publicized by Ryan's men on Radio Santiago y Maria. They had been able to boost its signal so that it was easily heard in both Montecristo and the outlying provinces.

Towards mid-afternoon, despite the heat, the president began to feel a distinct cold lump in his gut. It was a sensation he had not experienced for many years – not since his early days in the Sierra Hiarra, where his tiny forces had been first pitted against the might of General Ramon. Now the wheel seemed to have come full circle. The dead dictator, in the person of his bitch-widow, was suddenly threatening not only Gallo's popular credibility, but the whole basis of his regime.

Down in the bunker the air-conditioning, even the fans, had failed. An emergency generator had been brought in, but for some technical reason this could only be connected to the strip lighting. A number of large unpleasant flies had somehow managed to penetrate the steel doors and shafts down into the bunker; and valuable time was lost spraying and swatting, between bitter arguments about tactics, logistics, hopes of success, the creeping prospect of failure and defeat.

It was here that Gallo received all afternoon, a steady procession of staff officers from every district of the Island – every echelon and department of his Armed Forces, Police and Security. As the day wore on, the faces of these men became more gloomy, their communications more evasive, often degenerating into plain untruths.

By four o'clock Gallo knew the worst: the Fifth and Fifteenth Armoured Brigades – his finest and best-equipped troops not on the African Continent – were reported to have defected to the rebels, taking most of their tanks with them.

Before La Vuelva's speech it was known in Montecristo that there had been an invasion of the Island, and that the rebels had seized the radio station in Santiago y Maria; but during that first night, and even for part of the next day, the full extent of the uprising had not been fully established. Gallo's propaganda had made effective use of the delay by reporting that the attacks had been financed by Washington and was officered by foreign mercenaries; that a few Fascists on the Island had gone over to the invaders; and that the enemy, taking cynical advantage of the earthquake disaster, had been able to gain a temporary advantage.

But when La Vuelva's shrill, impassioned voice had come over the air-waves at noon, not even the stupidest or most fanatical follower of Gallo could doubt that this was no cheap, flash-in-the-pan rebellion. It was a full-blooded revolution. Or counter-revolution, as Gallo and his propagandists now preferred to call it.

By late afternoon there was one objective that Gallo had achieved – though to a far wider and more dismaying extent than he could ever have anticipated. He at least knew who was still loyal to him and who was not.

When darkness began to fall over the capital – now almost deserted except for scattered groups of police – the full tally was more or less known. The president could rely on rather less than a thousand regular officers and men, and perhaps three thousand SACA officials and 'Cobras'. The rest of his troops on the Island – including the entire People's Air Force – had either gone into hiding or joined La Vuelva.

Later that evening Gallo played his last card. It was a humiliating decision, made all the more cruel because he had formally and repeatedly assured both his country and the world that it was something he would never do.

Shortly after 10 p.m. the President of the Island's People's Republic emerged, sallow-faced, from the bunker. He was accompanied by his Chief Minister, Señor Emil Fares, and by Colonel Rodrigo Espada, the titular head of SACA. They were closely followed by their representative bodyguards. They then drove, in Gallo's Land-Rover and two bullet-proof Volga sedans, to the Soviet Embassy on the outskirts of the city.

The streets were mostly unlit and empty. All day, as the rumours multiplied, bringing with them a confusion of excitement, panic, hopes and doubts, the radio had been broadcasting a different kind of warning from that of the invasion. Monte Xatu – stoked up, as much of the population still believed, on the fires of Hell – was preparing to bring down on the capital its burning cloud of gas, '*el nube ardente*'.

Many people, especially from the poorer areas, had packed up a few household belongings and fled into the countryside before midday; then, with the news of La Vuelva's broadcast only exacerbating the situation, the municipal authorities had arranged for fleets of buses to start evacuating the more densely populated central areas. But many had still refused to go, and force had to be used to persuade them.

It was through this darkened, deserted city that the convoy of three, followed by two 'Cobra' outriders, rode on this decisive tropical evening. Gallo's Land-Rover headed the procession at a steady 60 m.p.h.

The arcades swept by like rows of empty eye-sockets. In the rear Volga, behind its smoked glass and curtained window, Colonel José Espada sat talking continuously on the car-telephone. He hung up only when they drove past the sentries at the stone gate-posts and pulled up in front of the dark turreted villa. A single light showed from one of its windows.

Gallo led the way, in silence. The door was opened to them before he had rung the bell. A man in a blue serge suit showed them in, up the mahogany stairs and along a corridor. Gallo walked first, absent-mindedly chewing a dead cigar, followed by Minister Fares, with Colonel Espada a few feet behind.

They were shown into a small, cosy room with chintz-covered furniture, a large desk and two ancient photographs of Lenin and Marx. Gallo entered with an air of solemnity, bowed, then embraced the little man with the spiky grey beard who welcomed them. Beside him sat a huge, thick-necked figure in an open shirt and sports jacket.

The man with the beard, who was the USSR's Ambassador to Montecristo, spoke in slow accurate Spanish: 'Mi Presidente, welcome! I am pleased to introduce to you Señor Sviatlo, who is our new military adviser. It is unfortunate that he only arrived four days ago, and that you have not had the opportunity of making his acquaintance.'

His companion stood up and gave Gallo a bone-crushing handshake; then did the same with Fares and Espada. He did not speak.

The ambassador waved them to a circle of chairs round the desk. He sat down and smiled. 'Mi Presidente, it is indeed a privilege to be visited by you in these difficult times. You have no doubt more news for us than we have for you?'

Gallo, who was very much aware of being on the privileged territory of his political mentors, removed the cigar from his mouth and said, 'These are indeed difficult times, Señor Ambassador. If I were not so angry – indeed, ashamed – at the disloyalty of so many of my compatriots, I would ask your pardon for what has happened. I am still the leader and commander-in-chief of my people and of their forces. As long as it is within my power, I will continue to fight these Fascist rebels who, with the assistance of the United States and their Central Intelligence Agency, are attempting to usurp my country.'

He looked the Russian hard in the face. 'I am here, Señor Ambassador, to ask for your help. The situation can no longer be tolerated, or disregarded. I need your help urgently, and I need it now.'

Behind him, Gallo's Chief Minister, Fares – an ageing fragile figure – pressed his hands together and stared at the floor; while beside him, Colonel José Espada sat back, shifting his calf-leather boots, and watched Gallo and the two Russians with fine dark eyes under thick eyebrows, black and glossy as horses' hair.

The ambassador nodded. 'We appreciate your problem, mi Presidente. You are in a delicate situation and you deserve sympathy. However, permit me to make certain observations. First – I must state that our own Intelligence Services informs us that this invasion of your country is not the work of the United States, or of its own Agency, the CIA. We are reliably informed that it is an indigenous rebellion – that its motivating force is the widow of your last president, General Ramon. Would you dispute that?'

Gallo's face had become flushed; it was hot in the little room, and he was sweating. 'Do you expect me, Señor Ambassador, to champion my enemies? To underwrite the credentials of those who wish to destroy the Democratic Republic of which I am proud to be leader and president?'

The Russian stroked his beard. 'Do not misunderstand us, please, Señor Presidente. The Soviet Union has many friends and many enemies. You are one of our friends. Let there be no mistake about that. But let us also be sensible – let us see this conflict in its broader, more global perspective.

'This woman who calls herself La Vuelva – this widow of the late General Ramon – carries with her much public support. The

Movement she represents did many good things for the workers and the peasants of this country. General Ramon himself was never a great friend of the Imperialist powers – of the United States in particular.'

He raised his hand before Gallo could speak. 'Please, you must understand, mi Presidente. As you know, the Soviet Union has a global strategy, which is to expand the frontiers of Socialism. But we also have the policy of détente to consider. If it is the true will of your people to change the government of this Island, the Soviet cannot impede that will.'

Gallo brought his fist down with a crash on the desk. 'Are you telling me, Ambassador, that you wish to wash your hands of the great Revolution that has been going on in this country for ten years? Are you not forgetting that I have sixty thousand of my compatriots at this moment risking their lives in the jungles of Africa, in the struggle to defeat White Imperialism? Do you think this woman – this whore from the cabarets of Caracas – is going to send *her* troops out in such a noble cause?'

The ambassador glanced at the bull-necked Russian at his elbow, murmured something, and the second man nodded his huge head, but said nothing.

'Mi Presidente. This is difficult, indeed painful, for me to say. But we have no reason to believe that the widow of General Ramon will rescind the duties of your Island towards our African brothers. Indeed, we have received assurances that – in return for certain guarantees, and with the promise of our continued aid programme – your country's courageous efforts in the African Liberation War will continue.'

Gallo was still standing, his great body in its slovenly jungle-green fatigues leaning forward, both hands now on the desk. His voice was a whispered shout:

'Ah! so you have already contacted her! Holy Mother of God! that I should ever find myself standing before a representative of the so-called First Socialist State in the world, and hear such blasphemies against the very name of Socialism! Hear my whole cause – the cause of my people, of comrades, brothers, sisters who have suffered and perished at the hands of the Ramonista Fascist filth – all betrayed so that you can flirt with this back-street slut who used to sit in the Palace here and sign death warrants in the morning, and cheques into her Swiss bank in the afternoon!

'And don't think that at the first whisper from Washington – the first smell of a few gringo greenbacks – she will not be wagging her little backside to the Yanquis' tune?'

He straightened up, his big hands on his hips. 'Señor Ambassador, I demand to speak to Moscow. To the minister himself.'

This time is was Sviatlo, the second Russian, who spoke. He sat there with his bulging neck, his little porcine eyes fixed unblinkingly on Gallo. 'Presidente, Moscow has already been consulted.' His voice was soft and flat. 'The first secretary himself has taken the decision. It is not merely a matter of political judgement – it is a problem of logistics. In the present situation it would require a major military operation to rescue you. It is not practical.'

'Not *practical*?' Gallo roared. 'So what's that fleet of Ilyushin 176s doing parked in the Peoples' Democracies of Eastern Europe? Those transport planes can ferry over two hundred men and equipment across the Atlantic in less than six hours! So what are you frightened of?

'Are you scared the gringos will hit back with nuclear weapons? You know the Americans have grown fat and soft, and that where I am concerned they are impotent!'

Not a muscle in the big Russian's face had moved. 'We have listened to you, Presidente. But we repeat, the decision has been taken. The Government of the USSR has followed events in this country during the last forty-eight hours.' This time his small eyes shifted from Gallo to Colonel José Espada, who sat quietly on the left, looking like a well-polished knife. 'Unless your chief of security here can assure us that he has the resources to repel the invaders and suppress the counter-revolution, I am forced to conclude that your position is no longer tenable—'

Gallo broke in with another shout: 'So you admit that it is a counter-revolution!'

The ambassador raised his hand. 'Please, Presidente. These are mere semantics. The fact of the matter is, the Soviet Union is not, at this present time, prepared to embark on a military adventure in the Caribbean. That is our last word.'

Colonel Espada had stood up, his slim hands folded in front of him, as neat as a pair of napkins. 'I consider it useless to prolong this discussion.'

Gallo rounded on him, his hands clenched into two enormous fists. 'So you're running out too? Or maybe you think that you can make a deal with the bitch? That before long she'll be in need of your special services? So be it. But remember, I'm not finished yet.'

He turned back to the desk, his teeth bared in a fierce humourless grin, while Colonel Espada walked hurriedly out of the room. The two Russians sat facing Gallo with closed faces. The ambassador spoke. 'I have one last thing to say to you, Presidente. A Soviet aircraft is at your disposal. It will fly you direct to the German Democratic Republic. But it is scheduled to leave not later than midnight.'

'Go to the devil.' Gallo turned now to his Chief Minister, Fares, who sat below him, looking old and shrunken. 'And you, Emil? Do you want to run to the hospitality of our German comrades? The Fascists will hang you by your *cojones* if you stay!' He started towards the door.

The little man stood up. 'I will do as you do, mi Presidente.' And he followed Gallo out of the room. Neither the ambassador nor Sviatlo stirred.

When Gallo reached the forecourt he saw that Colonel Espada's car, together with his two 'Cobra' motor-cycle escorts, had already left. He got into his Land-Rover, with his chief minister in the car behind; took a fresh cigar from his breast pocket, bit the end and lit it. 'Return to Command Headquarters.'

'At once, mi Presidente!' The driver started the engine. Neither he nor the bodyguard spoke. Gallo sat back and stared at the road ahead.

It was a privileged suburb, consisting of big Spanish colonial houses set back behind lush gardens. Most of the residents were either Government officials or belonged to the diplomatic corps from the 'fraternal' countries; yet even here there were few lights to be seen.

They came to a wide roundabout with a bronze statue of Bolivar on a horse, his hair and sideburns white with bird-droppings. A pair of 'Cobra' motor-cyclists waited in a side turning, their lights on full-beam. Two more cars, also with their lights on, stood in the next street.

As the Land-Rover slowed into the roundabout, a burst of machine-gun fire shattered the windshield. The driver, with two bullets in his throat, slammed his foot down on the accelerator and the front wheels swerved wildly and mounted the central reservation.

A second burst ripped through the side-windows and the bodyguard was dead before he could get his gun out. The driver had slumped forward across the wheel and the Land-Rover came to a shuddering halt against the stone plinth beneath the statue.

Gallo crawled out of the door, down on all fours, his cigar still gripped between his teeth. His curly black hair was thick with pieces of white glass, like crushed ice, from the shattered windshield. There was the crack of a rifle and the front of his head disappeared.

The steps leading up to Bolivar were spattered with glass and blood and splinters of bone. The president's heavy body twitched for a moment, his buttocks jutting into the air. Then he flopped down lifeless under the hooves of the prancing bronze horse. His cigar was still alight.

CHAPTER NINE

'Twixt Cup and Lip

The news of the president's death was announced on the National Radio thirty minutes later. Colonel Espada wrote the text of the bulletin himself. The president had died in combat against counter-revolutionary forces. He had been on guard to the last, fearlessly defending the capital against the international Fascist conspiracy. His memory would live forever in the annals of the Island's glorious history. 'Long live the Democratic People's Republic!' – and the radio went off the air.

An hour later the Democratic People's Republic was officially pronounced dead by Radio Santiago y Maria, which now became the only source of information on the Island.

Shortly after midnight it proclaimed a state of national emergency, and declared that a Provisional Government had been set up by La Doña 'La Vuelva' Ramon. All troops who had served in the People's Defence Forces were ordered to stay at their posts and to bear allegiance to their new president. The bulletin ended with the brief announcement that General Romolo had been appointed responsible for Internal Security – a post which Ryan knew to be the most notoriously strategic, and the most menacing to any young government.

Ryan also knew that from now on he was going to have to tread carefully with Romolo. Between the two of them there existed no oath of loyalty, no bond of blood or faith; and now that Gallo was gone, they did not even have a common enemy.

At dawn, on the morning after Gallo's assassination, Ryan, La Vuelva and General Romolo took off from Santiago y Maria in one of the Soviet transport planes, with No-Entry at the controls. They landed forty minutes later at Montecristo. Except for one Czech airliner, and an Ilyushin from *Aeroflot*, in an advanced state of disrepair, the field was empty of all civilian aircraft.

Even the control-tower was deserted, and No-Entry had to land blind. There was low cloud and it was raining. At one end of the field, away from the terminal buildings, stood a row of marooned MiG 23s, wings unfolded, ready for take-off.

No-Entry came in on one of the furthest runways, away from the jet-fighters and hangars; then taxied across the wet tarmac to the terminal buildings. A solitary Indian woman, with a brown face as taut as the skin of a drum, was padding about with a mop and pail; and an unshaven man in uniform was eating an orange in the locked doorway. Otherwise there was no reception.

Ryan knew – as did the rest of the party – that the city had been evacuated, while their own forces were pushing north from Santiago y Maria. They were not expecting to be greeted by a massive crowd; yet after the intoxicating atmosphere of yesterday this wet abandoned airfield visibly subdued them – especially La Vuelva.

She looked exhausted. Behind her a couple of soldiers carried the same set of smart luggage with which she had travelled from Europe; and she was wearing another close-fitting trouser suit of light chequered wool. In the rain her hair looked dank and lustreless.

Both Ryan and No-Entry Jones were in uniform – the Negro now established as Ryan's aide-de-camp. General Romolo was still in his black suit.

The unshaven man in the terminal doorway tossed away his orange and now came to attention, bringing his hand up in a vague salute, evidently uncertain whether or not to clench his fist.

Ryan demanded to know if there was any transport. The man shrugged and spat out an orange pip, and Ryan slapped him hard across his dark jowls. He rocked backwards and blinked; his breath smelt of stale rum.

They walked past him, through steel gates in a high cantilevered barbed-wire fence. Outside the terminal stood a couple of empty jeeps and a very old Dodge with a flat tyre.

La Vuelva turned to Ryan. 'Do you really expect me to ride into my capital city in one of these filthy vehicles?'

'You can try hitchhiking, if you like.'

General Romolo growled from behind: 'You will show more respect to La Doña Presidente!'

Ryan looked at them both wearily. This was their revolution, not his. From now on, Romolo and his boys would make all the running. La Vuelva would just be a figure-head – an elegant face on the new postage-stamps, and on the walls of the government offices, where she would look good next to the slim dashing portrait of Bolivar.

There was no further argument. No-Entry managed to get both jeeps going by crossing the wires in the engines; a few minutes later they drove slowly into the silent city.

There was still a number of troops around, some disorderly and obviously drunk, others trying to prevent looting. As the party neared the centre they heard gunfire, echoing like whip-cracks under the arcades and off the shuttered housefronts. It was impossible to tell where it was coming from. No-Entry, who was driving the first jeep, with Ryan, La Vuelva and General Romolo, increased speed, shooting a couple of traffic-lights that had stuck on red.

They reached the central square, which was crowded with soldiers. As the jeeps drove through them a few raised a cheer; but for the most part they stood mute and puzzled.

It began to rain again; and many hurried off the square to the shelter of the arcades. The rain blew in through the canvas side-flaps of the jeeps and La Vuelva's face and suit were soon glistening with damp. It was a thin, clinging rain that only added to the atmosphere of desolation.

La Vuelva was swallowing hard, having difficulty checking her tears. It was more than a decade since she had last seen this city – once famed as the 'Pearl of the Caribbean' – now shabby and derelict: its fine white boulevards and squares grown grey and flaking: pavement-cafés gone, bright lights long extinguished: shop-windows flyblown and empty: its fountains dry and statues green with neglect.

They drove from the Plaza Bolivar straight to the Presidential Palace. Here there were many more soldiers, including several high-ranking officers. Ryan took charge and explained who they were. Except for a few sullen stares, they were generally welcomed – though the enthusiasm was at a markedly lower temperature than that in Santiago y Maria.

Accommodation was found for La Vuelva in one of the fine, musty rooms in the old wing, which had remained deserted since Gallo had come to power. Gallo himself, with a show of brutish simplicity, had usually slept on a camp-bed in his office, and made his ablutions in the guards' quarters of the Palace.

La Vuelva was as shocked by the state of the building as by that of the city outside; but she restrained her emotions until she was alone. As soon as the dusty four-poster bed had been stripped and remade, and her luggage laid out in the rococco sofas, she summoned an officer from outside and gave a simple order.

He saluted and withdrew. Little did he know that he was about to commit one of the most fateful acts of the whole Revolution.

Meanwhile Ryan and his staff, together with General Romolo, had been ordered by La Vuelva to make their headquarters on separate floors in the Hotel Nacional.

Her attitude towards Ryan had remained remote, and there was now a distinct chill between him and her entourage. However, he was not a man to be upset by the changing moods of a woman. He was determined to fulfil the duties for which he had been so handsomely paid.

His first act on arrival was to confirm that the radio and television station was operating normally again, and that a fresh bulletin was being regularly broadcast, reassuring the population that the reports about Monte Xatu had been total fabrications invented by Gallo and his clique to confuse the people and distract them from the Revolution.

It was decided that La Vuelva should speak next day, again at noon, in the city's vast football stadium. By then it was hoped that a degree of normality would have returned to the city.

Ryan spent the rest of the day, and much of the night, working on the telephone, in a fury of frustration as he grappled with the imbecile incompetence of the now defunct National People's Telecommunications, one of Gallo's legacies to the city. By late afternoon he had ensured that most of the evacuated population had either returned, or had means laid on to to so; and that by tomorrow, all but a few thousand stragglers would be ready to acclaim La Vuelva as their new president and saviour.

Later that night a storm broke over the city, relieving some of the static tension. Ryan was in his hotel room eating a scrappy meal off a tray when he received the first reports that General Romolo had also been active, and his new police had started making arrests.

At nine o'clock that night thirty-seven men and two women

were executed by firing-squad in the square behind the former People's Army Cadet College. They had been tried together, by a five-man tribunal headed by Romolo himself, and each accorded a three-minute hearing, with the assistance of a lawyer.

Ryan went up to the General's floor, where he was greeted by dance music. The air was hazy with cigar smoke and Romolo was doing the tango with a large woman wearing a great deal of cheap jewellery. He laughed at Ryan and offered him some rum. Ryan tried to reason with him, then to threaten him, promising that he would bring in troops to stop such excesses which could only dirty the whole image of the Revolution. Romolo told him to go and drink his mother's milk.

Ryan withdrew, called up No-Entry and told him to get the jeep out. They then drove to the Palace. Here Ryan was relieved to see that security had been tightened, with three armoured cars at the gates and a half-track at the main doors, while the rich shrubbery all round was being patrolled by armed troops.

He had difficulty getting in, since his identity was not immediately known to the troops at the doors; and he had also signed both his own and No-Entry's safe-conducts.

Once inside, a major from the crack Paratroop Regiment, which was guarding the Palace, informed him, politely but firmly, that the Dona Presidente could not be disturbed.

Ryan was angry. He needed La Vuelva's signature on a number of decrees. Above all, he wanted her authority to put an end to Romolo's savage zeal.

Because Ryan – perhaps without even realizing it – had already been infected by a certain idealism. The Island's six million inhabitants had suffered for ten years under a drab, cruel autocracy dictated by the interests of the Kremlin. Their miserable history, illuminated by so many shafts of hope that had been extinguished almost immediately, deserved better than men like Romolo.

He returned to the Nacional in a sour mood; finished what work he could without La Vuelva's signature, then fell into a deep dreamless sleep.

He was awakened by bright sunlight. It was still early, but the street outside had taken on a festive air. The national flag, with a hole cut in its side, was everywhere, along with red and green scarves and bandanas.

A few cafés had opened and there were even tables out in the sun. The people were reading the main newspaper, renamed *La Tribuna del Popolo Liberado*. It had appeared on the streets a couple of hours ago, carrying a full front-page declaration which had been drawn up, in La Vuelva's name, by Ryan himself.

He went out, bought a copy, ordered a coffee and brandy, and read the page through. It contained a multitude of clichés, but considering it was his first excursion into journalism the result was not bad: and the people reading it round him seemed to draw encouragement from it.

An hour later he checked that the preparations at the football stadium were complete. La Vuelva was to make her speech from the Presidential box; and Ryan's task was to ensure that every possible precaution had been taken: all roofs, boxes, stands and terraces fully checked, and that plain-clothes men with concealed hand-guns would be mingling with the crowds.

For the two miles' ride from the Palace he had commandeered a fleet of closed cars – one of them armoured, in which La Vuelva would ride. She would leave the Palace at precisely 11.45 a.m., and reach the stadium only a few minutes before her speech was scheduled.

Ryan would not be collecting her. That privilege had already been claimed by General Romolo. Instead he would greet her in the VIP room behind the Presidential box, and from then on stay in the background. Ryan, after all, was only a foreign mercenary – and an expensive one at that – who had won the war for them. When the Island's history books came to be written yet again, he was likely to be deleted.

He had become dispensable.

Ryan had intended to be at the stadium an hour before the proceedings began, but he was interrupted at his hotel by one of the guards who announced that Commandant Moulins wished to see him.

The Frenchman was again dressed immaculately – riding breeches, white polo-necked sweater, black knee-high boots polished like dark mirrors. Ryan wondered why he was not in uniform, and he could only guess that the Frenchman considered the badge of a foreign army, and a rebel army at that, unbecoming to a former French officer – albeit one who had been cashiered for attempting to murder his Head of State.

He removed the long pipe from his mouth and bowed, without saluting. 'Colonel Ryan, I am glad to see you. It seems that I owe you an apology.'

Ryan said nothing. The Frenchman looked at him through a coil of smoke. 'I have been holding the southern tip of the Island. Fortunately – or perhaps unfortunately – I have still encountered no resistance.'

Ryan waited for him to go on; but the man just sucked at his pipe. 'Why do you say "unfortunately", Commandant?'

The Frenchman was still standing. He took his pipe from his mouth and smiled at the floor. 'I am a soldier, Colonel, and I enjoy the fruits of battle as any other good soldier does.' He looked up. 'I am now looking for the rewards of this battle.'

'Why don't you discuss this with La Vuelva? Go and ask her for your pay-off.'

Moulins took a step back. 'There is no need to be offensive, Colonel. I am a soldier – a soldier who has done his duty.'

'Then continue to do it.'

The Frenchman shifted his weight from one boot to the other. 'I was promised responsibility,' he said at last. 'I was promised the responsibility of leading La Vuelva to victory. Now I wish to be rewarded. And I do not mean by money.'

Ryan looked at him with a dull smile. He was too tired to argue with this ageing, arrogant officer who was more concerned with the trappings of triumph than with the spoils of victory.

'Look, Commandant, it is too late to give you military glory. If you want publicity, talk to the press. Tell them how you commanded Operation *Belladonna* – that you held out against the superior forces of President Gallo – while I was merely leading a diversionary tactic.'

Moulins had removed his pipe again. He held himself very straight. 'You know the truth, Colonel Ryan. I risked leading an incompetent and ill-equipped body of men to invade the Island. I undertook this venture against immense odds. While you had the good fortune to steal the victory, I was left in a filthy dungeon of a block-house, without even the honour of an attack.'

'You appear, Commandant, to have preserved your wardrobe

in remarkably good condition,' Ryan said.

Moulins pulled back his shoulders. 'You are in a good position to joke, Colonel. You were dealt all the good cards, and you played them well. I admit that.'

'So?'

'I want some reward. I want authority – command. I want a position in which I can influence events.'

Ryan yawned. 'You took on this job, Commandant, either for power or for money. I am not going to act as your broker. Go and see the new president. Ask her either to promote you or to give you a cheque. But for Christ's sake don't bother me anymore. I'm busy.'

The telephone was winking on the emergency button. Ryan answered it.

A group of senior ex-SACA officers, under a Brigadier Gavra, was seeking a political arrangement with the High Command of the Revolutionary Forces.

A few seconds later he received another call, this time informing him that the Provisional Revolutionary Government had given permission for Gallo's funeral to take place at three o'clock that afternoon, with the ceremony to begin at the Trade Union House of Recreation, in the working-class suburb of Barracas. The hour had been deliberately chosen in the middle of siesta-time, so that numbers might be depleted and passions lulled. Nevertheless, several thousand mourners were expected, and extra riot police had been laid on.

Ryan looked up at Moulins. 'So – you want a responsible job? Go and supervise this funeral. It won't be easy, but it should be instructive.' He scribbled the address and passed it over to the Frenchman. 'And don't go strutting around in those fancy clothes as though you were at Longchamps or in the Jockey Club. And take Hausmann – he's at least reliable.'

Moulins winced at the oblique slur on his own ability, saluted and left.

Ryan now made several urgent telephone calls, satisfying himself that a sufficient number of riot-police were on hand for La Vuelva's appearance; then set off for the stadium.

He had been allowed the use of a chauffeur-driven, bullet-proof Zil limousine – the Soviets' clumsy attempt to copy the Packard – a long black brute of a car which Ryan considered hardly tactful under the circumstances.

The chauffeur, a surly man with a bulging jacket, drove with the skilled, selfish defiance of one long used to driving those in authority.

The stadium stood on the site of the old Plaza de Toros. Under Gallo it had been enlarged to serve not only as a bull-ring, but also a football and baseball stadium – baseball having ironically been the late President's favourite sport. The oval-shaped structure had a capacity of more than a hundred thousand.

Ryan reached the building twenty minutes before La Vuelva was due to arrive. He made his way straight to the VIP lounge behind the president's box, past steel-helmeted troops at all the gates, doors and staircases.

The crowd was enormous, swelling all the time. A match between the Island and Real Madrid would not have required half as many police to control the besieging fans.

Ryan watched the crowds taking their seats. For the first few minutes they were orderly; then scuffles broke out. There were flags, banners – the simple hieroglyphics of the extreme Left and extreme Right: *'The Falangist Ramonista Movement!' 'Marxist-Leninist Ramonista Workers' Brigade!' 'The Pan Socialist International!'* And everywhere the red-and-white slogan, *'Gracias La Vuelva!'*

For a few moments the crowd looked like a field of corn, swaying and rippling under a breeze. There were swirls, channels, eddies of shadow among the pools of sunlight. Occasionally a banner toppled and was trampled under foot, while all round, in the 'calejon' between the stands and the ring, stretched a grey-black belt of riot-police, shoulder-to-shoulder, batons drawn, faceless behind their perspex visors.

Ryan turned from the Presidential box into the VIP room, and found No-Entry Jones. The Negro saluted and handed him a message. 'This jus' come in, Colonel. It's from the Commander o' the Barracas District – that's where they're buryin' Gallo, so ah heard – at fifteen hundred hours. Seems they already got a pretty big turn-out. The commander says they gonna get trouble.'

Ryan read the message and handed it back. 'Tell the commander that on no account is the crowd to be prevented from seeing Gallo off. And any counter demonstrations are to be held back.'

No-Entry saluted and left.

The room was now filling with dignitaries, most of them in resplendent uniform. Ryan felt a little dowdy, out of place. A whisper went round; a young officer touched Ryan's arm. 'She is arriving, mi Coronel!'

Ryan looked towards the door of the little room. The news must have also reached the crowds outside, for the fighting seemed to have subsided, and all passions and energy were now directed towards the Presidential box from which an enormous banner was now draped, with the red letters on gilt-edged white: *'VIVA LA VUELVA!'*

There were no lifts in the stadium, and Ryan knew that she would have to climb five flights of stairs. Four minutes later she had not appeared. He supposed that she was stopping to greet people on the way up: for the whole place would be swarming with ambitious officers greedy to insinuate themselves into her favour.

Five minutes later there was still no sign of her. He went to the rear door leading on to the stairs. The whole place was unnaturally quiet. Then he heard footsteps, several of them, on the landing below. Steel-helmeted guards stood all round, gripping their Kalashnikovs. Ryan saw her a moment later: walking stiffly between two officers who stood so close to her that at first he thought they were supporting her.

She was dressed entirely in white – white linen trouser-suit, white shoes and white gloves, white scarf knotted round her throat, and a huge white sun-hat; half her face was again hidden by dark glasses. Yet there was something oddly rigid and immobile about the set of her cheeks and mouth. Ryan was reminded of someone trying to suppress a yawn or a laugh.

He stepped forward to greet her; but at first she did not seem to recognize him. When she did, she reached out. For an unpleasant moment Ryan thought she was going to miss his hand and stumble. Her mouth was clamped shut, but her handshake was limp, and dropped away as soon as he released it.

She said nothing; but as she was about to enter the VIP room one of the officers beside her dropped back a step, and her shoulder brushed – very slightly – against the side of the door.

She smelt strongly of scent. The best scent, but there was still too much of it. Ryan grabbed one of her accompanying officers. 'Tell me,' he whispered: 'has she been drinking?'

The man looked at him with nervous brown eyes. 'I do not know, mi Coronel. I only came on duty downstairs.'

'Who does know then?'

The officer glanced behind them, to where Romolo stood with his plain-clothes men. Ryan went up to him. 'General, what has happened to La Doña Presidente?'

As he spoke, he looked back and saw La Vuelva moving in a stiff strutting walk towards the double doors leading out to the Presidential box. At the last moment she failed, and had to steady herself against the arm of the officer nearest her, before carefully planting her neat haunches on the sofa beside the doors.

'La Doña Presidente has not been well.' General Romolo's smug fat face reminded Ryan of a hunk of salami.

'What do you mean – not well?'

The general shrugged, and a hint of patronizing pleasure showed in his cold-capped smile. 'I speak in all confidence, Coronel, but yesterday our lady president sent out for some champagne. French champagne. And a bottle of French brandy. Later some of the officers found a box of Russian vodka in the late Gallo's study. I understand there was a party. And why not?' He spread his thick hairy hands. 'Is this not a moment for celebration?'

'And you let her drink?' Ryan's watch said one minute to noon. He looked back again and saw La Vuelva sitting upright like a stiff doll, staring in front of her through her black glasses.

Romolo gave a confident smirk. 'I am not the president, mi Coronel. Perhaps *you* would like to order the lady not to take her pleasures?'

Ryan's rage and dismay were fortunately deflected from the general to the woman on the sofa behind him. For despite all the well-practised reactions of the alcoholic, how could she possibly step out now and deliver a speech that was going to be televised round the world? – and which would change the whole complexion of Caribbean politics?

Ryan left Romolo and went over to her. Scarcely thirty seconds were left now, before she was due on the balcony. He leant down and said, in a sharp undertone, 'Mia Doña Presidente! Do you feel well enough to speak?'

Her head turned slowly to face him. He could still not see her eyes, but her mouth opened and she spoke, with immaculate clarity. 'I feel very well, Señor Ryan. I am delighted to have you with me. You observe, do you not, that your poor little patient, Madame Achar, is not so unimportant after all?' She enunciated these last words with a slow deliberation close to hysteria.

'Doña Presidente, do you want some coffee?'

She flung her head back so that the cords in her throat showed through the translucent whiteness of her skin.

'Coffee! – Before you offer me coffee, find me some! Find me some beautiful coffee that Gallo has kindly left for my people!' She brought her head up suddenly. 'You find it for me, you Irish peasant—' and there was a fleck of saliva at the corner of her crimson lips. Her dark glasses had dropped down her nose so that he could see the red linings of her eyes.

He answered gently, in English: 'Madame, you are not ready to speak from that balcony. Let me announce that you are ill. That the ceremony cannot go on without you, and will have to be postponed.'

For a couple of seconds her face remained brittle, her jaw muscles twitching under the skin; then her features seemed to collapse like a crumpled sheet of paper. She fell forward and began to shake.

Ryan could hear that familiar echoing howl from the stadium – the one-two dactylic beat of the slogan '*La Vuelva*'. He did not move. The woman on the sofa wiped her lips on the back of her hand and laughed.

'Madame, I am giving you ten seconds. Then I shall go out on to the balcony myself.'

She put out her hand, placed it on his thigh and pushed him, slowly but firmly, away from her; then stood up and walked towards the windows leading out to the Presidential box.

Her slim body was held erect, her movements perfectly co-ordinated. As she drew level with the microphone she lifted both hands in the familiar gesture that had driven the crowds so wild in Santiago y Maria.

She was greeted by that same howling roar, as more than a hundred thousand throats bellowed her name. But at the final second, just as she stepped forward to touch the balcony rail, her high heel caught on the frayed matting. She tripped; her glasses again fell off her face, and her huge hat dropped absurdly over her eyes.

The incident might have just passed off without embarrassment had not a young officer behind her dashed forward and tried to catch her. He slipped too, and his head collided with her buttocks. She swung round, tried to slap him, lost her balance and sat down on the floor.

The cheering below became ragged, broken by bursts of uneasy laughter. For some seconds La Vuelva remained hidden behind the balcony. Ryan had tried to run forward but was held back by a circle of officers under the orders of General Romolo, whose oily features bore an expression of odious satisfaction.

Out in the Presidential box La Vuelva had collected herself. She stood up, adjusted her hat and dark glasses, but had lost one shoe, which she now clumsily bent down to retrieve. This critical pause was enough to allow the crowd to become restive. For a moment there was a dead hush. Everyone in the room behind was staring out at her, waiting. Even General Romolo appeared tense.

La Vuelva had steadied herself against the parapet; but instead of lifting her arms again in that potent gesture that had so captivated her audience in Santiago y Maria, this time she leant down until her face was only an inch from the microphones. She belched.

The sound was amplified into a curious growling roar which echoed clearly, unambiguously, round the whole stadium. A second later the jeering and booing and whistling began.

Anyone with experience of a Caribbean mob knows how mercurial are its moods, how violent its reactions. La Vuelva knew as well as anyone. But in that moment she was neither normal nor rational. She was not embarrassed, not frightened, not overawed. She reacted with a ferocious rage at this ugly mob that dared to laugh at her in her hour of triumph.

She grabbed one of the microphones and pronounced into it, in a clear voice, the single obscenity that is rarely heard on the mouth of a woman, even in the meanest whore-house. Then she laughed. She threw back her head, with her arms flung wide at her side, and she gave a long peal of demented, humourless, laughter.

A group of officers moved forward and bundled her quickly inside the VIP room. General Romolo hurried forward. They were half leading, half supporting her. Ryan, realizing that the situation was lost, did not move.

La Vuelva's features had again disintegrated, this time into a grotesque mixture of weeping and giggling. A handsome young aide-de-camp, splendid in white piping, a sash and ceremonial sword, bent over her as they laid her on the sofa, and offered her a glass of water. Another officer produced a handkerchief, which she seized and flung on the floor.

Ryan found himself standing again next to Romolo. The general's face was puffed with righteous indignation. 'Colonel, the woman is suffering from shock.'

'She's drunk.'

Romolo peered at Ryan with his small wet eyes. But as he spoke the terrible roar reached them from the stadium, followed a few seconds later by a screaming, baying chant which was taken up from every side, every stand and terrace: 'La puta a la linterna!' – 'The whore to the lamp-post.'

Ryan stepped forward. 'Get her out of here – quick! – before they tear her to shreds!'

It needed four of them to get her down the five flights of stairs and into Ryan's waiting bullet-proof Zil. For a moment he thought she was going to have a fit. He pushed three fingers into her mouth, wedging down her tongue, and she bit him savagely. He told the driver to head with all speed for the Palace.

As they drew away Ryan could hear – even through the closed windows – the noise of the crowd from inside the stadium, punctuated now by the popping of gas-grenades and by panic-stricken screams. He reflected bitterly how the fruits of triumph had turned rotten before his eyes. He could even smell it, on La Vuelva's breath, mixed with her overpowering scent.

During the drive she had become quite passive, lolling back on the rear seat with eyes closed, a trickle of saliva running from between smeared lips. None of them spoke until they had driven through the marble gates, past the brilliant flora, and drawn up in front of the bronze doors of the Palace. As they got out Ryan was joined by No-Entry Jones, who had been in the car behind.

'Some charade, Colonel!'

'Just a minor Latin American fuck-up.' Ryan and Romolo carried La Vuelva up the steps into the Palace. Here they were relieved by the handsome young officer with the ceremonial sword, who disappeared with their semi-conscious burden down the flaking corridors of the building.

One of her shoes had again come off and lay at the top of the steps. Ryan picked it up, as though in a last vain attempt to salvage her dignity. He smiled sadly at No-Entry. 'She'd have done better to have stayed at home. At least she'd have had proper servants to look after her.' As he spoke a tall man in uniform, with iron-grey moustaches, strutted up to them.

'Señores, you will please leave.' He did not even salute.

Coldly, Ryan identified himself; but the man just shook his head. He did not bother to ask for Ryan's written credentials, just repeated: 'You will please leave here.'

'Who are you?'

'I am Brigadier Gavra, Special Security.'

Ryan nodded. 'Yes, I know about you, Brigadier – you and your staff have an appointment with me at the Nacional at five. Now, I would like to speak to La Doña Presidente.' Ryan again made to pass the brigadier, but the man's gloved hand moved swiftly, automatically, to the holster at his belt.

'I regret, Coronel. No one is permitted to see the Señora until the situation is normalized.'

Ryan tensed himself, holding his temper. 'I would remind you, Brigadier, that I am still acting Commander-in-Chief, directly responsible to La Doña Presidente and no one else. As for you, aren't you one of the smart boys who've spent the last ten years in Dr Gallo's SACA – wearing two coats, eh? Or maybe just the same one turned inside-out?'

He grinned as he saw the man's face turn white round the eyes. But it seemed a bad place to start a squalid wrangle with a senior officer. Brigadier Gavra had turned and snapped his fingers, and two helmeted men with machine-pistols stepped forward, one on each side of Ryan and No-Entry, and guided them back out through the bronze doors.

Together they got back into the bullet-proof car, and Ryan gave the driver the address of the Nacional.

'I guess the lady'd be under house-arrest?' said No-Entry.

'Either that, or they're waiting for her to sober up. Either way, it probably won't make much difference. She's destroyed herself. And probably us with her.'

Less than an hour had passed since the outrage at the stadium;

yet the news had spread, even to those who had not heard the vile phrase on their radios.

An ugly change of mood had come over the city. The crowds along the streets and boulevards were no longer waving flags; in the newly-opened cafés people had stopped chatting and smiling and exchanging newspapers. Faces had become sullen, uneasy; they seemed to be waiting for something, without knowing what it was.

Several men turned to watch Ryan's Russian limousine glide past, and one stepped forward and spat at it. Ryan watched the thick gob slide down the smoked window and reminded himself that it was not him they hated but the woman who had just reduced their glorious deliverance to a squalid farce.

He just hoped that Brigadier Gavra's security at the Palace would be applied as rigorously to others as it had been to himself.

It was only when he got back to the hotel that he began to calculate his own chances.

He had been at La Vuelva's right hand, and could justifiably claim to have done more than anyone to defeat the Gallo regime. Yet now his role had not only been tainted by his association with her: it had become superfluous.

Romolo and his friends would control all means of communication and propaganda; and so far the publicity surrounding Ryan's exploits had been so modest as to be almost obscure. There were any number of ways in which he could disappear, violently or otherwise, and very few people would either notice or care.

Meanwhile, at the Nacional – the largest hotel in the Island – he and No-Entry found there was no room-service; the restaurant and bar had been closed; the lifts no longer worked.

Next, Ryan found himself unable to get through on the telephone either to High Command, Brigade Headquarters, or to the Radio and Television Centre. The operator explained that the lines were either engaged or out of order.

Over the past twenty-four hours, Ryan had become resigned to the vagaries of the local telephone system: but now, for the first time, he began to feel a distinct constriction in his gut. It was only the presence of No-Entry Jones, as sanguine as ever, that steadied his resolve.

It was now 3.20 p.m. – exactly two hundred minutes since

La Vuelva had disgraced her country and her cause; and twenty minutes after the people had been due to pay their last respects to the late President Gallo.

Down in the hotel lobby there was chaos, with a noisy, opulent injection of foreign newsmen and TV cameras. Ryan also noticed other individuals. Quiet men, alone, not in uniform – except for grey suits, too long in the arm, too short at the neck – who waited in corners, by doorways and the stairs, some pretending to read the morning's paper, others pretending to do nothing.

Outside, the air was heavy under a bilious sky. Then suddenly the crowded streets were sliced by a panting scream of sirens, as a convoy of riot trucks careered through the centre of the city.

The first news reached the hotel a few minutes later. Either the telephones were working again, or someone was operating mile-a-minute relay between the hotel and the Trades Union House of Recreation half a mile away.

The reports were garbled, but there was a convincing thread throughout them all, which even the wildest rumours did not contradict.

The crowd at Gallo's funeral – estimated at more than ten thousand – had been deliberately kept waiting after the ceremony had been due to begin. Then strident Communist and Galloista songs had been played over the loudspeakers; and as the mood began to ferment still further, an announcement was made that the funeral had been officially cancelled and that Gallo's body had already been burnt.

The mourners – made up largely of the poor and the peasants, Indians, mestizos and mulattoes – were now joined by that gruesome spectacle of 'los decamisados', 'the shirtless ones', and had spontaneously run amok. The few troops guarding the building had been butchered. Some were hacked to death, some decapitated, others hanged from lamp-posts or palm-trees.

At this point – strategically late – the riot-police had turned up – reinforced, some said, by several hundred well-armed anti-Gallo demonstrators who had either arrived by car or been driven direct in Army trucks.

The battle had been swift and the carnage efficient. All exits to the square had been blocked. By 3.40 it was reported that at least two to three hundred were dead, and between seven hundred and a thousand either wounded or in captivity.

Ryan and No-Entry reached the Zil and told the chauffeur to head for the Trades Union Recreation House. It took them nearly an hour to press their way through the convoys of trucks – some open, others ominously closed – between the grey tenement blocks that gave off a stench of drains and rancid cooking.

They had to leave the car in a side-alley, several blocks from the square, which lay under a white fog of tear-gas smoke. Across the façade of the Recreation House hung a huge, hideously coloured portrait of Fulgencio Gallo, the lower half of his beard partially burned away.

Ryan and No-Entry ran, doubled-up and choking through their handkerchiefs, hoping that their uniforms would make them immune to the sporadic fire from the riot-troops, who were now wearing grotesque rubber snouts.

They found Commandant Moulins close to the steps up to the building. His AK-47 lay a few feet away from him. Nobody had bothered to touch it, although later it turned out that it had not been fired.

The body had been horribly mutilated. According to an eye-witness among the military, the Frenchman had stayed hidden in the House until the first riot-police appeared, and had then emerged on the mistaken assumption that he was safe. But it seemed that his elegant appearance had only driven the 'decamisados' to further fury. They had removed his boots, after chopping off his legs at the knees; and when they had finished with the rest of him his half-naked body lay beside a steaming coil of intestines. Near the stump of one of his legs Ryan saw what looked like a small bunch of shrunken fruit. It took him a couple of seconds to realize that they were the Frenchman's genitalia.

It was some time, through the stinging gas, before they found Hausmann. His gun was empty, and so too were his spare clips. They had impaled him on a long wooden spike, up through his ragged trousers and out of his mouth. The expression on his face, Ryan remembered, was as gaunt as ever.

He grabbed No-Entry's arm. 'Let's get the hell out of this filthy little country.'

'Yeah, but how?'

'Leave that to me.' They reached the Zil, where the driver was surprisingly still waiting. Ryan was relieved that at least someone, besides No-Entry, remained loyal to him.

On the drive back he noticed, above the city to the north, that the dark cone of Monte Xatu seemed to be smoking more than usual.

The centre of the city was still packed with waiting crowds, indecisive and threatening. Food was being distributed by the Army, but in a haphazard way, and in insufficient quantities, so that the wealthier centres benefited, thus causing greater lawlessness among the poorer areas. Riots and looting broke out in several quarters and by late afternoon the official death-toll – besides that at Gallo's funeral – had risen to between five and six hundred, with thousands in make-shift hospitals, already overcrowded and understaffed from tending the earth-quake victims from the coast towns.

The sky had darkened with a storm that never broke. Rumours were again spreading like an epidemic; and the troops – mostly battle-weary conscripts on leave from Africa – were exhausted, confused by the change of orders, by the shift of allegiances.

Ironically, as the day drew on, it was not so much these itchy-fingered troops or the wanton mobs, or even the increasing state of uncertainty, which provoked the greatest dread. Since midday the plume of smoke above Monte Xatu – usually no more than a brown smudge against the blue sky – had grown steadily taller, until by late afternoon it formed a high dark pillar, reaching even above the storm clouds.

But this time the little authority still existing in the city did not make the mistake of creating more panic by trying to evacuate the population for a second time – even if they had had the means and organization to do so. Instead, they had placed the capital in a state of quarantine. The airport was closed to all out-going flights; the railway line cut; and all along the main arteries there were road-blocks and barricades – besides those set up by rampaging peasants and deserters in the outlying shanty-towns.

The radio continued to function, but all it broadcast was a steady stream of martial music, interspersed with insipid dance rhythms, and the occasional exhortation to the populace to remain calm.

Ryan was one who did remain calm; but he also knew that his time was running out.

By 5.30 when the delegation of former SACA officers under Brigadier Gavra had not yet arrived, and the telephones were still not working, Ryan made his decision.

He left No-Entry on guard in his room, with instructions to open the door to no one: not even to answer the phone. If Ryan was not back within one hour, the Negro was to fend for himself.

In the corridor outside Ryan noticed the two silent grey watchdogs. The lifts were still not working, and there were more men on the stairs and the floors below, as well as in the crowded lobby; but Ryan was quite as skilled in their craft as they were, and made sure – in the continuing confusion of the lobby – that he was not followed.

The Zil was parked outside the hotel, locked and empty, Ryan having dismissed the driver after the riot at Gallo's funeral. On this busy boulevard he was mildly surprised to find the long, shiny-black limousine – reserved for the elite – totally unblemished. He would have preferred something less ostentatious, like a jeep; but was at the same time reassured by the car's armour-plating, bullet-proof glass, and self-sealing tyres.

He drove fast, feeling the hard bulge of the Stechkin, fully loaded, under the fold of his tunic.

The streets were still full of people, together with concentrations of troops and police. He knew that it would only need one jittery soldier, one green recruit to loose off, and the city would explode in mayhem.

The troops round the Palace had been doubled. There were now also tanks and armoured personnel carriers parked in the grounds and in the streets outside. Ryan drew up directly in front of the bronze doors, just behind an APC; and with his pistol in his hand marched up the steps and into the foyer before he was stopped by a young captain who seemed more apologetic than officious.

Ryan ordered to be conducted at once to the apartments of La Doña Presidente. The officer saluted and asked him to wait. A major was called, and had begun asking to see Ryan's written authority when he was anxiously called away by some other officer.

Ryan did not wait, but slipped away into the labyrinth of dilapidated corridors. Once inside, no one challenged him. He found a smartly-dressed lieutenant who directed him at once to the old wing of the Palace.

When finally he was challenged it seemed more a matter of routine. They were two smart young officers with white sashes and ceremonial swords whom Ryan took to be the traditional Palace Guard. But unlike the men outside, they seemed less interested in guarding the Palace than in preening themselves in their proud tailor-made uniforms. They hardly looked at Ryan's credentials as they raised their swords in a salute, and pointed them to a pair of tall ormolu doors. These were unlocked.

It was a long, high, cheerless room, with curtains drawn across the windows, so that it took Ryan several seconds to adjust to the dark. Despite the muggy heat outside, the whole room had a cool dank smell, like a cellar. There was no carpet and little furniture; and what there was, he guessed to be expensive reproduction antiques, all badly in need of repair.

La Vuelva lay on a sofa at the far end. Her face was turned to the wall, on which the wine-red silk wallpaper was blotched and blistered with white mould. A strip of it had come loose and curled down just above her head. She was dressed as he had last seen her after the stadium in a white trouser-suit, but without the hat, scarf and shoes.

He knew that she had heard him come in, for she moved her head slightly, but still without looking at him. The bare boards creaked as he came towards her.

'Mia Doña Presidente.' He had stopped a few paces from her, but still she did not turn.

'Señor Ryan? – What do you want?'

'I have come to see how you are. To ensure that you are being treated correctly.'

'That is not true. You have come to laugh at me – like all the others. Do not lie to me, Señor Ryan. You do not care. Nobody cares. You least of all. You, after all, have been paid.' She continued to stare at the silk wall.

'Mia Presidente, you are mistaken. I have been paid, but I do not believe in leaving a job until it is finished. It is also true that both our fortune, and our salvation, are bound up together.'

'You are saying that without me you are afraid for your safety, Señor Ryan? Or is it just that you wish to see how far I have sunk? Knowing, perhaps, that my disgrace could be a danger also to you?'

Ryan moved forward until he was standing over her. 'Mia Presidente, I am still an officer in your employ, and under your orders. I also have an obligation to ensure your personal security.'

'Even at a time like this?'

'Particularly at a time like this.'

'Go away, please. There is nothing you can do.'

'You are mistaken. I can at least try to arrange a safe-conduct for you out of the country.'

'I am sure you could! Romolo and his scum long to be rid of me. I am an embarrassment to them. What they would give to see me scurrying away in the arms of a foreign impostor! Unfortunately, Señor Ryan, I do not wish to leave my country.'

'I am only suggesting it for your own good.'

'It is kind of you. But it is useless. My place is here, with my people. My destiny has taken me so far, and I must follow it to the end. Now please, I am tired. Leave me.'

He stepped forward and touched her shoulder, and felt it flinch as though in pain. 'Do as I say. Go' – her words came in a quick hoarse whisper – 'go, or I will order the guards to expel you.'

'This is probably your last and only chance. All your other friends have abandoned you. Romolo is greedy for power. Moulins was lynched this afternoon by a mob. And young Pedro has disappeared.'

'Don't talk to me about him! Señor de Sanchez is a child. A clever delinquent child – but one who also interested me. I believed that he could help our cause. Instead, he used me – as an amusing diversion. He thought it would be clever to steal those poison capsules and blackmail Gallo into surrender. But when he saw that we were winning without his help, he lost interest. He has no real interest in revolution, in victory, in responsible government. Only in power – the struggle for power, and the power to destroy.

'Now, please – go. Go, before I call the guards!'

Ryan stood for several seconds looking down at her with pity and contempt. He had succumbed to her coarse advances; taken her money; carried out her orders; won the supreme prize for her; and now – after she had so wantonly, ridiculously squandered it – his offer to help her had been peevishly rejected.

As he left the room, still without having looked her in the face, he felt a morose sense of guilt.

He had done nothing disloyal, nothing dishonourable; even as a lover he had behaved more or less like a gentleman. Yet he still felt that he owed her something. Respect, perhaps? For despite her flawed character, broken, irretrievably ruined – he recognized for the first time some of the power and legendary magic which she had exercised for so long, over so many. Even in this hour of ultimate degradation, she had managed to retain a wounded dignity.

Outside, in the hot stormy evening, as he climbed into the Zil and headed back to the hotel, he could still feel the chill of that room.

Ten minutes after he reached the Nacional – at 6.30 p.m. – the political vacuum was broken. General Romolo came on the radio and pronounced himself head of the provisional Revolutionary Government.

He also declared a state of martial law, and a twenty-four-hour curfew which would commence when he stopped speaking. Any unauthorized person found on the streets after that time would be shot. The responsibility for the restoration of law and order had been entrusted to Brigadier Gavra, who would head the new 'United National Committee of Public Safety'. There was conspicuously no mention of La Vuelva.

But even before this, as Ryan had entered the hotel, he had noticed that the drab grey goons, with long arms and short necks, had multiplied. There were now two more, at each end of his corridor, and another two at the top of the stairs.

He let himself into his room where he found No-Entry covering the door with his AK-47. 'Thank the Lord! I been gettin' ready to split.'

'Anything happened?'

'Nuts! That's the trouble. Phone's dead – fuzz outside. We're prisoners, Colonel.'

'Fuck that,' said Ryan, and touched the pistol under his

make it to the airport, can you fly one of those Russkie transports?'

'Hell, man, ah flew you up here in one jus' yes'day mornin'!'

'I know that. But could you fly one out tonight – without clearance, and without keys?'

'I guess ah can fix the electrics.' He shrugged. 'Shit, what choice we got?'

There was another long boom, and to the north the sky was etched with a jagged vermilion mushroom of poisonous gas, powdered rock and lava-bombs. It all suddenly looked very close, like the backcloth to some grotesque melodrama.

The boulevard now reminded Ryan of the aftermath of a violent football-match: people charging in all directions, their faces stretched, distorted, wild-eyed. He saw a group of soldiers throw down their rifles and run.

'Let's go,' he said quietly. He again had one hand on his pistol, the other holding the car-keys. As he unlocked the Zil, he saw a couple of the grey watchdogs eyeing them both from the hotel steps.

He turned the headlamps on full-beam, and with his hand pressed down on the horn swerved out into the massing crowd. 'Just let's hope that volcano keeps stoked up.'

'Burn on, volcano!' No-Entry intoned, and adjusted his AK-47.

'And let's also hope those bastards of Romolo's back at the hotel haven't put the finger on us. I didn't quite manage to shake them off this time. A couple of them saw us leave.'

No-Entry just nodded and sank deeper into the wide leather seat.

It was when they reached the shanty-towns to the south of the city that they began to run into trouble. The narrow streets were already choked with handcarts laden with pitiful household chattels, from crude cooking utensils to elaborate crucifixes. Women ran wailing and screaming, with children wedged under their arms like packages; and groups of men were fighting over decrepit bicycles.

Here there were no police, no troops in sight. Ryan still had his hand down on the horn, and No-Entry had slipped off the safety-catch of the gun on his lap. They were nosing their way between the carts, at no more than fifteen kilometres an hour now, when the first stones thudded against the bullet proof windows.

tunic. 'That fat little sod Romolo may be in the driving-seat, and he may find a couple of mercenaries like us a bit of an embarrassment. But we're still armed, we've still got our papers, and I've still got the car. On the other hand, the whole city seems to be completely sealed off. And with this curfew it's not going to be easy to break out – even as far as the perimeter.'

No-Entry stood stroking his smooth jaw. 'I guess we shouldda tried before the curfew. I mean, the crowds wouldda helped.'

'I know. But we didn't. I had some unfinished work to attend to.'

As he spoke, the heavy silence outside was broken by what sounded like a clap of thunder, followed by a long dull rumbling. Ryan took it to be the storm breaking; then realized that there had been no lightning, and no rain. Instead, shouts and screams rose through the open windows. Within seconds – despite the curfew – he could hear the people pouring out on to the boulevard below. Then came a second rumble, accompanied by a slight but unmistakable tremor. Outside there was a loud concerted gasp.

He grabbed No-Entry, who already had his rifle at the ready. The corridor outside was full of people, hesitant, terrified; even the plain-clothes goons seemed in disarray. Ryan and the Negro headed down the stairs at the double. No one stopped them.

Out in the street, above the rim of houses to the north, the fading light was fanged by two boiling streams of yellow flame coursing down the flanks of Monte Xatu. It was not the apocalyptic disaster of the *nuée ardente*, as prophesied by Pedro over Santiago y Maria Radio, and repeated in Montecristo with such effect. But those warnings, despite the official denials, had combined with the traditional dread of the volcano to produce a highly combustible atmosphere which now ignited into total panic.

General Romolo's efforts to enforce a curfew were stillborn. Within minutes the streets were once again jammed; even the troops were trying to flee. People poured out of their houses clutching infants, carrying valuables, dragging children.

Ryan saw the solid black shape of the Zil still parked in front of the hotel entrance. He said to No-Entry: 'If we can

A moment later the front bumper collided with one of the carts and sheared off its wheel. Someone leapt on to the bonnet and for a moment Ryan's view was obstructed by a savage Indian face. Quite deliberately he accelerated, and felt first the front wheels, then the rear, bump over something soft. There were more men on the bonnet now, and one of them was hacking ineffectually at the windshield with a machete. Ryan began to swing the power-steering hard over, first to the left, then to the right. Most of the men dropped off the bonnet. The man with the machete tried to stand up and brought down a hacking blow on to the roof; then lost his balance and fell off too. The crowds were now running in terror before them, half-blinded by the swerving on-coming headlamps: scrambling over each other to make a ragged passage ahead.

No-Entry glanced back through the rear window and let out a long whistle. 'Jesus H. Christ on a bicycle! It's like a fuckin' battlefield back there!'

Ryan had no idea how many men, women or children he had maimed, even killed, before they ran into a wall of people that stretched across the whole street. He realized he had not touched the brake-pedal once since leaving the hotel; and he was not going to start now.

Somewhere he remembered hearing a story about the Eastern Front, where a German artillery unit had been captured only after so many dead Russians lay piled up in front of the muzzle of the 88mm that the shells began exploding in the gunner's faces.

It took all the power of the huge four-litre Zil to bump and lurch its way through the crush of human beings. Then, just as the road seemed to be at last clear, Ryan caught a flash in his mirror. It was the beam of a powerful spot-light, held low between two smaller lights which were approaching fast.

It was not yet quite dark, with that colourless gloom that makes all distance deceptive; while above them the glow of Monte Xatu rose like some great distorted sunset.

Ryan accelerated; hit a dog, heard someone scream, pressed his foot down further. 'Behind us – coming up fast!'

No-Entry looked back through the shaded bullet-proof windows. 'Looks like an APC, Colonel.'

Ryan calculated quickly. An armoured personnel carrier meant heavy machine-guns and perhaps as many as a dozen armed men inside; while on these rough roads it could easily keep up with the Zil, which had been designed for more leisurely highways. Even if he did manage to out-distance the vehicle, it would no doubt be equipped with a radio to call in reinforcements. On the other hand, he had still not reached the main outer-city road to the airport, and could – for all the men in the APC knew – be heading for the mountains.

The spotlight, weaving giddily between the straggling crowds, was coming closer. But no sound of a siren, no warning shots. They must be hanging back to see which route he took.

The moment he turned off for the airfield, they could either intercept him then and there, or radio ahead that he was coming. However, there was another, more unpleasant possibility: that they intended getting clear of the crowded shantytown to where they could catch up with him on some quiet stretch of road, and write off the big Soviet car as an accident of war. Ryan knew that even with the armoured coachwork and bullet-proof glass, he and No-Entry would not stand a chance. These cars were built against a stray assassin's bullet, not a fully equipped armoured vehicle.

He was just deciding whether to pull over and try to bluff his way out when two things happened, simultaneously. They were driving down a broad, half-made road lined with shacks and mud hovels. The APC, with its eight huge wheels, was gaining rapidly. Ryan could now just make out its ugly squat shape, with the long slit above the bonnet, and the two heavy machine-guns on either side. One burst from them, and the Zil wouldn't be worth its weight in scrap metal.

But just then a vast truck, as long and high as a pantechnicon, pulled slowly, deliberately out into the road. A second later the APC ploughed into it. Ryan could almost hear the crash and rending of metal as the armoured vehicle sliced half through the truck, then stopped. Its spotlight had gone out.

There was a single burst of small-arms fire, then the whole APC exploded in boiling flames. Ryan could only hope that the wretched crew had not yet alerted the guards at the airfield.

Then, suddenly, the road widened and was clear. A couple of miles ahead their headlamps picked out the high cantilevered wire-fence round the airport perimeter. At the gates stood two armoured cars and a line of helmeted troops with machine-pistols.

An officer stepped into the middle of the road and waved the Zil to halt, Ryan complied, reaching for his wad of papers; and as the officer came round his side touched the button to open the automatic window. The officer saluted. Ryan said, 'I am a colonel attached to the General Staff. Open the gates.'

The man held out his hand. 'Your documents.' He had a hard unyielding face, and Ryan guessed that he and his men were serious. He handed him his papers, which were all counter-signed by La Vuelva. The officer studied each one carefully; then gave them back, this time without saluting. 'I am authorized to allow no one to enter the airport. Those are the personal orders of General Romolo.'

Ryan looked at him steadily and said, 'What is your name and rank?' The officer was wearing battle-dress, without insignia.

'Capitano Marcos. Twelfth Infantry Battalion, Bolivar Division.'

It was one of the crack units that had recently served in Africa. Ryan nodded. 'Capitano, you will have the courtesy to address me as "Coronel". You will also understand that I and my colleague here have been dispatched on a vital diplomatic mission on behalf of the new Provisional Revolutionary Government. Please open the gates.'

'I regret, Coronel, but the airport is closed to all outgoing flights until further notice.'

'For what reason?'

'To prevent the escape of political undesirables and criminal elements from the former regime.' The officer recited the phrases as though he had only just learnt them.

'Read those documents again, Capitano. Read them carefully. And read the signature.'

The captain's expression did not alter. 'Coronel, these documents are not in order. They must be signed by General Romolo – those are my orders. The signature of ex-Presidente La Doña Ramon is no longer valid.'

Ryan's voice hardened. 'Capitano Marcos, you are an officer and therefore a man of responsibility. I trust you are also one of intelligence?'

The man looked grimly back at him, but said nothing.

'I should also remind you that not only has there been a revolution in this country, but General Romolo assumed power as head of the Provisional Government less than two hours ago. Do you expect that he should have the time to countersign every official document issued by the former president?'

One of the soldiers, who had been prowling round the back of the car, came quickly up to the officer and whispered something. Without a word the captain also went round to the back of the car. When he returned he was holding something in his hand. He held it out to show Ryan, who flinched. On the man's palm were three severed brown fingers.

'These were caught between the bumper and the chassis, Coronel. There is also blood on the car.'

Ryan nodded. 'That is quite possible. You are lucky, Capitano. The mob has not yet got here. When they do, you and your men are going to have to do more than concern yourselves with paper-work.'

The captain took out a khaki handkerchief, wrapped the three fingers inside it and put them away in his tunic pocket. 'Coronel, I am prepared to allow you to wait in the guardhouse while I check your credentials with my superiors. What is your destination?'

'That is classified. And your superiors will not be aware of my mission. It is top-secret.'

At that moment he felt No-Entry lean across him. The Negro had discreetly laid his AK-47 down under the dashboard, and was holding out a soft-covered green passport with rounded edges and the gilt emblem of the spread-eagle, with the inscription UNITED STATES OF AMERICA – E PLURIBUS UNUM. He passed it through the window. 'Speak English – inglés – Capitano?'

The captain frowned and shook his head; then took the passport tentatively, as though it were some illicit gift. As he stood looking at it, No-Entry turned to Ryan, 'Translate for the sonofabitch, will you?' – then looked out again at the officer and spoke slowly and deliberately in his Southern drawl.

'Captain, ah'm engaged on a highly confidential mission on behalf of the US State Department to arrange diplomatic recognition and foreign aid for your new Government. Ah'm actin' personally' – and Ryan translated with suitable authority – 'on behalf of your new Head of State, General Romolo.' He paused, and for the first time the officer looked uneasy.

'Captain Marcos – Twelfth Battalion, Bolivar Division?' No-Entry repeated, and gave a slow nod, without moving his eyes from the officer's face. 'I got no wish to threaten you, Captain, but if mah mission is impeded in any way, ah shall be obliged to explain the reasons not only to mah own superiors, but to yours too, ah guess.'

Ryan spoke the Spanish words in a flat, menacing monotone. The officer hesitated, glanced at the passport again, then handed it back, saluted, and shouted an order. The gates were opened. Ryan saluted back, then closed the window and drove through, out on to the dark deserted airfield.

'That was fast thinking, Major.'

No-Entry grinned in the dashboard light; only his teeth showed. 'I told yah – there's some advantages in bein' a nigger and possessin' one o' Uncle Sam's passports!'

Ryan was heading for the corner of the field where they had left the Tupolov transport plane on that damp yesterday morning. It had been refuelled in Santiago y Maria and therefore offered them a wide range of destinations: though Ryan had already decided on Jamaica, since it had the closest links to Britain, and he knew – wearing the uniform of a colonel in a foreign army, and flying in without clearance in a Soviet aircraft – that he would have some explaining to do.

The plane had not been moved. They drew up close to the tail of the fat grey fuselage; and No-Entry leapt out and climbed nimbly up through the cockpit door. As Ryan followed, he sniffed the warm northerly breeze and, from the direction of the volcano, caught the faint sickly stench of sulphur.

They landed at Kingston's Michael Manley Airport, Jamaica, shortly before midnight; and, as Ryan had anticipated, were immediately detained.

At this hour there was no one on duty senior enough to deal with their case. After a chaotic fifteen minutes – at the end of which the local officials gave up in complete bewilderment – they were both consigned to a detention-room with two camp-beds and a lavatory.

It was not until after eleven next morning that Ryan was visited by an official from the British High Commission – a cheerful, beery-faced little man called Walter Beecham – 'Call me Wally, Mr Ryan!' – who arrived with a fresh set of clothes, including a brand-new ill-fitting tropical suit. He seemed highly entertained both by Ryan's outfit and by his whole story, and was able to expedite his release before lunch-time. 'Mind you, you'll have to be on the next plane back to UK. I expect those hush-hush wallahs in Whitehall are going to have a few questions for you!'

The American Consul was more suspicious; and although No-Entry – unlike Ryan – still carried a genuine passport, the official still regarded with grave doubts any US citizen who visited the Island, especially one wearing the uniform of the national army. But since he was evidently unaware of No-Entry's past record, and after some subtle prompting from Ryan, he too finally arranged the Negro's release.

At the airport bar Ryan and No-Entry had a last drink together. The Negro had booked himself on the next flight to Mexico City, which was due to be called in twenty minutes. He was drinking orange juice, and seemed unexpectedly morose.

'Come on, what's biting you?' Ryan said, sucking at a large daiquiri.

No-Entry sank his woolly head down over his glass. 'Jus' that ah ain't got paid, that's all. She promised me the money as soon as she got settled into the Palace.'

'You bloody idiot. And you didn't even ask for a downpayment?'

'Ah'm not good at money matters, Colonel. But ah was told that if ah waited, they would fix me up with some fancy deal through the Cayman Islands or some such place – to avoid the Revenue boys, if y'understand.'

'I understand. How much were you promised?'

No-Entry told him. Ryan nodded and ordered himself another drink; then scribbled out a promissory note, guaranteeing to pay Major Robert Jones the sum of US $50,000, to be drawn on Ryan's numbered Swiss account, and passed it along the bar. 'You'll have to put a stamp on that before it's valid. What are you going to do then?' he added.

'I guess ah'll buy meself a piece o' action in a golf club – one where they allow us dark boys in.' He looked up and his eyes were moist.

* * *

It was a black wet night at London Airport when Ryan landed and passed through Immigration. The man at the desk took his passport away, returned a moment later and said, 'Would you come this way, please, sir?'

He was held for nearly five hours. There were four of them altogether. They were very polite, very interested; and between the relays of coffee and sandwiches they did not object to his drinking three-quarters of a bottle of duty-free Chivas Regal, although they touched none themselves.

Ryan was fairly truthful about almost everything. The only details he omitted were his part in the death of the two men on Alderney, and the existence of his Swiss bank account. Officially he had agreed to the operation out of an infatuation for La Vuelva, as well as a latent sense of adventure. He knew they did not entirely believe him; but he also knew that with his record they were unlikely to risk digging too deep.

Towards 3.00 a.m. a snappily-dressed blond man joined them. 'Good morning, Mr Ryan.'

'Good morning, Detective-Sergeant. Sorry about Oxford – afraid I rather lost my way.'

The Special Branch man took off his coat and sat down. 'I hear you've been having rather an exciting time, organizing one of these little Latin American revolutions. Pity it went sour on you. Personally I've never trusted those Latins – too hot-blooded for my taste.'

He declined Ryan's offer of whisky. 'Seems you got out in the nick of time?' he added. 'This new fellow – General Romolo, isn't it? – sounds a rather nasty piece of work. I wouldn't fancy that woman's chances much.'

'Is that all you came to tell me, Sharp?'

'Not quite. I'm here to try and tie up a few loose ends. The Jersey police have been onto us about a couple of murders on Alderney. Two boys with Colombian passports who are supposed to have been on your lady-friend's pay-roll. You wouldn't happen to know anything about it, would you?'

'Sorry. I've killed rather a lot of people in the last week, but fortunately they were all well outside your manor, Detective-Sergeant. As for for Alderney, I'd hazard a guess that La Vuelva had a little disagreement with her hired help, and had them quietly knocked off.'

Sharp sat looking at him, saying nothing.

'What's the next item, Sharp?'

'I also wanted to clear up that little matter of the break-in at the Rushdale Research Centre. It was all a lot of fuss about nothing. The stuff our friend Pedro stole turns out to have been a new experimental vaccine against whooping-cough.'

Ryan chuckled and slopped more whisky into his glass. 'Any news of young Pedro? The last I heard of him, he'd broadcast some crazy warning about a volcano about to erupt. Funny thing is, the damn thing did erupt after all. Seems he's not only a genius at doing a vanishing trick, but he's a bloody clairvoyant as well.'

The detective said, in his flat toneless voice: 'According to our latest information, Señor Fraga de Sanchez, alias Pedro, has formed his own guerrilla group on the Island and has declared on the new Government. Unofficially, we're delighted. At least it'll keep him out of our hair – for the time being, at any rate.'

'Anything else?'

'Yes, there is just one thing. About your chum, Miles Merton. We haven't been able to track down who killed him yet. Which is embarrassing, because there's a lot of official heat being turned on. Fortunately, it's not my case. But if I had to make a guess, I'd say that whoever did it also had a hand in the murder of the Mayfair doctor.'

He paused, but his eyes did not move from Ryan's face. 'Unless it was those two Colombians they found on Alderney. But then, of course, you don't know anything about that, do you, Mr Ryan?'

Ryan stood up and pushed the bottle of Chivas Regal into his pocket. 'If they're not your cases, Sharp, why so many questions?'

'Routine. Habit, if you like. My job's to clear up any diplomatic shit.' He paused again. 'Oh yes – you'll be glad to know that we've recovered your Lagonda. Beautiful piece of work, I must say. We cleaned some vomit off the driving-seat, but apart from a few scratches you'd think it was brand-new. If you ring Oxford Central, they'll arrange for you to collect it. And one last thing, Mr Ryan. Don't do it again.'

'Thanks,' said Ryan.

CHAPTER TEN

Exit

There were four men in the café. The clock on the belltower had just struck noon with its usual eleven cracked chimes, which caused the resident vultures to raise their bald heads and stir their dusty black wings like old umbrellas.

The Plaza was otherwise deserted: the newspaper vendors were gone, because there were no longer any newspapers; and the lottery touts had turned to precarious begging and pimping, since the proceeds of La Loteria Nacional had just been paid into the late finance minister's numbered bank account in Basel. Most of the cafés and bars had again been closed by decree of the new Revolutionary Government; and the dust lay undisturbed by the bare feet of vagrant women who used to parade their hideous, deliberately-mutilated infants – all chased away by the whips of the riot police. Even the statutory figure of the albino Creole who used to be seen every evening pushing his curious contraption under the arcades – a tricycle-like machine with two handles and a battery which, for fifty centavos used to offer the client a mild electric shock to stimulate him against the torpor of the dead hour – even he had now vanished, believed to have been yet another arbitrary victim of CUNSP, the United National Committee of Public Safety.

The four men in the bar sat listless round a bare marble table. The fan hung motionless from the ceiling; and the hot stagnant air smelt faintly of drains, and Russian petrol fumes.

When they had first come in, nearly an hour ago, the barman had approached them cautiously and begun to apologize that there was no coffee, only rum and a cheap local brandy. Coca-Cóla – along with all other American drinks – was still prohibited. The four men had ordered nothing, said nothing, stared at him with their dead eyes until he retreated gratefully into the backroom behind the bar.

The eleventh chime from the belfry had died away, and one

of the man yawned. He was a big bald mulatto with a complexion like burnt cork. In common with his three companions he wore a plain uniform the colour of dried mud, with no insignia, just a gun-belt and a cracked leather holster. The others carried Kalashnikov AK-47 assault-rifles slung over their shoulders.

Outside, one of the vultures settled lazily in the dust and stood pecking at a green cigar-butt. The big mulatto pushed his chair back, spat fastidiously between his legs, stood up and strode out under the arcades, paused to unbutton his holster, drew his gun and blew the vulture's head off. The report carried slowly round the square like a series of whip-cracks. He buttoned the gun back inside and squinted across the glaring emptiness of the square. He thought he detected several quick movements behind windows. Above him the vultures waited patiently for him to return to the bar before going down to enjoy their companion.

The man had reached the cool of the arcade when he heard the car. It made the loud rasping noise of a reconditioned diesel engine. It came round the Plaza fast, leaving a wake of yellow dust. The man waited for it to pull up. At the same time his three companions joined him, and together they walked towards it. The driver got out and opened both rear doors.

No words were spoken. The four men squeezed into the back seats unslinging their weapons and holding them between their knees.

The car sped diagonally across the Plaza, under an arch in one corner which led into a steep alley of filthy festering walls plastered with layers of political posters, each carrying some violent exhortation, now torn one from another like gigantic scabs.

It took them five minutes to reach the high marble gate-posts where the car slowed to walking pace, while two helmeted guards inspected them, each with his finger pressed to the trigger, safety-catch off: then on into the spacious gardens, all jaundiced and bloodshot, full of fleshy bilious leaves and the wild fauna of the rain-forest which a succession of tyrants had failed to tame within the confines of the Palace gardens.

A group of soldiers waited on the forecourt. Several of them wore piping and white sashes and carried ceremonial swords. As the car drew up, they watched with the same indifference which the four men had shown since leaving the café.

One of the soldiers stepped forward and opened the car doors. The men climbed out. The soldier motioned with his sword towards the steps leading to the double bronze doors: issued a single order and stepped aside, as the bolts were shot soundlessly out and the doors swung inwards.

The bald mulatto led the way down the long, cool, flaking corridor. He had drawn his gun, and his rubber-soled boots, like those of his three companions, made only a soft padding rhythm on the marble floor. They reached a pair of folding ormolu doors. Here another soldier came to attention. He was facing down the corridor and did not have to shift his gaze as the four men approached. When the mulatto was within a couple of yards of him, he turned abruptly, without speaking or saluting, and flung open the doors. The mulatto walked silently through, followed by his three companions.

The room was large and high. In comparison, the woman who rose from the sofa looked small and fragile and very lonely. She was dressed entirely in black, and her face was half-concealed behind a pair of dark glasses. Her finely-shaped hands were clasped in front of her. She wore no rings, no jewellery of any kind. The four men who now approached her were too ignorant to perceive that her clothes and shoes had been chosen with immaculate taste.

The mulatto stopped half way across the room and grinned – an ugly, gap-toothed, embarrassed smirk. The woman stepped towards him.

'You are ready?' She unfolded her hands and took another step forward, anticipating his reply. Her voice was steady, quiet, with a well-tutored accent which did not quite succeed in concealing her origins.

The mulatto looked obscurely reassured. He bowed and said, in his heavy patois, 'Everything is in order, Señora. Please, to accompany me.'

He walked behind her through the doors, followed at a discreet distance by his three armed companions. The man outside with the sword stood aside, eyes averted.

They made an incongruous group as they crossed the marble hall, went out through the bronze doors, down the steps, and past the troops again on the forecourt, who waited round the old diesel-driven car. The mulatto gave an order and the party climbed in, as though by rehearsed arrangement: the woman in the back, seated between two of them, who still kept their Soviet weapons on their knees.

They drove through the empty white streets without speaking. The men sniffed the woman's scent and felt uneasy, and each shifted away from her. It was not an overpowering smell, and certainly not unpleasant: but to an unsophisticated nostril it created the same sense of malaise as the arrogant elegance of her appearance had done in that chamber of the palace. Only the vulgar insinuations of her voice could now dispel the antagonism which she aroused among her escort.

The bald mulatto in front did not once turn to look at her. Without asking her permission, he drew from his top pocket a fat cigar, one of the finest the Island produced – for export only. He had got out a box of cheap matches, and was about to light up when he paused, swallowed a gob of phlegm that he had been about to spit out and said, without moving his head, 'Señora, there is still a chance. You have not made an offer.'

She said quietly, almost inaudibly against the rattle of the diesel: 'You have your orders. Are you now about to change your mind?'

The mulatto drew on his cigar and sank back with a slow hissing of breath. There was no further conversation.

They drove through the foreign district, with its fine stone embassies set back behind rich vegetation: thinning into even finer, Spanish Colonial residences: then into the hot brown wasteland north of the city, sprinkled with the occasional white hacienda. And now they reached the spoon-shaped valley, where the dim horizon rose into the long smoking wall of the volcanoes. In the middle of this wasteland stood the massive dark cone of Monte Xatu, its distant summit smudged with a sulphurous brown cloud, while down its steep flanks crept a giant charcoal-black lava-flow in the shape of a hand, each finger higher than a house, their tips glowing dull-red even in the sunlight.

All the men in the car, including the driver, looked up at it with awe. Only the woman seemed not to notice it.

Twenty minutes later they drew up at a farmhouse with a chicken-run and maize fields beyond. Nobody came out as the car stopped. The four armed men, and the woman, walked into a bare tiled room and waited.

Presently a short squat man in a black suit came in. Both his hands were held out in welcome. 'Señora!' His two brown palms closed round the hand of the woman; and without a word, the other four retreated through the door.

He gave a little bow, then paused. 'The situation has been explained to you? It is difficult for both of us. It is difficult for all of us. But for you, most of all—' He sighed, shedding his hands from hers. 'The crowd is furious, it is in revolt. The Movement itself is totally divided, one side against the other. I regret, Señora, but you are left with few options. However, it is still possible for you to leave the Island.'

She stood in front of him and said, 'I will not leave the Island. I will die here – die rather than face the horrible publicity that awaits me outside. My husband would have preferred it that way.'

He nodded and lowered his head. 'You must, please, excuse those ruffians who brought you here.' He paused. 'You had no trouble at the Palace?'

She said nothing, and he went on: 'I was worried that the men might insult you.' When she still made no reply, he gave a small deprecating smile, then seemed to hesitate, as though a last doubt had seized him.

She spoke at last: 'No, General Romolo. They were quite correct. I would like the situation to be terminated.'

He nodded again, turned and shouted an order. He then led the way to the back door of the room, into a yard with a concrete wall on both sides, and a third one rich with red creeper. He stood for several seconds quite motionless, his hands spread at his sides; then he said, with his back still turned to her: 'I wish there could be some other solution, Señora. This will bring no credit to our country.'

She said, with sudden quiet fury, 'You mean it will bring no credit to you, General! All you think about is your image – what they will write about you tomorrow in the world's newspapers. Well, they will not be kind – but that mustn't stop you.' And she added an obscenity which made him wince. 'The play is over, General. Finish it.'

He made a slight apologetic sloping of the hand. 'I am sorry—' he began.

'Shut up.' She turned her back to him and walked towards the far wall.

General Romolo gave a small shrug, turned and, without

looking at them, made a gesture to the four men who had brought her here. They came forward. Only the mulatto stepped aside at the last moment.

The woman had walked towards the far wall. She now turned and faced them.

The three men with the AK-47s raised them and fired loosely from the hip. The woman jerked and fell sideways. There was a pause. She began to move. The general gave a nod to the mulatto, who walked up to her and fired his pistol three times into her head.

'Get her buried,' the general said. 'You will be paid the usual bonus.'

THE END